Also by Taylor Jenkins Reid
Available from Random House Large Print

Daisy Jones & The Six

Malibu Rising

Malibu Rising

A NOVEL

Taylor Jenkins Reid

RANDOM HOUSE
LARGE PRINT

Copyright © 2021 by Rabbit Reid, Inc.

All rights reserved.
Published in the United States of America by Random House Large Print in association with Ballantine Books, an imprint of Random House, a division of Penguin Random House LLC, New York.

Cover design: Laura Klynstra
Cover images: Ty Sheers/Getty Images (aerial view of surfers), Trevor Williams/Getty Images (female surfer)
Author photograph: © Deborah Feingold

The Library of Congress has established a Cataloging-in-Publication record for this title.

ISBN: 978-0-593-39576-9

www.penguinrandomhouse.com/large-print-format-books

FIRST LARGE PRINT EDITION

Printed in the United States of America

10 9 8 7 6 5 4 3

This Large Print edition published in accord with the standards of the N.A.V.H.

Malibu Rising

Malibu catches fire.

It is simply what Malibu does from time to time.

Tornadoes take the flatlands of the Midwest. Floods rise in the American South. Hurricanes rage against the Gulf of Mexico.

And California burns.

The land caught fire time and again when it was inhabited by the Chumash in 500 B.C.E. It caught fire in the 1800s when Spanish colonizers claimed the area. It caught fire on December 4, 1903, when Frederick and May Rindge owned the stretch of land now called Malibu. The flames seized thirty miles of coastland and consumed their Victorian beach house.

Malibu caught fire in 1917 and 1929, well after the first movie stars got there. It caught fire in 1956 and 1958, when the longboarders and beach bunnies trickled to its shores. It caught fire in 1970 and 1978, after the hippies settled in its canyons.

It caught fire in 1982, 1985, in 1993, 1996, in 2003, 2007, and 2018. And times in between.

Because it is Malibu's nature to burn.

• • •

At the city line of Malibu today stands a sign that reads, MALIBU, 27 MILES OF SCENIC BEAUTY. The long, thin township—an area that hugs the slim coast for almost thirty miles—is made up of ocean and mountain, split by a two-lane throughway called the Pacific Coast Highway, or PCH.

To the west of PCH is a long series of beaches cradling the crystal blue waves of the Pacific Ocean. In many areas along the coast, beach houses are crammed along the side of the highway, competing for views, narrow and tall. The coastline is jagged and rocky. The waves are brisk and clear. The air smells of fresh brine.

Directly to the east of PCH lie the immense, arid mountains. They dominate the skyline, sage green and umber, composed of desert shrubs and wild trees, brittle underbrush.

This is dry land. A tinderbox. Blessed and cursed with a breeze.

The local Santa Ana winds speed through the mountains and valleys from the inland to the shore, hot and strong. Myth says they are agents of chaos and disorder. But what they really are is an accelerant.

A tiny spark in the dry desert wood can grow to a

blaze and run wild, burning bright orange and red. It devours the land and exhales thick black smoke that overtakes the sky, dimming the sun for miles, ash falling like snow.

Habitats—brush and shrubs and trees—and homes—cabins and mansions and bungalows, ranches and vineyards and farms—go up in smoke and leave behind a scorched earth.

But that land is young once again, ready to grow something new.

Destruction. And renewal, rising from the ashes. The story of fire.

• • •

The Malibu fire of 1983 started not in the dry hills but on the coastline.

It began at 28150 Cliffside Drive on Saturday, August 27—at the home of Nina Riva—during one of the most notorious parties in Los Angeles history.

The annual party grew wildly out of control sometime around midnight.

By 7:00 A.M., the coastline of Malibu was engulfed in flames.

Because, just as it is in Malibu's nature to burn, so was it in one particular person's nature to set fire and walk away.

Saturday, August 27, 1983

Part One

7:00 a.m. to 7:00 p.m.

7:00 a.m.

Nina Riva woke up without even opening her eyes.

Consciousness seeped into her slowly, as if breaking the morning to her gently. She lay in bed dreaming of her surfboard underneath her chest in the water, before she began remembering reality—that hundreds of people were going to descend upon her house in just over twelve hours. As she came to, it dawned on her once again that every single person who would show up tonight would know the indignity of what had happened to her.

She lamented it all without even peeking through the curtains of her own eyelashes.

If Nina listened closely, she could hear the ocean crashing below the cliff—just faintly.

She had always envisioned buying a home like the

one she and her siblings grew up in down on Old Malibu Road. A shabby beach bungalow off of PCH, built on stilts, extended out over the sea. She had fond memories of sea spray on the windows, of half-rotted wood and rusting metal holding up the ground beneath her feet. She wanted to stand on her patio and look down in order to see high tide, hear the waves crashing loudly underneath her.

But Brandon had wanted to live on a cliff.

So he'd gone and bought them this glass-and-concrete mansion, in the cliffside enclave of Point Dume, fifty feet above the coastline, a steep walk down the rocks and steps to the breaking waves.

Nina listened as best she could for the sounds of the water and she did not open her eyes. Why should she? There was nothing for her to see.

Brandon was not in her bed. Brandon wasn't in the house. Brandon wasn't even in Malibu. He was at the Beverly Hills Hotel, with its pink stucco and its green palm trees. He was—most likely at this early hour—cradling Carrie Soto in his sleep. When he woke up, he would probably take his big paw of a hand and move her hair out of the way, and kiss her neck. And then the two of them would probably start packing together for the U.S. Open.

Ugh.

Nina didn't hate Carrie Soto for stealing her husband because husbands can't be stolen. Carrie Soto wasn't a thief; Brandon Randall was a traitor.

He was the sole reason Nina Riva was on the cover

of the August 22 issue of **Now This** magazine under the headline NINA'S HEARTBREAK: HOW ONE HALF OF AMERICA'S GOLDEN COUPLE GOT LEFT BEHIND.

It was an entire article dedicated to the fact that her tennis pro husband had publicly left her for his tennis pro mistress.

The cover image was flattering enough. They had pulled one of the photos from her swimsuit shoot in the Maldives earlier that year. She was wearing a fuchsia high-leg bikini. Her dark brown eyes and her thick eyebrows were framed by her long brown hair, lightened from the sun, looking a tad wet, a faint curl still in it. And then, of course, there were her famous lips. A billowy bottom lip topped by her thinner upper lip—the Riva lips, as they had been dubbed when they were made famous by her father, Mick.

In the original photo, Nina was holding a surf board, her yellow-and-white Town & Country 6' 2" thruster. On the cover, they had cropped it out. But she was used to that by now.

Inside the magazine, there was a picture of Nina in the parking lot of a Ralphs grocery store from three weeks prior. Nina had been wearing a white bikini with a flowered sundress thrown on over it. She'd been smoking a Virginia Slims and carrying a six-pack of Tab. If you looked closely, you could tell she had been crying.

Next to it, they'd put a photo of her father from the midsixties. He was tall, dark, and conventionally handsome in a pair of swimming trunks, a Hawaiian shirt, and sandals, standing in front of Trancas Market, smoking a Marlboro and holding a bag of groceries. Over the photos ran the title THE APPLE DOESN'T FALL FAR FROM THE RIVA TREE.

They'd framed Nina as the dumped wife of a famous man on the cover, the daughter of a famous man on the inside. Every time she thought about it, her jaw tensed up.

She finally opened her eyes and looked at her ceiling. She stood up out of bed, naked except for a pair of bikini underwear. She walked down the concrete stairs, into the tiled kitchen, opened the sliding glass doors that looked onto her backyard, and stepped out on the patio.

She breathed in the salt air.

It was not yet hot that morning; the breeze that stalks all seaside towns was running offshore. Nina could feel the wind across her shoulders as she walked onto the perfectly cut grass, feeling the stiff edges of the blades between her toes. She walked until she got to the edge of the cliff.

She looked out onto the horizon. The ocean was as blue as ink. The sun had settled into the sky an hour or so ago. Seagulls chirped sharply as they dove and rose over the sea.

Nina could see the waves were good, a clear swell was moving in toward Little Dume. She watched a set come in, watched them go unridden. It seemed like a tragedy. Those waves hitting the break all by themselves, no one there to claim them.

She would claim them.

She would let the ocean heal her like she always had.

She may have been in a house she never would have chosen. She may have been left by a man she could not even remember why she'd married. But the Pacific was her ocean. Malibu was her home.

What Brandon had never understood was that the glory of living in Malibu was not living in luxury but raw nature.

The Malibu of Nina's youth had been more rural than urbane, the rolling hills filled with dirt paths and humble shacks.

What Nina loved about her hometown was how ants found their way to your kitchen counters, pelicans sometimes shit on the ledge of your deck. Clumps of horse manure sat along the sides of the unpaved roads, left there by neighbors riding their horses to the market.

Nina had lived on this small stretch of coast her entire life and she understood she could do little to prevent it from changing. She had seen it grow from humble ranches to middle-class neighborhoods. Now it was becoming a land of oversized mansions on the beach. But with vistas this beautiful, it had been only a matter of time before the filthy rich showed up.

The only real surprise was that Nina had married one of them. And now she owned this slice of the world, she supposed, whether she liked it or not.

In a moment, Nina would turn around and walk back into the house. She would put on her swimsuit and head right back to this spot, where she would descend the side of the cliff and grab her board from the shed she kept on the sand.

But right that second, Nina was thinking only of the party tonight, having to face all of those people who knew her husband had left her. She didn't move. She wasn't ready to turn around.

Instead, Nina Riva stood on the edge of the cliff she'd never wanted, and looked out onto the water she wished was closer, and for the first time in her quiet life, screamed into the wind.

"Stay here." Jay Riva hopped out of his CJ-8, jumped the five-foot gate, walked down the gravel drive, and knocked on the door of his older sister's house.

No response.

"Nina!" he called out. "You up?"

The family resemblance was striking. He was slender and tall like she was, but more powerful than reedy. His brown eyes, long lashes, and short, rumpled brown hair made him the kind of handsome that breeds entitlement. With his board shorts, faded T-shirt, sunglasses, and flip-flops, he looked like what he was: a championship surfer.

Jay knocked again, slightly louder. Still nothing.

He was tempted to pound on the door until Nina got out of bed. Because, he knew, eventually, she'd come to the door. But now was not the time to be a dick to Nina. Instead, Jay turned around, put his Wayfarers back on, and walked back to his Jeep.

"It's just you and me this morning," he said.

"We should wake her up," Kit said. "She'd want in on these waves."

Tiny Kit. Jay started the car, and began his three-point turn, careful to make sure their sticks stayed put in the back. "She watches the same forecast we do," he said. "She knows about the swell. She can take care of herself."

Kit considered this and looked out the window. More accurately: She looked out where a window might have been if the car had doors.

Kit was slim and small and tightly built, all sinew and tanned skin. She had long brown hair, lightened with lemon juice and sunshine, freckles across the bridge of her nose and onto the apples of her cheeks, green eyes, full lips. She looked like a miniature version of her sister without any of the grace and ease. Beautiful but maybe a bit awkward. Awkward but maybe beautiful.

"I'm worried she's depressed," Kit said, finally. "She needs to get out of the house."

"She's not **depressed**," Jay said, as he came to the intersection where the neighborhood roads met PCH. He looked to his left and then to his right, trying to time his turn. "She's just been dumped is all."

Kit rolled her eyes.

"When Ashley and I broke up . . ." Jay continued. They were now flying north up PCH, the base of the mountains to their right, the vast clear blue ocean to their left, the wind so loud Jay had to shout. "I was upset about it, but then I got over it. Just like Nina will soon. That's how relationships are."

Jay seemed to be forgetting that when Ashley had broken up with him, he was so upset that he wouldn't even admit it had happened for almost two weeks.

But Kit wasn't going to mention that and risk him bringing up **her** love life. At the age of twenty, Kit had not yet kissed anyone. And it was a fact that she felt every day, every moment, some more acutely than others. Her brother often talked to her as if she were a child when it came to love, and when he did, she found herself reddening—equal parts embarrassment and rage.

The car approached a red light and Jay slowed down. "I'm just saying, getting in the water is probably what she needs right now," Kit said.

"Nina will be fine," he said. With no one else at the intersection, he put his foot on the gas and drove on, even though the light had yet to change.

"I never liked Brandon, anyway," Kit said.

"Yes, you did," Jay said, catching her eye out of the corner of his. He was right. She had. She had liked him so much. They all had.

The wind roared as the car sped up and neither of them spoke until Jay pulled a U-turn and took a spot on the side of the road at County Line, an expanse of sand at the very northern edge of Malibu where surfers hovered in the water all year round.

Now, with the southwest swell, there would be waves hollow enough to get barreled. And maybe show off a little if they were so inclined.

Jay had taken first and third in two United States Surfing Championships. He had three **Surfer's Monthly** covers in as many years. A sponsorship with

O'Neill. An offer from RogueSticks to shape a line of Riva brand shortboards. He was a favorite going into the first ever Triple Crown later that year.

Jay knew he was great. But he also knew that he attracted attention based in part on who his father was. And sometimes, it was hard to tell the line between the two. Mick Riva's shadow excelled at haunting each one of his children.

"Ready to show these kooks how it's done?" Jay said.

Kit nodded with a sly smile. His arrogance both infuriated and amused her. By a certain population, Jay might have been considered the most exciting up-and-coming surfer on the mainland. But to Kit, he was just her older brother, whose aerials were getting stale.

"Yeah, let's go," she said.

A short guy with a gentle-looking face and a wet suit half undone around his hips spotted Jay and Kit as they started to get out of the car. Seth Whittles. His hair was wet, slicked back. He was wiping his face off with a towel.

"Hey, man, I thought I might see you here this morning," he said to Jay as he came around the side of his Jeep. "The tubes right now are classic."

"For sure, for sure," Jay said.

Seth was one year younger than Jay and had been one grade behind him in school. Now, in adulthood, Seth and Jay ran in the same circles, surfed the same peaks. Jay got the sense that felt like a victory for Seth.

"Big party tonight," Seth said. His voice had the slightest edge of bravado to it and Kit instantly understood Seth was confirming he was invited. Kit caught Seth's eye as he was speaking and he smiled at her, as if just now realizing she existed.

"Hey," he said.

"Hi."

"Yeah, man, party's on," Jay said. "At Nina's place in Point Dume, just like last year."

"Cool, cool," Seth said, one eye still watching Kit.

As Seth and Jay continued talking, Kit got the boards out of the back and waxed them both down. She started dragging them to the shoreline. Jay caught up with her. He grabbed his board out of her hands.

"So I guess Seth is coming tonight," Jay said.

"I gathered," Kit said, tying her leash onto her ankle.

"He was . . . checking you out," Jay said. He hadn't ever noticed someone checking Kit out before. Nina, sure, all the time. But not Kit.

Jay looked at his little sister again, with fresh eyes. Was she hot now or something? He couldn't stand to even ask himself the question.

"Whatever," Kit said.

"He's a good guy but it's weird," Jay said. "Somebody scoping out my little sister in front of me like that."

"I'm twenty years old, Jay," Kit said.

Jay frowned. "Still."

"Yeah, well, I'd rather die than suck face with Seth

Whittles," Kit said, standing up and grabbing her board. "So don't lose sleep over it."

Seth was an all-right-looking guy, Jay figured. And he was nice. He was always falling in love with some girl or another, taking them out to dinner and shit. Kit could do worse than Seth Whittles. Sometimes she made no sense to him.

"You ready?" Kit said.

Jay nodded. "Let's go."

The two of them headed into the waves as they had countless other times over the course of their lives—laying their bodies down on their boards and paddling out, side by side.

There were already a handful of people in the lineup. But it was easy to see Jay's prominence as he made his way past the breakers, as the men in the water saw him coming toward them. The lineup spaced out, made room.

Jay and Kit saddled up right at the peak.

Hud Riva, short where his siblings were tall, stocky where they were lithe, who spent the summer getting sunburned as they grew bronze, was the smartest one of the bunch. Far too smart to not understand the true ramifications of what he was doing.

He was eight miles south on PCH, going down on his brother's ex-girlfriend Ashley in an Airstream illegally parked on Zuma Beach.

However, that was not how he would have phrased it. For him, the act was making love. There was simply too much heart in all of it, in every breath, for it to be anything cheaper than love.

Hud loved Ashley's one dimple and her green-gold eyes and her gold-gold hair. He loved the way she could not pronounce **anthropology,** that she always asked him how Nina and Kit were doing, and that her favorite movie was **Private Benjamin.**

He loved her one snaggletooth that you could only ever see when she laughed. Whenever she caught Hud looking at it, she'd get embarrassed, covering her mouth with her hand and laughing even harder. And he loved that about her, too.

In those moments, Ashley would often hit him and say, "Stop it, you're making me self-conscious," with the sparkle still in her eye. And when she did that, he knew she loved him, too.

Ashley often told him she loved his broad shoulders and his long eyelashes. She loved the way he always looked out for his family. She admired his talent—the way the world looked more beautiful through his camera than it did right in front of her. She admired that he could get in just as dangerous waters as the surfers did, but that he swam, or balanced on a Jet Ski, holding up a however-many-pound camera, capturing in perfect light and motion what Jay could do on the board.

Ashley thought that was the more impressive feat. After all, it wasn't just Jay who had made the cover of **Surfer's Monthly** three times in as many years. So had Hud. All of the most famous shots of Jay were by Hud. The wave breaking, the board cutting through the water, the sea spray, the horizon . . .

Jay might be able to ride the wave but Hud was the one making it look beautiful. The name Hudson Riva was in all three of those issues. Ashley believed that Jay needed Hud as much as Hud needed Jay.

Which is why, when Ashley looked at Hud Riva, she saw a quiet man who did not need attention or accolades. She saw a man whose work spoke for itself. She saw a man instead of a boy.

And in doing so, she made Hud feel like more of a man than he ever had before.

Ashley's breath got shallower as Hud moved faster.

He knew her body, knew what she needed. This wasn't the first or second or tenth time he'd done this.

When it was over, Ashley pulled Hud up to lie next to her. The air was muggy—the two of them had shut all the windows and doors before they had even kissed, for fear of being seen or heard or even **sensed.** Ashley sat up and cracked open the window near the bed, letting the breeze in. The salt air cut the humidity.

They could hear families and teenagers on the beach, the waves rolling onto the shore, the sharp whistle of a lifeguard at the nearest tower. So much of Malibu was restricted beach access, but Zuma— that wide stretch of fine sand and unobstructed coast against PCH—was for everyone. On a day like this, it attracted families from all over Los Angeles trying to squeeze one last memorable day out of summer vacation.

"Hi," Ashley said softly, shy and smiling.

"Hi," Hud said, charmed.

He grabbed the fingers of Ashley's left hand and played with them, weaving his own fingers between them.

He could marry her. He knew that. He'd never felt this way about anyone before but he felt it for her. He felt like he'd known it since the day he was born, though he knew that couldn't possibly be right.

Hud was ready to give Ashley all of him, anything he had, anything he could give. The wedding of her dreams, however many babies she wanted. What was so hard about dedicating yourself to a woman? It felt so natural to him.

Hud was only twenty-three but he felt ready to be a husband, to have a family, to build a life with Ashley.

He just had to find a way to tell Jay.

"So . . . tonight," Ashley said as she sat up to get dressed. She pulled up her yellow bikini bottom and threw on a white T-shirt that said UCLA in blue and gold across the chest.

"Wait," Hud said, sitting up, his head almost hitting the ceiling. He was wearing navy blue corduroy shorts and no shirt. There was sand on his feet. There was always sand on his feet. It was the way he and his brother and sisters had grown up. Sand on their feet and on their floors and in their cars and bags and shower drains. "Take your shirt off. Please," Hud said as he leaned over and grabbed one of his cameras.

Ashley rolled her eyes, but they both knew she would do it.

He pulled the viewfinder down, looked at her directly. "You're art."

Ashley rolled her eyes again. "That is such a lame line."

Hud smiled. "I know but I swear I've never said it to any other woman on the planet." This was true.

Ashley took her hands and crossed them over her chest. She grabbed the bottom edge of her shirt, and pulled it off her head, her long sandy hair falling down her back and around her shoulders. As she did all of that, Hud held down the shutter, capturing her in every state of undress.

She knew she would look beautiful through his lens. As he clicked, she grew more and more comfortable, blooming at the idea of being seen by him. Ashley slowly took her hands and put them on her bikini bottom and untied the strings holding it on. And in three swift clicks, it was gone.

Hud stopped for an imperceptible second, stunned at her willingness, at her initiative, to become even more bare in front of his camera than he'd ever asked of her. And then he continued. He photographed her over and over and over again. She sat down, on the bed, and crossed her legs. And he moved closer and closer to her with the camera.

"Keep shooting," she said. "Shoot until we're done." And then she pulled at his shorts, and let them fall down, and put her mouth on him. And he kept photographing her until they were done, when she looked up at him and said, "Those are just for you. You have to develop them yourself, all right? But now you'll have them forever. Because I love you."

"OK," Hud said, still watching her, stunned. She was so many incredible things at once. Confident enough to be this vulnerable. Generous but in control. He always felt so calm around her, even when she thrilled him.

Ashley stood up and tied her bikini bottom back

on, put her shirt on with conviction. "So, like I was saying, about the party tonight . . ." Ashley looked at Hud to gauge his reaction. "I don't think I should go."

"I thought we decided—" Hud started but Ashley cut him off.

"Your family has enough problems right now." She started slipping her feet into her sandals. "Don't you think?"

"You mean Nina?" Hud said, following Ashley to the door. "Nina's going to be fine. You think this is the hardest thing Nina's had to go through?"

"That's even more to my point," Ashley said as she walked out of the Airstream, her feet hitting the sand, the sun hitting her eyes. Hud was one step behind her. "I don't want a spectacle. Your family . . ."

"Attracts a lot of attention?" Hud offered.

"Exactly. And I don't want to be one more problem for Nina."

It was this kind of thoughtfulness for his sister, despite having met her only a few times, that Hud had found so enchanting about Ashley from the beginning.

"I know but . . . we have to tell them," Hud said, pulling Ashley toward him. He put his arms over her shoulders, tucked her head underneath his. He kissed her hair. She smelled like tanning oil—fake coconuts and bananas. "We have to tell Jay," he clarified.

"I know," Ashley said. She rested her head on Hud's chest. "I just don't want to be this person."

"What person?"

"The bitch, you know? That comes between brothers."

"Hey," Hud said. "Me falling in love with you is my fault. Not yours. And it was the best thing I ever did."

Fate trips up sometimes. That's the conclusion Hud had come to. It's how he made sense of a lot of things that had happened in his life. Whatever hand was guiding him—guiding everyone—toward a certain future . . . there's no way it could work without error.

Sometimes the wrong brother meets the girl first. It doesn't have to be any more complicated than that. Hud and Ashley . . . they were simply correcting fate.

"It doesn't even make sense I was with Jay," Ashley said, pulling back from him except for where her hands interlaced with his.

"That's what I thought the first time I saw you," Hud said. "I thought, **That girl doesn't belong with Jay.**"

"Did you think I belonged with you?"

Hud shook his head. "No, you're far too good for me."

"Well, at least you recognize it."

Ashley pulled far away this time, sinking her heels into the sand, letting Hud's grip on her be the only thing keeping her from falling down. Hud let her hang for a moment and then pulled her back to him.

"You should come tonight," he said. "And we will tell Jay and it will all be OK."

There was an unspoken pact between them that

what they were going to "tell Jay" was going to be a lie. A half-truth.

They were going to tell Jay they were together. They were not going to tell him they had started sleeping together one night six months ago, when they ran into each other on the Venice Boardwalk. Back when Ashley and Jay were still together.

Ashley had been wearing a denim jacket over a coral dress that was floating up with the breeze. Hud was in white shorts and a blue short-sleeved button-down, a pair of old Topsiders on his feet.

Each had been out drinking with friends when they found themselves passing each other just outside a tourist shop, selling tank tops with cheesy catch-phrases and cheap sunglasses.

They stopped to say hi and told their friends they would catch up in a moment. But "a moment" seemed to get longer and longer until they realized they weren't going to catch up with their friends at all.

They kept talking as they slowly started walking together down the boulevard, going into shops and bars. Hud tried on a straw cowboy hat and Ashley laughed. Ashley jokingly grabbed a Wonder Woman lasso and pretended to twirl it in the air. And Hud could tell, the way Ashley smiled at him, that the night was becoming something bigger than either of them intended.

Hours later, after a few too many drinks, they crammed themselves into one of the bathroom stalls of a bar called Mad Dogs. Ashley whispered into

Hud's ear, "I always wanted you. I always wanted you instead." **She'd always wanted him instead.**

A second after she'd said it, Hud had kissed her and grabbed her legs, pulling her up around his waist and against the wall. She smelled like a flower he couldn't name. Her hair felt fine and soft in his fingers. No one had ever felt as good against him as she did that night.

When it was over, they both felt exhilarated and satiated and light as air, until the anvil of guilt settled in their stomachs.

Hud liked thinking of himself as a good guy. And yet . . . sleeping with your brother's girlfriend was exactly the sort of thing a good guy would never do.

Certainly not more than once.

But there was that night and then another. Then dinner in a restaurant four towns up the coast. And then a few discussions of how, exactly, Ashley should break up with Jay.

And then, she did it.

Five months ago, Ashley had shown up at Hud's Airstream at eleven o'clock at night and said, "I broke up with him. And I think you should know that I love you."

Hud had pulled her inside and taken her face in his hands and said, "I love you, too. I've loved you since . . . I don't know. Well before I should have."

And now they were just biding their time, trying to create the perfect moment in which to tell Jay the half-truth. A half-truth between half brothers, though Jay and Hud never thought of themselves as **half** brothers at all.

"Come to the party," Hud said to Ashley. "I'm ready to tell everyone."

"I don't know," Ashley said as she put on her white sunglasses and grabbed her keys. "We'll see."

8:00 a.m.

Nina was out in the surf, having a hard time finding the kind of long, slow right-handers she was looking for.

She wasn't there to shred. And the waves weren't right for it that morning anyway. All she wanted was to ride her longboard gracefully, cross-stepping up to the nose until the waves knocked her off.

The beach was quiet. This was the glory of a tiny, exclusive cove, protected on three sides by fifty-foot cliffs. While technically the beach was public, the only people who knew how to get to it were those who had access to private stairs or those willing to hike the jagged coastline and risk high tide.

That morning, Nina was sharing the cove with two teenage girls in neon swimsuits who were sunbathing and reading Jackie Collins and Stephen King.

Since Nina was the only one in the water, she hung out on her board just past the peak, unhurried. As she floated there, the wind chilling her wet skin, the sun crisping her bare shoulders, with her legs dangling in the water, Nina was already getting a small slice of the peace she'd come out here for.

An hour ago, she had been dreading the party. She'd even fantasized about canceling it. But she couldn't do that to Jay, Hud, and Kit. They looked forward to this party every year, talked about it for months afterward.

The party had started out as a wild kegger years ago, a bunch of surfers and skateboarders from around town gathering at the Rivas' house the last Saturday in August. But in the time since, Nina's own fame had risen and she'd married Brandon, garnering even more attention.

With each passing year, the party seemed to attract more and more recognizable people. Actors, pop stars, models, writers, directors, even a few Olympians. Somehow, this once small get-together had become **the** party to be seen at. If only to be able to say you were there **when.**

When, in 1979, Warren Rhodes and Lisa Crowne got naked in the pool. When, in '81, the supermodels Alma Amador and Georgina Corbyn made out with each other in front of their husbands. When, last year, Bridger Miller and Tuesday Hendricks met for the first time, sharing a joint in Nina's backyard. They got engaged two weeks later and then Tuesday left him at the altar back in May. **Now This** ran a head-line that said, WHY TUESDAY COULDN'T CROSS THAT BRIDGE WITH BRIDGER.

There was no end to the stories people would tell about what happened at the Riva party, some of which Nina wasn't even sure were true.

Supposedly, Louie Davies discovered Alexandra Covington when she was swimming topless in Nina's pool. He cast her as a prostitute in **Let 'Em Down Easy** and now, two years later, she had an Oscar.

Apparently, at the party back in 1980, Doug Tucker, the new head of Sunset Studios, got plastered and told everyone that he had proof Celia St. James was gay.

Did Nina's neighbor Rob Lowe sing all of "Jack & Diane" with her other neighbor Emilio Estevez last year in her kitchen? People claimed so. Nina never knew for sure.

She didn't always catch everything that happened in her own home. Didn't see every person that showed up. She was mostly concerned with whether her brothers and sister had a good time. And they always did.

Last year, Jay and Hud had smoked weed with every member of the Breeze. Kit spent the entire night talking to Violet North up in Nina's bedroom, a week before Violet's debut album hit number one. Since then, Jay and Hud had tickets to the Breeze's shows whenever they wanted. And Kit did not shut up about how cool Violet was for weeks afterward.

So Nina knew she couldn't cancel a party like that. The Rivas might not be like most families, being just the four of them, but they had their traditions. And anyway, there was no good way to cancel a party that never had any invitations. People were coming, whether she wanted them there or not.

She'd even heard from her close friend Tarine, whom she'd met at a **Sports Illustrated** shoot, that Vaughn Donovan was planning on coming. And Nina had to admit Vaughn Donovan was perhaps the hottest guy she'd ever seen on-screen. The way he smiled as he took off his glasses in the mall parking lot in **Wild Night** still got her.

As Nina watched a swell come in just west of her, she decided the party was not a curse, but a blessing. It was exactly what she needed. She deserved a good time. She deserved to let loose. She could share a bottle of wine with Tarine. She could flirt. She could dance.

Nina watched as the first wave in a set crashed just beyond her. It peeled slowly, consistently, beautifully to the right, exactly as she'd hoped. So when the next one came in, she paddled with it, caught the feel of the tide underneath her, and popped up.

She moved with the water, thinking only of how to compensate, how to give and take in perfect measure. She did not think of future or past, but only present. **How can I stay, how can I hold on, how can I balance? Better. Longer. With more ease.**

As the wave sped up, she hunched farther down.

As the wave slowed, she pumped her board. When she had her bearings, she danced, lightly, up to the nose, moving with a softness that did not compromise speed. She hovered there, on the tip of the board, her feet balancing, her arms out to steady her.

Throughout it all, this grace had always saved her.

1956

Our family histories are simply stories. They are myths we create about the people who came before us, in order to make sense of ourselves.

The story of June and Mick Riva seemed like a tragedy to their oldest child, Nina. It felt like a comedy of errors to their first son, Jay. It was an origin story for their second son, Hud. And a mystery to the baby of the family, Kit. To Mick himself it was just a chapter of his memoir.

But to June, it was, always and forever, a romance.

• • •

Mick Riva first met June Costas when she was a seventeen-year-old girl on the shores of Malibu. It was 1956, a few years before the Beach Boys got there, mere months before **Gidget** would begin to beckon teenagers to the waves in droves.

Back then, Malibu was a rural fishing town with only one traffic signal. It was quiet coastline, crawling inland by way of narrow winding roads through the mountains. But the town was coming into its adolescence. Surfers were setting up shop with their tiny shorts and longboards, bikinis were coming into fashion.

June was the daughter of Theo and Christina, a middle-class couple who lived in a two-bedroom ranch home off one of Malibu's many canyons. They owned a struggling restaurant called Pacific Fish, slinging crab cakes and fried clams just off the Pacific Coast Highway. Its bright red sign with cursive type hung high in the air, beckoning you from the east side of the highway to look away from the water for just one moment and eat something deep fried with an ice-cold Coca-Cola.

Theo ran the fryer, Christina ran the register, and on nights and weekends, it was June's job to wipe down the tables and mop the floors.

Pacific Fish was both June's duty and her inheritance. When June's mother vacated that spot at the counter, it was expected that it would be June's body that filled it. But June felt destined for bigger things, even at seventeen.

June beamed on the rare occasion that a starlet or director would come into the restaurant. She could recognize all of them the second they walked in the door because she read the gossip rags like bibles, appealing to her father's soft spot to get him to buy her a copy of **Sub Rosa** or **Confidential** every week. When June scrubbed ketchup off the tables, she imagined herself at the Pantages Theatre for a movie premiere. When she swept the salt and sand off the floors, she wondered how it might feel to stay at the Beverly Hilton and shop at Robinson's. June marveled at what a world the stars lived in. Just a few miles away and yet impossible for her to touch because she was stuck serving french fries to tourists.

June's joy was something she stole between shifts. She would sneak out at night, sleep in when she could. And, when her parents were at work but did not yet need her, June would cross the Pacific Coast Highway and rest her blanket in the expanse of sand opposite her family's restaurant. She would bring a book and her best bathing suit. She would fry her pale body under the sun, sunglasses over her eyes, eyes on the water. She would do this every Saturday and Sunday until ten-thirty in the morning, when reality pulled her back to Pacific Fish.

One particular Saturday morning during the summer of '56, June was standing on the shoreline, her toes in the wet sand, waiting for the water to feel warmer on her feet before she waded in. There were surfers in the waves, fishermen down the coast, teens like her laying out blankets and rubbing lotion on their arms.

June had felt daring that morning and put on a blue gingham strapless bikini. Her parents had no idea it even existed. She'd gone into Santa Monica with her girlfriends and had seen it hanging in a boutique. She'd bought it with money she'd saved from tips, borrowing the last three dollars from her friend Marcie.

She knew if her mother saw it, she'd be forced to return it or worse yet, throw it out. But she wanted to feel pretty. She wanted to put out a signal and see if anyone answered.

June had dark brown hair cut into a bob, a button nose, and pert bow lips. She had big, light brown eyes that held the giddiness that often accompanies hope. That bikini held promise.

As she stood at the shoreline that morning, she felt almost naked. Sometimes, she felt a little guilty about how much she liked her own body. She liked the way her breasts filled out her bikini top, the way her waist pulled in and then ebbed out again. She felt alive, standing there, partially exposed. She bent down and ran her hands through the cold water rising up to her feet.

A twenty-three-year-old, as-yet-unknown Michael Riva was swimming in the surf. He was with three of the friends he'd made while hanging out in the clubs of Hollywood. He'd been in L.A. for two years, having left the Bronx behind, running west in search of fame.

He was finding his footing coming out of a wave when his gaze fell on the girl standing alone along the shore. He liked her figure. He liked the way she stood there, shy and companionless. He smiled at her.

June smiled back. And so Mick ditched his friends and headed toward her. When he finally made his way over, a drop of ice-cold water fell from his arm onto hers. She found herself flattered by his attention even before he said hello.

Mick was undeniably handsome with his hair slicked back from the ocean, his tan, broad shoulders shining in the sun, his white swimming trunks fitting him just so. June liked his lips—how the bottom was so full it looked swollen, and the top was thinner and had a perfect little v in the center.

He held out his hand. "I'm Mick."

"Hi," she said, taking his hand. The sun was beating down on them and June had to put her left hand over her eyes to block the glare. "I'm June."

"June," Mick said, holding on to her hand just a bit too long. He did not feed her a line about June being a beautiful name. He conveyed the sentiment clearly enough by the cool joy he took in saying it out loud. "You are the prettiest girl on this beach."

"Oh, I don't know about that," June said, looking away, laughing. She could feel herself reddening and hoped he would not notice.

"I'm sorry to say it's a fact, June," Mick said as he caught her gaze again and then let go of her hand. He slowly leaned forward and kissed her cheek. "Maybe I'll take you out sometime?"

June felt a thrill run through her, from her heart to her legs.

"I would like that," she said, straining to keep her voice flat. June did not have much experience with men—the few dates she'd been on had been to school dances—but she knew enough to hide her eagerness.

"All right, then," he said, nodding at her. "You've got yourself a date."

As Mick walked away, June felt confident he had no idea she was giddy with delight.

That next Saturday night, at a quarter to six, June wiped her last table at the restaurant and quietly slipped off her red apron. She changed her clothes in the dimly lit, dingy bathroom. She waved her parents goodbye with a shy smile. She told them she was meeting a friend.

As June stood in the parking lot in her favorite A-line dress and a buttoned-up pink cardigan, she checked her reflection one more time in a hand mirror and smoothed her hair.

And then there he was at six on the dot. Mick Riva in a silver Buick Skylark. He was wearing a well-fitted navy suit with a white shirt and a thick black tie, not unlike the look he would be known for only a few short years later.

"Hi," he said as he got out of the car and opened her door.

"Hi," June said as she got in. "You're quite the gentleman."

Mick smiled out of only one side of his mouth. "Mostly." June forbade herself from swooning.

"Where are we going?" June asked as Mick pulled out of the lot and headed south.

"Don't you worry," Mick said as he smiled at her. "It's gonna be great."

June sat back in her seat and pulled her purse into her lap. She looked out her window, facing the twilight ocean view. It was easy, in moments like this, to appreciate how beautiful her hometown was.

Mick pulled into the parking lot of the Sea Lion, built against the rocky shoreline, with its oversized swordfish sign proclaiming it WORLD FAMOUS.

June's eyebrows went up. She'd been there a few times before with her parents on special occasions. There were hard-and-fast rules in her family for places like this: only water to drink, one appetizer, split an entrée, no dessert.

Mick opened up her car door and took her hand. She stepped out of the car.

"You look gorgeous," he said.

June tried not to blush. "You look very handsome, as well," she said.

"Why, thank you," Mick said, smoothing his tie and shutting the door behind her. Soon, she could feel the warmth of his hand on the small of her back, guiding her toward the front door. She immediately surrendered to his touch. His command of her felt like relief—as if, finally, there was someone who would usher her toward her future.

Once inside, the two of them were led to a table by a window, looking out over the Pacific.

"This is lovely," June said. "Thank you for bringing me here."

She watched Mick's face loosen and brighten into a smile. "Oh, good," he said. "I took a chance you'd want seafood but I wasn't sure. Since it sounds like your family owns Pacific Fish, right?"

"Yes." June nodded. "My parents own it and run it. I help out."

"So are you sick of eating lobster?" Mick asked.

June shook her head. "Not at all. I'm sick of lobster **rolls.** If I never see another lobster roll it will be too soon. But we almost never have a full lobster. And we certainly don't have steak or anything like that. It's all burgers and fries and clams and stuff. Everything's fried. My father has not met a single thing he can't fry."

Mick laughed. And June hadn't been expecting it. She looked up at him and smiled.

"When they retire, I'm supposed to take over." Her parents had recently expressed a very unappealing idea to June: that she should marry a man who wanted to be in the restaurant business with them.

"And I take it you're not excited about that?" Mick asked.

June shook her head. "Would you be?" Maybe he would be. Maybe marrying a man who wanted to take over the restaurant wouldn't be so bad.

Mick looked June in the eye and held her gaze for a moment. "No," he said. "I would not be excited about that."

June looked down at her water and took a sip. "No, I suspected not."

"I've got my eyes on a bigger prize is all," Mick said.

June looked up. "Oh?"

Mick smiled and put down his menu. He repositioned himself, leaning forward, sharing with June a secret, a sales pitch, a magic spell. "I'm a singer," he said.

"A singer?" June asked, her voice rising. "What kind of singer?"

"A great one."

June laughed. "Well, then, I'd like to hear you sing sometime," she said.

"I've been making my way in Hollywood a little bit, doing a couple of clubs on the circuit, meeting the right people. I don't make much yet. I mean, I barely make anything, honestly. I paint houses during the days to pay the bills. But I'm getting somewhere. My buddy Frankie knows an A & R guy over at Runner Records. I figure I wow him, I might just get my first record deal."

The words **Hollywood** and **circuit** and **record deal** made June's pulse speed up. She smiled, not taking her eyes off him.

The waiter came and asked for their orders but before June could speak, Mick took over. "We will both have the surf and turf."

June stifled her surprise as she folded her menu. She handed it back to the waiter.

"So am I going to be able to say I knew you when?" she asked.

Mick laughed. "Do you think I can do it?" he asked. "Do you think I can get a record deal? Hobnob around with all the stars? Tour the country selling out venues? Make the papers?"

"You're asking me?" June said, smoothing out the napkin on her lap. "I'm not in the business. Nobody cares what I think."

"I do," Mick said. "I care what you think."

June looked at him, saw the sincerity plastered across his face. "Yes," she said, nodding. "Yes, I do think you can do it."

Mick smiled and drank the ice out of the bottom of his glass.

"Who knows?" he said. "Maybe a year from now I'll be an international sensation and you'll be the girl on my arm."

This, June knew, was a line. But she had to admit, it was working.

Later, as the waves rolled in just beyond their window, Mick asked June a question no one had asked her before. "I know you don't want to take over the restaurant, but what **do** you want?"

"What do you mean?" June said.

"I mean, if you close your eyes . . ." he said.

June closed them, slowly but at once, happy to do as she was told.

"And you imagine yourself happy, in the future, what do you see?"

Maybe a little glamour, a little travel, June thought. She wanted to be the sort of woman who, when someone complimented her fur coat, could say, "Oh, this? I got it in Monte Carlo." But that was all wild stuff. Fit for a daydream. She had a real answer, too. One she saw in vivid color. One that was almost real enough to touch.

She opened her eyes. "A family," she said. "Two kids. A boy and a girl. A good husband, who likes to dance with me in the living room and remembers our anniversary. And we never fight. And we have a nice house. Not in the hills or in the city but on the water. Directly on the beach. With two sinks in the bathroom."

Mick smiled at her.

He wanted a career touring all over the world—but he'd also always imagined having a family waiting for him when he got home. He wanted a wife and kids, the kind of house where there was space to breathe and peacefulness even when it wasn't quiet. He wasn't sure if he could ever have that sort of life. He wasn't sure what it looked like or how one went about making it. But he wanted it. He wanted it just like she did. "Two sinks, huh?" he said.

June nodded. "I always liked the idea. My friend's parents had two sinks in their home over by Trancas Canyon. They had a ranch behind the marketplace there," she said. "We used to play dress-up in her parents' room. I noticed they had two sinks in their master bathroom. And I just thought, **I want that when I'm an adult. So my husband and I can brush our teeth at the same time.**"

"I love that," Mick said, nodding. "I'm not from a two-sink world either. Where I'm from, we couldn't even afford lobster rolls."

"Oh, I don't care about that," June said. She wasn't sure if it was true or not, in general. But she felt it when she said it.

"I'm just saying . . . I don't come from any money at all. But I don't think what you're born into says anything about where you're headed."

Mick had grown up in a glorified tenement, sharing a bathroom with other families. But he'd decided a long time ago that there would be no more squalor in his future. He would have **everything** and it was how he would know he'd outrun it all.

"I'll be rich one day, don't worry," he said. "I'm just advising you that I'm a penny stock."

June smiled. "My parents' restaurant is on the verge of bankruptcy every two years," she said. "I'm in no position to judge."

"You know if we ever make our way into the two-sinks world, those two-sinks people are gonna call us New Money."

June laughed. "I don't know. They might be too busy tripping over themselves for your autograph."

Mick laughed, too. "Cheers to that," he said. And June lifted her drink.

For dessert, Mick handed the decision to June. And so she nervously perused the menu, trying to pick the perfect thing, as the waiter looked on. "I'm on the spot!" she said. "Bananas Foster or baked Alaska?"

Mick gestured back to her. "It's your choice."

She hesitated a second longer and he leaned over and stage-whispered to her. "But get the bananas Foster."

June looked up. "The bananas Foster, please," she said to the waiter.

When it showed up, the two of them tangled their forks over the same plate.

"Watch it, mister," June said with a smile on her lips. "You're hogging the whipped cream."

"My apologies," Mick said, leaning back. "I have a mean sweet tooth."

"Well, so do I, so I guess we'll have to compromise."

Mick smiled at her and pushed the plate to her side of the table, giving her the rest of the dessert. June took it.

"Thank you for finally being a gentleman," she said.

"Oh, I see," Mick said. "You just wanted me to **say** that I would split the dessert but then let you eat it all."

June nodded as she continued to eat.

"Well, I'm not that kind of guy. I want in on the desserts. I want my half. And if this thing has legs, you're gonna have to get used to it."

If this thing has legs. June tried her best not to blush.

"All right," she said, handing the rest back to him, content to give it up. "Fair's fair."

When the waiter put the check down on the table, Mick picked it up immediately.

"Do you want to freshen up before we go?" he asked her.

"Yes," June said, hopping up from the table. "Thank you. I'll be out in just a moment."

She went into the bathroom, where she reapplied her light pink lipstick, powdered her face, and checked her teeth. **Was he going to kiss her?** She opened up the bathroom door to find Mick waiting for her.

"Ready to roll?" he said, putting his arm out for her to grab.

As they hastily made their way back to the car, June got a sense that Mick might have skipped out on the bill. But she put the thought out of her mind just as quick as it had come in.

That night, after they left the restaurant, they parked on the side of the road by the beach. Mick took June's hand and pulled her out into the cool evening air, the two of them running their bare feet through the chilled sand.

"I like you, June," Mick said as he held her close, wrapping her tight in his arms. He wanted a woman he could make happy. "You're one in a million."

He began to sway with her, as if they could hear music.

June wasn't quite sure what Mick thought was so exceptional about her. She hadn't played it as cool as she'd meant to. She was sure she'd made it obvious how charmed by him she was. She was sure he could sense how naïve she felt about all of this—about love, about sex. But if he believed she was special, then maybe she could dare to believe she was, too.

"Can I sing to you?" Mick said.

June grinned and said, "I get to hear this great voice?"

Mick laughed. "I was talking a big game back there. Maybe it's not so great."

"Either way, I'd love to hear it."

There, just off the Pacific Coast Highway, they were miles away from the nightclubs of Hollywood, isolated from the movie studios farther inland, far up the coast from the hustle and bustle of Santa Monica. The lands of Malibu back then were only half-tamed, all ocean and desert, navigated by half-paved roads. Everything could still feel quiet and wild.

June pushed her body up against his and pressed her cheek to his chest and Mick starting singing a quiet song on a quiet beach with his beautiful voice to a beautiful girl.

I'm gonna love you, like nobody's loved you, come rain or come shine.

His voice was buttery and gentle. She couldn't detect even an ounce of effort. The notes left his throat like breath out of lungs, and June marveled at how easy it all was, how easy the world felt when she was near him.

She understood then that she'd been right, back at dinner, when she said she believed he could do it. The man in her arms right now was a star. June was sure of it. And it thrilled her.

I'm with you always, I'm with you rain or shine.

When the song was over, June didn't lift her cheek or stop swaying. She simply said, "Will you sing Cole Porter next?" She had loved Cole Porter from the time she was a baby.

"Cole Porter is my favorite," Mick said. He pulled away from her for a moment and looked her in the eye. "A beautiful woman who will fight me over the bananas Foster and who has great taste in music, too?" he asked. "Where did you come from, June Costas?"

Mick didn't want to go through the world alone. He had one of those hearts that stick to things. And he wanted to stick to her. She seemed like such a good one to stick to.

"I've been right here," June said. "In Malibu. This whole time."

"Well, thank God I finally came to Malibu," he said before he started singing again.

Mick wanted a woman with an entirely tender heart, not an edge in sight. A woman who could never yell, never raise her hand. Who would radiate warmth and love. Who would believe in him and encourage his career.

He was starting to think June could be that woman. And so, in a way, you could say that this is when Mick fell in love with June, if falling in love is a choice. He chose her.

But for June it wasn't a choice at all. For June it was a free fall.

And after Mick took her face in his hands and kissed her that night on the beach, June Costas was a goner.

9:00 a.m.

Nina's hair was wavy and wet. Sand clung to the edges of her feet, settled in the pockets behind her knees and the roots of her hair.

She put her board back in the shed and fastened the lock. She did not want to get out of the water, but there was so much to be done.

As she started up the long, steep path to her house, her legs felt wobbly, her back and chest just as tired and sore as they were every time she came out of the ocean. Still, she made it easily up the hillside to her yard.

She headed directly for the outdoor shower. It was made of teak panels and a faucet along the side of the house. As she pulled off her dark green halter bikini, she didn't even need to shut the shower door. There was no one and nothing to see her naked body but the ocean and the bougainvillea.

She let the water warm her iced skin, washing away the brine, rendering her once again a clean slate. Then she turned off the faucet, grabbed a fresh towel, and walked into her house.

Her huge, quiet, echoing house. Full of space and light.

The home was all open hallways, glass walls, ivory couches, and ecru carpets. It was intimidatingly casual, as if its excellence was entirely without effort. Paintings Brandon had collected—a Warhol, a Haring, a Lichtenstein—hung on the walls, adding a scribble of red or a dash of orange to an otherwise aggressively pale home.

Nina dried her hair as she walked toward the stairs to her bedroom. But as she passed the kitchen, she saw the red light blinking on her answering machine. Worried that Jay, Hud, or Kit needed her, she pushed the button and started listening.

"Hey, Nina, it's Chris. Travertine. Looking forward to the big party tonight. Wanted to give you the heads-up before I see you: There's nothing we can do about them releasing extra photos from your calendar shoot. They own them. And you are technically not nude, you are wearing a bikini. Anyway, look, you look hot, all right? Onward and upward. And let's talk tonight about **Playboy**! All right, buh-bye, love. See you soon."

Nina erased the message and walked up the steps to her bedroom.

She looked at herself in the sliding mirrors that covered her closets. She looked like her mother. She could see June in her eyes and eyebrows, the way her cheekbones rounded her face. She could see her mother in her body, could feel her in her heart, could sense her in everything she did, sometimes. The older she got, the more obvious it became.

Nina was twenty-five now. And that felt young to her because she was so much older than twenty-five in her soul. She had always had a hard time reconciling the facts of her life with the truth of it. Twenty-five but she felt forty. Married but she was alone. Childless and yet, hadn't she raised children?

Nina threw on a pair of cuffed jeans and a faded Blondie T-shirt that she'd cut the arms off of. She left her hair damp and dripping slightly down her back. She grabbed her silver watch and put it on, noticing that it would be 10:00 soon. She was meeting her brothers and sister for lunch at the restaurant at noon.

While technically all of the Riva kids had inherited it, it was Nina who felt an obligation to make sure it continued to thrive. She did it not only for the people of Malibu but for her mother and her grandparents, who ran it before her. The weight of their sacrifices to keep it standing pushed her to do the same.

And so she usually went over for an hour or two Saturday mornings, to do the spot checks and greet customers. This morning, she didn't really feel like going. Lately, she almost never felt like going. But her mere presence brought in customers and she felt an obligation to be there.

So Nina slid her feet into her favorite leather flip-flops, grabbed the keys to her Saab, and hopped in the car.

1956

Every Saturday night for three months, Mick took June to dinner.

They went out for burgers and fries, or Italian, or steak. And they always shared dessert afterward, fighting for the last bite of pie or ice cream. It had become a joke between the two of them, their mutual love for sugar.

Once, Mick picked June up for a date with his hand closed into a fist. "I have a gift for you," he said with a smile.

June pried open his fingers to find a sugar cube on his palm.

"Sugar for my sugar, sweet for my sweet," he said.

June smiled. "Quite the charmer," she said as she took the cube from his hand. She'd put it right into her mouth and sucked on it. "I understand you brought it as a joke but I'm not going to let it go to waste."

He kissed her, right then, still tasting it on her lips. "I brought a whole box actually," he said, gesturing to the front seat, where a box of Domino sugar cubes was resting against the back of the seat next to a bottle of rye.

They didn't even go out for dinner that night. They drove up the coast eating sugar cubes, drinking whiskey right out of the bottle, and teasing each other over who could control the radio. When the sun set, they parked at El Matador—a pristine and stunning beach hidden under the bluffs, home to rock formations so massive and breathtaking it looked as if the ocean had made its own Stonehenge.

Mick's windshield framed the waves coming in down the shore, a beautiful movie they weren't watching. The two of them were drunk and sugar-rushed in the backseat.

"I love you," Mick said in June's ear.

June could smell the whiskey on his breath, could smell it coming out of her pores. They'd had so much, hadn't they? Too much, she thought. But it had gone down so easy. It scared her sometimes, just how good it tasted.

His body was pressing against hers and it was, she thought, the most miraculous feeling. If only he could press into her farther, hold her tighter, if only they could fuse together.

Mick put his hand up her skirt slowly, testing the waters. He got up to the top of her stockings before she pushed him away.

"I'm starting to feel like I can't live without you," he said.

June looked at him. She knew that was the sort of thing men said to women just to get what they wanted. But what if she wanted it, too? They didn't give you any answers for that part. All they said was to bat his hand away until you were married. Nobody told you what to do if you felt like you'd die without his hand pushing farther up your legs.

"If you can't live without me," she said, regaining some control of herself, "then you know what to do."

Mick released his head onto her neck, in defeat. And then he pulled away ever so slightly and smiled. "Why are you saying that? Are you saying that because you think I won't ask you to marry me right now?"

June's heart began to beat light and fast as if trying to fly. "I have no idea what you'll do, Mick. You're going to have to show me."

Mick buried his head into her shoulder once more and kissed her collarbone. She hummed with the delight of his lips on her.

"I want to be your first," she said. She knew exactly what she was doing, making a statement like that. It would allow him to give her the answer she wanted and make her think it was the truth.

"You will be," he told her. He would tell her whatever she wanted to hear. That was the way that he loved her.

June kissed him. "I love you," she said. "With all of my heart."

"I love you, too," he said, as he tried one more time. She shook her head and he nodded and let up.

That night, when he dropped her off, he kissed her and said, "Soon."

•   •   •   •

Mick and June walked along the Santa Monica Pier, the roller coaster and carousel just ahead. The worn boards creaked underneath their feet.

June was wearing a white dress with black polka dots. Mick was in trousers and a short-sleeved button-down. They looked good together and they knew it. They could feel it in the way people responded to the sight of them, the way cashiers perked up to serve them, the way passersby took an extra second to glance.

As they walked toward the water, with the Ferris wheel dominating the sky to their left, they were peeling pink sticky wisps of sugar off the mound of cotton candy Mick was holding. It had tinted June's lips a rose-colored hue. Mick's tongue was dyed as red as a raspberry.

He threw the empty paper cone of the cotton candy in the trash and turned to June. "Junie," he said. "I wanted to run an idea by you."

"OK . . ." June said.

"Here goes," Mick said, as he got down on one knee. "June Costas, will you marry me?"

June gasped so hard she gave herself the hiccups.

"Honey, are you OK?" he asked, getting up off his knee. June shook her head. "I'm fine," she said, trying to gain control of her breathing again. "I . . . just . . . I wasn't expecting this today. Do you mean it? Really?"

Mick pulled out a tiny ring, a thin gold band, a diamond smaller than an apple seed. "It's not much," he said.

"It's everything," she told him.

"But one day, I'll get you a huge ring. So big it will blind people."

"Oh, wow," she said.

"I'm on my way, I'm going places."

"I know you are."

"I can't do it without you."

"Oh, Mick . . ."

"So is that a yes?" he said. He was surprised to find himself finally nervous. "You're saying yes, aren't you?"

"Of course I'm saying yes," she said. "I think I was put here on this earth to say yes to you."

Mick lifted her into his arms and spun her around. And June suddenly felt as if human flight was no big thing at all.

"I know that I can make you happy," he told her as he put her down and put the ring on her finger. "I promise you won't ever have to step another foot in that restaurant once you're mine. And I'll get you the house of your dreams one day. Two sinks in the bathroom, bedrooms for as many kids as you want, the beach at your front door."

All she had ever wanted.

"Of course I will be your wife," June whispered, tears in her eyes.

"It's me and you, baby," Mick said, as he pulled her close to him. She buried her head in his neck, inhaled his scent, pomade and aftershave. They held hands as they made their way up the pier and Mick kissed

June with a passion and gravity that he'd never kissed anyone with before.

His parents had died when he was barely eighteen. But now he was building his own family. His own piece of the world. And they would be different, he and June.

When they got to his car, they quickly made their way to the backseat. And this time, when Mick slipped his hand up her dress, June let herself rejoice. She let herself be touched, the way she had so desperately yearned to be touched by him.

People act like marriage is confinement, June thought, **but isn't this freedom?** She was thrilled to finally be able to say yes, to feel everything she wanted to feel.

As they pushed against each other, June guessed—from the confident way Mick held her, the finesse with which he moved—that it was not his first time. Her heart ached a bit to know he'd lied to her. But hadn't she asked him to? She found herself drawn to him that much more, quenching a need to be the only one who mattered. She let him push himself into her, pulled him as close as she could, and she let it all go.

June was shocked—surprised, stunned—when he put his hand on her while he was inside her. She felt embarrassed and shy about being touched like that. But she did not want to tell him to stop, could not bear the thought of him stopping. And moments later, bliss ran through her like a bolt.

And somehow, as she lay there next to him in the back of the car, the two of them breathless, June understood that she could never go back to who she was even a moment ago, now that she knew what he could do to her.

"I love you," she said.

And he kissed her, and looked her in the eye, and said, "I love you, too. God, Junie. I love you, too."

• • •

The next day, Mick came over and held her hand as they stood in her parents' kitchen and told them they were getting married.

"I wasn't given much of a choice, it seems," her father said, frowning.

"Dad—"

Theo nodded. "I'll hear him out, June. You know me well enough to know that. I'll always hear a man out." He nodded to Mick. "C'mon, son, let's talk about your plan to take care of my daughter."

Mick winked at June as he followed Theo into the living room. She felt a tiny bit more at ease.

"Get the chicken out of the fridge, honey," her mother said. "We'll make chicken and rice for supper."

June did as she was told, moving quietly, trying to hear what her father was saying to Mick. But she couldn't make out a single word.

As Christina lit the stove, she turned to June.

"He's certainly as handsome a man as I've ever seen," she said.

June smiled.

"My God," Christina said. "He looks like a young Monty Clift."

June got the carrots out and put them on the cutting board.

"But that's just all the more reason to be cautious," Christina said, shaking her head. "You don't marry the boys who look like Monty Clift."

June looked back down at the carrots in front of her and started chopping. She knew her mother would never understand. Her mother never bought new dresses, never tried a new recipe, never watched TV except the news. She watched her mother reread her old, worn copy of **Great Expectations** over and over every year, because "why take a chance on another book when I already know I like this one?"

If June didn't want her mother's life, then she couldn't take her mother's advice. Plain and simple.

Twenty minutes later, as Christina was stirring the rice and June was nervously setting the table, Mick walked in, Theo's hand on his shoulder.

Theo smiled at June. "You might have picked a good one after all, honey."

June, overcome, ran to Mick and her father and hugged them both.

"You have my blessing," Theo said, turning his gaze to Mick. "With the caveats we talked about, son."

Mick nodded.

"Thank you, Daddy," June said.

Theo shook his head. "Don't thank me. Mick here's got a few years in him to try to make it big and then he's ready to do the right thing and take over the restaurant."

Theo shook Mick's hand and Mick smiled and shook it back. "Yes, sir," he said.

Theo went over to Christina and June pulled Mick aside. "We're going to take over the restaurant?" she whispered.

Mick shook his head. "He just needs to hear what he needs to hear right now. And so I gave it to him. But did you hear the first part? A few years to make it big? I don't need a few years. Don't worry, Junie."

Over dinner, Mick complimented Christina's cooking and Christina finally smiled. Mick asked Theo for advice on car insurance and Theo gladly stepped in to consult.

And over dessert, strawberry shortcake, Theo asked Mick to sing.

"June says you sing Cole Porter better than Cole Porter," Theo said.

Mick demurred and then acquiesced. He put his napkin on the table and stood up. He starting singing "I've Got You Under My Skin." And before he got to the bridge, Theo was nodding along, smiling.

Mick felt a lump in his throat and so he carried on, but he pushed harder out of his sternum, held the notes a bit longer than normal. And when he was done, Mick caught his breath, unable to look at Theo as he tried to steady his pulse.

June clapped. Theo joined her. "Nicely done," he said. "Nicely done."

Mick looked at him, finally took in his approval.

Christina smiled wide but June noticed she neither parted her lips nor scrunched her eyes. "Lovely," she said.

Mick said good night to everyone shortly after dinner. He kissed June on the cheek in the driveway. "We're really going to be something together. You know that, don't you?" he asked her.

And June beamed. "Of course I know that."

He held her hand tight as she tried to walk back into her house, as if she could drag him with her. He dropped it at the very last second, not wanting to say goodbye. He stayed in his car until she waved at him from her bedroom window. Then he backed out and went on his way.

Christina found June in the bathroom moments later, washing her face. Christina was already in her robe; she'd set her hair in rollers to sleep in.

"June, are you sure?" Christina asked.

June felt her shoulders begin to slump. She straightened them out. "Yes, I'm sure."

"I know he's handsome and I know he's got a great voice but . . ."

"But what, Mom?" June asked.

Christina shook her head. "Just make sure he knows how to run a restaurant."

"Did it ever occur to you," June said, feeling her voice getting higher, "that I might be meant for something bigger than a restaurant off the side of the road?"

Christina's face tightened, her lips pursed together, as if she was guarding herself against her daughter's sharp tongue. June braced herself for a moment, unsure how her mother would react. But Christina softened once more.

"I know you like all this flash, honey," she said. "But a good life is knowing people care about you, knowing you can take care of the people that count on you, knowing you're doing a little something in your community. The way your father and I do that is by feeding people. I truly can't think of much bigger than that. But that's just me."

June apologized and kissed her mother good night. And then she picked up a copy of **Sub Rosa** and imagined, one day, reading about Mick in those pages.

• • • •

Mick started getting paying gigs at restaurants in Hollywood and Beverly Hills singing standards while rich people ate dinner. Then he booked a few clubs in Hollywood with a backup band he'd put together called the Vine.

With each show, June became prouder and prouder, telling anyone who would listen that she was marrying a **professional musician.**

Mick and the Vine booked a show in a small casino in Las Vegas, a week on a cruise to Ensenada, a wedding for the head of Sunset Studios.

Then the Mocambo called with an offer for Mick to do two shows there solo. June jumped up and down when he told her. Mick picked her up and swung her in the air.

The first night at the club, June came with him and stood behind the curtain as he sang, staring at the stars who came and took seats. She thought she saw Desi Arnaz. She could have sworn Jayne Mansfield was there.

When Mick finished at the Mocambo, he was invited to play at the brand-new Troubadour in West Hollywood. And suddenly, there it was, his name on a marquee. MICK RIVA: ONE NIGHT ONLY.

June delighted in it all. "I'm marrying Mr. Mick Riva," she would say to Mrs. Hewitt, who ran the grocery; Mr. Russo, who delivered the clams to the restaurant; Mrs. Dunningham at the bank. "He just did two nights at the Mocambo. Don Adler was there. I saw him there with my own eyes. The night before he was there, Ava Gardner had come in. Ava Gardner!"

She showed off her tiny ring to her childhood best friends and the girls who picked up shifts at the restaurant sometimes. "He's going to be a big singer one day, already is practically," she'd say.

Two months later, Mick finally got his meeting with Frankie Delmonte at Runner Records. A week after that, he came to June's house with a record deal and a new ring. This one twice the size of an apple seed.

"You didn't have to do this," June said. It was so brilliant, so bright white.

"I wanted to do it," Mick said. "I don't want you walking around with a tiny little something. You need bigger, you need better."

June had liked the small little ring. And she liked this one, too.

"Just wait," Mick said. "We're gonna have so much money it's gonna be embarrassing."

June laughed but that night, she went to bed dreaming about their future. **What if they could have a king-sized bed? And a Cadillac? What if they could have three kids or even four? What if they could get married on the sand, under a huge tent?**

When she confessed these ideas to him, asking if he thought any of it was possible, he always told her the same thing. "I'll give you the world."

He would whisper it in her ear as he took off her dress. He would pledge it to her as he put his leg between hers. "Anything you want. I'm going to make sure you get it." He would run his hand down her back, kiss the skin behind her ears, grab her hips.

Who could blame June for how often she lay naked beside him before they were married? When he knew so well how to touch her?

When they realized June was pregnant, neither of them was surprised.

• • •

"June," Christina said as she shook her head, standing in the kitchen of Pacific Fish, whispering her frustration. "I thought you were smarter than this, honey."

"I'm sorry," June said, nearly in tears. "I'm sorry."

Christina sighed. "Well, you're going to have to move up the wedding. That's first. And then I guess we will get you a forgiving dress. And figure out the rest as we go."

June dried her eyes.

"You're not the first woman in the world to lose her head over a man," Christina said.

June nodded.

"C'mon, now," Christina said. "Cheer up, buttercup. It's a beautiful thing." She pulled June into her arms and kissed the top of her head.

Mick and June said "I do" in a tent under the stars, right there on the sands of Malibu. Family on her side. Some music executives on his.

That night, Mick and June danced cheek to cheek as the band played standards. "We're gonna do it all right," Mick said to her. "We're gonna love this baby. And we're gonna have more of them. And we're going to have good suppers and happy breakfasts and I'll never leave you, Junie. And you'll never leave me. And we'll have a happy home. I promise you that."

June looked at him and smiled. She put her cheek back to his.

Toward the end of the evening, Mick got up in front of the crowd. He grabbed the microphone. "If you'll indulge me," he said, with a half smile. "I have a song I'd like to sing for you all tonight. I wrote it for my wife. It's called 'Warm June.'"

Sun brings the joy of a warm June
Long days and midnights bright as the moon
Nothing I can think of but a warm June
Nothing I can think of but you

June sat right in the front as he sang to her. She tried not to cry and laughed as she failed. If this was their beginning, my God, how high could they fly?

• • •

Nina was born in July 1958. Everyone pretended she was premature. Mick drove them both home from the hospital directly to a new house.

He had bought them a three-bedroom, two-story cottage, right over the water. Baby blue with white shutters on Malibu Road, the back half extending out over the sea. There was a hatch in the floor, on the side patio, that led to a set of stairs that went directly to the beach.

As if a new house wasn't enough, there was a brand-new teal Cadillac in the driveway.

When June first walked through the house, she found herself holding her breath. A living room with windows that opened to the water, an eat-in kitchen, hardwood floors. Surely it couldn't have everything, could it? Surely each one of her dreams hadn't come true all at once?

"Look, Junie, look," Mick said, leading her excitedly into the master bedroom. "This is where the king-sized bed will go."

Holding tiny, delicate Nina in her arms, June followed her husband through the bedroom and soon made her way to the master bathroom. She looked at the vanity.

She ran her right hand along the side of the sink, felt the smooth porcelain curve down, level out, and curve back up. And then she kept running her hand along the cold tile and rough grout, until she hit the curve of porcelain of her second sink.

Nina pulled into the parking lot of the restaurant and shut off her engine. As she got out of her car, she glanced up at the sign and wondered if it was time to have it redone.

Riva's Seafood, once known as Pacific Fish, was still very much old Malibu, complete with a faded sign and peeling paint. It was no longer just a roadside dive but an institution. The children who used to come with their parents now brought their own children.

Nina walked through to the kitchen entrance with her sunglasses still on. She found herself leaving them on more and more lately. It wasn't until she saw Ramon that she took them off.

Ramon was thirty-five and had been happily

married for over a decade with five kids. He had started as a fry cook and had worked his way up over the years. He'd been running Riva's Seafood since 1979.

"Nina, hey, what's up?" Ramon asked her as he was simultaneously keeping an eye on a fry cook and getting shrimp out of the freezer.

Nina smiled. "Oh, you know, just making sure you haven't set the place on fire."

Ramon laughed. "Not until you add me to the insurance policy."

Nina laughed as she came around to his side of the counter and took a sliced tomato off the cutting board. She salted it and ate it. Then she braced herself and headed out to the picnic tables to smile and shake hands with a few customers.

As she stepped outside, the sun was already bright on her eyes and she could feel the false version of herself coming to life. Her face took on an exaggerated smile and she waved at a few tables full of people who were staring at her.

"Hope everyone is enjoying lunch!" she said.

"Nina!" shouted a boy not much older than fifteen. He rushed toward her in madras shorts and an Izod polo. Nina could already see the rolled-up poster in his right hand, the Sharpie in his left. "Will you sign this?"

Before she responded, he started unrolling it in front of her. She could not count the number of people who had showed up at the restaurant with a poster of her surfing in a bikini, asking for her signature. And despite how bizarre she felt it was, she always acquiesced.

"Sure," Nina said, taking the Sharpie from his hand. She wrote her name, a perfectly legible "Nina R.," in the top right-hand corner. And then she put the cap back on the pen and handed it over to the boy. "There you go," she said.

"Can I get a photo, too?" he asked, just as his father and mother got up from their table, armed with a Polaroid.

"Sure." Nina nodded. "Of course."

The boy sidled up right next to her, reaching to put his arm around her shoulders, claiming the full experience for himself. Nina smiled for the camera as she inched away from the boy ever so slightly. She'd perfected the art of standing close without touching.

The father hit the shutter and Nina could hear the familiar snap of the photo being printed. "You all have a wonderful day," she said, moving toward the tables in the front, to greet the rest of the customers and then head back inside. But as the boy and his mother looked at the photo coming into existence, the boy's father smiled at Nina and then reached out and smoothed his hand over the side of her T-shirt, grazing her ribs and hips.

"Sorry," he whispered, with a confident smile. "Just wanted to 'see for myself that it's soft to the touch.'"

It was the third time a man had tried this line since her ad for SoftSun Tees launched last month.

Nina had posed for it at the top of the year. It had been her biggest payday to date. In the ad, she stood, in red bikini bottoms and a white T-shirt, her hair wet, her hips jutted out to the left, her right arm up against a doorframe. The T-shirt was threadbare. You couldn't see her nipples but if you stared enough, you might be able to convince yourself you could.

The photo was suggestive. And she knew that. She knew that's why they wanted her in the first place. Everyone wanted the surfer girl to take her clothes off—she'd made her peace with that.

But then they had added that tagline without telling her. **See for yourself, it's soft to the touch.** And they'd placed it right under her breasts.

It had invited a level of intimacy that Nina didn't care for.

She grinned insincerely at the boy's father and moved away from him. "If you'll excuse me . . ." she said as she waved to the rest of the customers and went back into the kitchen, closing the door behind her.

Nina understood that the more often she posed—most likely for even more high-profile campaigns—the more people would show up at the restaurant. The more often they would want her photo, her signature, her smile, her attention, her body. She had not quite figured out how best to handle the sense of ownership that people felt over her. She wondered how her father had tolerated it. But she also knew they didn't touch him the way they touched her.

"You don't have to go out there and shake all their hands," Ramon said when he saw her.

"I don't know . . . I wish that were true," Nina said. "Do you have time to go over the books?"

Ramon nodded, wiped his hands on a towel, and followed her into the office.

"The restaurant's doing OK," he said to her as they walked. "You know that, right?"

Nina shook her head from side to side, a yes and a no. "It's the **keeping** it doing OK that I worry about," she said, as they both sat down and began to go over the numbers. It was a complicated endeavor.

The building was old, the kitchen had needed to be brought up to code recently, business ebbed and flowed with the seasons.

Fortunately, it had been a good summer. But the off-season was approaching and last winter had been brutal. She'd had to keep the place afloat with an influx of her own cash back in January, just as she'd done a few times before.

"We've pulled it out of the red from the top of the year," Nina said, turning the book toward Ramon for him to see. "So that's good. I'm just a little worried we'll fall back in once the tourists dry up."

It occurred to her at times that she was using modeling to subsidize a restaurant in which people came to take her photo and often didn't even buy a soda.

But she loved the staff, and some of the regulars. And Ramon.

"Regardless, we will figure it out. We always do," she said.

She wasn't going to be the one, three generations in, to let Riva's Seafood go to shit. She just wasn't.

"Can we stop at home before we head to the restaurant? I want to take a shower," Kit said, over the sound of the road.

"Totally," Jay said as he put on his blinker to turn down the street they'd grown up on.

Jay and Kit were the only two Rivas still living in their childhood home. Nina was in the mansion at Point Dume and often traveling for photo shoots. Hud liked living in his Airstream. But Jay and Kit stayed in the beach cottage they had grown up in, the one their father had bought their mother twenty-five years ago.

Jay had taken over the master bedroom. But he traveled a lot, too. He was often at surf competitions all over the world, with Hud by his side.

Soon, the two of them were supposed to leave for the North Shore of Oahu. Jay was scheduled to compete in the Duke Classic, the World Cup, and Pipe Masters. Then they'd be off to the Gold Coast of Australia and Jeffreys Bay in South Africa. O'Neill would foot a lot of the bill and have their name plastered across Jay at every turn. Hud would be snapping photos of him all the while.

The two of them were due for another cover, were planning on selling off the rights for posters and calendars. But to do so, they had to roam the earth. The life of a professional surfer and his entourage required a light foot, a sense of spontaneity. Jay's and Hud's passion, their livelihood, their lives, depended on chasing the ever-changing, unpredictable combination of wind and water.

And so, as much as Jay considered California his home, lately he didn't think of himself as necessarily living anywhere.

Kit, meanwhile, was still sleeping in her childhood bed, looking at a junior year at Santa Monica College, spending her nights and weekends behind the register at the restaurant. The only bright spot she could see would be when she could ditch to take trips with her friends up to the breaks in Santa Cruz. The waves were big up there, some double overhead. But that was about as far as Kit's life was taking her right now, just a few hours up the coast.

Her siblings were out there seeing the world while Kit was still slinging crab cakes.

She wanted some of the glory, too. Some of the glamour of Nina's life, some of the thrill of Jay's and Hud's. She had spent so much of her childhood following them all into the water. But she suspected that even if none of them had ever picked up a surfboard, she still would have.

She was great on a board. She could be legendary.

She should be out there, getting accolades, too. But she wasn't taken as seriously as her brothers and she knew she wasn't as gorgeous as her sister, so where did that leave her? She wasn't sure. She wasn't sure if there was a spot in the limelight for someone like her. A chick surfer who wasn't a babe.

Jay pulled up in front of the garage and let Kit hop out.

"I'll be back," he said.

"Wait, where are you going?" she asked. She had gotten a tiny bit of a sunburn on the apples of her cheeks and the bridge of her nose. It made her seem younger than she was.

"It's going to take you forever to shower and I need to get gas," Jay told her. He looked at his gas gauge to see whether he was even telling the truth. The indicator was hovering at just under half. "I only have a quarter tank."

Kit gave him a skeptical look and then left, heading into the house through the garage.

Jay pulled the car back onto the road and put his foot on the pedal a bit heavier than he needed to. The car roared over the barely paved street. He checked the clock on the radio. If he sped, he had time.

The Pacific Coast Highway was the most comfortable place on land for him and practically the only road in town. There were small offshoots of neighborhoods dotted along the highway, canyons branching out, shopping centers nestled in one direction or the other. But you could not go anywhere, could not do anything, could not visit anyone in Malibu, without your wheels hitting the pavement of PCH. Your ability to get to a restaurant, shop at a store, make a movie on time, claim your patch of sand, take your spot in the waves, all depended on just how many other people were pulling onto the same road as you every day. It was the price you paid for the view.

Jay navigated traffic as best he could, sped up through changing lights, stayed in the left lane until mere seconds before he needed to be in the right one, and soon, he pulled onto Paradise Cove Road.

Paradise Cove was a startlingly gorgeous inlet hidden from PCH behind palm trees and valley oak. Jay turned right onto the narrow road and slowed. Once his Jeep rounded the corner, a cove of blond sand came into view, surrounded by magnificent cliffs and clear blue skies.

There was a community of mobile homes on the bluff looming over it all with land fees so outrageous that only the Hollywood elite could afford them.

But the restaurant at Paradise Cove was the reason Jay was here. The Sandcastle was a beach café, where one could buy an overpriced daiquiri and drink it while looking out onto the pier. Jay parked his car and checked his pockets. A five and four ones. He had to at least go through the motions of ordering something.

Jay walked into the restaurant, putting his sunglasses on top of his head, and approached the bar counter. He was greeted by a blond guy with a tan darker than his hair, whose name Jay could not remember.

"Hey, Jay," the guy said.

"Hey, man," Jay said, giving him an upward nod. "Can I get an order to go?"

The man turned and Jay checked his name tag. Chad. **Right.**

"Sure thing. What can I get you?" Chad took out a notepad.

"Just a uh . . ." Jay glanced at the specials listed on the board and chose the first thing he saw. "Slice of chocolate cake. To go."

Jay tried not to look around too much, be too obvious. If she didn't come out, he'd resolved not to ask if she was there. Maybe she wasn't working today. Whatever. That was fine.

Chad clicked his pen in a way that implied he was excited about Jay's order. "One choco cake, coming right up, dude."

And Jay remembered that Chad was a dork.

He sat down on a stool as Chad walked back into the kitchen. Jay looked down at his own shoes— beat-up slip-ons—and decided that it was time for a new pair. His big toe on his right foot was starting to peek out from a hole in the top. He would go into town and visit the Vans store next week, get the exact same pair. Black-and-white checkered, size twelve. No sense in messing with perfection.

That moment, Lara walked out with a Styrofoam container she was putting into a plastic bag.

"Chocolate cake?" Lara said. "Since when does Jay Riva eat chocolate cake?"

So she **was** working today. So she **was** paying attention to him.

Lara was six feet tall. Actually a full six feet, just an inch and a half shorter than Jay. She was skinny, all hard edges. And, if Jay was being completely honest, not particularly beautiful. There was a harshness to her, an oval face with a sharp jaw. A thin nose. Thin lips. Yet somehow, when your eyes landed on her face, it was hard to look away.

Jay had not been able to stop thinking about her. He was infatuated and smitten and nervous, like a teenager. And he had never been lovestruck as a teenager. So this was all new to him, all uncomfortable and nauseating and thrilling.

"Gotta change it up, sometimes," he said.

Lara put the bag down next to the register and rang him up. He handed over his cash. "You coming to the party tonight?" he asked. The words were out and he was satisfied with his performance. Casual, not too eager.

Lara opened her mouth to speak, Jay's entire day and night resting on her answer.

• • •

Three weeks prior to that moment, Lara and Jay—until then only vaguely acquainted—had found themselves the only two people outside of Alice's Restaurant. Jay had been walking back to the shoreline after smoking a joint at the end of the Malibu pier. Lara had been leaving the bar. Her lame date had left an hour ago and she'd been nursing her disappointment with Coronas.

When Jay saw her, she was sitting down on a bench in denim shorts and a tank top. She was in the middle of attempting to retie her white Keds, fully buzzed.

Jay spotted her and smiled. She pleasantly smiled back.

"Lara, right?" he'd said, lighting a cigarette to try to hide the smell of weed.

"Yes, Jay Riva," Lara said, standing up.

Jay smiled, humbled. "I knew your name was Lara. I was just trying not to seem like a creep."

"We've met at least three times," she said, smirking. "It's not creepy to remember my name. It's polite."

"Lara Vorhees. You work at the Sandcastle, mostly behind the bar, sometimes waiting tables."

Lara nodded her head and smiled. "There you go. See? I knew you could do it."

"There needs to be some room to play it cool, don't you think?"

"People that are cool don't really need to play cool, do they?"

Jay was used to women that hung around and waited for him, women that made it clear they were available, women that laughed at his jokes even if they weren't funny. He was not used to women like Lara.

"All right," he said, "I get your point. Tell me. If I'm cool, what do I say next?"

"I guess, next you ask me if I'm doing anything

right now," she said. "And then I tell you I'm not. And you ask if I want to go finish your joint, which you clearly have because you're high and smell like bud."

Jay laughed, caught. "Are you doing anything right now?"

"No."

"Do you want to go somewhere and finish my joint? I'm high and I smell like bud."

Lara laughed. "Let's go to my place."

And so they did. Lara lived in a studio apartment in a complex a quarter of a mile inland at the foot of the mountains. Her place had a view of the water on a clear night. The two of them stood on her tiny balcony, nestled between two houseplants, sharing a beer and a roach, and looking at the moon over the sea.

When Lara said, apropos of absolutely nothing, "How many people have you slept with?" Jay was so disarmed he told the truth. "Seventeen."

"Eight, for me," she said, looking forward, toward the horizon. "Although, I guess it kind of depends on what we are defining as sex."

He was surprised by her. Where was the shyness? The coyness? Jay was smart enough to know that these traits weren't necessarily natural for women, but he was also bright enough to know that they were learned. That most women knew they were supposed to perform them as a form of social contract. But Lara wasn't going to do that.

"Let's say we define it as an orgasm," Jay said.

Lara laughed at him. Actually laughed at him.

"Well, then, three," she said, breathing out the smoke of the joint, passing it back to Jay. "Men don't give women as many orgasms as they think they do."

"I guarantee I would give you one," he said, as he put the joint to his lips.

This time she didn't laugh. She looked at him, considered him. "What makes you so sure I'd let you?"

He smiled and then pulled back, moving away from her, letting her feel his absence. "Look, if you don't want to feel an orgasm that starts in your toes and shakes your whole body, it's no skin off my back."

"Oh, this is impressive, actually," Lara said, playing with the label on the beer bottle. "How you've managed to make sleeping with me seem like a favor. Let's be explicitly clear about something, Riva. You wouldn't be here if I wasn't interested. But you're **lucky** I'm interested. It's not the other way around. I don't care who your daddy is."

Jay figured it was then. That moment. When he fell in love with her. But there were other moments, too, that night. Moments it could have been.

Did he fall in love with her when she took her clothes off right there on the balcony? Maybe it was when she touched his face, and she looked directly into his eyes, and moved on top of him.

Maybe he fell for her as they interlocked themselves together, legs pretzeled, bodies pulled tight until there was no space left between them. They moved together like they knew exactly what they were doing. No fumbles, no mistakes, no awkward moments. And Jay thought, maybe that was love.

Or maybe he fell in love with her later, when it was pitch dark out, and the two of them were pretending to be asleep but each knew the other one was also awake. She had lain there bare, no gesture toward covering up. And her skin was the only thing he could see in the dark.

It was then that he took a deep breath and, for the first time, told someone else his big new secret. The one that was eating him alive.

"I was just diagnosed with a heart problem," he said to her. "It's called dilated cardiomyopathy."

This was the first time he'd ever said the phrase out loud since he'd heard it from the doctor the week before. It sounded so strange coming out of his mouth that he wondered if he'd mispronounced it. The word repeated, over and over in his mind, until it sounded like nonsense. That couldn't be right, could it? **Cardiomyopathy?** But it was. He'd pronounced it just like the doctor had.

He'd been having chest pains for weeks. He'd noticed them starting shortly after he got thrown off his board and then caught in a two-wave hold down in Baja. He'd been underwater so long he thought he might die. He struggled and struggled against the current, trying to decipher up from down. He pushed himself against the weight of the water, desperate to reach the sky. But he just kept tumbling and tumbling, pulled by the riptide. And suddenly, he broke through the surface and there it was: air.

Ever since, these pains appeared from time to time, as a tightening that took him by surprise, arriving out of nowhere and stunning him silent and then passing on, leaving as quickly as they came.

The doctor wasn't sure what was causing them until suddenly the doctor became very sure indeed.

Lara put her hand on his chest, moved her warm body closer to his, and said, "What does that mean?"

It meant that Jay's left ventricle had been weakened and would not always function the way it should. It meant that anything that might cause over-exertion and adrenaline, especially something like being thrown underwater, was no longer in his best interest. Putting his heart into overdrive by almost drowning had triggered it, but the underlying condition was hereditary, given to him by all of the people who came before him, lying in wait in his blood.

Jay spared Lara any more of the details, but told her the worst part. "I should stop surfing. It could kill me." His glory, his money, his partnership with his brother . . . One little defect in his body would take it all.

But on hearing that, Lara said, "OK, so you'll find something else to be." She had made it seem so simple.

Yes, Jay thought, that was when he'd fallen in love with her. When she made what had felt like a fatal blow seem easily overcome. When she'd cracked open his bleak future and shown him the light shining in.

When Jay woke up the next morning, he'd found a note from Lara saying that she'd had to go to work. He didn't have her number. Since that day, he'd been down to the Sandcastle three times, trying to find her.

• • •

"I wasn't sure how it worked," Lara said, handing him his chocolate cake. "With the invites, I mean."

Jay shook his head. "No invites. It's a pretty simple system: If you know about the party and you know where Nina's place is, you're invited."

"Well, I don't actually," Lara said. "Know where her place is."

"Oh," Jay said. "Well, luckily you know me."

He wrote down his sister's address on a napkin and handed it to her. She took it and looked at it.

"It is OK," she asked, nodding toward the other server, "if I bring Chad?"

She was into Chad? Jay started burning up from the inside, on the verge of humiliation and heart-break. The drop was so long, so treacherous, when you started from this high up.

"Oh, sure," he said. "Yeah, sure."

"I'm not sleeping with him, if that's what you're thinking," Lara said. "I prefer men who don't spend four hours a day sunbathing with a foil reflector."

Relief came to Jay like ice on a burn.

"He's depressed because his even-more-orange girl-friend dumped him," Lara continued. "Somebody at your party's gotta have a thing for pretty boys, right? Can we pawn him off on someone?"

Jay smiled. "I think we will have a lot of options for getting Chad laid."

Lara folded the napkin with the address and put it in her apron pocket. "Guess I'm going to a party tonight."

Jay smiled, pleased. There it was. What he came for. When he left, he forgot to take the cake.

1959

June had been due with Jay on August 17, 1959. Smack in the middle of Mick's tour for his debut album, **Mick Riva: Main Man.**

June and Mick had fought about the tour dates all through her first trimester. June had insisted Mick reschedule the second half of the tour. Mick had insisted what she was asking was virtually impossible.

"This is my **chance,**" Mick told her one afternoon as they stood out on the patio, watching the tide pull away. Nina was napping and they were trying to keep their voices down. "You don't get to just reschedule your chance."

"This is your **child,**" June said. "You cannot reschedule your child."

"I'm not asking to reschedule my child, Junie, for crying out loud. I'm asking for you to understand what's at stake here. What I'm building for our kids. What I'm building for this whole family. I can't do all of this alone. I need your help. If I'm going to go out there and be great, I need you to be here, keeping things together, being strong. This life we want . . ." Mick sighed and calmed down. "It requires things from you, too."

June sat down, resigned. This reasoning made sense to her, as much as she hated it. And so somewhere in the time that Jay went from the size of a lime to the size of a grapefruit, they found a compromise.

Mick could perform wherever he wanted, whenever he wanted, but when June called him home, he had to come.

They shook on it one night when they were going to bed and as they did, Mick pulled June's arm toward him and pulled her on top of him. She laughed as he kissed her neck.

When Mick took off for his Vegas shows four days before June's due date, he promised to head home the moment she called to say she was in labor. "And I'll be home as soon as I can," he said as he kissed Nina's forehead and June's cheek. He put a hand on June's belly and then made his way out the door.

But when the time came—June's mother called him an hour and ten minutes before his Saturday night show began—Mick didn't run to the airport like he'd promised. He hung up the phone and stood there, backstage in his suit and tie, staring at the bulbs around the mirror.

It was his last Vegas stop on the tour. And impressing the guys at the Sands meant a lot of things. It meant he could get booked out for whole months at a time, which would mean some financial stability. This was his last booking for two weeks. Two weeks! Just like Junie had asked.

Think of all that time he'd have to be home. Junie and the kids would have him all to themselves. He'd pay full attention to their every waking need.

And so, he turned away from the mirror, straightened his tie, and finished his sound check.

June's second labor developed with lightning speed, her body kicking into gear, remembering with precision exactly what it had done only a little over a year before.

Mick was in an impeccable black suit, leaning over and winking at a young woman in the front row, at the very moment that his first son, three hundred miles away, cried at the shock of the world.

Mick arrived back in L.A. seven hours after Jeremy Michael Riva was born. And Mick could see, just looking at June in her hospital bed, that she was angry.

"You have a lot to explain," his mother-in-law said, the moment Mick came through the door. She began grabbing her things. She shook her head at him. "I'll let you get to it," she said as she took Nina with her and exited the room.

Mick looked at June, his eyes resting on the baby swaddled tightly in her arms. He could see only the tiny tip of his son's head and marveled at the dark swirl of hair.

"You were supposed to be here before," June said. "Not half a day later. What is the matter with you?"

"I know, honey, I know," Mick said. "But can I hold him? Now?"

June nodded and Mick swooped in, ready to take him. The boy was light in his arms and the sight of Jay's fresh face stunned Mick silent for a brief moment. "My son, my son, my son," he finally said, with a level of pride and warmth that melted June's tired heart. "Thank you for my boy, Junie. I'm sorry I couldn't be here. But look what you have done," he said. "Our beautiful family. I owe it all to you."

June smiled and took it all in. She looked at her glamorous husband and thought of her darling daughter out in the hall and reached out and touched her beautiful new baby boy. She felt that she had so many of the things she had ever wanted.

And so she let them go, the things she did not have.

A few weeks after they brought Jay home, as June was brushing her teeth, Mick kissed her on the cheek and told her he had a surprise. He had recorded the song he'd written for her. "Warm June" was going to be the first single off of his second album.

She spit out her toothpaste and smiled. "Really?" she said. "'Warm June'?"

Mick nodded. "Everyone in the country is going to know your name," he said.

June liked that idea. She also liked the idea that everyone would know he loved her. That he was spoken for.

Because June was starting to suspect Mick wasn't keeping to himself on the road.

11:00 a.m.

Kit was sitting in the driveway, waiting for Jay. She checked her watch again. He'd been gone for almost an hour. Who took an hour to get gas?

Her hair was wet and combed, grazing her bare shoulders. She was wearing an old dress of Nina's, seersucker and strapless.

Kit wasn't really into dresses but she'd seen it hanging in the closet and decided to try it on. It was comfortable and cool and she thought maybe she liked how she looked in it. She wasn't sure.

Jay pulled up to the cottage like a man who'd only twenty seconds ago stopped speeding.

"What took you so long?" Kit asked.

"Since when do you wear dresses?" he said, the second he saw her.

"Ugh," Kit said, frowning. How were you supposed to change—in ways both big and small—when your family was always there to remind you of exactly the person you apparently signed an ironclad contract to be? She turned around and started walking through the garage.

"Where are you going?" Jay called out.

"To change my clothes, you asshole."

Once inside, she pulled off the dress, leaving it there on the wood floor. She slipped into jeans, put her arms through a T-shirt.

"Nice job pretending you were getting gas," Kit said, as she hopped in the car. She leaned over the center console to confirm her suspicions. The tank was still half full.

"Oh, shut up," Jay said.

"Make me."

Jay sped out and headed back up the Pacific Coast Highway. The Clash came on the radio and, despite feeling annoyed with each other, neither Jay nor Kit could resist singing along. As with most of their disagreements, they found the anger dissipated as soon as they forgot to hold on to it.

Just as the car approached Zuma Beach, they saw Hud in his shorts and T-shirt and Topsiders, waiting for them on the east side of the road. Jay pulled over and gave Hud a second to jump into the backseat.

"You guys are late," Hud said. "Nina's probably waiting for us."

"Jay had to run some secret operation," Kit said.

"Kit had to change her clothes four times," Jay offered.

"Once. I changed my clothes once."

"What secret operation?" Hud asked as Jay looked at passing traffic and then gunned it into the right lane.

"It's nothing," Jay said. "Lay off." And that's when everyone knew it was a woman.

Hud felt his shoulders loosen. If Jay was interested in someone new, that would soften the blow. "Consider me officially laying off then," he said, both hands up in surrender.

"Yeah," Kit said. "Like anyone gives a shit anyway."

Hud turned his head and watched the world stand still as they whizzed past it. The sand, the umbrellas, the burger stands, the palm trees, the sports cars. The dudes at the volleyball nets, the bottle blondes in bright bikinis. But he was barely paying attention to what he was looking at. He was guilt-ridden and sick over how he was going to confess to his brother what he had done.

Hud's entire life, he'd always felt that Jay was not just his brother but his closest friend.

The two of them were forever tied to each other, twisting and turning both in unison and in opposition. A double helix. Each necessary to the other's survival.

1959

It was late December 1959, just a few days after Christmas. Mick was at the studio in Hollywood. June was home with Nina and Jay, roasting a chicken. The house smelled like lemon and sage. She was wearing a red-striped housedress and had curled the ends of her hair into a perfect bob, as she did every day. She never let her husband come home to a woman with her hair out of place.

Sometime after four in the afternoon, the doorbell rang.

June had no idea that in the ten seconds it took for her to make her way from the kitchen to the entryway, she was experiencing her very last moment of naïveté.

With four-month-old Jay in one arm and seventeen-month-old Nina clinging to her leg, June opened the door to see a woman she recognized as a young starlet named Carol Hudson.

Carol was small—tiny really—with big eyes and fair skin and delicate bones. She was wearing a camel-hair coat and pink lipstick, expertly applied to her thin lips. June looked at her and felt as if a hummingbird had shown up on the windowsill.

Carol stood on June's doorstep holding a baby boy only a month or so younger than Jay. "I cannot keep him," Carol said, with only the thinnest edge of regret.

Carol handed the baby over to June, pushing him into June's already crowded arms. June was frozen still, trying to catch up. "I'm sorry. But I cannot do this," Carol continued. "Maybe . . . If it was a girl . . . but . . . a boy should be with his father. He should be with Mick."

June felt the breath escape her chest. She gasped for air, making a barely audible yelp.

"His birth certificate," the woman said, ignoring June's reaction and pulling the paper out of her black pocketbook. "Here. His name is Hudson Riva." She had named the child after herself but would leave him all the same.

"Hudson, I'm sorry," Carol said. And then she turned and walked away.

June watched the back of her, listened as the woman's black pumps clicked faintly on the pavement.

Rage began to take hold in June's heart as she watched the woman run down her steps. She was not yet angry at Mick, though that would come. And not angry at the situation either, though that frustration would set in almost immediately. But at that moment in time, she felt a grave and seemingly never-ending amount of fury at Carol Hudson for knocking on her door and handing over a child without having the courage to say the words "I slept with your husband."

Carol had treated the betrayal of June's marriage as

an afterthought, the smallest piece of the puzzle. She did not seem to care that she was not only handing June a child but also breaking her heart. June narrowed her eyes as she thought of the unique combination of audacity and spinelessness that this woman possessed. Carol Hudson was a bold one indeed.

June continued to watch Carol walk away while the two baby boys in June's arms started crying—in alternating tracks, as if refusing to be in unison.

Carol backed out of the drive. Her clearly brand-new Ford Fairlane was crammed to the roof with suitcases and bags. If June had any doubt, the image of a packed car made it clear that this was not a game. This woman was leaving Los Angeles, leaving her son in June's arms, leaving him for June to raise. Her back was turned, quite literally, to her flesh and blood.

June watched Carol drive off, until the car disappeared behind the curve of the mountains. She kept looking awhile longer, willing the woman to turn around, to change her mind. When the car did not reappear, June's heart sank.

June shut the door with her foot and guided Nina to the television. She tuned it to a rerun of **My Friend Flicka** in the hope that Nina would sit there quietly and watch. Nina did exactly as she was told. Even before the age of two, she knew how to read a room.

June laid Jay down in his crib and let him cry as she unwrapped Hudson from his swaddle.

Hudson was small and puny, with long limbs he had not grown into, could not yet control. He was red and screaming, as if already angry. He knew he'd been abandoned, June was sure of it. He cried so hard and so loud for so long—so very, very long—that June thought she might lose her mind. His cry just kept repeating over and over like an alarm that never ceased. Tears started falling down his newborn face. A boy without a mother.

"You have to stop," June whispered to him, desperate and aching. "Sweet boy, you have to stop. You have to stop. You have to stop. Please, little baby, please, please, please. For me."

And for the first time since they began this peculiar and unwelcome journey, Hudson Riva looked June right in the eye, as if realizing suddenly that he wasn't alone.

It was then, June holding this strange boy in her hands—staring at him, trying to process just what exactly was happening to them both—that she understood everything was far more simple than she was making it.

This boy needed someone to love him. And she could do that. That would be a very easy thing for her to do.

She pulled him close to her, as close as she could, as close as she'd held her own babies the days they were born. She held him tight and she put her cheek to his head and she could feel him start to calm. And then, even before he was silent, June had already made up her mind.

"I will love you," June told him. And she did.

• • •

Evening came around and June took the chicken out of the oven and steamed the broccoli and fed Nina dinner. She rocked the boys, gave Nina a bath, and put all three of them to bed—a process that took a full two and a half hours.

And as she performed each one of these tasks, June was forming her plan. **I will kill him,** she thought as she washed Nina's hair. **I will kill him,** she thought as she changed Jay's diaper. **I will kill him,** she thought as she gave Hudson a bottle. **But first I will lock him out of the goddamn house.**

When the kids were asleep—Nina in her bed and the two boys sharing a crib—June poured herself a shot of vodka and threw it back. Then she poured herself one more. Finally, she called a twenty-four-hour locksmith out of the yellow pages.

She did not want Mick to step one foot in their house, did not want him to ever again sleep in their king-sized bed, or brush his teeth in one of their master bathroom sinks.

When the locksmith—a Mr. Dunbar, sixty years old in a black T-shirt and dungarees with yellowing blue eyes and wrinkles so deep, you could lose your change in them—got there, June hit her first roadblock.

"I can't change the locks without an agreement from the master of the house," Mr. Dunbar said. He frowned at June, as if she should know better.

"Please," June said. "For my family."

"Sorry, ma'am, I can't change the locks if the house isn't yours."

"The house is mine," she said.

"Well, not **only** yours," he said, and June guessed his own wife might have locked him out of the house a time or two.

June continued to plead to no avail but the truth was, she was only a little surprised. She was a woman, after all. Living in a world created by men. And she had long known that assholes protect their own. They are faithful to no one but surprisingly protective of each other.

"Good luck to you, Mrs. Riva. I'm sure it will all work out," he said as he left, having done nothing but extort a fee for being dragged out of his bed.

So June used the only tool she had at her disposal: a dining room chair. She lodged it underneath the knob of the front door and then sat on it. And for the first time in her life, she wished she were heavier. She wished she were broad and tall and stout. Hefty and mighty. How silly of her to have worked so hard to stay trim and small this whole time.

When Mick came home at 1:00 A.M., after recording—his collar undone, his eyes vaguely bloodshot—he found that the door would open a crack but budge no further.

"June?" he said, into the thin space between the door and the frame.

"The thing that upsets me the most," June said,

plainly, "is that I think I knew it, already. That you weren't being faithful. But I put it out of my head because I trusted what you said more than I trusted myself."

"Honey, what are you talking about?"

"You have a third child," June said. "Your girlfriend dropped him off here with us. Apparently, she's not ready to be a mother."

Mick remained silent and June found herself desperate for him to say something.

"Oh, Junie," he said, finally. June could hear his voice give, as if he were about to cry.

Mick fell to the ground, shaking his head and then burying it in his hands. **Jesus,** he thought. **How did it come to this?**

• • •

It had all felt so simple to him before Carol.

He could have the beautiful house with the beautiful wife and the beautiful children. He could love them with all of his heart. He could be a good man. He had **meant** to be a good man.

But women were flocking to him! Good God, you'd have had to see it to believe it. Backstage at his shows, especially when he was appearing on a bill with guys like Freddie Harp and Wilks Topper, it was like Sodom and Gomorrah.

June never understood that. The way the young girls looked up at him from below the stage, with their big, bright eyes and knowing smiles. The way young women would sneak into his dressing room, their dresses open two buttons too far.

He said no. He said no **so many times.** He'd let them get close or touch him. Once or twice, he'd even tasted the schnapps on their lips. And then he always said no.

He would push their hands away. He would turn his head. He'd say, "You should go. I've got a wife at home."

But every time he said no, he worried he was that much closer to the one day when he would say yes. And he wasn't sure quite when it had been, but sometime when Nina was still just a tiny little something, he realized he was saying no the way you decline a second helping of dessert. You say no while knowing that if it's offered one more time, you're going to say yes.

That yes finally came in the parking lot of the recording studio during his first album. Her name was Diana. She was a twenty-year-old redhead backup singer with a beauty mark drawn above her eyebrow and a smile that made you think she could see you naked through your suit.

Heading home one night, Mick ran into her by his car and she met and held his glance just a second too long. Before he caught himself, he was kissing her against the side of the building, pushing her up against the stucco, pushing his body against hers as if it would save them both.

Seven minutes later, he was done. He pulled away from her, fixed his hair, and said, "Thanks." She smiled and said, "Anytime," and he knew, in his bones, he was going to do it again.

The thing with Diana lasted for two whole weeks and then he got bored. But he found that once it was over with Diana, the guilt made him want June more. He needed her love the same way he'd needed it when he first met her. He craved her acceptance, couldn't get enough of her big brown eyes.

It was that much easier to cross the line a little while later with Betsy, the waitress at the bar across from his producer's office.

And then there was Daniella, a cigarette girl in Reno. Just a one-time thing. It meant nothing.

And what did it matter?

He could still be a good husband to June. He could show up on time to every recording session. He could sell out crowds. He could charm the young and the old, wink at the old ladies who showed up with their husbands to have a good time listening to the hip young man. He was giving June everything they had dreamed of for themselves. They had their two sinks and they were starting a great family. And anything June could think of, he would give her.

He just had this one thing for himself.

But then he met Carol. It was the Carols that ruined everything. And he'd known that. That's what was so maddening about it. He'd learned this all already, watching his father.

He'd met Carol at a show at the Hollywood Bowl. She'd been there with a studio executive. She was so tiny but her attitude filled the room. She didn't want to be there, didn't even know who Mick was—a distinction that was becoming more and more rare. She shook his hand politely and he smiled at her, his very best smile, and he watched the edges of her thin pink lips start to curl up ever so slightly, like she was trying hard to dislike him but couldn't quite muster it.

Forty minutes later, he had her right there in an unlocked limo they found behind the venue that night. Just before they both finished, she screamed his name.

When they were done, she got up and left with little more than a "see you around." And ten minutes later, she was back on the arm of the exec she came with, not giving him a second look.

Mick was sunk. He needed to see her again. And again. He would call her agent's office. He showed up at her apartment. He could not get enough of her, could not help but be enchanted with her passive charm, her indifference to almost everything— including him. He could not get enough of the way she could talk to anyone about anything but did not hang on a single person's word. Even his.

Oh, God, he thought a few weeks into it. **I'm falling.**

They had been seeing each other during late nights and long lunches for three months when Carol told Mick she was pregnant.

They had run into each other at Ciro's. Mick had been having dinner with his producer. Carol was there with another man.

Mick had lured her into the men's bathroom and taken her right there in the stall, so overcome with jealousy seeing her with someone else that he needed to own her.

Afterward, as he smoothed his hair and prepared to leave the bathroom, Carol fixed her skirt and made herself presentable. Then she said, "I'm pregnant. It's yours."

He looked up at her, hoping she was joking. It was clear she wasn't. And before Mick could say anything, she left him there alone.

He closed his eyes and then opened them up to see his slack-jawed face staring back at him in the mirror. **You fucking idiot.** In an instant, he punched his own reflection, shattering the glass and cutting his hand open.

He did not see Carol again after that night. He'd sent her money but stopped calling her, forced himself to stop thinking of her, and he had not bedded another woman since then.

Now here he was, nearly a year later, barricaded from his own house. But he'd known from the very moment he punched the mirror that this was looming. Maybe he'd known long before that, too. Maybe he'd always known he couldn't escape himself.

• • •

"Junie, I'm so sorry," Mick said, starting to cry. It was so unbearable, to hate yourself the way he hated himself just then. "I tried to do the right thing, I swear."

June refused to be moved by the weak sound of his voice.

It was not difficult for her to maintain her anger, but whenever she feared she might falter, she would think of herself being pregnant and retroactively change the memory, shading it with the knowledge that there had been another woman nearby, carrying another one of her husband's children, almost as far along as she. How sad to not be the only one carrying your husband's child at that very moment. It seemed to June that privilege was the very least you could ask of a man.

"I was weak," Mick said, pleading with her. "It was a moment of weakness. I just couldn't stop myself. But I am stronger now."

"I don't want you here," June said, undeterred. "I don't want you around these kids. I'd hate for these boys to grow up to be anything like you."

She'd said "boys." Not **boy. Boys.**

"Sweetheart," Mick said. He saw it now. The way he could convince her to let him fix everything for all of them. "I'm Hudson's father. If you want him, you have to take me, too."

June and Mick were silent for a while after this, June unsure what to do. Mick waited with bated breath. There was no way she was going to allow a baby to be handed over to Mick. He didn't even know how to change a diaper. That baby needed June. That boy needed a mother. They both knew that.

June opened the door. Mick fell into the house.

"Thank you," he said, as if she had granted him clemency. "I will make this up to you. I will do right by you every moment from this day forward."

At just that moment, Mick looked up to see that Nina had woken and found them there.

"Hi, honey," he said to her.

From the bedroom, Jay and Hud started crying at the same time. June scooped up Nina and went to tend to her babies. Mick peeked over her shoulder, looking at the newborn son he was meeting for the first time.

June was unable to bear it, witnessing Mick's connection to this child. She swatted him away and he backed off.

When she was done with the children, she went to the bedroom and saw that Mick had lain down on the far edge of the bed, as if the left side of it was still his.

"Junie, I love you," he said.

She said nothing in return.

But as June looked at him, she felt fatigue take her down. He was not going to make it easy on her. He wasn't going to leave of his own will. He was going to make her scream it and shout it and force him to go. She was going to have to rage against him and even then, she might not win.

Anger extracts such a toll and suddenly, June was so

tired. She sighed, giving her body over to her breath. She could not fight him now because she could not fight him now and win.

And so, she lay down next to him, saving her indignation for daylight, when she could think straight. All of this would still be there to fight in the morning.

But in the morning, her anger had lost its edges. It had morphed into sorrow. She was now overtaken by the dull ache of grief, expansive and tender like a whole-body bruise. She had lost the life she had believed she'd been granted. She was in mourning.

So when Mick turned over and put his arm around her, she could not summon the energy to shrug it off.

"I promise you all of that is over," Mick whispered, tears forming in his eyes. "I will never do anything to hurt you again. I love you, Junie. With all of my heart. I'm so sorry."

And because June had not shrugged off his arm, Mick felt confident enough to kiss her neck. And because she had not shrugged off the small request, she did not know how to shrug off the larger one. And on and on it went. Small boundaries broken, snapped like tiny twigs, so many that June barely noticed he was coming for the whole tree.

With every move Mick made, as he held her, as he kissed her, June lost sight of the exact moment to speak up and then resigned herself to the pain of having never spoken up at all.

And soon, on the horizon appeared a resolution—one that even June started to welcome if for no other reason than needing the return of normalcy, even if it was a lie.

At midnight the following night, Mick whispered sweet nothings into June's ear. June, despite herself, relished the feeling of his breath on her neck. And the two of them talked it through, in the hurried and hushed tones reserved for secrets.

Mick would be forever faithful and they would raise Hud as one of theirs. They would intimate that Jay and Hud were twins. No one would dare question it. After all, they were about to enter another social stratum with Mick's second album. They would have new friends, new peers. They would be, now, a family of five.

June felt, that night, as if she and Mick were mending their own broken bones together. Laying the cast perfectly in the hope that one day she would not even remember she had been broken.

●   ●   ●

And the crazy thing was that it worked.

June loved her children, loved her older girl and her twin boys. She loved her house on the water and watching her kids play on the shore. She loved people stopping her at the market, two infants and a toddler in the cart, saying, "Aren't you Mick Riva's wife?"

She liked the money and the Cadillac and the minks. She liked leaving the kids with her mother and putting on one of her smartest cocktail dresses and standing backstage for some of Mick's shows.

She liked hearing "Warm June" on the radio and having Mick's attention when he was home. He always did make her feel like the only woman in the world, even when she knew—knew for certain now—that she wasn't.

So, despite the ulcer she was growing, June had to admit, she could stomach it all more easily than she thought. Vodka helped.

Unfortunately, Mick simply couldn't stop himself.

There was Ruby, whom he met on the Sunset lot. And then there was Joy, a friend of Ruby's. They meant nothing to him and so he saw no real betrayal.

But then, Veronica. **And oh my God,** Veronica.

Black hair, olive skin, green eyes, a body that set the standard for hourglasses. He'd fallen again, despite every attempt to keep his heart out of it. He fell for her crimson smile and the way she liked to make love in the open air. He fell for her slinky dresses and her sharp wit, for the way she refused to be intimidated by him, the way she made fun of him. He fell for just how famous she was getting, maybe more famous than him, when she starred in a hit domestic thriller called **The Porch Swing.** Her name was above the marquee in big bold letters and yet still, in the quiet of the night, it was his name she called out.

He could not get enough of Veronica Lowe.

And June knew exactly what was happening.

When Mick didn't come home until four in the morning, when Mick had a tiny trace of lipstick behind his ear, when Mick stopped kissing her good morning.

Mick started having dinner with Veronica in public places. Sometimes, he stopped coming home altogether.

June had her hair done. She lost weight. She humbled herself to the level of asking her girlfriends for sex tips. She made his favorite roast beef. In the rare moments she held his attention, she tried to subtly remind him of the duty he had to his children.

And still, he could not be torn away.

Mick told himself he was nothing like his own father. His own father who would come home smelling like other women's perfume, his own father who would leave for weeks at a time, his own father who would smack his mother for asking too many questions.

He told himself he'd done right by marrying June, a woman nothing like his own mother, who would smack his father back. But he was lost in Veronica's hair, the way it smelled like vanilla. He was lost in her laugh. He was lost in her legs. He was lost.

And then one night, when the boys were ten and eleven months old, Mick came home at four in the morning.

He was drunk but he was unconfused. He bumped into his nightstand pulling out his passport. The lamp crashed onto the floor.

June woke up and saw him there, hair flopping in front of his face, eyes bloodshot, jacket draped over his arm. There was a suitcase in his hand.

"What's going on?" she said. But she already knew. She knew the way people know they're about to be robbed, which is to say acutely, right at the last second.

"I'm taking Veronica to Paris," he said, before he turned and left for the door.

June chased him to the driveway in her sheer nightgown. "You can't do this!" she screamed. "You said you wouldn't do this!" She mortified herself, begging for something she never wanted to beg for.

"I can't be this person!" Mick yelled at her. "Some family man or whatever it is that you thought I was. I'm not! I've tried, all right? And I can't do it!"

"Mick, no," June said as he shut the car door. "Don't leave us."

But that's exactly what he did. June watched him back up the car. And then she crumpled down onto the driveway, heavy and dead, like an anchor tied to nothing.

Mick drove away, headed to Veronica's house in the hills, where, he told himself, he could finally get things straight. With Veronica, he would do better.

He was not a good man. Not an honest man. It was how he was born, how he was raised. But a good woman could save him. He'd thought that was June, but he now understood, it was Veronica. **She** was the answer. His love for her was strong enough to cure him. He'd call his kids once things settled down. Years from now, when they were old enough, they'd understand.

June cried in her driveway for what felt like a lifetime. Cried for herself and her children, cried because of how much of herself she had compromised in order to keep him, cried because it had never been enough to make him stay.

She cried because she was not surprised that he had left, only that it was happening now, in this moment. And not tomorrow or a month from now or ten years from now.

Her mother had been right. He had been too bold a choice, too handsome a man.

Why were all of her mistakes that had been so hidden from her as she was making them so clear to her now?

And then, for one brief second, she gasped and broke down, thinking of the fact that, if he was truly gone, there might never be another man who could touch her the way he did. He took so much with him when he went.

The sun started to rise and June caught her breath. She walked back to the house, determined. She would not be shattered by this. Not in front of her children.

She walked into the kitchen and put two cold spoons on her eyelids, trying to reduce the puffiness. But when she caught a glimpse of herself in the side of the toaster, she looked just as frightful a mess as she'd feared.

June poured herself a glass of orange juice and then

popped the top of the vodka she kept in the cabinet and tossed that in, too. She smoothed her hair, tried to summon the dregs of her dignity.

"Where Daddy go?" Nina asked, standing in the doorway.

"Your father doesn't know how a man's supposed to act," June said, walking past her. She grabbed Mick's albums off the record player and threw them into the trash, his cocksure face staring back up at her.

She poured the rest of the carton of orange juice over it all. "Wash your hands and get ready for breakfast."

June and her three children ate eggs and toast. She took them all down to the sand. They spent the day in the water. Nina showed June she could sing the alphabet all the way through. Jay and Hudson had both started pulling themselves up. Christina came by around lunchtime with tuna melts and June pulled her aside.

"He left, Mama," she said. "He's gone."

Christina closed her eyes, and shook her head. "He'll come back, honey," she said, finally. "And when he does, you'll have to decide what to do."

June nodded, relieved. "And if he doesn't?" she asked. Her voice was small and she could barely stand to hear it.

"Then he doesn't," Christina said. "And you have me and your father."

June caught her breath. She looked at her children. Nina was building a sandcastle. Jay was about to eat a handful of sand. Hudson was sleeping under the umbrella.

I will be more than just this, June thought to herself. **I am more than just a woman he left.**

But when the lights went out that night, and all of them lay in their separate beds, staring at the ceiling, June knew that she, and Nina, and Jay, and Hudson all had lost something. They were now living with a different-sized hole in each one of their four hearts.

Noon

Nina stood in the packed kitchen as the three cooks managed the oversized grill and two fryers. She quietly began what was arguably her most important task at Riva's. She grabbed a few handfuls of fried clam strips, a bowl of cold shrimp, a bottle of tartar sauce, three slices of cheese, and four rolls. And she began making each one of her siblings what they all called "the Sandwich."

It was a mess of cold seafood, smooshed between bread. One for each of them, hers with no cheese, Jay's with extra sauce, Hud's with no clams, Kit's with a lemon wedge.

The Sandwich didn't exist without Nina. When Nina was sick, she still went in and made the Sandwich. When she was out of town on a shoot, no one ate the Sandwich. It would never have occurred to Jay, Hud, or Kit to make the Sandwich themselves, to make the Sandwich for Nina.

Nina didn't mind. She took care of her siblings and they thanked her for it, loved her for it, and they all left it at that.

When the Sandwiches were done, Nina grabbed four red baskets and four pieces of parchment paper. She nestled each one in and filled the remaining space of the baskets with fries. Except for hers, which she filled with salted sliced tomatoes.

She checked her watch. Her brothers and sister were late.

"Party tonight, right, girl?"

Nina looked up to see Wendy coming into the kitchen. Wendy was an aspiring actress who took shifts at Riva's Seafood between driving into Hollywood for auditions. So far, Wendy had done a recurring role on a soap opera and been featured in a music video.

"Yeah," Nina said. She liked Wendy. Wendy showed up for all of her shifts, was kind to customers, and always remembered to clean the soda fountain. "Are you coming?"

Wendy raised an eyebrow. "Do you honestly think I would miss it? The Riva party is the one time of year that you truly never know what you'll end up doing."

Nina rolled her eyes. "Oh, God," she said. "You make it sound so . . ."

"Rad?" Wendy offered.

Nina laughed again. "Sure, rad."

"I'll be there, with bells on."

"I'm coming, too, by the way!" Ramon shouted from the fryer.

Nina laughed as she put the fried clams on each of the rolls. "I will believe it when I see it," she said to him.

"Psssh," he said, waving her off as he pulled two baskets of shrimp out of the fryer. "You know I've got a life. I can't go to some Richie Rich party, spend my time bumping elbows with some famous assholes. No offense."

"I would expect nothing less than for you to decline my invite," Nina said. She was pretty sure Ramon was one of the only people who didn't consider being invited to the annual Riva party a perk of the job.

Meanwhile, she was positive the kid currently manning one of the grills, Kyle Manheim, a local surfer just out of high school, had taken the job this summer **just** to get the invite. She could practically sense his resignation coming next week.

"Where are your good-for-nothing siblings?" Ramon asked. And just as he did, Kyle lit a grilled cheese on fire. The kitchen erupted in controlled chaos and Nina put the baskets of sandwiches on a tray and slipped out. She made her way to the break room in the back.

Nina sat down and picked a magazine up from the desk behind her. **Newslife.** She flipped through the pages. Reagan and Russian dissidents and MTV is ruining children and **should she buy a videodisc player?**

There were ads for the Chevy Malibu and Malibu coconut rum and Malibu Musk body spray. Nina wondered for the millionth time why everyone outside of town thought the place evoked something exotic and preternaturally cool, as if it were a sun-bleached utopia.

Sure, your neighbor might be in a few movies, but Malibu was a place to live, like any other. It was where you brushed your teeth and burned dinner and ran errands, just with a view of the Pacific. **Someone should tell them all,** Nina thought, **paradise doesn't exist.**

And then she turned the page and came face-to-face with her husband, yet again. "BranRan and Carrie Soto: Love–Love." **Ugh, the tennis puns.**

Nina put the magazine down, disgusted. Then she picked it back up and read the article twice over. There were photos of Brandon and Carrie together all over the pages. The two of them getting into a silver Porsche on Rodeo, the two of them walking into a country club in Bel Air.

The photos haunted her. Not because Brandon looked happy with Carrie. Although, he did. And it also was not because he looked **different** with Carrie—although, again, this was true. Brandon had replaced his T-shirts with polo shirts, his boat shoes with loafers.

But no. What haunted Nina was that this all just felt so familiar. She'd long ago watched her mother scour magazines filled with images of her father and his new wife.

"We're here!" Hud called to her before they even made their way through the door.

Nina got up and hugged each one of her siblings as they joined her.

"Sorry we're late," Kit said.

"It's fine," Nina said.

"It was Jay's fault," Kit offered.

"We're barely late anyway," Jay said as he looked at the clock on the back wall. It was 12:23 P.M.

The four of them sat down at the table and Kit immediately started eating her fries. Nina knew they had to be cold by now but appreciated that none of her siblings mentioned it.

"So, what's up with the party?" Kit said, putting a fry in her mouth. "Do you need us to do anything?"

Nina picked up a slice of tomato. **God, she wanted a fry.** "No," she said, shaking her head. "It's all managed. I'm meeting the cleaning crew at the house in a few hours. The caterers will be showing up at five. The bartenders should get there at . . . six? I think? Party's at seven but people should start showing up around seven-thirty, I'd think. I have it all under control."

Jay shook his head. "It's so different from the old days."

Hud laughed as he was chewing. He wiped his

mouth and swallowed. "You mean when Nina cleaned the house and Kit was putting out the bowls of pretzels . . ."

"And you and I were convincing Hank Wegman at the liquor store to sell us three kegs," Jay said. "Yeah, that's exactly what I mean."

"By the way, I'm mostly focused on beer and wine this year," Nina said. "I mean, obviously the bar will have a few bottles of liquor for cocktails but I don't want to go crazy. I don't need somebody thinking it's a good idea to jump off my top balcony into the pool again."

"Oh, my God," Kit said, laughing. "Jordan Walker's nose still looks terrible! Remember when we saw **Pledge for Eternity**? Every time he came on-screen it looked like he had Silly Putty on his face."

Hud laughed.

"But that wasn't because he had a whiskey," Jay said. "The guy was hopped up on mushrooms."

"Still," Nina said. "The caterer said beer and wine is cooler anyway."

"Yeah, all right," Jay said. And then he briefly glanced at Hud and in that nanosecond of time they both knew they were going to drive down to the liquor store and stock the bar the way they wanted.

"Guys, what if Goldie comes this year?" Hud asked.

Jay shook his head. Nina smiled.

"Would you stop?" Kit said, laughing. "You can't call her Goldie—you don't even know her."

"I do know her."

"Standing behind someone in the grocery store is not knowing her. Just call her Goldie Hawn like the rest of us," Kit said.

"I lent her my basket!" Hud said. "Because her hands were full with her kids. And she said, 'Hi, I'm Goldie!'"

Nina, Jay, and Kit all looked at each other, trying to decide whether or not to give it to him.

"I haven't heard anything about Goldie Hawn coming," Nina said, diplomatically. "But I do think Ted Travis is coming again."

Kit smiled and rubbed her hands together, excited. "Yes!"

Ted Travis lived four streets over in a house built in the shape of a donut with a tiki bar and a grotto in the middle. Kit and her best friend, Vanessa, never missed an episode of his show, **Cool Nights,** about a cop in Orange County who slept with everyone's wives and solved murders wearing a blazer and swimming trunks. "He jumped two speedboats on water skis last week and Van and I wanted to ask him about it."

"Is Vanessa coming tonight?" Nina asked. "I know you said she might have to go to San Diego with her family."

"No, she's coming," Kit said. Vanessa had been in love with Hud since Kit and Vanessa were thirteen. So Kit knew she wasn't going to miss an opportunity to be near him. Kit kept hoping the crush would fade but it never did. Hud didn't help matters by being so sweet to her.

"But is anyone surprised Ted's coming?" Jay said. "He'd never miss an opportunity to come hit on Nina."

Nina rolled her eyes. "Ted is, like, old enough to be our dad," she said, getting up from the table to grab a napkin off the counter. "And anyway, I don't even want to think about getting hit on. I'm not sure I'm feeling my spunky best lately."

"Oh, come on," Jay said.

"Maybe just leave it," Hud offered.

"You're gonna let some tennis asshole make you feel bad about yourself?" Jay said, looking directly at Nina. "The guy's a complete douchebag and, I'm sorry, but his backhand sucks. And I always thought that. Even when I liked him."

"I mean," Kit said. "Jay's kind of right. Also, are we now allowed to acknowledge that he was balding?"

The last part made Nina laugh. Hud caught her eye and laughed with her.

"He really was balding," Nina said. "Which would have been fine if he realized it. But he had no clue! It was, like, right on the top of his head and he'd wear those visors—"

"That just made him look more bald," Jay said, plainly. "Why did you let him wear those visors?"

"I didn't know how to tell him he was balding!"

Kit shook her head. "That is brutal. You let him walk out of the house and onto national TV with a bagel of hair on his head."

And they all started laughing. The four of them,

erupting, at the image of Brandon Randall unknow-ingly balding on ESPN.

They were good at this, they had experience. This was how they began the process of forgetting the peo-ple who turned their backs.

"At least it's Carrie Soto's problem now," Nina said. "Let her find a way to tell him."

The good thing about getting dumped by a dick-head is that you don't have to deal with the dickhead anymore. At least, that's how it's supposed to work.

1961

The day after Mick and June's divorce went through, Mick married Veronica. Within weeks, Mick and Veronica bought a penthouse apartment on the Upper East Side of Manhattan and moved across the country.

They had been married for four months before he started sleeping with the wife of a sound engineer he'd been working with, a redhead with blue eyes named Sandra.

When Veronica figured it out—she'd found an auburn bobby pin in his suit jacket—she threw a dinner plate at him. And then two more.

"Fuck, Ronnie!" Mick screamed. "Are you trying to kill me?"

"I hate you!" she screamed as she threw another one. "I hope you die! I really do." Her aim was terrible; not a single dish so much as grazed him. But he was startled by the violence of it. The flush of her cheeks, the craze in her eyes, the cacophony of dishes breaking and a woman screaming.

The next morning, he had his lawyer file divorce papers.

As he had movers pack his things, Veronica stood in her robe screaming at him, mascara running down her face. "You are an awful man," she cried. "You were born a piece of shit and you'll die a piece of shit just like every other piece of shit on this planet!"

When he told the movers to take the bedside lamp, she hit him across his back and scratched his shoulder.

"Veronica, stop it," he said, as calmly as he could. "Please."

She grabbed the lamp out of the mover's hand and threw it against the wall. Mick's pulse started to race, as he watched her unravel. He grew nauseated and pale. She lunged at him and he ducked from her last grasp as she fell to the floor crying. He threw a few hundred bucks at the head mover and ran out of the apartment.

As he lit a cigarette there on the street corner, about to hail a cab to his hotel, Mick thought fondly of June.

· · ·

June learned about the divorce from the pages of **Sub Rosa** magazine. As she read the headline, she felt some semblance of pride. She'd lasted longer on the bull than Veronica had.

Maybe, June thought, **he'll get his head straight now. Maybe he'll at least call his kids.** But the phone never rang. Not on Christmas. Not on anyone's birthday. Never.

· · ·

Still, in the rare quiet moments backstage . . .

In the deafeningly sober seconds before the first drink at his after-parties . . .

In the blindingly bright mornings before his first glass of bourbon . . .

Mick thought of his children. Nina, Jay, and Hud.

They would be fine, he figured. He had chosen a good mother for them. He had done that right. And he was paying the bills for all of them. He was keeping that roof over their heads, sending child support payments that were sky high. They would be fine. After all, he'd been fine with far less than they had. He gave no thought to the idea that he might break his children just as someone had broken him.

• • •

Carlo and Anna Riva had been tall, stocky, formidable people. They had one child, Michael Dominic Riva, and had tried for more but came up empty. In other families that might have meant Mick was the star, but for the Rivas it meant Mick was the beginning of a failed project, one they were sometimes tempted to abandon.

Carlo was an unremarkable barber. Anna was a mediocre cook. They often were not able to pay their rent or put anything that tasted good on the table. But they were in love, the kind of love that hurts. They hit highs so high neither of them could quite stand it, and lows so low they weren't sure they'd survive them. They smacked each other on the face. They made love with a sense of urgency and mania. They locked each other out of the house. They threatened to call the cops on each other. Carlo was never faithful. Anna was never kind. And neither of them spent much time remembering there was a child.

Once, when Mick was only four years old, Anna was making dinner when Carlo came home late smelling like perfume.

"I know exactly where you've been!" Anna shouted, furious. "With the whore from the corner." Tiny Mick ducked at the sound of her raised voice. He already knew when to find cover.

"Anna, mind your business," Carlo snapped.

Anna grabbed the pot of boiling water in front of her with both hands and flung it at her husband.

The scorching water hit the kitchen floor and a spot across Carlo's neck. Mick watched from the living room floor as his father's skin began to puff at the collarbone.

"You crazy bitch!" Carlo screamed.

But by the time the burn had blistered, Carlo and Anna were snuggled up together on the tattered sofa, laughing and flirting as if they were alone.

Mick watched them, eyes wide and staring, unworried they would see him gawking. They never looked at him when they got like this.

The next month, Carlo was gone again. He'd met a

blond seamstress on the subway. He stopped coming home for nine weeks.

During times like those, when his father was gone, his mother could often be found alone in bed, crying. There were some mornings, far more often than to be called occasional, when Anna did not get out of bed until the sun had passed its zenith and started its way back around.

On those mornings, Mick would wake up and wait for his mother to come to him. He would wait until ten or eleven, sometimes even one. And then, understanding that it was one of those days, he would eventually begin to fend for himself.

Anna would later open her bedroom door and join the world of the living, often to find her baby boy cross-legged on the floor, eating dried spaghetti. She would run to him and sweep him up in her arms and she would say, "My boy, I am so sorry. Let's get you something to eat."

She would take him to the bakery, buy him every roll and donut he wanted. She would fill him with sugar, ply him with laughter. She would pick him up into her arms with glee, cradling him to her, calling out "My Michael, my Michael, fast as a motorcycle" as she ran with him through the streets. People would stare and that made it all the more fun.

"They don't know how to have a good time," Anna would tell her son. "They aren't special like us. We were born with magic in our hearts."

When they got home, Mick would have an ache in

his stomach, and he would crash from the sugar and fall asleep in his mother's loving arms. Until the chill settled into her again.

Soon enough, Mick's father would come home. And the fighting would resume. And then they would lock themselves in their bedroom.

But eventually, whether it was weeks or months or even a year, his father would leave again. And his mother would stay in bed.

And Mick would have to fend for himself.

• • •

Mick married again, shortly after he divorced Veronica. The biggest star in Hollywood. It was a huge scandal, the talk of the town when they had it annulled the next day.

Nina saw the headlines in the grocery store while June was buying milk and bread. She couldn't read the words on the cover of the magazine and June wasn't even sure if her daughter recognized the face of the man that was her own blood. After all, June had cleansed their home of his music and photos. She had changed the channel the few times his face invaded their TV screen. But still, Nina stared at the picture on the front of the magazine as if she could sense its importance.

June picked up the stack of magazines and turned them around.

"Don't worry yourself with that garbage," she

said, her voice steady. "Those people don't mean a thing."

June paid for her groceries and told herself she didn't care what he did anymore. Then she took the kids home and poured herself a Sea Breeze.

• • •

Then came the spring of 1962.

Mick was single and in Los Angeles for a show at the Greek, one of the last on his third world tour.

In his dressing room backstage afterward, Mick loosened his tie and threw back his fifth Manhattan of the night.

"You ready to come out and play?" said his makeup girl with a glint in her eye.

Mick was already bored with her and he hadn't even touched her. He rolled his eyes and grabbed his drink. He was getting so sick of all the people around him all the time. And yet, he didn't want to find out what his soul had to say when he was by himself. And so, he came out and charmed the VIPs and beauties who had made their way backstage.

There were so many girls. So many women. For some reason, all of them seemed too easy lately. The way they clamored for their chance to hang on his arm, the way their makeup was all the same, their hair all sprayed in the same styles. Even their beauty seemed meaningless—what is one beautiful woman if you've slept with hundreds already? What does it matter if the pretty teenager in the corner is batting her eyes at you when you've had the world's most famous woman in your bed?

Mick had started getting into the backs of his limos alone at night, drunk and already half-asleep. The night after the Greek was no different. Just him and his driver and a bottle of Seagram's.

Mick rested his head against the window, watching Los Angeles whiz by as his driver sped farther toward the Beverly Wilshire. Mick was now drinking his whiskey right from the bottle. Perhaps it was the sights of his old city, perhaps it was the smell in the air, perhaps it was the reckoning that was emerging in his soul. But when he closed his eyes, June's face appeared in his mind. Round, wide-eyed, gentle. She was making him dinner, pouring him a drink, hugging the children. Beautiful, patient, kind.

Things had been easier, then. When he had relaxed into her, in their life together. However small and simple it was. She was a good woman. With her, he was as close as he got to being a good man.

"Let's go down to the 10," he said to the driver, before realizing what he was even doing. "The 10 to PCH, please. Up to Malibu."

Forty-eight minutes later, he arrived at the front door of the first house he had ever owned, the home of the only woman he ever truly loved.

• • •

June woke up to the sound of the waves crashing and someone pounding on the door. She put on her dressing gown.

Somehow, she knew who it was before she turned the knob, but she couldn't quite believe it until she saw it. And then there he was at the threshold, in a stylish black suit, with a white shirt, and his thin black tie undone, hair tousled just so. "Junie," he said. "I love you."

She stared at him, stunned.

"I love you!" he shouted so loud she startled. She let him in, if only to get him to quiet down.

"Sit down," she said, gesturing to the dinette, the same vinyl chairs he had sat on before he'd left them almost two years ago.

"How did you get even more beautiful?" he asked as he obeyed.

June waved him away and brewed him some coffee.

"You are everything," he said.

"Yeah, well," June deadpanned. "You're a whole lot of nothing."

He had expected this. She had a right to be angry. "What have I done with my life, June?" he said, his head in his hands. "I had you and I ruined it. I ruined it because I got distracted by cheap women, women who don't hold a candle to you." He looked up at her, his eyes watering. "I had you. I had everything. And I gave it all away because I didn't know how to be the man I want to be."

June was not sure how to respond to the words she'd been dying to hear.

"I cannot live without you," he said, realizing he had come here to get back what he'd lost. "I cannot live without all of you, my family. I have been such an idiot. But I need you. I need you and our children. I need this family, Junie." He got down onto his knees. "I was sorry the moment I left you. I've been sorry ever since. I am so sorry."

June tried, desperately, to make the lump in her throat go away, to hold back the tears forming in her eyes. She did not want him to know how broken he had left her back then, just how desperate she felt now.

"Give me one chance to fix it all," he said, "I'm begging you." He kissed her hand with humility and reverence, as if she alone could cure him. "Take me back, Junie."

He looked so small to June then.

"Think of the life we could give the kids. The five of us, vacations in Hawaii and barbecues on the Fourth of July. We could give them a childhood of everything you and I ever dreamed of for ourselves. Anything we can think up, we can give to these kids."

June felt a pinch in her heart. And Mick did, too.

"Please," he said. "I love our children. I need our children."

He was picking the lock on her heart like a burglar at the front door. **Almost, almost, almost,** and then,

"I'm ready to be the dad they need," he said. **Click.**
It slid open.

June took his hand and closed her eyes. Mick
kissed her on the cheek. "Mick . . ." she sighed.

There, in her pajamas, Mick still in his suit, June
moved her mouth toward his and let him kiss her. His
lips were full and warm and tasted like home.

When Mick pulled back to look at her, June
looked away but took him by the hand. She led Mick
into the bedroom. They fell to the bed, as June pulled
Mick onto her. They rushed as they clung to each
other, their hearts swelling as they moved, their lips
pressed against each other, their breath one breath.
They both were under the same spell, that delicious
delusion that they were the two most important souls
to meet.

This was what June had ached for, every day since
he left. The feeling of his attention on her, the way he
moved his body with hers. He touched her in just the
way she had grown desperate to be touched.

Mick fell asleep soundly moments later, complete. June stayed awake the rest of the night, watching his chest move with his breath, watching his
eyelids flutter.

When morning came, she felt as if the next chapter
of her life was starting, the part where the family lives
happily ever after. As June started preparing breakfast,
Nina woke up and walked into the kitchen.

She could not quite make sense of the sight before
her. Her mother was making eggs and toast for this

strange man seated at the table. He was in trousers and an undershirt, drinking a cup of coffee. He looked eerily familiar and yet she could not place him.

She asked what she did not know. "Hi," she said. "Who are you?"

And Mick, undeterred, smiled at her and said, "Hi, honey, it's Daddy. I had to go away for a little while. But I'm back now. Forever."

Jay rolled up his trash and walked it over to the garbage can. "I have an idea," he said, with a grand pause.

"So spit it out," Kit said.

"When was the last time we were all riding together? Like, actually, all of us," he asked.

So often now things got in the way of the four of them just being out there on the water. Jay and Hud were traveling all over the world and Nina was always on some shoot. But they were all here now. They all had the afternoon free.

"I'm in," Kit said.

Hud nodded. "Me, too," he said. "Family shred."

Nina looked at her watch. "Let's do it. The waves are great at my place. We can head there. Especially since I can't stay out too long; the cleaners are coming.

I should be there to let them in, make sure they're all set."

"Can't you just leave the door unlocked with a note?" Jay asked.

"No, I mean, you know, I should greet them. Make them comfortable."

"Make them comfortable? They are going to clean your house," Jay said. "You are paying them to make **you** comfortable."

"Jay . . ." Nina started. But then that was it. "Are we gonna hit the surf or what?"

"Fuck yeah we're gonna hit the surf," Kit said, offering a high five to Hud, who took her up on it.

The four of them cleaned up their lunch and said goodbye to the staff and made their way to their cars.

It would be the last time they all surfed together. Even though Jay did not know what would happen over the course of the evening—did not know just what awaited them all—he did know that.

1962

Mick's life came into focus for him during the summer of 1962. He was on hiatus from touring. His new record was already in the can. And he had moved back in with his family.

Every day, he woke up with the satisfaction of being the man he meant to be. He was paying the bills and buying June and the kids whatever they wanted. He took June out for romantic dinners, he read stories of heroes and soldiers to his boys.

Still, his daughter held a piece of herself back from him.

Nina was not charmed by Mick like June was and she was not aching for his presence quite like the boys. But Mick remained determined to win her over. He would tickle her in the living room and offer to sing her to sleep at night. He would make her cheeseburgers on the grill and make sandcastles for her on the beach. He knew, over time, she would soften.

One day, he believed, Nina would come to understand that he was never leaving again.

"Marry me, Junie. One more time, this time forever," Mick said to June in the dark one night after they'd made love quietly, as the rest of the house slept.

"I thought last time was forever," June said. She

was half-joking, and still angry, but entirely happy to be asked.

"I was a boy pretending to be a man when I married you the first time. But I am a man now. Things are different," Mick said, pulling her toward him. "You know that, right?"

"Yes," June said. "I do." She'd seen it in the way he kept close to her, the way he never stayed out late, the way he drank half a pot of coffee in the morning to get up with the kids and almost no booze at night.

"Will you let this new man marry you?" he asked, pushing the hair away from her face.

June smiled, despite herself, and gave him the answer that both of them knew was never really in doubt. "Yes," she said. "I will."

• • •

That September, June and Mick remarried at the courthouse in Beverly Hills with the kids by their side. June wore a pale blue sheath dress with white gloves and three short strands of pearls around her neck. Mick wore his signature black. When the judge declared them married again, Mick grabbed June and dipped her, planting a kiss on her lips. Theo, Christina, and the kids watched as June laughed with her whole body, so delighted to have once again given him her soul.

"Be the man you tried to tell us you were," Christina said to him, just after the ceremony.

"I am that man now," Mick said. "I promise you that. I promise to never hurt her like that again."

"Them," Christina said. "Never hurt **them** like that again."

Mick nodded. "Believe me," he said. "I promise."

As the family walked out of the courthouse, Mick winked at Nina and grabbed her hand. She smiled just the tiniest bit in her lavender dress, so he lifted her up into his arms and ran with her through the parking lot.

"Nina, my Nina! Cuter than a ballerina!" he sang to her, and when he put her down, she was laughing.

Afterward, Mick and June did not leave for a honeymoon but, instead, drove home to the beach. They said good night to Theo and Christina. June heated up a leftover casserole for dinner. Mick put the kids to bed.

June took off her dress and hung it up in the closet in a plastic garment bag, dreaming of giving it to her daughter one day. It would be a physical testament to second chances.

June was pregnant before the year was out. And by the time Katherine Elizabeth Riva was born, Mick had stayed for so long, been so doting, that he had even won over tiny little suspicious Nina.

"I don't remember now when you were gone," Nina said to him one night as he was putting her to bed before leaving to do a few kickoff shows in Palm

Springs. His new album was about to be released, he was back in the spotlight. His publicity team was churning out the story of his redemption. "Ladies' Man Becomes Family Man." He was dressed up in his black suit. His hair was slicked back, showing his faint widow's peak. He smelled like Brylcreem.

"I don't remember it, either, honey," Mick said, kissing her on the forehead. "And we don't ever have to worry about those things again."

"I love you this much," Nina said as she reached wide with both her arms.

Mick tucked the blanket tight around her. "I love you double that."

Nina was in it with all of her heart now, as only those who have been hurt and learned to trust again truly can be. It is as if once your heart has been broken you learn of the deepest reserves it carries. And she had given up her reserves as well this time.

Her dad was here and he was staying and he loved her. She was his girl, his "Nina-baby." And every once in a while, when Mick was feeling emotional, he would pick her up and give her a hug and admit to her the truth: **She was his favorite.**

In the comfort of that love, Nina bloomed. She started singing Mick's songs with him around the house. "Sun brings the joy of a warm June . . ." they would sing together. "Long days and midnights bright as the moon . . ."

Nina became entranced by his voice, fascinated by his ties, riveted by the polish of his shoes, smitten to tell her friends at school who her dad was. She was proud that she had inherited his eyelashes, so full and long. She would sometimes stare at him, as he read the paper, watching him blink.

"Stop staring at me, sweetheart," Mick would say, not even moving his eyes off the page.

"OK," Nina would say and move on to something else.

So casual was their affection, so comfortable were their bodies and souls next to each other that there could be no rejection, no discomfort.

Now and then, in the early hours of morning, before everyone else was up, Mick would wake Nina up to fly a kite as the sun rose. Sometimes he would be fresh and clean, having just showered and shaved. Other times he would be getting home from a show, still tipsy, smelling a little sour. But either way, he would gently sit on Nina's bed and he'd say, "Wake up, Nina-baby. It's a windy day."

Nina would get out of bed and put on a cardigan over her nightgown, and the two of them would walk down, under the house, onto the beach.

It was always early enough that almost no one was there. Just the two of them sharing the dawn.

The kite was red with a rainbow in the center of it, so bright you could see it even in the fog. Mick would let it get sucked up into the sky and he'd hold on tight. He'd pretend he could barely hold on. He'd say, "Nina-baby! I need your help. Please! You have to save the kite!"

She knew it was an act but she delighted in it anyway and she would reach out, grabbing the string with all of her might. She felt strong, stronger than her father, stronger than anyone in the world as she held on to that kite, keeping it tied to the ground.

The kite needed her and her dad needed her. Oh, how good it felt to be important to somebody the way she felt important to him.

"You've got it!" he would say, as the kite teetered in her hands. "You've saved the day!" He would scoop her up in his arms and Nina knew, knew in her bones, that her father would never ever leave her again.

●　●　●

A year later, Mick Riva was performing in Atlantic City when in walked a backup singer named Cherry. He never flew home.

2:00 p.m.

The four Rivas were straddling their boards in the ocean, floating at the peak, all in a row like birds on a wire. And then, as the waves curled in, they took off, one by one.

Jay, Hud, Kit, Nina. A revolving team, with Jay the self-appointed leader of the pack. They soared past one another and paddled back out together, and when a wave took one of them too far down the shore, they worked their way back to their four-man lineup.

The first wave in a gorgeous set came in and Jay was primed for it. He got himself into position and popped up on his board, and then out of nowhere, Kit dropped in, cut him off, and stole his wave.

She smiled and held out a sisterly middle finger as she did it. Hud watched, mouth agape.

Kit knew that you can only bogart a wave from someone you are confident will not beat the ever-living shit out of you. Because waves that beautiful are rare. That is the thing about the water, it is not yours to control. You are at the mercy of nature. That's what makes surfing feel like more than sport: It requires destiny to be on your side, the ocean must favor you.

So when you are granted a sick wave like the one Jay thought was his—chest high, with a hollow face, peeling quick and clean—it is not only a bull's-eye but a jackpot.

"What the fuck!" Jay said, after cutting back quickly to avoid colliding. He grabbed the rails of his board to slow down. He hung there in the water, watching his little sister take off down the face of the wave until it slowly let her go, like her spot on the Ferris wheel was touching down.

She laid her chest down on the board and started toward Jay.

"You really can't pull that shit anymore," he called to her as Kit paddled out, duck-diving under the swells.

"Oops," she said, smiling.

"Seriously. Cut it out. Somebody's gonna get hurt," Jay followed up. "I can't always tell if you're about to drop in on me."

"I'm in full control," Kit said. "I don't need you to make room. I've got it." He really didn't understand, did he? How **good** she was.

But Hud saw it. Her confidence, her control, the chip on her shoulder.

"Kit, I'm seriously pissed at you," Jay said. "Like, apologize at least."

Hud took a wave out and then bailed once it all started to crumble. When he popped back out of the water, he saw Jay and Kit both floating on their boards, bickering. He spotted Nina walking out of the ocean. He watched her walk her board back over to her shed. She made her way up the steep stairs that led to her home.

Hud knew she was heading in to welcome the cleaning staff. She was going to offer them all a glass of water or iced tea. If one of them broke a plate or a vase, if they forgot a room, if they didn't make the beds the way Nina liked, she would still thank them profusely. She would overtip them. And then she would fix it herself.

It made Hud sad. The way Nina lost herself in always putting others first. Sure, Hud tried to put other people first. But sometimes he was selfish. Clearly.

But Nina never said no, never stood in anyone's way, never took anything. If you offered her five bucks, she'd give you ten. He knew he was supposed to like that about her but he didn't. He didn't like it about her at all.

Hud lifted himself over a soft wave, letting it buoy both him and his board, and paddled out to where Jay was. "Nina went in," Hud said. "For the cleaners."

Jay rolled his eyes. "For fuck's sake. Would it kill her to live a little?"

1969

In the late sixties, the counterculture had discovered the beauty of rustic Malibu and settled in along the mountains. The beaches were overrun with surfers on their brand-new shortboards—cooler and more aerodynamic than their older brothers' longboards. Teams of young dudes and the honorary dudette took over the water, running in packs, claiming coves for themselves, rushing poseurs out of town.

The air smelled like Mary Jane and suntan oil. And yet, still, you could smell the sea breeze if you took a moment.

Mick Riva's career—rocky tabloid headlines, a new hit album, a sold-out world tour—had taken off like a rocket, leaving hordes of young women screaming his name, millions of car radios playing his music as they sped down the freeway.

And so, to his children, he was both inescapable and never there.

Nina, Jay, Hud, and little Kit knew their father as a ghost whose voice visited them over the loudspeakers at the grocery store, whose face peered out at them from their friends' parents' album collections. He was a billboard in Huntington Beach on a road trip. He was a poster in the record stores their mother never wanted to go to. When he tried his hand at acting, he was a movie they never saw. But they almost never thought of him as theirs—he was everyone's.

And so, they never thought of the smell of whiskey on his breath, or the way his smile had once made them smile, or the way their mother used to blush with his kiss.

It was hard to remember their mother had ever blushed at all. To them, June was stress and bone.

In their second divorce, Mick had paid off the house and granted it to June. And he was supposed to resume the child support and alimony payments of their first divorce. But months after their divorce was finalized, June kept going out to the mailbox every day, looking for the checks and leaving empty-handed. None ever came. June suspected it was an oversight. She was almost positive that if she picked up the phone and called him—reminded him what was owed—he'd have an assistant or an accountant set up the recurring payments as he'd been instructed.

But she couldn't bring herself to ask him for one goddamn thing. She refused to let him see her squirm, to see her need.

When he finally came back to her again, he was going to respect her. He was going to bow at her feet and grovel, in awe of her strength.

So, instead of asking Mick to pay for the needs of his own children, June finally turned to her parents. She took a job at the restaurant.

June ended up in the exact place she had hoped Mick Riva would save her from.

• • •

By the summer of 1969, June's father had been dead two years. It was now only her and her mother running Pacific Fish. Nina was almost eleven. Jay and Hud were nine. Kit was six. And every day during the summer, they came with June to the restaurant.

One particular July morning, it neared a hundred degrees. People were coming in out of the sun in droves. They wanted cold beers and big sodas and shrimp rolls. The kitchen staff was overwhelmed and June, in a moment of crisis management, took the busboys off duty, put them in the kitchen to help out, and handed a rag to Nina, asking her to clean the tables.

Hud and Kit were playing Go Fish on a bench on the side of the restaurant by the parking lot. Jay was trying to flirt with a twelve-year-old girl, not above invoking his father's name in order to get a hello and a smile. And Nina was inside, watching the customers, making her way to their tables to clean up before they had barely left their seats.

Nina worked fast, with a sense of duty and pride in a job well done. She was efficient rather than perfect, just as her mother had instructed. And, without being asked, Nina grabbed a bin and pulled empty plastic baskets and cups and brought them over to the dishwasher. She was a natural. Born to serve.

As June rang in orders on the second register next to Christina, she looked up from the sea of customers to spot her daughter, wringing out the rag and getting to work on a just-vacated table. Nina's long brown hair had golden highlights from the sun just like June's had when she was a child, and her eyes were big and brown and open, just like June's had always been. Watching her daughter standing there, scrubbing down a table, June saw herself, only twenty years younger, and suddenly had the feeling she was going to jump out of her skin.

"Nina!" she called to her. "Take your brothers and sister to the beach."

"But—" Nina began to protest. She wanted to clean the tables because who else would clean them?

"Go!" June said, her voice impatient.

Nina thought she was in trouble. June believed she was setting her free.

• • •

Nina gathered her brothers and sister and pulled their swimsuits out of the back of the Cadillac that was now over a decade old. The four of them changed in the bathrooms behind the restaurant. Afterward, Nina took Kit's hand and the four of them stood on the side of the Pacific Coast Highway, waiting for an opportunity to cross over to the beach.

Nina was wearing a navy blue one-piece. She had sprouted that summer, now tall and lanky. She'd already begun to notice the way people looked at her, a second or two longer than they used to. The suit was now just a bit too small, the straps making indentations into the terra-cotta burn of her shoulders.

Jay, refusing to come inside all summer, had turned downright bronze, a fact made that much more apparent by his yellow swimming trunks. And Hud, faithfully beside Jay all season, had a sunburn, as always, and a new crop of light freckles across his nose and cheeks. His shoulders had begun to peel.

Kit, all of six years old, had begun insisting upon wearing T-shirts over her bathing suits because she didn't like boys looking at her half-naked. She stood on the side of the road with a yellow Snoopy T-shirt hiding a pink flowered suit, purple flip-flops on her feet.

Each one of them held a towel over their shoulder.

Nina held her siblings back from the road with one arm outstretched, forcing Jay and Hud to wait to cross the highway until she gave them the go-ahead. When she nodded, the four of them ran across, holding one another's hands. When their feet hit the hot sand, they pulled off their sandals and dropped their towels. They ran as fast as they could toward the water. And then the four of them came to an abrupt stop as their toes hit the foam, eight little feet sinking into the cold wet sand.

"Kit, you have to stay right next to me," Nina said.

Kit frowned but Nina knew she would do as she was told.

"All right," Jay said. "Ready? Set. Go!"

The four of them charged into the ocean like soldiers heading into battle.

They swam out, past the small breaking waves that were gently rolling onto the shore, preparing to body-surf to the sand. The ocean was something they had lived in their entire lives. In the water outside their home, they had swam while their mother cleaned the bathrooms, done somersaults in high tide as she made dinner, tried to find fish as June poured herself another Cape Codder. The Riva kids lived with water-clogged ears and salt-crusted faces.

Jay claimed the first good wave coming in. "Hud," he said. "Let's go."

"Right behind you," Hud called.

They took off. Jay's long, gangly arms paddled as fast as they could, Hud's thick legs kicked with all of their might. They coasted through the water, side by side, each one inching ahead and then falling behind.

These two had no real understanding of doing anything alone. They had come together at such a young age that they knew of no world but the one they inhabited alongside each other.

But they were not twins. And they had no illusions that they were, despite what their mother pretended in polite company. Each one of the children knew how Hud had joined the family. June had always told the kids the story with a sense of awe and destiny. She told them sometimes wild circumstances help fate unfold.

Jay and Hud. An apple and an orange. They did not have the same abilities or wear the same virtues. And yet, they still belonged side by side.

Jay coasted until his body hit the sand. Hud got clobbered at the last second, the wave turning him over and over in its grasp until he got his bearings and stood up. He looked to find Jay.

It felt as if Jay would always be the one who had made it to the sand and Hud would be the one thrown off the wave. But even before ten years old, Hud was managing this, redirecting his interests.

"Nice one!" Hud said, giving Jay a thumbs-up. This was something Hud took pride in, his lack of ego, his ability to appreciate the success of others, even when he had failed. His mother called it "good character."

Jay pointed out to the distance. Nina and Kit were coming in on a second wave. Nina had chosen a slow one, a small one. One that a six-year-old like Kit could handle. Nina was not looking at the shoreline or at Jay or at Hud. She was watching her sister, making sure if Kit went under, she knew where. Kit, even then, was irritated by her gaze.

They rode the calm wave in and were kicked off it only when they lost their momentum and landed butt first on the wet sand.

The four kids stood there in the shallow water,

about to go back out, when Jay happened to spot a lone surfboard resting against the grassy dunes to their left. Pale yellow with a cherry red stringer, beat up across the deck, the board stood there casually, as if it was waiting for someone.

"What if we surfed?" Jay asked.

These kids had been watching people on surfboards for as long as they could remember. There were surfers all down the waterline at that very moment, riding waves along the shore from cove to cove.

"We **are** surfing," Nina told him.

"No, with a **surfboard,**" Jay said, as if Nina could not possibly get any dumber.

They didn't have money for a surfboard. They had just enough money to pay the bills and eat three square meals a day. There was no money for new toys, new clothes. Nina was well aware of this. She was aware that, some months even the necessities weren't a guarantee. Children who grow up with money have no idea it exists. But children who don't understand that it powers everything.

"We are never going to have surfboards," Nina said.

"But what if we used **that** surfboard?" Jay said, pointing to the one that remained unclaimed.

"That isn't ours," Nina said.

"But what if," Jay said, walking over to it, "we just used it for a few minutes." Two preteen girls in crochet bikinis were in the process of laying down a blanket, preparing to sunbathe. Jay and Hud were both momentarily distracted.

"What are we gonna do when the guy who owns it comes looking for it?" Hud asked, pulling himself away.

"I don't know," Jay shrugged.

"That's your plan?" Kit said. "'I don't know'?"

"If he shows up and wants it back, we'll say we're sorry," Jay said. And before Nina could tell him no, he ran to the board and put his arms around it.

"Jay—" Nina began.

But Jay was already dragging it toward the water-line. He laid it down in the water, maneuvered himself on top of it, and began to paddle.

"Jay, come on," Nina shouted. "You shouldn't do this! It's lunchtime anyway, we should go back in!"

"No way! Mom said to stay out here!" Jay shouted back.

Nina looked at Hud, and Hud shrugged. Nina grabbed Kit's hand.

Kit took her hand reluctantly, and looked up at Nina, watching her sister's face scrunch into tiny folds. "Can I go out there, too? I want to try," Kit asked.

"No," Nina said, shaking her head. "It's not safe."

"But Jay is doing OK," Kit said.

Jay was now past the breakers, but he was having trouble handling the full weight of the board. It was hard to turn, hard to control. And then he couldn't get his legs around it quite right. The deck was wider than his straddle.

Nina grew more and more anxious with every second. He could fall off, he could lose the board, he could break his leg or his hand or go under. Nina quietly calculated how she would save him, or what she would say if the owner showed up, how she could handle all of this if it went south.

"I'm going out there," Kit said, taking her hand from Nina's and running into the water. Nina grabbed Kit with both arms and held her back.

"You always catch me," Kit said, aggrieved.

"You always run away," Nina said, smiling.

"Look, he's got it," Hud said, pointing at Jay.

Jay was standing on the board but then he swiftly slipped back, falling into the water. The board floated toward them with the current, as if it didn't need him to catch a wave. Nina waited for Jay to pop his head out of the water. And it was only once he did that she dared to take another breath.

By the time Jay made his way back to them, Hud had grabbed the board and saved it.

"Nina," Hud said, pushing the board over to her. "Take it."

"Just put it back where it was," Nina replied.

"Take it out!" Kit said.

Jay made his way back, put his hands on the board as if it was his.

"No," Hud said. "Nina's gonna take it out."

"No, I'm not."

"No, she's not," Jay said, taking it again. "I am."

"You're not either," Nina said.

"Yes, I am."

And it was then—this one moment in time—that Nina realized things were going to happen whether she relaxed or not. Whether she rode the surfboard herself or just watched Jay do it, the surfboard wasn't going back where it belonged. And so, Nina put her hands on the board. "Fine, I'm taking it."

Jay looked at her, stunned. He took his hands off of it. "It's heavy," he said.

"All right," Nina said.

"And it's hard to balance," he said.

"All right."

"When you fall off, it's my turn again," he said.

"Lay off, Jay," Hud said.

And Jay did.

Nina laid her body across the board and stretched her arms as far as they would go to paddle out. It was harder to get past the waves on the board. She kept getting pushed back, having to start all over again. But then she pushed her chest up off the board when the next wave came for her, the crest of it hitting her chest instead of her face, and she finally busted through.

She turned herself around, pushed her arms up, sat down on the board. She could feel it teeter underneath her and she straightened herself out.

When a wave approached, Nina weighed her options. She could try to stand up on the board or she could lie down and ride it in that way. Having watched Jay fall trying to stand up, she decided to lie low. Just before the wave bloated underneath her,

Nina started paddling as hard as she could. When she felt the water lift her, she didn't let up. She kept swimming until suddenly she couldn't swim anymore. Because she was in the air.

Lying across the board, she felt weightless and free, the wind blowing past her. What glory it was to feel the ocean move with you, to ride the water. The wave delivered her, softly, onto the sand.

Nina looked at her hands, now grazing the bottom. She'd done it. She'd ridden a surfboard all the way in.

When she stood up, she looked down the beach to see her siblings all cheering for her. Her brothers stood there with their mouths open.

"You have to keep paddling your arms as hard as you can until you catch it," Nina said, as she caught back up with them. "It takes more effort than just with your body. But then you move faster, once you catch it."

"You didn't stand up though," Jay said.

"I know but I think we can work up to that."

And so, that's what they did.

Nina, Jay, and Hud took turns riding the surfboard into the shore with varying degrees of success, sometimes letting Kit tag along on their backs.

They rode the surfboard all afternoon, crashing and gliding in equal measure. They inhaled water as they crashed, cut their toes on rocks, bruised their ribs simply from the weight of their bodies against the board. Their eyes stung with the salt of the ocean and the glare of the sun.

Until finally, hours into their adventure, Jay took the surfboard out on his own as the three of them watched from the wet sand. "I'm gonna stand up," he said. "Watch me."

Jay had fallen off enough times now to believe he understood the rules. He paddled out, faced the shore, and lay on the board, waiting. He waited for one slow, small wave, just big enough to carry him.

When he saw what he wanted, he paused until just before it swelled right behind him and he started to paddle. He used his arms harder than he had ever used them before. He could feel the board catch on the wave, feel it steady itself. And he slowly got onto his knees, and then his feet, and stayed low. He was doing it. He was **surfing.**

He could see Nina, Hud, and Kit watching him from the distance, could feel their anticipation. It was moments like this, all eyes on him, when he understood himself the best.

Beaming, he crouched as still as he could, until the wave started to knock him off. And then, feeling the board begin to betray him, Jay jumped off and landed, half gracefully, into the water. A champion.

Nina and Hud started running toward him, Kit leading their way. And Jay started laughing so hard that tears were forming in his eyes. "Did you see that?" he yelled to them. He was lost in pure, fresh joy. The kind that keeps you weightless even after you've touched ground.

"Pretty cool," Hud said, as he gave Jay a high five. Kit wrapped her hands around his neck and jumped up onto him. Nina smiled. He had been right. The whole afternoon had been exhilarating. The trying and crashing, the trying and doing, the trying harder, doing better.

• • •

Soon after, the extended lunch rush had ended and the real dinner rush had not quite started and so June snuck out of the restaurant. In her navy high-waisted shorts and white sleeveless button-up, she ran across the highway, to the beach. She found all four of her children taking turns on a surfboard that she knew wasn't theirs.

She put her hands on her hips and said, "Now where did this come from?"

"Mom, I'm sorry we—" Nina started to explain, but June put her hand up.

"It's all right, sweetheart," June said. "I was teasing. It doesn't seem like it belongs to anyone anyhow."

"Can we keep the surfboard?" Kit asked. "So we can do this together every day?"

All four of her children looked toward June, waiting for an answer.

"No, I'm sorry, honey, I don't think so," June said.

"Just in case someone is looking for it." June watched as all four of her children deflated. "But I'll tell you what. If it's here tomorrow, we'll bring it home."

That night, as the kids ate dinner in the break room in the back of the restaurant and June sipped her Cape Codder, they spoke of nothing but the water. June, with her cup in hand, listened patiently as her children described wave after wave. June kept them talking, asking questions about even the most trivial facts of the day. None of the kids stopped to wonder whether she actually found them fascinating or was just very good at pretending. But the truth was, June simply adored her children. She loved their thoughts and ideas, loved to hear about their personal discoveries, loved to watch them as they began to take the shape of fully formed people.

She thought of her children like the magic grow capsules you got at gift shops at the science museum. These tiny little nothings that you drop into water and then watch as they slowly reveal what they were always destined to be. This one a **Stegosaurus,** this one a **T. rex.** Except, instead, it was watching them become dependable, or talented, or kind, or daring.

June knew that her children had found a previously undiscovered part of themselves that day. She knew that childhood is made up of days magnificent and mundane. And this had been a magnificent day for all of them.

That night, they went home and watched **Adam-12** together and then dispersed. Kit went to bed. Jay and Hud went to their room to read comics. Nina got under the covers and pretended to read a book from the summer reading list.

But all of them felt as though their bodies were still rising with the surf.

For Jay, the feeling was almost an obsession. His brain couldn't stop focusing on how it had felt to ride a wave with that much power. To glide that smoothly. To ride, to float, to soar. He was lost in the thought of it when he heard Hud speak up from his bed.

"If that board's not there tomorrow," Hud said, "what are we going to do?"

Jay sat up. "I was wondering the same thing. Should we try to sneak out? And go get it so no one else does?"

"No," Hud said. "We can't do that."

"OK," Jay said. "Yeah, you're right."

Jay lay back down and stared up at the ceiling. They were quiet for a moment and Jay knew Hud was still considering it. When Hud didn't speak up, Jay knew it was final.

"It was awesome, though," Jay said.

"I bet we looked so cool," Hud added, his head on his pillow.

"Yeah," Jay said, smiling. "We totally did."

The two of them fell asleep soundly, both hoping and planning.

Kit, meanwhile, had drifted off to sleep the moment

her head hit the pillow, dreaming all through the night of the four of them surfing together on their own boards.

But it was Nina who was consumed by it, living the experience in her body. Her chest could feel where the board had been. Her arms ached from the resistance of the water. Her legs felt like rubber from the force with which she had slammed them down, used them to propel herself forward. She could feel both the ocean and its absence across her skin.

She wanted to **go back.** Right then and there. To try again. She wanted to stand up on the board like Jay had. She was determined now. She remembered a photo she'd seen in a magazine a few months ago, a guy on a surfboard somewhere in Europe. **Was it Portugal?** She wondered if she could be that sort of person when she grew up. A real surfer. Who went places just for the waves.

She tried to make herself fall asleep. But well after ten, still wide awake, she walked down to the kitchen and saw her mother sitting in the living room, sipping vodka right out of the bottle while watching the Saturday Night movie in her pajamas.

When June saw her elder daughter, she moved the vodka onto the floor, sliding it behind the sofa's arm with her foot.

"Can't sleep, honey?" June said as she put her arm out, inviting Nina onto the sofa with her.

Nina nodded and curled into the side of her mother's body, the cradle that often felt like it was hers and hers alone. Her mother smelled like Shalimar and sea salt.

"Can I get a job working at the restaurant?" Nina asked.

June looked at her. "What do you mean?"

"Well, maybe I could earn money," she said. "And buy us all surfboards."

"Oh, honey," June said, as she rubbed her daughter's arm, pulled her closer. "I will get you all surfboards, OK? I promise."

"You don't have to, that's not what I meant."

"Let me get you surfboards. Let that be my job."

Nina smiled at her and put her head back on June's shoulder.

It was not easy, being a parent. It was not easy raising your four children on your own. But what made June the most frustrated at her husband—her twice ex-husband—was that she had no one to swoon over her children with.

Her mother would listen, obviously. Christina loved them. But June wanted someone on the couch next to her at night, to smile with her when they thought of the kids. She wanted someone who would laugh with her about Kit's attitude, and commiserate with her about Jay's stubbornness, who would know how to teach Hud to stand up for himself a bit more, and teach Nina to relax. She, especially, wanted someone to light up along with her on a day like this, when her kids had found a sense of wonder and joy in the middle of her chaos.

Oh, what Mick was missing, wherever he was.

He did not know how good it felt for your eleven-year-old daughter to want nothing more than to lay her head against your shoulder. He did not know how good it felt to love like this.

She knew that when it came to the two of them— she here with these kids and he out there somewhere with God knows who—she had the better end of the deal. She would choose to be here with these four kids over anything in the world.

But she hated that, even in this blissful quiet moment, she was still thinking of him.

Nina fell asleep in her mother's arms and when she did, June picked the bottle of vodka back up. She needed that bottle to go to sleep, but she rarely drank past the invisible line she had in her head of where to stop for the night.

The next day, the surfboard was gone. And the kids went back to bodysurfing, trying to hide their frowns.

• • •

A few months later, on Christmas morning, Nina, Jay, Hud, and Kit woke up to see the tree they had decorated was gone.

"Where's the Christmas tree?" June asked, in mock confusion. "You don't think it just up and walked away, do you?"

The kids all looked at one another, cautiously excited for something they could not even guess.

"Maybe we should check by the water," June said.

The kids ripped open the door and ran down the steps to the beach. They shrieked when they saw it.

There, stuck lopsided in the sand, was their Christmas tree.

And beside it were four surfboards lined up in a row. Yellow, red, orange, and blue.

3:00 p.m.

Hud's hair was barely dry when he parked his car in front of the art studio at Pepperdine University. He grabbed his camera from the front seat and walked in despite the fact that, formally speaking, he wasn't supposed to be there. He wasn't a student.

But Hud had found that one of the nice things about spending his entire life in a small town was that he knew people. The cashier at the market, the guy who took the ticket stubs, the assistant to the head of photography at Pepperdine, Hud loved talking to them all. He liked to ask them questions about themselves and hear how they were doing. He liked to make jokes with the guy behind the register at the soft-serve stand about chocolate ice cream with extra whipped cream being "low-calorie."

He loved small talk. A quality he knew was in low supply. It certainly wasn't a trait he shared with any of his siblings or his mother. They, especially Jay and Kit, were always rushing him from one thing to the next. Sometimes, Hud wondered if he got it from Mick, but that seemed unlikely. Which led Hud to wonder if it came from his birth mother, Carol.

Carol was a mystery to Hud. He did not know anything about her other than what she had named him and where she had left him. All he could do was imagine what she might be like, wonder if there were things about himself that he'd recognize in her, things in her that would make him recognize himself.

A few years earlier, Hud had seen a photo of Mick in a magazine where Mick was looking directly at the camera and smiling. The headline said THE MAIN MAN IS BACK, and the article was about Mick topping the charts again after all these years. But Hud barely noticed any of that. He kept staring at Mick's right eyebrow, the way it was raised just the tiniest bit, the same way Hud raised his when he smiled.

Hud had felt as if the world was closing in on him. If he had Mick's eyebrow, what else of his did he have? Was Hud capable of what Mick was capable of? Did Mick's callousness live dormant inside him, choosing its moment to reveal that Hud, too, was capable of caring for no one but himself? That Hud, too, could leave the people he loved on the side of the road?

Our parents live inside us, whether they stick around or not, Hud thought. They express themselves through us in the way we hold a pen or shrug our shoulders, in the way we raise our eyebrow. Our heritage lingers in our blood. The idea of it scared the shit out of him.

He knew that Carol must live in him, too. Most likely in some way he could not see. And so he prayed it was something like this, the way he loved to speak to people. His tenderness. Let it be that he inherited that from her, or her laugh, or her gait. Anything but her cowardice.

"Hey," Hud said to the guy behind the front desk as he pulled his shades off his face and threaded them over the edge of his collar.

"Hey, man," Ricky Esposito said. Ricky was in charge of opening and closing the darkroom every day and he would let Hud use the facility whenever it was free.

Ricky had been two years behind Hud and Jay in school and thought of them as the very pinnacle of cool. Handsome brothers, surfers, sons of a famous singer. To the scrawny, acne-scarred Ricky Esposito, it was hard to believe Hud and Jay Riva had any problems at all.

"Mind if I . . ." Hud lifted his camera ever so slightly to indicate his intentions.

Ricky nodded toward the darkroom. "Have at it, buddy," he said. "Party on for tonight?"

Hud smiled. He'd been unaware that Ricky knew of the party. Jay would have said that Ricky Esposito was not cool enough to attend. In fact, many people would have said this. But Hud maintained that if you were cool enough to know about the party, you were cool enough to come to the party. Those were the rules. And Ricky knew about the party.

"Yeah, for sure," Hud said. "You coming?"

Ricky nodded coolly, but Hud saw that Ricky's hands were shaking ever so slightly. "You know it. Can I bring anything?"

Hud shook his head. "Just yourself."

"All right," Ricky said. "You got it."

Hud slipped through the door and into the darkroom. He had been thinking about the photos all morning. **Ashley.**

If he had to, would he screw up his relationship with Jay for her? Was he capable of it? Both possible answers scared him.

He shut the door tight and he got to work.

1971

June drank Screwdrivers in the morning like other people drank orange juice. She drank Cape Codders at lunch in the break room.

She had sea breezes with dinner, she and the kids sitting around the table eating meatloaf or a roast chicken. The cups on the table were always the same. Milk for Kit, soda for Jay and Hud, water for Nina, and a highball filled with vodka cut with the coral hue of ruby red grapefruit juice and cranberry cocktail poured over ice for Mom.

Nina had begun to notice the alcohol after they had to evacuate the year before. There were fires in the canyons, people's homes were burning, and you could smell the smoke in the air.

June woke them up early in the morning and calmly but firmly told them to each grab the things they absolutely could not live without.

Each one of the kids asked to strap the surfboards to the car roof. Kit brought her stuffed animals. Jay and Hud brought their comics and baseball cards. Nina brought her favorite jeans and a few records. June packed up the family albums. But then, as they all got in the car, Nina noticed June had grabbed the vodka, too.

Days later, when they returned to their home,

unscathed except for some soot covering the counter-tops, Nina noticed that there was a new, fuller bottle of vodka in her mother's purse. Nina watched as June snuck it into the freezer, the very first thing she unpacked.

These days, June had started falling asleep on the couch in her nightgown, hair in curlers. She never quite made it to her bedroom after spending her nights in front of the TV with that bottle.

But she still kept her charm and wits about her. She kept her smile. She got the kids to school on time, showed up for every single one of their plays and games. She made their Halloween costumes by hand. She ran the restaurant with diligence and honor, paying her kitchen and service staff well.

It was the beginning of a lesson her children would learn by heart: Alcoholism is a disease with many faces, and some of them look beautiful.

• • •

Christina died of a stroke in the fall of 1971, at the age of sixty-one.

June watched the nurses take her mother's body away. Standing there in the hospital, June felt like she'd been caught in an undertow. **How had she ended up here?** One woman, all alone, with four kids, and a restaurant she had never wanted.

The day after the funeral, June took the kids to

school. She dropped Kit off at the elementary building and then drove Nina, Jay, and Hud to junior high.

When they pulled into the drop-off circle, Jay and Hud took off. But Nina turned back, put her hand on the door handle, and looked at her mother.

"Are you sure you're OK?" Nina asked. "I could stay home. Help you at the restaurant."

"No, honey," June said, taking her daughter's hand. "If you feel up for going to school, then that's where you should be."

"OK," Nina said. "But if you need me, come get me."

"How about we think of it the other way around?" June said, smiling. "If you need **me,** have the office call me."

Nina smiled. "OK."

June felt herself about to cry and so she put her sunglasses over her eyes and pulled out of the parking lot. She drove, with the window down, to Pacific Fish. She pulled in and put on the parking brake. She took a deep breath. She got out of the car and stood there, staring up at the restaurant with a sense of all she had inherited. It was hers now, whatever that meant.

She lit a cigarette.

That goddamn restaurant had claimed her from the day she was born and now she understood that she would never outrun it.

Some of the lights on the sign were broken. The whole exterior needed a power washing. That was solely up to her now. She was all this restaurant had left. Maybe it was all she had left, too.

June rested against the hood of her car, crossed her arms, and continued smoking, taking stock of the new shape of her life.

She was overworked and overtired and lonely. She missed the parents who had never truly understood her, missed the man who had never truly loved her, missed the future she thought she had been building for herself, missed the young girl she used to be.

But then she thought of her children. Her exhausting, sparkling children. She must have done something right if life had brought her the four of them. That much seemed crystal clear.

Maybe she had done something with her life after all. Maybe she could make something of what she had left.

June put out her cigarette on the ground, crushing it with the toe of her black flat. And then, as she looked up at the Pacific Fish sign, June Riva got a wild idea. She'd earned her name through heartbreak and consequences—wasn't it her right to do with it anything she wanted?

Two weeks later, three men came to put up the new sign. Bright red cursive: RIVA'S SEAFOOD.

When it was done, June stood by the front door and looked at it. She was drinking vodka out of a soda cup. She smiled, satisfied.

It was going to bring in a lot more customers. It

might even get her some press. But more important, when Mick finally came back, he was going to love it. June was sure of that.

• • •

Soon, Jay and Hud also began to understand that she was an alcoholic—even if they didn't know the word for it or didn't know it was something with a word at all.

Their mom always made more sense first thing in the morning, tired and sluggish but lucid. She made less and less sense as the day went on. Jay once whispered to Hud, after June told him to "go bath and shower," that "Mom starts acting nuts after dinner."

It got so that by 6:00 P.M., the kids all knew to ignore her. But they also tried to keep her home, lest she embarrass them in public.

Nina had even started pretending to love the idea of driving at the young age of fourteen. She would ask her mom if she could drive them all to the store, if she could take the boys to the movie theater instead of June dropping them all off, if she could chauffeur Kit and Vanessa to the ice cream stand so June could stay home.

Nina was actually terrified of driving. It felt overwhelming and nerve-racking, trying to merge onto PCH with all of those cars flying by. She would white-knuckle the steering wheel the whole way, her heart racing, her confusion rising as she tried to time her turns. When she eventually got them all to the chosen destination and got out of the car, she could feel the tension she'd been holding in between her shoulder blades and behind her knees.

But as afraid as Nina was of driving, she was more afraid of her mother behind the wheel after lunch. Nina sometimes couldn't fall asleep at night, tallying June's surging number of near hits, her slow reactions, the missed turns.

It was easier, despite how hard it was, for Nina to drive them all herself. And soon it started to feel to Nina that it was not just easier but rather **crucial** that she prevent what felt like an inevitable calamity.

"You really like driving," June said, handing over the keys one evening, after June realized they were out of milk. "I don't get it. I never liked it."

"Yeah, I want to be a limo driver one day," Nina said, immediately regretting the pathetic lie. Surely she could have come up with something better than that.

Hud caught Nina's eye when he heard her. "I'll go with you," he said. "To get the milk."

"Me, too," Jay added.

As the three of them headed out, June lit a cigarette and closed her eyes on the couch. Kit was playing with Legos in front of the TV. June's arm relaxed as she stretched out, the tip of her lit cigarette grazing Kit's hair. Nina gasped. Jay's eyes went wide.

"Kit, you're coming with us," Hud said. "You need more toothpaste. For your . . . teeth."

Kit looked at them quizzically, but then shrugged and got up off the shag rug.

"What's going on?" Kit asked when they got to the car.

"Don't worry about it," Hud said as he opened the door for her.

"Everything's fine," Nina told her as she got in the front seat.

"You never tell me anything," Kit said. "But I know something's up."

Jay got in the passenger seat. "Then you don't need us to tell you. Now, who wants to buy the cheapest jug of milk and spend the rest on a pack of Rolos?"

"I want at least a fourth of the pack!" Kit said. "You always take more than your share."

"You can have my share, Kit," Nina said, putting the gear in reverse.

"Everyone be quiet now. Nina needs to concentrate," Hud called out.

As Nina slowly backed the car out of the driveway and did a three-point turn onto the road, Kit looked out the window and wondered what it was that her brothers and sister wouldn't tell her, what it was that she already knew.

In the end, it was the TV that gave her the words.

• • •

About a year later, when Kit was ten, she was with June on the couch, watching a TV show. In the scene, two brothers were confronting each other about a murder. And Kit saw one brother take a whiskey bottle out of the other's hand and call him a "drunk." "You're a drunk," he said. "And you're killing yourself with this stuff."

Something clicked in Kit's head. She turned to look at her mother. June caught her eye and smiled at her daughter.

Suddenly, Kit's body started to burn with rage. She excused herself and went to the bathroom, shut the door behind her. She looked at the towels hanging on the door and wanted to punch through them, punch through the door itself.

She had a name for it now. She understood what had been nagging at her, scaring her, unsettling her for so long.

Her mother was a drunk. **What if she was killing herself with that stuff?**

• • •

The next week, June burned dinner.

There was smoke in the house, a flame in the oven, the smell of burnt cheese settling into the tablecloth and their clothes.

"Mom!" Nina yelled, running through the house as soon as she noticed the smoke. June sprang to attention as her children invaded the kitchen.

"Sorry! Sorry!" she said, pulling her head off the table, where she'd fallen asleep. Her movements were stiff, her processing slow.

Kit clocked the bottle of Smirnoff on the counter. She wasn't sure if it was the same bottle that had been almost full yesterday, but now there was barely any left.

Nina ran to the oven, put on a glove, and pulled the casserole dish out. Jay ran in and got up on the counter, immediately disabling the smoke detector. Hud opened all the windows.

The macaroni and cheese was nearly black on the bottom, scorched on the sides and top. You had to cut it open with a knife to find the familiar pale orange it was supposed to be. June served it anyway.

"All right, kids, eat up. It's not so bad."

Nina, Jay, and Hud all sat down as they were told, prepared to act as if everything was fine. They passed around plates, put their napkins on their laps, as if this were any other meal.

Kit stood, incredulous.

"Do you want milk with dinner, Kit?" Nina said, getting up to serve her younger sister.

"Are you kidding me?" Kit said.

Nina looked at her.

"I'm not eating this," Kit said.

"It's fine, Kit, really," Hud said. Kit looked at Hud and watched his face tense, his eyes focus in on her. He was trying to tell her to drop it. But Kit just couldn't do it.

"If she doesn't want to eat it, she doesn't have to eat it," Jay said.

"I'll go make us all something else," Nina said.

"No, Nina, this is fine. Katherine Elizabeth, sit down and eat your food," June said.

Kit looked at her mother, searched for some embarrassment or confusion. But June's face showed nothing out of the ordinary.

Kit finally snapped. "We're not going to pretend you didn't just burn dinner like we pretend you're not a drunk!"

The whole house went quiet. Jay's jaw dropped. Hud's eyes went wide in shock. Nina looked down at her hands in her lap. June stared at Kit as if Kit had just slapped her across the face.

"Kit, go to your room," June said, tears forming in her eyes.

Kit stood there, silent and unmoving. She was awash in a tumbling cycle of guilt and indignation, indignation and guilt. Was she terribly wrong or had she been exactly right? She couldn't tell.

"C'mon, Kit," Nina said, getting up and putting her napkin on the table. Nina grabbed her hand gently and led her away. "It's OK," Nina whispered to her as they walked.

Kit was quiet, trying to figure out if she regretted what she'd said. After all, regret would imply she felt like she'd made a choice. And she hadn't. She felt she'd had no other option but to say out loud what was hurting so much within her.

When Nina and Kit disappeared down the hall, Jay and Hud looked back at their mother.

"We will clean up, Mom," Hud said. "You can go lie down."

Hud caught Jay's eye. "Yeah," Jay said, despite the dread growing within him that it was going to be his job to clean up burnt cheese. "Hud and I have this under control."

June looked at her two sons, already fourteen. They were almost men. How had she not noticed that?

"All right," she said, exhausted. "I think I'm going to go to sleep." And for the first time in a long time, she walked into her bedroom, put on her pajamas, and fell asleep in her bed.

The boys cleaned up the kitchen. Jay scrubbed the Pyrex as hard as he could to get the char off. Hud poured out the full glasses and wiped down the light dusting of ash on the counter where the smoke had settled.

"Kit's right," Jay said in a whisper as he stopped scrubbing for just a moment and caught Hud's eye.

Hud looked at him. "I know."

"We never talk about it," Jay said, his whisper growing louder.

Hud stopped cleaning the counter. He took a deep breath and then let it out as he spoke. "I know."

"She almost set fire to the kitchen," Jay said.

"Yeah."

"Should we . . ." Jay found it difficult to finish his sentence. **Should we call Dad?** Jay wasn't even sure how they would do such a thing. They didn't know where their father was or how to contact him. If they did, Jay would have liked the chance to see him. But once, years ago, when Hud had broken his nose falling off the monkey bars at school and needed surgery to have it straightened, Jay overheard June tell his grandmother, "I would sooner turn tricks off the highway than call Mick and ask him for anything." So even saying it out loud, even suggesting it, seemed to dishonor his mother. And he wouldn't do that. He couldn't. "I guess I'm saying, what are we supposed to do?"

Hud frowned and sighed, searching for an answer. He finally sat down at the table, resigned. "I have no idea."

"I mean, this whole thing with Mom . . . She's just in a bad, like, moment, right?" Jay asked. "This isn't a forever thing?"

"No, of course not," Hud said. "It's just a phase or something."

"Yeah," Jay said, assuaged. He picked up the scrubber again, grinding away at the cheese. "Yeah, totally."

The brothers looked at each other, and in one flash of a second, it was perfectly clear to both of them that there was a big difference between what you needed to believe and what you actually believed.

When they were done, they brought a half-eaten bag of chips and a box of Ritz crackers into Kit's room, where Nina and Kit were sitting on the floor, talking.

The four of them sat there, eight greasy hands being rubbed off on eight pant legs.

"We should get napkins," Nina said.

"Oh, no, are there crumbs on the floor?" Jay teased her. "Call the cops!"

Kit started laughing. Hud pretended to dial a phone. "Hello? Crumb police?" he said. Jay got so hysterical, he nearly choked on a Ritz.

"Yeah, uh, Sergeant Crackers here," Kit said, as if she was speaking into the handheld radio. "We've heard reports of loud crunching."

Something broke inside of Nina too, causing a wild and loud laugh to escape her mouth. The bizarre sound of it made them all laugh harder.

"All right, all right," Nina said, calming down. "We should get to bed."

They got up and put the food away. They put their pajamas on. They brushed their teeth.

"Everything's going to be OK," Nina said to each of her siblings as she said good night that evening. "I promise you that."

Upon hearing it, Jay's shoulders relaxed one tenth of a percent, Hud exhaled, Kit released her jaw.

Despite having long ago learned some people don't keep their promises, all three of the younger Rivas knew they could believe her.

4:00 p.m.

Nina stood in her bedroom at the very top of the mansion. It had been rendered spotless. The floor-to-ceiling windows that faced southeast to the ocean were so clean that, were it not for the frames themselves, you would have thought you were looking at open air. In still and perfectly clear moments like this, when Nina could see out past the cliffs, across the rippling sea, as far as Catalina Island, she had to admit there were things to love about this house.

Her bed had been made with military precision. A birch-wood platform bed with a white quilt spread out across it, tucked tightly under the mattress. A comforter lay folded in a perfect crease at the foot of the bed. Every type of pillow and coordinating sham that you could imagine was displayed at the headboard.

How did she own so many expensive things?

The cleaners had moved on to the downstairs. They were washing the stone tile floors and whitening up the walls. They were getting the cobwebs from the crooks of the high ceilings and the dust bunnies from the far corners of the hallways and bookshelves and cabinets.

Nina could hear them vacuuming her area rugs and she wondered if there was any real point to it. They would be sandy and dingy by ten. By midnight, her whole downstairs would be in disarray.

She walked into her master bathroom to find the vanity pristine, the floor flawless; taupe cloth hand towels were piled in neat triangles.

Nina opened up the double doors to the walk-in closet and ran her hand along the left wall, feeling the textures of her dresses, her pants, her shirts. Cotton and silk and satin. Velvet and leather. Nylon and neoprene.

She had so many clothes—so many clothes she had never wanted, never needed, never worn. She had so much **stuff.** Lately it felt as if that was supposed to be the whole point of everything—how many things you could buy—as if some magical life waited for you on the other side of all of it. But it made her feel nothing.

When she got to the end of her things, she started on the other side, running her hand along what was remaining of Brandon's clothes. She could feel the gaps in between the shirts, could see the empty hangers left behind. Brandon did believe in the glory of all that **stuff.** And now Nina was keenly aware of what **wasn't** on his side of that closet anymore. His stiff polos and soft Levi's and broken-in Adidas. His Lacostes and his Sperrys. The things he loved, the things he felt he needed. They were gone.

It hurt. It hurt so bad that there was a part of her that wanted to get out a bottle of Smirnoff and fix herself a Sea Breeze.

1975

It was late 1975. The kids all had sleepovers planned on the same weekend. It was the first time that had ever happened.

Nina was seventeen and had plans to go out to a party at a friend's house and spend the night there. Jay and Hud had an overnight with the water polo team. Kit was sleeping over at her friend Vanessa's.

Before Nina left the house that afternoon, she wondered if it was a bad idea, all of them leaving at once. "I don't want you to be here all alone," Nina said to June. Nina was in the kitchen, looking at her mother sitting on the living room sofa.

"Honey, go out with your friends, please."

"But what are you going to do tonight?"

"I'm going to enjoy myself," June said with a smile. "Do you have any idea how exhausting you four are? Don't you think I might be eager for a little time by myself? I'm going to run a bath and sit in it as long as I want. Then I'm going to lie out on the patio and watch the waves roll in."

Nina looked unconvinced.

"Hey," June said. "Who's the mom here? Me or you?"

"You're the mom," Nina said, amused. It had

become a familiar refrain. She answered the next question before it was even asked. "And I'm the kid."

"And you're the kid. For at least a little while longer."

"OK," Nina said. "If you're sure."

June got up off the couch and put her hands on her daughter's arms and looked her in the eye. "Go, honey. Have fun. You deserve it."

And so Nina left.

June settled herself back on the sofa and turned on the TV. She grabbed the **TV Guide.** She planned out what she was going to watch. And then there he was on the nightly news.

"And in entertainment," the reporter said, "Mick Riva has married for the fifth time at the age of forty-two. His blushing bride, Margaux Caron, a young model from France, is twenty-four."

June lit a cigarette and sipped her vodka.

And then she buried her head in her hands and bawled her eyes out. The cry came from her stomach, bubbled over within her, and emerged from her throat in gasps and screeches.

She stubbed out her cigarette and threw herself onto the sofa. She let the sobs run through her body. He was never coming back. She should have listened to her mother all those years ago. But she'd been a fool since the day he'd shown up. She'd been a fool her whole life.

God, June thought, **I have to get my life together. For my children.**

She thought of Nina's bright smile, and Jay's cock-sure determination, and Hud's gentleness, the way he always hugged her tight. She thought of Kit, that spitfire, who might just one day rule them all.

She knew they knew she was losing it. It was clear from the way they doted on her, the way they no longer trusted her to remember what they needed for school, the way they had started whispering to one another in front of her.

But she could change that if she'd just stop waiting for that asshole to fix it all. If she'd just face that she had to fix it herself.

She breathed in deeply. And poured herself another glass.

She put on an old Mick Riva record, his second album. She listened to "Warm June" over and over and over again, and with each go-round on the record player she'd pour herself another glass. She'd meant something to him. He could never take that away from her.

June turned to the vodka bottle again to see she'd emptied it. She went through the kitchen to get more but, instead, found a dusty old bottle of tequila.

She opened the tequila. And then she drew herself a bath.

She watched the bathroom steam up from the heat of it and breathed in the mist. It felt comforting and safe. She untied her robe, stepped out of her clothes, and slipped into the water.

She rested her arms along the walls of the tub, relaxed her head back, and breathed in the warm air. She closed her eyes. She felt like she could stay in this bath for an eternity. And everything was going to be fine.

It was her last conscious thought. Forty-five minutes later, she drowned.

June Riva, that once tenderhearted dreamer, was gone.

• • •

When Nina came home the next morning, she found her mother in the bathtub, slack and lifeless.

She rushed to try to pull her mother's body from the water, to try to wake her. She could not process her mother's pallor or stillness. Terror clutched her chest.

She ran through who to call at lightning speed but came up empty. Grandparents (dead), father (deadbeat). There must be someone, anyone, who could fix this.

As Nina knelt there on the bathroom floor, she felt like she was falling, falling, falling, falling. The pain had no limit, the fear no boundary. There was no net to catch her, nothing to bounce off of, no ground floor to end her agony and distress.

The moment Nina fully understood that her mother was dead was the moment she understood there was no one left in the world to count on, to lean on, to trust, to believe in.

She held her mother's pale hand as she called 911. She held her tighter as the medics rushed over.

Nina watched as EMTs bolted into the house, hurrying to her mother's side. Nina stood by the door, breathless, as they told her what she already knew. Her mother was dead.

Nina watched her mother's body being carried away. And she thought, for certain, she would come back. Even though she knew that was impossible.

She called Vanessa's house and when Vanessa's mother answered, Nina summoned all of her strength to ask her to send Kit home right away. And then, unsure how to get ahold of Jay and Hud, she paced the floor.

The two boys came home shortly after and when they did, she forbade them from going inside.

"What happened?" Jay said, panicked. "Fuck, Nina! What's going on?"

Hud remained silent, in shock. Somewhere within him, he already knew. When Kit got there, moments later, Nina took them all down to the shoreline, just underneath the house.

She knew it was up to her to say what had to be said. To do what had to be done. When there is only you, you do not get to choose which jobs you want, you do not get to decide you are incapable of anything. There is no room for distaste or weakness. You must do it all. All of the ugliness, the sadness, the things most people can't stand to even think about, all must live inside of you. You must be capable of everything.

"Mom died," Nina said, and then she watched all three of her siblings fall to the earth.

And she knew, in a flash, that she had to be able to catch them. She had to be able to hold each of them up, as they screamed, as the water came and soaked their socks and squeaked into their shoes.

And so she did.

Do you know how much a body can weigh when it falls into your arms, helpless? Multiply it by three. Nina carried it all. All of the weight, in her arms, on her back.

5:00 p.m.

Kit was trying to get dressed for the party.

The sun was just beginning to set. The blue-and-orange sky was faintly turning purple. The tide was low, the seagulls were squawking down on the shoreline. Kit could hear the waves softly rolling from her opened window.

She was standing in front of the mirror in her bedroom, wearing a bra and a pair of light-wash jeans. She did not know what shirt she wanted to wear and was already second-guessing the pants. But tonight was important.

She was going to kiss a boy. Seth would be there. Maybe she could work up the interest to kiss him. Or maybe someone else. Hopefully somebody else. Surely there would be at least one dude at this party she could . . . feel something for. And if not, she just had to rip the Band-Aid off and do it anyway. But she should look good, right?

She wasn't actually sure how to look good, wasn't sure what she thought looked good on her. She'd never really tried to look beautiful before. That had been her mother's thing; it was her sister's job.

As she looked at herself in the mirror, she thought of her sister's long legs, the way Nina always wore short skirts and shorts. She thought of the way her mother used to sometimes take the better part of an hour to get dressed on her good days—curling her hair into a bob, applying lipstick with precision, choosing just the right top.

The two of them always looked so pretty.

Kit took her favorite T-shirt out of the closet and put it on. It was a men's white crewneck that said CALI in faded yellow letters. She liked it because it was soft and the collar had stretched out. She realized, looking at herself, that maybe those were not the best parameters for what she was trying to achieve.

And so, realizing she was out of her league, Kit grabbed her two options for shoes, and went to the head of the family, her swimsuit model sister.

1975

June's body was buried at Woodlawn Cemetery in Santa Monica.

As she was lowered into the ground, she was surrounded by her children, as well as the cooks and cashiers and waitstaff of Riva's Seafood, some of her childhood friends, and a smattering of acquaintances from around town—the mailman, the neighbors, the parents of her children's friends—who had always appreciated her sincere smile.

The Riva kids were lined up next to her casket, dressed all in black. Jay and Hud, sixteen, wore ill-fitting suits; Kit, twelve, pulled at the shoulders of her hand-me-down shift dress, chafing in her black flats; and Nina, seventeen, was dressed in one of her mother's long-sleeved wrap dresses, looking twice her age.

The four of them stood together, their faces stoic and detached. They were there but not there. This was happening but not happening.

Their mother was lowered fully into her grave. As Jay started crying, Kit started crying. Nina reached out for all of her siblings, and pulled them tight. Hud squeezed her hand.

Afterward, everyone gathered back at the house. The staff from Riva's catered everything. Ramon, having been hired by June just a month before as the new fry cook, stayed late to help them all clean up. He was ten years older than Nina and had a wife and two kids by that point. Nina knew he needed to go home to them.

"You don't have to do this," she had said to him as they put cold shrimp in Tupperware.

Ramon shook his head. "Your mother was a good woman. You're all good people. So yes, I do have to do this. And you have to let me."

Nina looked down at the table. There was still so much to clean, so much to do. And when it was all done, then what? She couldn't even begin to imagine.

That night, after everything was put away and Ramon had gone home, the Rivas sat together in the living room. And finally Hud said the thing no one had said all day. "I cannot believe Dad wasn't here."

"I don't want to talk about it," Jay said.

"Maybe he didn't get the message," Nina said. But there was no conviction in her voice. She had called his manager's office. She had put an obituary in the paper. He had been designated the executor of her mother's estate, which meant the courts had already called him. He knew. He just didn't show up.

"Do we need him?" Kit asked. "I mean, we've never needed him before."

Nina smiled forlornly at her little sister and put her arm around her, pulling her in. Kit rested her head on her sister's shoulder. "No," Nina said, breathing in deeply. "We don't need him."

Hud looked at her, trying to gauge her expression. Surely, she didn't believe that. And yet, still, it did make him feel better, the idea that they already had everything they needed right there in this room.

Jay kept staring down at his own feet, trying with everything he had not to cry ever again in front of anyone at all.

"We are going to be absolutely fine," Nina said, reassuring them. She was turning eighteen soon. "I'm going to make sure of it."

Nina didn't sleep that night. She tossed and turned in her mother's bed, smelling the sheets, trying to hold on to her mother's scent, afraid that once it was gone her mother was gone, too. As the sun rose, she was relieved to be free from the pressure of attempting to sleep. She could give up trying to be normal.

She stood out on the patio and watched some seals go by, four of them in a group, popping their heads out of the waves. She wished she could join them. Because presumably, they weren't living through one of the worst days of their lives, trying to figure out how to make sure their siblings weren't put in foster care.

Nina breathed in the salt air and then exhaled as hard as she could, emptying her lungs. She thought of going for a swim and felt guilty, as if it was a betrayal of her mother to want to enjoy herself at all. She knew her brothers and sister would feel the same way. That they would welcome their own despair and push away their own joy. She understood then, in a way that she never quite had before, that she did not have room to flail about. She had to model for her siblings what she wanted them to do for themselves. They would not be OK if she was not OK. So she had to find a way.

Once the sun fully woke, Nina went into their bedrooms and gently opened the windows. She handed each of them a wet suit as they rubbed their eyes open.

"Family shred," she said. "Come on, let's go."

And they all, groggy and heartbroken, their chests wounded, their brains foggy, put on their wet suits, grabbed their boards, and met her out on the shore.

"This is how we survive," she said. And she led them into the water.

•   •   •

Nina became what Nina had to become.

She went to the grocery store. She made dinner. She did math homework with Kit while she studied for her own chemistry test. She paid the property taxes. When one of her siblings broke down in tears, Nina held them.

When the roof started leaking, she put a pot underneath it and called a roofer. The roofer told her that, in order to do it right, the entire back half of the house would need to be repaired. So Nina called a handyman who came over and tarred the cracks in the shingles for a hundred bucks and stopped the leak. Imperfect, haphazard, but functional. The new Riva way.

There was a system put in place, each one of them asked to grow up overnight in specific and efficient ways.

Hud was in charge of cleaning the bathrooms and kitchen. He would leave them spotless every Sunday and Wednesday and then get upset when Jay got sand in the sink.

"It's the sink, man," Jay would say, exasperated. "It's easy to clean."

"Then you clean it! I'm sick of cleaning it and having you come in and mess it up again," Hud would say. "I'm not your maid."

"You are though," Jay would say. "Just like I'm the fluff and fold around here."

Jay was in charge of the laundry. He handled his sisters' underwear and bathing suits with chopsticks, unwilling to touch them whether they were clean or dirty. But Jay quickly became a wiz at stain removal, each mark a puzzle to solve. He threw himself into researching the right combination of liquids that would unlock the dirt from Kit's soccer shorts. He found the golden ticket by asking an older woman in the laundry aisle what she did to get out grass stains. Turned out, it was Fels-Naptha. Worked like a charm.

"Look at this, motherfucker!" Jay called out to the rest of the house one day from the garage. "Good as fucking new!"

Kit peeked her head in to see her white shorts bright as the sun, unblemished.

"Wow," she said. "Maybe you can open Riva's Laundry."

Jay laughed. They all knew there was only one future Jay would entertain for himself—and that was on a surfboard. He would go pro.

When he wasn't at school or running the wash cycle, he was in the water. Hud was usually out there with him, helping him perfect every single movement he could control in the waves.

Kit often tried to join. And Jay would tell her the same thing every time. "I'm not out here to play, Kit. This is serious."

Often, after having been rebuffed, she would watch Jay and Hud out in the water from her spot on the deck, a pair of binoculars in hand. She could do what Jay was doing. Someday, he'd understand.

"Go ahead and get out there," Nina would encourage her while vacuuming or making dinner or trying to speed-read a book for English class. Nina's A's and B's were quickly becoming C's and D's, a fact she kept to herself. "Jay doesn't own the ocean."

Kit would shake her head. If they didn't want her there, she didn't want to be there, even if she did. Instead, she would watch. And maybe learn.

When she was done watching, she would always put the caps back on the lenses, put the set of binoculars back in their case, and then put the case on the shelf in the living room. Because Kit was in charge of tidying up. And she took it very seriously.

Every single night, before she went to bed, she picked up all of the books and magazines and put them in stacks. She grabbed all of the glasses and put them in the sink. And if she couldn't see an imminent use for something, she was ruthless about what went into the trash bin.

"Where is my permission slip?" Hud asked one morning when he came to breakfast. Nutritional concerns had been thrown out the window the moment they lost their mother. Grocery store donuts and sugar cereal and chocolate milk took over the kitchen. Kit, not yet thirteen, had taken to drinking coffee with half-and-half and four sugars. Nina tried her best to get each of them to at least eat protein.

"What permission slip?" Kit asked.

"The one about the field trip to the Getty. For my art class. I needed Nina to make it look like Dad signed it. I left it on the coffee table."

"The yellow thing?" Kit asked. "I threw it away."

"Kit!" Hud said, irritated.

"I told you all: Keep it in your room or I'll throw it in the trash."

Hud went through the garbage and found it, wrinkled and stained with butter. "Where's Nina?" he asked.

Jay came in and saw Hud with the permission slip. "You know, any one of us can forge Dad's name."

"Nina's better at it."

Jay turned to Kit. "Do you think we should buy some of those headshots people have of Dad? And sign them? And then sell them?"

Hud looked at Jay, frowning. "Don't put that in her head."

"It's not a terrible idea," Jay said. "He **is** our dad."

Hud ignored him and went looking for Nina. He found her brushing her hair in the bathroom. "Can you sign this?"

Nina grabbed the pen out of his hand and scrawled "M. Riva" across it.

"Thanks," Hud said. But he stayed a moment longer. "People are going to figure it out. That he's not here. That he's . . . never been here."

"Everyone knows he's not here," Nina said. "The whole school administration knows he's not here."

Principal Declan had pulled Nina aside two months prior and told her that he understood her predicament. And as long as it **looked** like someone was home, he wasn't going to call the state. "You're almost eighteen. I don't want you all split up into different homes or anything else they might do. You've been through enough. So . . . make it look good and we'll be all set, all right?"

Nina had thanked him as casually as possible and then bawled her eyes out in the girls' bathroom.

"But I'm saying . . . how much longer can we really keep this ruse going?" Hud asked. "At some point, we're going to come up against a problem we really can't solve without help."

"I got it, Hud," Nina said. "Trust me. Whatever it is, whatever happens, whatever we run into or need . . . I will take care of it."

They were living off the profits from the restaurant, which was being run by a shift manager named Patricia, who Nina had promoted on the spot one day shortly after her mother died. Nina was flying by the seat of her pants.

But what other choice did she have? June had been gone for four months. Mick still hadn't so much as sent a sympathy card. And somewhere in all of those days and weeks and now months of the phone not ringing, Nina had given up on her father's humanity.

She'd consulted an attorney—a guy she found in the yellow pages—who told her that in order to force Mick to comply with his legal duty as their father, she would need to alert the authorities, who would most likely pursue child abandonment charges. Nina bristled at the idea of its making the papers.

"Or," the attorney told her gently, "if you stay under the radar until then, you can file for legal guardianship of them once you turn eighteen."

So it was Nina who signed permission slips, drove them to school, and sometimes answered the phone pretending to be an aunt they didn't have.

When Kit got called into the elementary school principal's office for an "attitude problem," after telling a teacher of hers to "eat it," it was Nina who smoothed things over after school, explaining that her father was "performing in New York right now," but that she, herself, would make sure Kit never behaved like that again.

Nina would sometimes have to sneak off the high school grounds during her lunches in order to get to the post office and the bank. Sometimes she'd have to skip school altogether in order to work at the restaurant when too many people called in sick.

Every week, she'd try to understand the accounting books, haphazardly kept by Patty. Nina would take what cash she could to pay what she had to.

The bills came in faster than the money. Past due notices showed up, the gas got turned off. Nina lost an entire two days negotiating with the gas company to turn it back on. She had to commit to a payment plan that she knew she could not follow.

She was flunking French and had three incompletes in English.

She worried herself sick—new symptoms popping up with every unpaid bill and failing grade. She worked through back spasms and eye twitches and ulcers that she was too young for. She held the stress in her body, suppressed it in her chest, clenched it in her shoulder blades, let it boil in her gut.

When Patty quit to move back to Michigan, Nina's heart sank deeper into her chest from the sheer weight of it all. On the one hand, it was one fewer person to pay. On the other, Nina would have to do Patty's job.

"I can't do this," she would cry to herself in her mother's bed at night sometimes, quietly and humbly, sure to not wake up anyone else. "I don't think I can do this."

She hoped to hear her mother's voice in those moments, hoped for some sort of guidance from the beyond, as if such things existed. But she heard nothing, just the shocking quiet of her desperation.

By April of her junior year, Nina's tardies and truancies had already tallied up to a number that meant she would have to repeat the year. It seemed clear to her then that she simply did not have time to get an education. Suddenly, English class, which had, for so long, seemed like a burden, was a luxury she could not afford. She dropped out.

And officially took over running Riva's Seafood.

She would wake every morning and get her brothers and sister up, make sure they packed lunches, and then get them to school.

"Did you do your homework?" she'd say to Kit as Kit hopped out of the backseat.

"Did you do your homework?" she'd say to Hud.

"Did you do your homework?" she'd say to Jay.

"Yes," they would all say. Sometimes Hud would give her a hug through the window. And then all three of them would walk off, into school. And Nina would drive up the coastline, and park in the parking lot of Riva's Seafood.

She would open the front door with her keys, turn the lights on, check the inventory, meet the deliverymen, sweep the floor, greet her employees as they trickled in.

And then she would take her place, just as her mother and grandmother had before her, behind the register.

• • •

The morning of Nina's eighteenth birthday, Jay went out to get bagels for her as a surprise and then crashed the car into the mailbox pulling back into the driveway.

Kit ran out at the sound of the crash and gasped when she saw the mailbox on the ground. The hood of the car was crunched into a tiny v in the center. "Nina's gonna kill you," she said.

"Thanks, Kit, very helpful!" Jay yelled. His chest was growing red, his cheeks started to flush.

"Why did you swing that way coming in?" Kit asked. "You took the turn too wide."

"Not now, Kit!" Jay said, trying to reattach the mailbox.

Hud came out and immediately checked the hood. The car was still drivable, even if it was now ugly.

Nina rushed out behind him and took one look at the situation: Jay embarrassed, Hud reassuring him, Kit with her arms crossed in judgment. She wanted to bury her head in her hands and start the day over. "It's all right," she said. "The car still runs, right?"

"Yeah," Hud said. "Totally."

"All right, well, everybody get in," Nina said, taking the keys from Jay. "We're late for the lawyer."

The four of them piled into the car and Nina started backing out of the driveway.

"I'm sorry," Jay said, sincerely.

Nina looked at him in the rearview mirror, catching his eye. "What doesn't kill us," she said.

She put the car in gear and they went on their way, to file the paperwork so that Nina could petition the court for custody of them all.

In a sworn affidavit, she testified that she had no knowledge of her father's whereabouts and that she was the only known relative in the country who could provide for them. She asked for the responsibility of three dependents.

She knew her father would be notified. He would be given the option of claiming his rights. And she wasn't sure what she expected him to do.

But after a few weeks, Nina got a letter in the mail saying the paperwork had been approved.

So, she reasoned, he either signed them away or didn't respond at all. Either way, she was now what he refused to be: a parent.

After it became official, the four of them went to Riva's Seafood to celebrate. They were hanging out in the break room while Nina made them the Sandwich for the first time.

"What is this?" Kit said, looking at it as she sat down.

"I put a bunch of stuff in the kitchen onto a roll," Nina said.

"It looks delicious," Jay said, taking a bite.

Hud picked up his sandwich and before he took a bite, he looked at his older sister, who, in becoming his legal guardian, had settled the stress that lived in him on an almost daily basis. Their day-to-day life would be no different now. It would be full of the same loss, the same challenges. But he no longer had to worry the state would come and take Kit.

"Thank you," Hud said.

Nina looked up at him. She could feel the weight of his gratitude. She had to keep herself from crying. The world seemed no more manageable to her today than it had yesterday. Only a little less unpredictable.

"Yeah," Jay said, nodding. And Kit piped in, too. "Seriously."

Nina smiled a small, slight smile. She didn't say, "You're welcome." She didn't think she could get the words out. And so, instead, she nodded toward their sandwiches and said, "All right, eat up."

6:00 p.m.

Kit opened the front door without knocking. Nina's expansive home was already filling with people.

There were cater waiters dressed in black pants and white button-downs with black ties. There were bartenders in black vests organizing bottle after bottle, punctuating the air with the sound of glass stinging glass as they moved.

A cocktail waitress with red hair and green eyes walked by Kit, and Kit stopped her. "Is Nina upstairs?"

"Oh," the waitress said, getting her bearings. "Nina Riva? Yes, I believe she went to get dressed."

Kit studied the waitress and wondered how she managed to be so pretty while being so plain. She wasn't wearing much makeup that Kit could see and her vibrant hair was pulled back into a low ponytail. And yet, it was undeniable, her allure.

"Thanks," Kit said. "I'm Kit, by the way."

The waitress smiled. "Caroline," she said. "Nice to meet you."

With her shoes in her hand, Kit ran up the stairs to Nina's bedroom. She gathered her breath and knocked on the door.

"Oh, hey," Nina said, seeing her.

"Hi," Kit said. She moved through the doorway into the warmth of the room.

Nina was wearing a black suede miniskirt and a silver-sequined sleeveless shirt, which hung effortlessly off her shoulders, showing her bare back.

Kit's beautiful sister. Whose calendar was on everyone's wall. Just standing next to her, Kit felt childish. In some ways, Nina made Kit feel loved and cared for and safe. In other ways, just looking at Nina made Kit feel desperately lonely, as if she was the only person in the world with her specific problems.

"What's up?" Nina asked.

Kit's shoulders fell. "I look like shit."

Nina frowned. "What are you talking about? You look great," she said, shuffling through her jewelry box, considering earrings for herself.

"No, I don't."

Nina turned to her sister, taking her in. "Of course you do. Stop saying that."

"Stop saying I look great when I don't," Kit said,

losing her patience. "What good does it do to lie to me?"

Nina cocked her head in the other direction, put her arms behind her, rested on the edge of the vanity. She gazed at Kit, expressionless, for what felt like ninety million minutes. It was four seconds. "You don't dress very sexy, is that what you mean?" she finally said.

Kit started to feel ill, curling in on herself like a poked porcupine. It felt terrible, simply terrible, to have the most vulnerable thing about you pointed out and given a name.

"Yes," she said, moving through the angst. "That's what I mean." And then she added, "But I want to. And I don't know what to do about it. I . . . I need your help."

"OK," Nina said.

"And I don't want to wear a tight dress," Kit spit out. "Or high heels or any of that. That's not me."

Nina considered her little sister. What a gift it was to know so clearly what you were not, who you did not want to be. Nina wasn't sure she'd ever asked herself that question.

"Well, OK. What **do** you want to wear? Is there a particular way you want to look?"

Kit mulled it over. She thought of the girls she'd been drawn to in high school. Julianna Thompson, the captain of the soccer team, who wore bell-bottoms and plaid shirts. Or Katie Callahan, the valedictorian, who always wore that headband and ribbons in her hair. Or Viv Lambros or Irene Bromberg or Cheryl Nilsson. But she never wanted to be those girls. She could never really see herself wearing their dresses or their skirts or anything. She just liked them, admired them. She didn't see herself in them. Maybe that was part of the problem. That she could never really see this side of herself in anyone yet.

"I don't know," Kit said. "I don't even know where to start."

"All right, never fear, my dear," Nina said. "I know exactly what to do." She opened the top drawer of her vanity and pulled out a pair of scissors.

"Give me your jeans," Nina said.

"Excuse me?" Kit said.

"Your jeans," Nina said, reaching her hand out. "Hand 'em over. Trust me."

Kit unbuttoned her pants and slipped out of them. She gave them to her sister and stood there in her underwear.

"I'm basically naked now," Kit said, uncomfortable.

"There's no difference between standing there in your underwear and standing there in a bathing suit, which you do every day," Nina said as she got to work. "Relax. I have this under control."

With two swift cuts, Kit's favorite jeans were now her favorite shorts. Nina had created an angled edge to them, shorter in the back, a bit longer in the front. The pockets hung lower than the hemlines. Nina pulled at the newly shorn edges, fraying them.

"There you go," she said, handing them back to Kit.

Kit stepped into the shorts and buttoned the fly. She looked at herself in the mirror. Her long, tanned, muscular legs looked good.

"Give me your shirt, too," Nina said.

"You're gonna cut my shirt?" Kit asked.

"Not if you don't want me to," Nina said.

"No," Kit said, intrigued. "Go ahead."

Kit lifted her shirt off and handed it over. She was standing in just her bra and the shorts. Kit could feel herself narrowing, curving her back, trying to hide her chest from her sister. Nina looked over at her.

"Don't stand like that. Stand like this." Nina stood behind Kit and grabbed her shoulders, pulled them wide. Kit's chest popped out.

"You've got a great rack," Nina said. And Kit laughed because she'd never heard her sister talk like that before.

"It's true," Nina said. "Us Riva women have great boobs. Mom had great boobs. I have great boobs. You have great boobs. Own your birthright."

Kit started blushing and Nina felt both gleeful and sad. Kit had never been willing to let Nina in in this way. Nina had always hit a wall trying to talk to Kit about boys and sex and her body. But she should have pushed her further earlier. They should have had this conversation earlier. It was Nina's job to make sure Kit learned how to be herself, all sides of herself.

Nina had been so worried about making sure Kit

was safe and protected, making sure Kit never felt like an orphan, that she'd babied her. Nina knew that. She was trying to stop. It just . . . wasn't that easy. To let go.

But Kit was an adult now. There wasn't much left for Nina to do. In fact, maybe the only true parenting left was to make sure Kit understood this very thing: how to be whatever type of woman she wanted.

Nina took the T-shirt and considered cutting the neckline, chopping one of the shoulders off. But no. "Are you OK showing your stomach?" Nina said.

Kit looked down, assessing.

"I think you would look good showing it off," Nina clarified.

"I guess," Kit said, going along. "Sure."

Nina took her scissors to the bottom half of the shirt, cutting it straight off. She handed the T-shirt back to Kit, now as a loose crop top.

Kit put it on and could feel the air on her abdomen. You could see the very bottom of her baby blue bra from certain angles.

"Wow," Kit said, looking down at herself. She liked that she looked both different and the same. She was herself, only with cooler clothes.

"All right," Nina said with a ponytail holder between her teeth. "One more step." She took Kit's long, wild hair into her hands and gathered it on the top of her head, creating a high pony. She then put mascara on Kit's lashes, blush on her cheeks, and handed her a tube of clear lip gloss.

"As for shoes, I think your huaraches are perfect," Nina said. And Kit felt a tiny flutter of joy, that she owned something that was actually OK as is. She turned and looked at herself in the mirror.

She thought she looked cool. **Like, actually cool.** She could feel herself starting to well up.

Nina came up behind her, put her arms around her, and said, "You look like a million bucks, babe."

This outfit made her feel like there were parts of herself she was just meeting for the first time. Kit could barely contain the smile on her face. She hung her own arms around her sister's and said, "Thank you."

Nina always knew just the thing, didn't she? Kit wished she could be that for someone, be that for Nina, the person who knows just the thing.

"Are you feeling all right?" Kit said. "About the party tonight? And, you know, people asking about Brandon?"

Nina waved her off. "It's okay," she said. "I'll be fine."

"You know . . ." Kit began, unsure exactly how to convey just how much she cared. "It's OK if you aren't OK. If you . . . need to talk or just want to cry about it. Or anything, really. I could listen."

Nina turned to Kit and smiled. "Thank you," she said. "You are the best. I'm OK, though. Really. I'll be fine."

Kit frowned. "All right, well . . . if you ever change your mind." But Nina wouldn't. They both knew that.

Too much self-sufficiency was sort of mean to the

people who loved you, Kit thought. You robbed them of how good it feels to give, of their sense of value.

But Kit put all of that out of her head. Because she was determined that this be the night she finally cut loose.

1978

Nina kept their family afloat week to week on the restaurant's income, one ill-timed emergency away from total disaster. They lived that way for three years.

Three Christmases trying to find a way to afford presents. Three years of birthdays, all celebrated with each of their favorite cakes, recipes re-created from memory because June never wrote them down. Three first days of school, three last days of school, for all of her siblings but her.

When a cute guy buying a hamburger at the restaurant asked her out on a date one afternoon, Nina froze, as if her brain had short-circuited. "Uh . . ." she said, dumbfounded that this guy thought she was normal, could be normal.

"I just mean . . ." the young man said, backtracking. He was tall and blond and had a humble smile. "That you are maybe the prettiest girl I've seen in my entire life and I thought, you know, if you're single and free, maybe we could . . . I don't know. See a movie."

She'd had two boyfriends before her mother died. She'd even called a guy friend or two since then when she was feeling particularly lonely. But a date? This guy wanted to take her out to do something . . . for fun?

"No, thank you," she said. She breathed it out with a sigh like a helium balloon. "I can't," she added, but she found no words to explain it further. And so she moved on to the next customer, trying, as she did every day, to sell more fries and sodas than they had the day before.

At the end of the day, that's what everything came down to: money. She could approximate her mother's German chocolate cake recipe. She could tell Hud the same things June had told her when she was having a bad day. She could sleep three hours in a night in order to fix Kit's science fair project. But money was the one thing she couldn't will into existence.

She had to run the car near empty so often she twice ran out of gas. She started postdating checks, taking out credit cards she couldn't pay back, and turning off all the lights in the house when no one else was home to save electricity.

When Jay's wisdom teeth needed to be taken out, Nina spent three weeks trading calls with insurance companies to get dental insurance through the restaurant. When Hud fractured his wrist after slipping off the roof of the car, he'd refused to go to the hospital because he knew they couldn't afford it. And so Nina, knowing the cost might break her, had to convince him to go regardless of the cost. She negotiated the bill to a sum she could not attain and then went to bed every night for weeks with a clenched jaw, thinking of what would happen when the late penalties added up.

Nina made them lemon roasted chicken when they missed June. She stayed up late watching TV with Kit even though she had to get up early the next morning. Nina encouraged Jay and Hud to get out there in the waves and practice, even if it meant the bathrooms didn't get cleaned or she had to do the laundry herself.

And every time Hud or Jay offered to drop out of school, too, in order to pick up shifts at the restaurant and help pay the bills, Nina forbade them. "Absolutely not," she said, with a seriousness that consistently disarmed them. "You quit school, I'll kick you out of the house."

They all knew she never would. But if she was serious enough to bluff that hard, then they felt they had no choice but to listen to her.

In the spring of 1978, Nina and Kit sat side by side on the bleachers as Hud and then Jay walked across the stage and accepted their diplomas.

Kit hooted and hollered. Nina clapped so hard she stung her hands.

When Jay and Hud pulled their tassels from one side of their caps to the other, Nina knew that the war wasn't over. But she let herself rejoice for a brief moment. A battle had been won.

• • •

After graduation, Jay worked at Riva's Seafood and a local surf shop. Hud got a financial aid package that made it feasible for him to go to college nearby at Loyola Marymount, by taking some side jobs and accepting some help from Nina.

On the weekends when they could, Jay and Hud would ride up the coast, chasing swells. Hud had already bought a used camera by then. The two of them had decided that Hud taking photos of Jay would help both of their portfolios.

And so, it was often just Nina and Kit at the house. Kit, nearing sixteen, did not want to be under her sister's thumb. She did not want to be told what to do or when to hold back. She no longer wanted to be reminded to be careful.

So, instead of hanging out at home, Kit went over to Vanessa's. Kit went to parties. Kit joined a club of girls who liked to surf in the early morning hours before school. She took a job assisting a housepainter up in Ventura and begged rides off her co-workers to get to job sites and back.

All of which meant that by the end of 1978 there were moments—finally—when Nina came home from working twelve hours and had no one to take care of.

It unsettled her, having these quiet evenings in the house, when all she could hear were the waves crashing beneath her and the wind blowing past the windows. She would sit down and balance the checkbook, nervously subtracting each sum, continually finding they were still overdrawn. She would go through Kit's report cards, trying to figure out a way, despite everything, to afford a tutor.

In the rare moments that she truly did not have anything she had to do, Nina would sometimes read Jay and Hud's old comics, trying not to think of her mother.

And then, one day, in February 1979, three and a half years after June died, Nina sat by herself on the rocks down the shore from her home and caught her breath.

It was just before the break of dawn. The air was chilly, the wind was running onshore. The waves were coming in fast and cold, foam claiming more and more of the dry sand.

Nina was in a wet suit, her long hair fluttering in the breeze. The sun started to rise over the horizon, peeking ever so slightly. She had gone down to the shore to surf before the start of the day.

But as she stood looking at the water, she saw a family of dolphins. At first, it looked like just one dolphin jumping. And then one more. And then two more. And then another. And soon the five of them were in a pack, together.

Nina sat down and began to weep. She was not crying out of stress or frustration or fear, although she had so much of those still in her bones. She was crying because she missed her mother. She missed her perfume, her meatloaf, missed the way she made impossible things happen. Nina missed lying in her mother's arms on the sofa, watching television late at night, missed the way her mother would always tell her everything would be OK, the way her mother could make everything OK.

She mourned the things that would never happen. The weddings her mother would never attend, the meals her mother would never make, the sunsets her mother would never see.

And she thought, for a moment, that maybe she could let herself be angry at her mother, too. Angry at her mother for the burnt dinners and lit cigarettes, for the Sea Breezes and Cape Codders. Angry at her mother for getting in that bathtub in the first place.

But she couldn't quite get there.

On the beach that early morning, Nina watched the tiny crabs digging deeper into the sand, she watched the purple sea urchins and pearl starfish holding steady in their tide pools, and she let herself cry. She allowed herself to grieve every tiny thing—every hair roller, every housedress, every smile, every promise. She wanted to empty herself of heartbreak, a task both possible and impossible. And when Nina dove deep into her own sorrow, shoveling it out like digging to the bottom of a hole, she found that this pain, which had seemed bottomless, did, in fact, have a bottom for now.

Nina sometimes felt as if her soul had aged at a rate ten times that of her body. Kit still needed to graduate. There would still be bills that Nina knew she might never be able to get out from under. She still didn't have a high school diploma. But she felt somewhat renewed in that moment. And so she wiped her eyes, and did what she had come out on the beach to do in the first place.

She grabbed her board, paddled out past the breakers, and took her position.

• • •

That April, Nina was spotted by a magazine editor on vacation while she was surfing First Point. It was hotter than she'd expected, so she had unzipped her wet suit, letting her yellow halter bikini top show through. The waves were larger than normal, and Nina was having one of those days when you are fully connected, when ease comes easy. She was taking wave after wave, compensating for their speed with the low crouch of her body, riding in long stretches almost to the pier.

The magazine editor—on the thicker side, with graying hair and a chambray short-sleeved shirt somewhat chicly unbuttoned to his chest, had made his way down to the beach from the pier from which he'd seen her. He approached her as she was coming out of the water and introduced himself just as her feet hit the sand.

"Miss," he said, moving toward her eagerly. He looked to Nina to be about fifty and she was afraid he was going to ask her out.

"You are a wonder to look at," he said to her, but Nina noted there was not an ounce of lasciviousness in his voice. He was merely presenting what, to him, appeared plain fact. "I want to introduce you to a friend of mine. He's a photographer looking to do a surf spread."

Nina was drying her hair with her towel and squinted slightly.

"It's for **Vivant** magazine," the man said, handing her a business card. The moment it was in Nina's hand it was already wet. "Tell him I sent you."

"I don't even know you," Nina said.

The man considered her. "You're a beautiful woman with great command of a surfboard," he said. "You should make money off of that."

He left shortly after and as Nina watched him walk away from her, she was surprised by how easy it had been for him to grab her attention.

When she got home, she sat at the phone, flicking the card with her thumb and forefinger. **Money,** she kept thinking. **How much money?**

Nina didn't love the idea of posing for photos, but what other options did she have? The restaurant was in the red from a slow winter. She knew for a fact it was going to fail a health inspection. Hud's tuition for next year was going up. Kit needed her cavities filled. The roof had started leaking again.

She called the number on the card.

• • •

The photographer and assistant kept insisting she wear these tiny bikinis during their shoot at Zuma. They shot for hours, her coming into and out of the water, her rolling around in the sand. She found it uncomfortable, the leering eyes of the men behind the camera.

But then she saw the photos. She stared at the negatives with the photographer's loupe and something ignited within her.

She was beautiful.

She'd known, on some level, her whole life, that she was pretty. She could tell by the way people sometimes lit up at the sight of her, the same way she'd seen them react to her mother all those years ago.

But was this really how she looked to other people when she was in the water? This gorgeous? This care free? This cool?

It was jarring, but altogether lovely, to see herself like this.

She was in the June 1979 issue of **Vivant,** a photo of her face—skin copper from the sun, hair slicked back by the water—set across from a headline that said, CALIFORNIA COOL: THE NEW BEACH BUM.

When everyone pieced together that she was the daughter of Mick Riva, the phone started ringing off the hook. **Where had this famous progeny been hiding?** Her fame took off like a wildfire.

A surf magazine, two men's interest magazines, ads for two different swimsuit companies, a wet suit shop, and a commercial for a surf shop later, Nina Riva was the face of women's surfing.

She wanted to enter surfing competitions and see if she could place, see if she could make a name for herself as an athlete out there in the water. But her new agents discouraged it.

"No one cares if you win contests," her modeling agent, Chris Travertine, had said. "In fact, it's better to not find out. You're number one to everyone right now. Let's not test it. Not put a different number on it."

"But I want to actually surf," Nina said. "Not just pose for photos."

"You **are** surfing. You're a surfer. We have the photos to prove it," he said, exasperated. "Nina, you're the most popular female surfer in the world. What more is there?"

Before the year was out, she was offered a calendar. Twelve shots, all her.

She took Jay, Hud, and Kit with her as she and her team set up shop at some of the best surf breaks in SoCal. She surfed the wild ripple of waves at Rincon, the crowded perfection of Surfrider, the isolated rugged cliffs at Torrey Pines, the larger waves at Black's Beach, the far-out reef breaks at Sunset Cliffs, and spots all in between.

It was watching Nina ride that showed Kit there was a future for female surfers.

And it was talking to Nina's photographers during

shooting breaks that allowed Hud to get serious about surf photography.

And it was the sting of the fact that Nina had gotten paid to surf before he had that made Jay realize he needed to get way more serious about going pro.

"SoCal Babe: Nina Riva Gets Wet" featured Nina in bikinis of ever-changing colors, catching waves from Ventura to San Diego.

When the calendar was done, Nina flipped through the final proof. Her at Trestles straddling a Lance Collins single fin in a red bandeau bikini, her at Surfrider hanging five as seven male surfers tried to get a wave behind her.

But the most startling photo was placed squarely in the dead of summer, July. Nina was riding a wave at Rincon. The ocean was crisp, the water indigo blue.

She was wearing a white string bikini on a hot pink surfboard. The angle of the camera allowed you to see the side of her face, smiling as she tackled the water—and you could also see the side of her ass barely contained in her swimsuit, and the side of her breast, escaping her top.

She realized, looking at the photo, that her bikini had not been as opaque as she had been led to believe. The wet white fabric left very little to the imagination. Her nipple and the line of her ass were faintly visible underneath.

Whenever Nina looked at the picture she felt uneasy. It was not a good wave, her stance was not great, and she knew that seconds later, she had fallen off the board. She was a better surfer than that photo could ever attest to. She was capable of so much more.

But naturally, it was that photo that became a sensation. The one where you could see her body, unintentionally exposed.

The photo made her career. It was blown up into posters that would hang in teenage boys' bedrooms and closets and lockers for years to come. The photo was phenomenal to everyone except the woman featured in it.

Nina had lived through enough trauma to know there were worse problems. So, instead of getting upset about it, she chose to go to bed every night thankful for the money.

The money the money the money.

The money that allowed her to promote Ramon to take over running Riva's Seafood for her. The money that allowed her to finally reroof the house, let her pay off Hud's tuition, pay for Kit's dentist, pay off their medical bills, pay Jay's first competition entrance fee. Get the restaurant kitchen up to code.

That photo of Nina's ass brought all of the Rivas security for the first time in their lives.

After all of the bills were paid, Nina sat out on the patio and stared at her checkbook, marveling at the balance. It was not much. But it was not zero.

And so, at the end of that August, when Jay, Hud, and Kit were all home, gathered around to grill some burgers, Nina said something they never thought they'd hear her say.

"Hey, guys?" she said to them, in a wild rush of impulsivity, as she brought out the chips and salsa. "What if we threw a party?"

Jay and Hud were on their way back from the liquor store with twelve bottles of Seagram's, ten bottles of Southern Comfort, and nine bottles of Captain Morgan loaded into the back of Hud's pickup truck. Also in the back of Hud's truck: the cashier from the liquor store.

The guy had pleaded for the address of the party. And then he had pleaded for a ride. Jay said no. Hud said yes. And so, Tommy Wegman was now in the back of the truck. He was smoking a cigarette, feeling the breeze on his face, reveling in the delight of knowing he was going to the Riva party, imagining he might get to hit on Demi Moore or Tuesday Hendricks.

"You're such a sap," Jay said, in the passenger seat, watching Tommy in the back through the side mirror. "Such a sap."

"There are worse things to be than a sap," Hud said. "For instance, I could be an asshole."

Jay turned toward Hud and smiled. "Fair point."

It was quiet in the cab of the truck, aside from the hum of the engine and the crackling of tires on the road. And this felt like the time for Hud to admit what he'd done.

Sweat instantly appeared along the edge of his forehead and his upper lip. This was a thing Hud's body sometimes did. Usually it was because he'd eaten too much of something he was mildly allergic to, like vinegar. But it also happened in instances such as this one, when he was so nervous he began to get clammy.

"Hey, there's something I wanted to talk to you about, actually," Hud said.

"OK . . ."

Hud breathed in deeply, preparing himself to say her name. "Ashley," he said finally.

Jay was caught off guard by the mention of his ex-girlfriend. He was still uncomfortable with the thought of her.

"What about her?" he asked. He didn't get every girl he wanted, no one did. But he usually saw his rare rejections coming. Ashley had dumped him out of nowhere.

Hud could hear the irritation in his brother's voice and he started to worry. What if Jay wouldn't give him his blessing? What would Hud do then?

He'd had a whole plan in place, a flowchart in his mind of what he would say depending on what Jay said. But in that second, it all went out the window. All he could see was that he was going to tell his brother that he was sleeping with his ex-girlfriend. And then, in a panic, Hud told a lie. "I was thinking of asking her out. Wanted to know if you were cool with it."

Within seconds of the words leaving his mouth, Hud had calmed down. **This could work.**

Jay whipped his head to look at his brother head-on. "Are you fucking serious, man?" he said.

Already, Hud had all but forgotten that what he was asking was a lie in the first place. "Yeah, is it that big of a deal? I didn't think you would care."

"I care, I definitely care."

It wasn't about Ashley, per se. The truth was that Jay did not see—had never seen—Ashley as a girl of any particular significance. It was nothing against her. He didn't see any girls to be of particular significance until he met Lara. Jay could see now—now that he had met the real thing—that the girls before her had been . . . well, **not** the real thing. Unimportant. Ashley had been unimportant.

But Jay just kept picturing Ashley going out with Hud. He pictured her welcoming his brother's advances. And that's when his brain shut down.

"Sorry, man, but I don't think it's a good idea. I just don't."

Hud froze. "All right," he said, as Jay turned in to Nina's driveway.

"Cool," Jay said, pulling his keys out of the ignition.

Jay got out of the truck, but Hud sat for an imperceptible second longer, processing the fact that he was—to put it mildly—completely fucked.

The doorbell rang.

Nina was teasing her hair in the bathroom. She looked at the clock: 6:51 P.M. **So eager,** she thought. But the world is full of all kinds of people and some are the kind who show up for a party before it even starts.

Nina opened her bedroom door and saw Kit considering herself in the mirror in the hallway and Jay coming up the stairs.

Jay was shocked to find his little sister in such a tiny shirt but, after this morning with the dress, he knew better than to say anything.

"Can you open the door?" Nina said to both Kit and Jay but to neither one of them in particular.

"Yeah, sure," Jay said, turning back around.

Hud was stacking the extra liquor in the pantry. He came into the foyer to answer the door at the same time Jay reached the bottom of the stairs. And so, somewhat embarrassingly, they opened the door together.

There, in a pair of Dockers and a Breton striped light sweater over a polo shirt, stood floppy-haired Brandon Randall.

Jay, with his hand holding on to the side of the door, had the impulse to slam it shut. Hud, with his hand on the inside door handle, was inclined to open it farther to see what the hell Brandon wanted. And so, with the push and pull of the two brothers, the door stayed where it was.

"Hi," Brandon said.

"Brandon?" came a voice from behind them. Nina had reached the foot of the stairs and was stunned at the sight in front of her.

"Hi, Neen," Brandon said, taking a step into the house.

"What are you doing here?" Nina imagined that he had come to pick up some clothes or grab something from the safe. But as she watched the look on Brandon's face—soft, hopeful—she felt a pit in her stomach, worried he was going to say . . .

"Can we talk?"

Nina breathed in deeply without even realizing it. "Uh . . ." she said. "Sure. Come on upstairs, I guess."

Jay and Hud watched as Brandon followed Nina up to the second floor. Kit, coming down, froze when she saw them. She stood there on the landing as Nina and Brandon walked past her, a look of disbelief on her face. When they were finally out of sight, Kit looked at Jay and Hud and said, very plainly, "What the fuck."

• • •

Nina walked into the master bedroom—her bedroom? their bedroom?—and gestured for Brandon to join her. She found herself unable to decide what to say to him, what to even think of his being there.

"What is going on?" she asked.

"I love you, Nina," Brandon said. "I want to come home."

1981

It was February '81. Brandon was doing a series of photo shoots for the cover of the **Sports Pages** April issue. It was timed to publish ahead of the French Open, one of many contests he was the favorite for in the upcoming year. The plan was to feature him playing tennis in what would look like exotic and unexpected locales. Fortunately, Southern California can deliver beaches, deserts, and snowcapped mountains.

After shooting a day in Big Bear and a day in Joshua Tree, Brandon and the **Sports Pages** team set up shop just in front of the Jonathan Club, a Santa Monica beach club right on the water.

At that very hour, Nina and Kit were seated at one of the tables at the restaurant by the sand. They had decided to go out for lunch—Nina's newfound cash flow making certain parts of the coast available to them that had never been available before. Such as a beach club with white cloth napkins and four different types of glasses at the ready. It was still unusual to them, not entirely natural. Nina didn't like how subservient the waiter was to her. Kit thought the other patrons were all assholes.

Brandon was down the beach a distance, in the sand, wearing his tennis whites, holding a black racket, angled in front of a camera, the ocean to his back. He was tall and sturdy, with sandy brown hair, and mild features—average-sized blue eyes, wide cheekbones, thick eyebrows. His face was attractive but forgettable, as if fate had not taken a single risk in composing it.

"Who is that?" Kit asked, watching him. There was a break between shots and Brandon sat down on a milk crate, holding a bottle of Perrier. "I know that I know him but I don't know where from."

"I think he's a tennis player," Nina said, picking at her salad. By this point, per her agent, Chris's instruction, Nina had already cut out all cheese, butter, and desserts. She'd lost eight pounds. "You stay slim, you get rich," he'd said to her. Nina had bristled when she heard it but still, she obeyed. And now she found herself quickly growing tense anytime she was hungry. Her body was their whole cash cow.

Brandon took a sip from his Perrier and then screwed the top back on. He stood up, ready to get back to work. And as he did, his sight landed on the patio in front of him and then zeroed in on Nina.

"Well," Kit said, as if offering bad news. "He's looking at you."

• • •

When Brandon told people the story later, he would say that the moment he saw Nina he **just knew.** He never realized what he was looking for until he saw it all in her: long gorgeous hair, lithe body, bright smile. She looked sweet without being soft.

"Uh . . ." the PA said. "Mr. Randall?" Brandon didn't respond. The PA raised his voice and continued talking.

"Sorry," Brandon said. "What?"

"Touch-ups. On your jawline."

"Oh, right," Brandon said, finally tearing himself away from the sight of Nina. But he continued to steal glances at her as his makeup was fixed and he was put back in front of the camera. The photographer started flashing and Brandon was still looking over there. **Did he know her from somewhere?**

"She's the girl in the poster," the photographer said, catching him staring. "Nina Riva."

Brandon was unsure.

"Mick Riva's daughter," the photographer added.

"That's Mick Riva's daughter?" Brandon said.

"Yeah, she's a surfer."

Brandon looked at her again, this time long enough to get her attention. Nina turned and glanced at him. He figured his chances were good. After all, he had eight Slam titles under his belt and was expected to grab a ninth.

"You said her name is Nina?" Brandon asked the photographer. Before the photographer could stop shooting and confirm it, Brandon called to her.

Nina turned toward him. Kit looked to see, too. That's when, in full view of the cameras flashing at him, with his racket now down by his side, Brandon shouted, "Can I get your number?"

Nina laughed. And it seemed genuine, the way her head fell back ever so slightly. Brandon thought then that her smile looked effortless, that joy must come to her with ease.

"I'm serious!" he called to her. Nina shook her head, as if to say, "You're crazy."

Brandon felt a little crazy. He felt like he'd discovered a hidden treasure and he had to make it his. He had to hold it in his hands.

"Would you excuse me?" he said to the photographer. "For just one brief moment?" And then, without waiting for an answer, he ran to her table.

Up close, Brandon felt that much more intoxicated. There was something casual about her, the way her bikini top was tied up around her neck under her T-shirt, the way her flip-flops were worn down. But there was grace there, too: the elegant shape of her feet, the smoothness of her skin, the warmth of her brown eyes.

Brandon hung there, on the rail that separated the beach from the patio.

"I'm Brandon Randall," he said, extending his hand.

"Nina Riva." Nina accepted his hand and then gestured to her sister. "This is Kit."

"Kit," Brandon said, bowing his head ever so slightly. "Nice to meet you."

"Charmed, I'm sure," Kit said, amusing herself.

Brandon smiled, fully aware that Kit was making fun of him. He turned to Nina. "Marry me," he said, with a smile.

Nina laughed. "I don't know about that . . ."

Brandon leaned toward Kit. "What you do you think, Kit? Do I have a shot here?"

Kit looked Nina in the eye, trying to gauge what her sister might want her to say. "I don't know . . ." Kit said, as if she was sorry to disappoint him but still entirely entertained. "I don't think it's looking good."

"Oh, no!" Brandon said. He put his hand on his chest, as if to protect his broken heart.

"I mean, do you know how many men come up to her on a daily basis and do exactly what you're doing?" Kit asked.

Brandon looked to Nina, raising his eyebrows to ask if this was true. Nina, mildly embarrassed, shrugged. Since the poster started selling in record shops and pharmacies, Nina had been getting hit on every time she left the house. It was a new reality she didn't much care for.

"She gets about four marriage proposals from strangers a week lately," Kit said.

"That's a lot," Brandon conceded. "Maybe I'm out of my depth here."

"Maybe you are," Kit said. "Although, you're at least one of the less annoying ones."

"Oh, good," Brandon said. "What a lovely distinction."

Nina laughed. "Kit is not an easy audience," she said.

Brandon looked at her. "I'm starting to get that."

"I'm actually a very easy audience," Kit said. "I just think you should probably ask my sister out to dinner and let her get to know you first before you ask her to spend the rest of her life with you."

Brandon looked at Nina and smiled. "I'm sorry if I came on too strong." Nina kept his gaze, found herself smiling back. "I really can be a pretty good dinner companion. Would you consider doing me the honor?" he said.

Kit nodded. "There you go."

Nina laughed. Even just three minutes ago, she had been ready to turn Brandon down. But now here she was, changing her mind. "OK," she said. "Sure."

• • •

Brandon had picked up a tennis racket for the first time at the age of six and had a perfect serve by his seventh birthday. And so his father, Dick, put him on the court every hour he wasn't in school or sleeping.

His father taught him two things: You always win and you always act like a gentleman. And at the age of twelve, Brandon started training with renowned tennis coach Thomas O'Connell.

Tommy was punishing in his exactitude. There was no almost, there was no good try. There was only perfection or failure. Brandon rose to the challenge, bought into the premise, hook, line, and sinker. Either you win or you are a loser. Brandon became relentless in his pursuit of precision.

He would triumph, always. And he would act like a gentleman, without fail.

Brandon hit the global stage when he made it to the finals of the Australian Open at the age of nineteen, courtesy of his signature slingshot serve, which ESPN was calling "the Snap."

He went on to win the title. And the very second he won the last point, Brandon did not drop to his knees and raise his racket to the sky. He did not pump his fists in glory. He did not rejoice in any way. He held back a smile, walked to the net, and shook the hand of his opponent, Henri Mullin. The camera, close up, could see him mouth the words "You played beautifully."

And the media called him "The Sweetheart."

By the time Brandon turned twenty-five, he had won the U.S. Open, Wimbledon, and the Australian Open, some multiple times. And the sportscasters no longer called him "The Sweetheart." They called him "BranRan" and they called him a phenom.

But they always kept the camera on him. And people tuned in to see him crush his opponents, as humbly and graciously as any athlete in the history of sports television.

Nina liked that about him. She liked it about him a lot.

"My father always said. . ." Brandon told her on their first date, sitting at a hole-in-the-wall Mexican restaurant in Santa Monica. "It's easy to be gracious when you're winning. So you have no excuse not to be."

His father had passed away just the year before and Nina admired how eloquently Brandon could talk about him. She found it hard to share anything about her mother without her voice catching.

"And if you lose?" Nina asked.

Brandon shook his head. "You just work harder to make sure you win on the next one. And then you haven't lost anything at all."

"And you can stay gracious then, too?" Nina asked.

Brandon laughed. "The cameras zoom right in on me when I lose," he said. "They're just waiting for me to slip up. So yes, I stay gracious then, too. But it's harder, I'll give you that. But we are talking about me too much. So, the first time you were on a surfboard. Tell me everything."

Nina smiled and told Brandon the story of all of her siblings on the beach that afternoon in '69. Brandon laughed when she told him about not letting Kit go on her own, but instead pulling her along on Nina's shoulders on the board. "I realize I barely know her," Brandon said. "But I feel like I already know that she hated that."

Nina laughed. "Oh, she definitely hated it," she said. And then she sipped her wine and caught Brandon's eye. **How nice it is,** she thought, **to laugh in this way.**

After Brandon drove her home that night, he kissed her on the cheek as they sat parked in her driveway.

"I like you, Nina," he said. "And I know you've got guys coming at you every which way nowadays. But I want to be the real deal. Can I see you again?"

Nina smiled and nodded.

"All right," he said. "I'll call you tomorrow and plan something good."

"OK," Nina said. "You do that."

Despite his fame and his fortune, Brandon did not woo Nina with expensive dinners. He did not ask very many questions about her fancy father. He did not whisk her away to penthouse apartments in foreign lands.

He made her stir-fry at his place in Brentwood. He showed up at her house with flowers. He went to the beach with her and watched her surf.

When she cut her arm on some coral, he pulled a first aid kit out of the back of his Mercedes and bandaged her up. When she said thank you, he kissed her on the temple and said, "I like taking care of you."

That April, the cover of **Sports Pages** was not BranRan in Big Bear or BranRan in Joshua Tree. It was BranRan with his back to the ocean, his racket down by his side, calling out to someone off-camera.

The headline said BRANRAN: TENNIS'S NICE GUY IS LOOKING FOR LOVE. It was the only issue of **Sports Pages** that sold out that year. Kit thought it was cheesy but she still bought Nina three copies.

By that point, Nina and Brandon had started

seeing a lot of each other. And Brandon almost always invited Kit, and soon Jay and Hud, out with them, too.

The five of them all went to see **Raiders of the Lost Ark** together. They went hiking together. They went on road trips to chase waves. Brandon drove and waited out on the sand for them.

When they all tried to teach him to surf one afternoon at County Line, he kept falling off the board. His strength and training from tennis didn't seem to help him with his balance in the waves just yet.

"Fall off nine times, get up ten, right?" Brandon said, after he bit it the first time.

Nina laughed and helped pull him up onto his board and he leaned over to her and kissed her and said, "I guess you're better at this than me."

Nina laughed. "I've been doing it longer."

"Still," he said. "It's sexy."

Kit had overheard him and smiled to herself.

"All right," Brandon said after falling off for the fourth time, frustration growing in his voice. "I'll be in charge of lunch, meet you all back here in an hour."

Jay and Hud laughed. Kit convinced him to order them all steak sandwiches. And when they came in from the water that day, he was there, with five steak sandwiches laid out on a towel. Nina's had no cheese, with a sliced tomato on the side. She kissed him on the cheek but found that she had to stop herself from welling up.

Later that evening, after Nina and Brandon had

gone home to his place, they made love in his bedroom, slowly and sweetly. And afterward, as they
lay in the dark together, sharing the secrets of their
hearts, Brandon told Nina that he wished he loved his
brother the way she loved her siblings. "I want you
to know that if we do have a future together . . . if we
ever . . . buy a house together, I know it needs extra
bedrooms, for all of them, just in case. I know they
are a part of the deal. And I love it about you."

Nina smiled and turned to him and kissed him.
"I love you," she said and she meant it with all of
her heart.

If she was totally honest with herself, she thought
he was sort of blandly handsome. She found his white-
bread style a little bit embarrassing. He didn't make
her laugh very hard and he didn't blow her mind in
bed. She didn't like how often he would simply refuse
to do something that he wasn't immediately good at.
And while she knew it mattered to him that he was
famous and talented and rich, none of those things
intrigued her.

But when she thought of a life with Brandon, her
muscles relaxed and breath came easier. He felt like
falling into a warm, soft bed. And she was so tired.

• • •

That fall, Nina and Brandon got engaged. They were
married in the spring of 1982. Nina wore a crown
of flowers in her hair, her bare feet buried in the

cool evening sand. Brandon wore a white linen suit, picked out by Hud.

Nina felt the hole where her mother should have been. All three of her siblings walked her down the aisle.

• • •

Brandon looked at homes with a real estate agent every day for six weeks before finding the perfect one. 28150 Cliffside Drive was big and airy like he wanted, with a tennis court that overlooked the ocean. It had just enough bedrooms upstairs and a pool that he imagined teaching his children to swim in.

"I've found exactly the place," he said to Nina that night at dinner in the city. He'd been taking her out to restaurants in a lot of areas of Los Angeles she had never thought to explore. This time they were in West Hollywood, eating at Dan Tana's. There had been a photo of her father on the wall and she'd chosen to ignore it.

"Tell me all about it," Nina said. "Is it on the water?"

"Better," Brandon said. And Nina could think of nothing better than to be right on the water but she listened anyway. "It's on the edge of Point Dume. You'll be able to surf Little Dume every day. You can walk down there from the backyard. Westward Beach is just a stone's throw away. It's literally on the edge of the cliff. It's on the edge of the world, honey."

"Oh, OK," Nina said, eating an undressed salad.

"Sounds cool. I'm excited to look at it. I can do it tomorrow if you think it will go fast."

"No need," Brandon said. "I put in an offer. It's ours. It's all taken care of."

"Oh," Nina said, breathing in deeply and hiding her annoyance by sipping her red wine. She would much rather have renovated her current place. Or bought something near it. She thought he knew that. But maybe she hadn't really explained herself well. "Great. I'm sure it's great. I'm sure it's perfect."

The next morning, Brandon took her to the new house and showed her around. "This is where the couch will go. And I'm thinking my Warhol will go here . . ."

He kept talking and talking and talking but Nina wasn't listening. This house was gorgeous but it was too much. Too big and too beige and too industrial and . . . there was no soul in here.

"What do you think?" he said. "Is it not perfect?"

What could she do about it? It was already done. "It's perfect," she said. "Thank you."

He pulled her into him, put his arms around her. He put his chin to her neck, buried his face by her ear. His body was always so solid. Every time he held her like that, she felt so much less alone.

"Pretty great party house, right?" he asked her. "You all can throw your end-of-summer party here every year for decades to come, I bet."

Nina smiled and pulled away from him ever so slightly. "You already thought of that?" she asked.

"Thought of it? I said to the realtor, 'It has to be walking distance to a great break, great for parties, and at least five bedrooms. Those were my stipulations. I wanted you to have the chance to surf every day, have room for Jay, Hud, and Kit, and be able to throw the Riva party every year."

Nina laughed. She looked at the home again. "It **is** great for a party."

"Stick with me, kid," he said, smiling at her. "I'm always going to make sure you have everything you ever wanted."

There wasn't much she wanted. But it enchanted her nonetheless. "I love you," she told him, grabbing his hand and pulling him up the stairs.

"I love you, too," he said, allowing himself to be pulled. "With all of my heart, forever."

When they made their way to the empty master bedroom of the home that was not yet technically theirs, Nina pulled Brandon down onto the plush carpet and made love to him. Sweet, and slow, never rushed, never wild, only tender and wholehearted.

And it was that very spot where Nina fell to her knees a year later when Brandon walked out.

• • •

He'd just come home from winning Wimbledon. They had a vacation to Bora-Bora planned with Jay, Hud, and Kit next week. She was reading a travel guide.

She heard him walk in the front door and heard

his footsteps coming up the stairs. But when Brandon walked into their bedroom, he wasn't smiling.

"I'm sorry, Nina," he said. "But I'm leaving."

"What are you talking about?" she said, laughing. She put down the book and stood up, wearing a T-shirt and a pair of his old boxer shorts. "Leaving for where? You just got here."

"I've met someone else," he said as he went into the closet and stuffed some shirts into a duffel bag.

Nina stared at him, her jaw slack. He walked out the door, now rushing down the stairs. Nina followed him.

"I don't understand," she said quietly. "What do you mean you've met someone else?"

Brandon did not turn around to answer her, he just kept walking away.

"Brandon!" Nina said finally as they got to the driveway. "Look at me, please."

"We'll talk about this more at another time," Brandon said as he got in his car. And then he drove off.

Nina stood there watching his car turn onto the road. She started gasping for air, stunned at what had just happened, what she'd just seen with her own eyes. "What?" she kept saying over and over, in between panicked breaths. "What?"

She sat down on the front stoop of her home to gather herself. Only then did it really sink in that her husband was leaving her for another woman.

She began to cry without even realizing it, wiping

her cheeks but unable to keep up with the tears. Her eyes grew red and swollen. She could not move from her place on the stoop, heavy and dead, like an anchor tied to nothing.

She cried until the sun started to set, until the birds settled into their trees. She'd have to tell her siblings he was gone. She felt embarrassed, thinking of how excited she'd been to take them to Bora-Bora. She grew cold, sitting outside in Brandon's underwear.

And then she stood up and dried her eyes. And she thought of June. She'd lived this all before, of course. Watching her mother go through it.

Family histories repeat, Nina thought. For a moment, she wondered if it was pointless to try to escape it.

Maybe our parents' lives are imprinted within us, maybe the only fate there is is the temptation of reliving their mistakes. Maybe, try as we might, we will never be able to outrun the blood that runs through our veins.

Or.

Or maybe we are free the moment we're born. Maybe everything we've ever done is by our own hands.

Nina wasn't sure.

She just knew that, somehow, after everything that had happened in her life, she had ended up all alone on the front stoop, left behind by a man she had dared to trust.

Part Two

7:00 p.m. to 7:00 a.m.

7:00 p.m.

The clock struck seven and Kit's best friend, Vanessa de la Cruz, pulled up to Nina's house, the first to arrive. She was immediately approached by one of the team of valets and stepped out of her car.

Vanessa was wearing a sky blue T-shirt, belted at the waist, with white shorts and white pumps. She had teased her hair at the crown and rimmed her eyes in black eyeliner. She had stolen her entire outfit idea from Heather Locklear, who'd been wearing the same thing on the cover of **Los Angeles** magazine last month.

This had seemed like a good idea, until right this very second, when it occurred to Vanessa that Heather Locklear might show up at the party. And then what was she going to do?

The valet put his hand out for Vanessa's keys.

"I mean . . . I can park it myself," she said. "If that's easier?"

"It's my job," he said, gently taking the keys from her.

Vanessa watched her AMC Eagle drive away from her. It was still strange to her that the Rivas were rich kids now. She remembered hanging out with Kit at the Rivas' house with all the lights turned off to save power. Now, Vanessa wasn't even sure if her shoes were nice enough. Not that any of them, especially Kit, would have ever noticed or cared.

Vanessa stepped to the front door and put her hand up to knock. Anxiety was settling in. Every year at this party, she hung back and made jokes in the corner with Kit. But this year, she wanted to get Hud's attention. Maybe this was the night he finally noticed her **in that way.**

She rapped her knuckles on the door and rang the doorbell.

The door opened and there he was. Vanessa was absolutely positive he was only getting better looking with every passing day and it crushed her.

"Oh, hey, Vanessa," Hud said, opening the door wider, a smile on his face. "Kit!" he called out to the rest of the house. "Vanessa's here!"

Kit came around the corner. "Hey!"

Vanessa's eyes went wide at the sight of Kit's outfit. She'd never seen her friend show so much skin outside of the beach. "Wow," Vanessa said. "You look great."

Hud patted Kit on the back and then walked toward the kitchen. Vanessa watched him go, her pulse slowing down with each step he took away from her.

"I do?" Kit said, looking down at her own torso. "Are you sure?"

Vanessa returned her gaze to Kit and laughed. "Yeah, you look hot."

"OK, good," Kit said. "You do, too."

"Thanks," Vanessa said, fluffing her hair as she peeked around for another moment, to see if maybe Hud was coming back.

The night was young.

The doorbell had started ringing every twenty seconds. Nina could hear Kit greeting people downstairs.

She could see the sky darkening through the windows, the stars beginning to brighten against the dusk.

"Please, Nina," Brandon said. "I got caught up in something. I got lost in my own . . . need to be . . . I don't know. I had shit I was going through and I handled it in the worst way possible. But . . . God, I'm so horrified by how I've acted the past few months. I don't even recognize myself in the mirror anymore, honestly. I've never just colossally fucked up like this before. But I'll do anything to make it right. Anything. I love you. Please, Nina," he said as he stood in their bedroom. "Give me another chance. You know I'm not a bad guy. You know that. You know me. You know if I did something this stupid, it's because I was going crazy, I wasn't myself."

Brandon got down on his knees and started kissing Nina's knuckles. Her hands were cold and he was warm. "I have missed your face," he said, looking up at her, his eyes growing glassy, his voice scratchy. "And the smell of your hair. I missed brushing my teeth next to you every morning and night. The way you look the most like yourself in your pajamas next to me at the sink. The way you smile with your whole face sometimes," he said. "I cannot live without you."

"I don't know what you want me to say," Nina said.

"Say you'll give me another chance."

Nina found herself looking at the floor and the ceiling, the bedspread and the closet doors. Anywhere but his face. At anything but his eyes.

"Come with me," Brandon said, taking her hand. "You deserve to know I'm serious." He began pulling her out of the bedroom into the hallway.

"Brandon, what are you doing?" Nina asked, running with him so as not to be dragged.

He led her down the stairs, where people were starting to gather in the entryway and living room. Nina caught eyes with Tuesday Hendricks just as she walked in the door.

"Brandon," Nina whispered. "You're embarrassing me."

"Everyone!" Brandon called out, his voice booming over the music that had just started playing. "I have an announcement to make."

Heads started to turn in their direction, including Hud's. He had been pointing out the nearest bathroom to an Olympic volleyball player. Nina didn't see Jay or Kit but she could feel everyone's eyes on her.

"If any one of you have read the papers, you might know that I've fucked up recently. That I forgot how lucky I was. That I haven't been such a nice guy."

"You've been a moron, man!" someone called out from the crowd. Everyone laughed and Nina wanted to evaporate into the air.

Brandon turned to her. "But I'm here to tell you, Nina, in front of everyone here tonight. That I love you. And I need you. That you are the most beautiful, kindest, most amazing woman on the planet. I am here to declare publicly, I am nothing without you."

Nina grinned reluctantly, unsure where to look or what to say.

He got down on one knee. "Nina Riva, will you take me back?"

Somebody whistled. Nina couldn't tell who it was but she thought it might have been her neighbor Carlos Estevez. The rest of the crowd starting clapping. Someone started chanting, "Take Him Back!"

Nina could feel the room shrinking, as if it could collapse on her.

"Take! Him! Back! Take! Him! Back!"

Suddenly, her voice was so small, she almost wasn't sure it was hers. "OK," Nina said, nodding, hoping everyone would stop looking. "OK."

Brandon swooped her up into his arms and kissed her. Everyone cheered.

Kit made her way to the commotion from the kitchen and saw Brandon there, a smile on his face, holding Nina in his arms. He looked so victorious.

Kit looked to Jay, who had come in by the stereo, and then to Hud, who was still by the door. It didn't take a genius to figure out what had happened. Kit's expression turned sour.

Nina glanced toward Kit at that very moment, saw how it all looked through Kit's eyes. She averted her gaze.

8:00 p.m.

Tuesday Hendricks was wearing baggy black linen pants with black suspenders, a white T-shirt, and a gray bowler hat over her long brown hair. She was fresh faced and slightly pale. The only makeup she had on was a hint of mascara.

She walked into the backyard with her hands in her oversized pockets. Within those pockets, Tuesday had four joints, two blunts, and a spliff.

She pulled out the spliff once she got to the open air and then lit it. She breathed in, she held the smoke in her lungs, and then she let it go.

She smiled at the people staring at her and then nodded, acknowledging them in the hope they would go back to their conversation.

"Tues, hey." Tuesday turned around to see Rafael

Lopez, her most recent costar, joining her and handing her a beer. She had not come with Rafael, had not been seeking him out. But she did not mind him. So far, during their current movie shoot, he'd kept his tongue in his mouth when they had makeout scenes and he never made her wait around for him when they were called to set. Plus, if he was standing next to her, perhaps people would be less inclined to interrupt.

She was not here to socialize. She was only here to show her face. To let everyone know she wasn't running away after her public scandal, hiding from what she'd done. She wasn't embarrassed. Bridger should be embarrassed. But the man had no shame.

"I thought you weren't coming," Rafael said.

"I didn't want to be the woman who couldn't hack showing up."

Rafael put his hand out, asking for the spliff. Tuesday handed it over. Tuesday was known for having the best weed. But she was known for this only within Hollywood. To the public at large she was supposed to be innocent and adorable and, **ugh,** peppy.

Well, that's what people had thought of her until she met Bridger. Now she was the girl who left him at the altar.

"It was exactly a year ago that you two met, right?" Rafael asked.

Tuesday nodded. "This very party. On this very night. One year ago."

Rafael took a hit. Tuesday watched a pop star and an MTV Veejay hang out by the barbecue and pretend they weren't going to screw later. But everyone already knew they were screwing. Tuesday laughed as it occurred to her. This whole town was just people who **weren't** screwing pretending they were and people who **were** screwing pretending they weren't.

"This is basically the anniversary of my very own hell," she added.

Rafael frowned at her. "The whole world thinks that guy is a saint."

"The whole world thinks I'm the daughter of a doomed astronaut who builds a time machine in order to visit him before he leaves for the moon."

Rafael laughed. "That's your fault. Next time don't be so convincing you win an Oscar at sixteen."

"Seventeen," Tuesday said.

Rafael raised his eyebrow at her. Tuesday watched the party begin to fill up. She smiled at people. She smoked her spliff. She checked her watch. She had told herself she'd stay for an hour. Just so everyone knew she wasn't afraid to see Bridger's face.

Twenty more minutes. And then she could go.

But then she heard a commotion behind her. And she heard Bridger's booming action-movie voice. That voice was fake. His real voice was higher pitched and nasal. Tuesday knew this because when he spoke in his sleep, the real voice came out. But even with her, even when it had just been the two of them eating takeout on the couch, he'd always used the fake voice.

"Hey, man, how's it hanging?" Bridger said to someone in the doorway.

Tuesday could feel him mere feet away now. She turned to Rafael, not wanting to look behind her. "He's coming up behind me, isn't he?" Her pulse started racing. Here was the problem: What she didn't want everyone to think about her was actually true. She **was** afraid to see his face.

She didn't think she could stand looking at him pretend to be hurt by her. She couldn't bear one more minute of his brilliant poor-me routine. He had crafted such a perfect performance as a victim that it unnerved the shit out of her.

Yes, she'd left him on the day of their wedding. And yes, she could have handled it better. And yes, she had owed him a heartfelt apology.

Which she had given him, in the bridal suite, in her wedding dress, ten minutes before they were both due to go out there.

She had said, "I think we are doing this for the wrong reasons."

And he'd said, "We don't have to be madly in love or anything. But we complement each other. Everyone loves us. And I do love you. I think you're the greatest actress of our generation."

"Bridge," Tuesday had said. "I want to marry the love of my life. I want to wait for someone that feels like my soulmate."

And Bridger had said, "C'mon. You of all people know the difference between real life and movies."

Tuesday had let go of his hands and begun to take off her wedding dress. "I just can't do this. I'm sorry. I can't marry you. I thought I could. I thought I wanted the magazine cover but . . . I can't do it."

"Tuesday, put your dress back on, the show starts in ten minutes."

Tuesday had shaken her head. "I'm not doing it. And I'm sorry."

She got her assistant to signal her parents, who were waiting for her in the first row. The three of them ran to her car and drove away.

Bridger went out to the chapel and pretended he expected Tuesday any minute. He started crying at the altar. And then sold the story to **Now This.**

That was four months ago. Tuesday had not seen him since.

And, just as she heard him coming closer, she decided she did not want to see him tonight either.

"Raf, God help me, I can't do it," she said and she started running again, this time toward the tennis courts. But when she got to the gate, she noticed she wasn't alone. Rafael had run with her.

"Quick!" he said, pulling the gate open. "Before the fucker sees us!"

Tuesday slipped in and Rafael followed her and then he locked the gate behind them. The two of them laughing.

Suddenly, they were alone, on Brandon Randall's tennis court, beachside in Malibu, a thousand stars in the sky.

Tuesday emptied her pockets, showing Rafael the

weed she'd brought. He nodded and emptied his own. Quaaludes and LSD.

"I think we're supposed to 'Just Say No,'" Tuesday said with a smirk.

"Say whatever you want," Rafael said. "But then let's get fucked up."

Suddenly, Tuesday's night didn't seem quite so bad after all.

The party was alive.

No one was counting but there were twenty-seven people in the formal living room, including Hud. There were twenty people milling around the kitchen, including Kit, and thirty-two people in the backyard, including Jay. There were couples and small groups migrating toward the family room, the dining room, the study.

There were seven people in the five bathrooms of the house. Two were peeing, three were snorting lines, two were making out.

Jay had been pretending to have a good time by the pool, talking to a few of his surf buddies from up in Ventura County. And then he pretended to have a good time in the living room, talking to a couple soap actresses, and then he pretended to have a good time absolutely everywhere else at the party, talking to anyone he could find. But, in fact, he was doing two specific things: watching the door and checking his watch.

When would Lara arrive?

Jay watched yet another group of people that did not contain Lara enter the house. He got frustrated and decided to go upstairs and take a piss.

So he did not see Ashley come in the front door.

He did not see her look around—clearly with the intent of finding Hud. He did not see her spot Hud in the very back of the house talking to Wyatt Stone and the rest of the band members of the Breeze.

And so, Ashley slipped into the party without being noticed by anyone except the man she came for.

Hud looked up from the guys he was talking to and instantly smiled, delighted by the very sight of her despite the complications. "You came," he said, as she made her way to him.

She was wearing a fuchsia tube dress and an oversized blazer with the sleeves rolled up. She had her blond hair in a deep side part, one side held back with a comb barrette. Her long earrings sparkled as the light hit them.

"I came," she said and then she hugged him, very lightly.

"What made you change your mind?" he asked.

"It felt silly," she said, a smile peeking out. "To hide a good thing."

Hud felt his chest tighten. He had to tell her how he'd screwed it all up. He would tell her in a moment.

Just not right then.

• • •

Nina was standing in the living room next to Brandon as they spoke to Bridger Miller.

"So even though it **looks** like I was scaling a thirty-foot building with my bare hands," Bridger said,

"I was actually just climbing about seven feet." He pointed at them both. "But it was cool, right?"

"It was completely awesome," Brandon said.

Despite the fact that she wasn't particularly charmed by Bridger, Nina had to admit she'd seen **Race Against Time** and the scene was, actually, pretty awesome.

As Bridger asked Brandon something about next year's Olympics, Nina turned her attention toward the front door. There were people funneling into the house, the door now propped open with a rock someone must have found near the doorstep.

She watched as people greeted one another with big smiles and outstretched arms. A Greek chorus of "You're here!" "You came!" and "How the hell are ya?"

Nina noticed a young girl in a purple jersey dress come in. She looked a little lost. Nina wondered who she knew, how she had heard of the party. The girl made her way awkwardly into the living room as a man came up to Brandon and Nina and said, "I thought you two were divorced."

Nina wondered what it was with some people, that they thought it was appropriate to say every single thought out loud.

Brandon said to the man, "Don't always believe what you hear," and then winked at him.

Chris Travertine, Nina's agent, walked in the door and spotted her next to Brandon. He was wearing a double-breasted blue suit with a T-shirt underneath, his jacket sleeves pushed up ever so slightly to reveal his gold Rolex. He smiled at Nina and came right to her. Kissed her on the cheek.

"Are you two back together?" he whispered in her ear. "Not a bad move."

Nina grinned as best she could. "Glad you could make it."

Chris put his hand on her waist. He leaned to her ear once more and said, "I will always show up for you, babe. Always. Did you get my message?"

Nina blew out a breath. "About **Playboy**?"

Chris raised an eyebrow. "I think it's a good play."

Nina smiled politely.

"Keep thinking on it," he said. "I have a feeling when you see the money, you're gonna come around." He gave her a sincere wink and a finger gun and then left to get a beer.

A cocktail waitress came by with a tray of glasses of white wine. Brandon took one and raised it. "Everybody, I'd like to raise a glass to my incredible wife, Nina. She knows how to throw one hell of a party, am I right?"

The early crowd raised their glasses and cheered.

"And with that, I say, have fun, get wasted, and don't wreck my stuff!"

9:00 p.m.

Ricky Esposito—the guy that ran the photography studio at Pepperdine—was in the kitchen eating cheese and crackers. He had seen Kit walk by four times and, each time, couldn't stop staring at her abs.

He'd had a thing for her for approximately three years now even though he'd never spoken to her and was absolutely positive she had no idea he existed. But when you live in the same town your entire life, you notice people. And everyone always noticed the Rivas.

Sometimes Ricky would go into Riva's Seafood and order fried clams with no bellies, a large Coke, and french fries. He'd take a seat out by the parking lot on one of the wooden benches. He'd hope to spot Kit Riva.

She was the most appealing person he'd ever seen in his life.

He liked that she never had to try to be beautiful. He liked that her body was so solid, so strong. He imagined she was the sort of girl that didn't need a guy to kill a spider and he liked that because, to be honest, Ricky was afraid of spiders.

He'd seen her surf at Surfrider Beach every once in a while. He liked to go down to the pier and take a seat on a bench and watch the fishermen. But he could always recognize Kit when she was in the water. She had a bravado that he liked. She was aggressive with the waves, never deferred to other people. Ricky had always imagined marrying a woman like that. His mother was like that.

He just needed to find the guts to talk to her.

Nina had wandered away from Brandon and was talking to a group of young runway models by the front door. They wouldn't stop asking her questions like who designed her skirt and what eyeliner she was wearing.

"Like, what are you doing for your skin? It's fucking . . . radiant," the tallest, lankiest one said. She was brunette with blue eyes and Nina had gathered, based on how often she kept bringing it up, that she'd walked in McLaren and Westwood's Fall show last year.

"Oh, thank you," Nina said, kindly.

"And what are you doing for crow's-feet?" the sweeter-looking woman asked.

"What am I doing for crow's-feet?" Nina asked.

"Like, to prevent it."

"Oh, you know, just zinc when I'm surfing sometimes. And moisturizer," Nina said.

"La Mer?" the taller one said.

"I don't know what you're asking me," Nina said.

"La Mer," said the sweeter-looking woman. "Crème de la Mer. The moisturizer?"

"I just use Noxzema," Nina said.

The taller woman looked at the sweeter woman and they exchanged glances. Nina became overtaken with the sense, one she had often, that she wasn't a very good model.

She pulled herself away from the group, as if someone had called for her. She continued to move through the party.

Brandon was holding court in the living room, talking to a crowd of photographers and artists that had gathered around the Lichtenstein hanging above the fireplacc.

She watched Brandon from a distance, seeing his hands gesticulating wildly, everyone in rapt attention. She decided she needed a glass of wine and so she made her way toward the kitchen.

She waved as she walked past the surfers up from Venice who were sitting on her living room sofa drinking beers. She smiled at the three actors trying to pretend they weren't doing cokc off of her entry table. She said hello to the four women talking to each other about **Dynasty** outside her guest bathroom.

Before Nina could make it to the wine bar set up in the kitchen, a cocktail waitress came by with a tray of merlot and Nina smiled at her and took one.

"You have a lovely house, if you don't mind me saying," the waitress said. She was a redhead with green eyes. Nina liked her smile.

"Thank you," Nina told her. "My husband picked it out."

And then the waitress kept walking and Nina stood right in place, people moving all around her.

Actresses, models, musicians. Surfers, skaters,

volleyball players. Agents and executives. Development assistants. Writers, directors, producers. Those two asshole comedians with that stupid movie everyone loved. Half the cast of **Dallas.** Three Lakers. It was barely nine o'clock and Nina already felt like everyone in the world was in her house.

She sipped the merlot in her hand slowly, with her eyes closed, breathing it in as much as tasting it. **Can I go hide in my bedroom?**

Suddenly, the DJ put on "1999" and it broke something open in Nina's chest. Just the sound of Prince's voice, the beat. This song, in this moment . . . Nina felt like she could leave the world behind—all the people, **Brandon**—and simply enjoy herself for a second.

She walked out onto her lawn to join the party-goers who had started to dance.

"All right! Nina! Gettin' down to boogie," a woman called to her from the mass of bodies moving. Nina looked up and saw Wendy, from the restaurant.

"You made it," Nina said, smiling. She started bopping her butt from side to side, sliding her shoulders. She wasn't much of a dancer but when you love the song, it doesn't matter.

"It's nice to see you like this," Wendy said. Wendy was a much better dancer than Nina, a much more sexual dancer. Nina marveled at the freedom it took to hump blindly in midair like that.

"See me like what?" Nina called out, over the music.

"I don't know, you seem lighter, maybe. Carefree?"

Nina wondered if everyone secretly thought she lived with a stick up her ass. And then she wondered if maybe she did.

"It's Prince," Nina said. "He does it for me."

"Oh, he does it for everybody," Wendy said.

Nina saw Hud by the firepit and she called to him, tried to wave him over, but he was talking to a woman. Nina looked closer. Who was her brother flirting with?

It was Ashley. Hud was talking to Ashley.

He's screwing her.

It seemed so obvious. The way they were standing so close to each other, their lack of reticence about their bodies brushing together. It is discernible, when two people feel complete comfort with each other's skin. It is plain for anyone to see if they are looking.

And that's exactly what they had: an electric sort of peace between them.

Nina instantly understood that Jay would not take this well. Jay didn't have the benevolent confidence necessary to absorb this blow with ease. And Nina felt a sense of doom, as she imagined how the night would play out. The conflict, the mess.

This night, Nina could feel in her gut, was not going to end well.

Jay was coming down the stairs when he saw her.

There she was. Lara. His Lara, if people could belong to other people.

She was standing by the door, next to Chad, wearing a plain white T-shirt tucked into a black miniskirt. She looked about eight billion feet tall, her legs the full length of her. All Jay could think about was running his hands from her ankles all the way to her ass, how smooth the journey would be, how long it would take him.

He pulled it together and walked up to Lara, affecting nonchalance. "You guys made it," he said. "What are you having to drink?"

"Why don't I head over to the bar?" Chad suggested. "You two can wait here."

Lara asked for a white wine spritzer. Jay took Chad up on the offer to get him another Jack and Coke. And then Chad was gone.

Jay looked at Lara, with her gigantic eyes and her thin lips. He felt as if it was just the two of them there together even though there were now close to two hundred people in his sister's house. But who cared about the rest? Who cared about the music and the people and the noise?

Jay pulled Lara toward him. "I'm going to kiss you," he said.

"All right," she said. "So kiss me then."

He leaned over and put his lips to hers. She tasted like spearmint and he tasted like whiskey.

Jay grabbed her hand and felt a whoosh through his head. It was the booze. He knew that. But it was also the thrill of letting yourself get swept away. It felt so good to fall.

Vanessa was watching Hud through the window as he spoke to a blond woman out in the yard. "Who is Hud talking to?" she asked, as casually as possible. "I mean, not that it matters."

"I don't know," Kit said, distracted. This guy Ricky kept looking at her. There were a few guys that had been looking at her all night. Seth had smiled at her again, that guy Chad from the Sandcastle was looking at her. Dressed as she was, she could feel a difference in how the rooms she entered made space for her.

She was still trying to figure out how she felt about it. All she knew for sure was that she didn't want to strike up a conversation with Seth or Chad. They seemed too . . . cool, like they'd expect something of her she wasn't ready to deliver.

Vanessa continued to watch Hud out the window as he smiled at the woman he was talking to and snuck a kiss on her neck, right behind her ear. The woman closed her eyes and then touched Hud's face tenderly.

Vanessa's heart sank.

"Do you see this guy over here?" Kit said. "I think he's friends with my brother. Ricky something?"

Vanessa looked in the direction Kit was indicating, trying to distract herself, pretending she wasn't thrown. "Oh, wow, OK, that guy is checking you out," Vanessa said.

"Don't look right at him!" Kit said, hoping Vanessa would quiet down.

"He's cute," Vanessa said. But from the way that she said it, it was clear she thought it was a qualified sort of cute.

Vanessa stole another glance at Hud. Now he and this woman were playing with each other's hands covertly, as if no one could see them.

Vanessa closed her eyes, unable to look anymore. What had she honestly thought was going to happen tonight? That Hud was going to fall in love with her? How ridiculous. How completely and utterly ridiculous. She thought she might cry.

"Should I talk to him?" Kit asked. "Like, if he comes to talk to me?"

"Hm?" Vanessa asked, turning back to Kit and trying to catch up. "Yeah, totally talk to him." **I will not cry over this,** Vanessa thought as she kept her tears back. She had to meet someone else. She couldn't sit around pining away for someone who barely noticed her after this many years. She was just learning what type of woman she was but she decided she wanted to be the sort of woman who didn't do that. She turned her full attention to Kit. "You should go up to him and start the conversation yourself."

Kit sipped her water from a Solo cup. She'd never had a drop of alcohol, never smoked pot once. Had no plans to. She pulled the cup away from her mouth and glanced in Ricky's direction. She looked at the way he hovered by the window, pretending to look out of it but, in fact, looking nowhere at all. He looked comfortable being in the middle of a party completely alone.

There was something about him.

He was the one she was going to kiss.

10:00 p.m.

Seth Whittles was standing by the edge of the pool, a bottle of beer in his hand, talking to Hud and Ashley.

Seth's jeans were cuffed, his high-top Chuck Taylors were new. His hair was shellacked to his head with a preposterous amount of mousse.

"When are you and Jay leaving for Hawaii?" Seth asked.

"Soon, man," Hud replied. "Hoping Jay takes all three events."

"You guys will probably get another cover," Seth said.

"We'll see," Hud said. "Fingers crossed."

"You will," Ashley assured him. "I know you will."

"For sure," Seth said. But then it occurred to him

it was odd for Ashley to be there at all. Hadn't she and Jay broken up recently?

Ashley noticed Seth considering her. Hud noticed it, too.

"I'm going to go get another beer," Hud said. "Anybody want anything?"

"I'll come with you," Ashley said, as if the idea had just come to her.

And the two of them walked away, pretending it was a coincidence they were headed in the same direction.

Seth, now abandoned, sipped his beer awkwardly and looked for someone else to talk to. He scanned faces for any familiarity, tried to make eye contact with any cute girl he could find.

He was—at every party, at every bar, on every beach—living with his heart wide open, looking for the One. His soulmate, his other half. The love of his life.

And yet, he could never find Her. He always found women who thought he was a nice guy but weren't very interested or women who were interested only until something better came along. But he never could quite find what he was looking for: true love.

And, unfortunately, this party was no different.

He tried to catch the eye of a girl he recognized from **General Hospital,** which he secretly watched sometimes when he had an afternoon off. He'd been watching more this summer because Luke was back in Port Charles.

He'd thought the actress was gorgeous every time he saw her on the show. And now here she was, smoking a cigarette over by the barbecue.

When she glanced at him, he smiled.

She took a drag of her cigarette without acknowledging him and then looked back to her friends.

If only Seth would make his way out to the driveway. His perfect match was standing right outside.

She was on the first step of the front stoop talking to a group of women about whether Lionel Richie was an asshole. She was arguing that he was not.

Her name was Eliza Nakamura. She was wearing a belted jumpsuit and high heels. Her father was Japanese. Her mother was Swedish. She was a development executive at the Geffen Company. She hated it when people called her a D-Girl.

Every morning she woke up and donned a leotard, leggings, and leg warmers and then made her way to the gym for the 5:45 aerobics class. Afterward, she showered, ran mousse through her hair, blew it dry, teased her bangs, set it all with hairspray, and then put on her nude hose and one of her power suits. She always doubled up on the shoulder pads.

And then she got in her white convertible and hopped into bumper-to-bumper traffic on the 101.

At work, she read spec scripts and recommended the good ones to her bosses. She gave writers notes. She took lunches with agents and directors at Spago and the Ivy. She scheduled drinks for herself every weeknight with other executives at places like Yamashiro.

She kept a Rolodex of every business card she collected. She wanted to run a studio one day. She knew she would be good at it. She knew she could not let anything derail her.

When her boss slipped his hand up the skirt of her suit, she smiled at him and moved away. When a producer chased her around the watercooler, she laughed it off as best she could.

On weekends, she'd hang out with her girlfriends and find a bar on the Sunset Strip—the Roxy, the Rainbow, maybe join the party at the Motley House—and make out with whatever eyeliner-clad metal rocker suited her fancy until the early hours of the night.

Eliza was not looking for love, necessarily. She had other things on her mind. Both long term and short term. She was angling for the head of production opening at work. She was saving up money to buy her own condo in West Hollywood. She had not yet decided if she ever wanted to have children.

But she would welcome a certain type of man in particular: a good man, who was a nice guy, who didn't play games and understood that her career was important to her, that she could never quit the business, that she was living her dream. A man that could give her an orgasm every night and not expect her to make breakfast in the morning. **That** Eliza Nakamura would have welcomed with open arms.

But as Eliza stood in the gravel driveway—now listening to her friend Heather and two other girls ponder whether or not to go talk to some actors inside—she was perfectly happy not finding love at all. She had two scripts back at her apartment that she was supposed to finish by Monday morning. She was looking forward to getting that done tomorrow.

And so, she did not go inside. Instead, she hung out in the front yard, talking to her friends.

And Seth hung out in the backyard, looking for love.

Hud grabbed Ashley's hand. "C'mere," he said, as he nodded toward the worn path and stairs down the side of the cliff.

"To the beach?" Ashley asked.

"Just for a second, just to talk," Hud told her. "With no one else around."

He led her over to the steps gently and when they got down to the beach, the two of them sat on the sand. It was cold, almost wet, having released the heat of the sun.

Hud put his arm around Ashley and confessed. "I fucked up," he said.

"What do you mean?" she asked.

Hud shook his head, buried it in his hands. He should have told Jay long ago. He should have confessed it all to him the moment he realized he had feelings for Ashley, when she and Jay were still together, before he ever slept with her, before he fell in love with her, **before before before.**

What sort of man sleeps with his brother's girlfriend?

"I lied to Jay," Hud said. "I made it seem like I wanted to ask you out instead of . . . well, you know."

Ashley braced herself. "And what did he say?"

Hud looked at her. "He said he'd rather I didn't."

Ashley frowned and turned her head toward the

water. She watched it ebb and flow at its own pace, entirely unhurried.

She hadn't wanted to push him on this. She hadn't wanted him to feel like he had to choose. But he might have to. That was becoming clearer to her by the minute.

"I'm going to talk to him tonight," Hud said. "Again. I really am. I'm going to be firm about it. Explain that I'm very serious about you. And he's going to understand."

Ashley watched the waves come in to the shoreline, watched the moonlight bounce off the water, creating ripples like stripes. She caught her breath.

"Hud," she said. "I'm pregnant."

Bobby Housman came through the door looking like he'd raided Jordache. He had on black acid-washed jeans, a yellow patterned button-down shirt, and a jean jacket with the collar flipped up.

He was not handsome. He was portly and had a slightly cartoonish nose. He had always known if he was going to make it in Hollywood, it was going to be behind the scenes. That was fine with him. He'd been studying films since he was old enough to watch them, holed up in his parents' finished basement out-side of Buffalo.

And now he was the guy writing some of the biggest hits of the decade so far. **Gorgeous, Baby. Summer Break. My Mia.** Bobby Housman was thirty-two and considered Hollywood's new "It" screenwriter. He'd always imagined that if the day ever came when he was the hottest screenwriter in town, he'd shed his crippling inhibitions and have the time of his life. But in reality, success had not done enough to change him.

Three blockbuster comedies under his belt and he still felt like the weird wallflower at the movie premiere, the guy not making eye contact with anyone at the Golden Globes.

But he always liked the Riva party. He'd been invited to tag along with a producer the summer **Gorgeous, Baby** came out. That night back in '80, he'd smoked a joint with Tuesday Hendricks and made her laugh. Every year he came since then, he felt a little bit more like he belonged.

That night, when Bobby set foot on the landing of Nina Riva's front steps, he saw that the party was packed. He was, in fact, the first person to comment out loud that things were getting a bit crazier than in years past. His exact word was "Whoa."

He looked through to the kitchen to see Nina Riva and that tennis guy. She was sipping a glass of wine and talking to a woman next to her.

Bobby couldn't help but smile just looking at her. He'd loved her T-shirt ad, with her hair hanging long and her arm up against the doorframe. That see-through shirt and red underwear. **Soft to the touch.** That was gold. He'd come to Hollywood, in part, to meet a girl like that, so tall and lean and tan. California Girls, man. Heartbreakers, all of them.

Bobby watched Nina touch her husband's arm and

then leave the kitchen, out of his sight. He remembered his mission and got to work. He had spent the day procuring an obscene amount of coke and he was going to give it out to everybody. Wallflower no more.

As Bobby stood in the foyer, he saw a cocktail waitress—Caroline—walking by with a tray of shrimp.

"Coconut shrimp?" she asked when Bobby caught her eye. She moved the tray toward him, grabbing him a napkin.

The very fact of her beauty made Bobby nervous. He tried not to think of it. "Can I . . . Can I have your tray?" he asked.

"My tray?" she said.

"Yes, please. If you don't mind."

"I can't just give you my tray."

"Because it has shrimp on it?" he said.

"Uh . . ." she said. "Yeah."

Bobby, in a moment of inspiration, took each one of the three remaining shrimp and ate them. And then he said, "Now it doesn't have shrimp on it."

"I guess so," Caroline said. She handed it to him and smiled and then started to walk away.

"Wait," Bobby said. "I have a gift. For you. If you want. Just hang on." He looked at her for only a split second, but in that split second he felt the spark of something strong enough to give him hope in himself.

He wiped the tray down with a napkin. And then took half a brick of cocaine from the inside of his jacket. There was another full brick in his car.

"Oh my God," Caroline said.

"I know." Bobby poured a little out and started cutting it into as many lines as he could using his Amex Gold. And then he rolled up a hundred. He was embarrassed it was the smallest bill he had.

Then, he held the tray up like a cater waiter would, and he looked at her. She probably went for the smooth guys with the nice hair. Probably didn't give a second glance to the awkward, chubby ones like him. But somehow, in this moment, he didn't feel foolish for at least trying. And he briefly considered that maybe that had been the problem all along: that he spent so much time feeling foolish instead of just letting go and risking looking like a fool. "Care for a line?" Bobby said.

Caroline was enchanted by the reversal. It was more effective than Bobby ever could have imagined. She would so much rather be the one being served than the one doing the serving.

She smiled at him and took the rolled-up hundred he'd extended. She leaned in. It felt cold in her nose, burned her sinuses. She lifted her head back up and said, "Thank you."

Bobby smiled at her. "Sure, anytime." Then he added, "Just to be clear, for you, I would do absolutely anything at absolutely any time."

She blushed.

What was it about him? He wasn't cute. He didn't seem cool. But he did make her feel admired. It was as if he understood that she was the true star of this party. And she had come out to Los Angeles all the way from Maryland in search of that very thing: to feel like a star.

"You're a nice guy," Caroline said. "Aren't you?"

Bobby gave her a lopsided smile. "Cripplingly so."

"Can I get in on that?" asked Kyle Manheim, who appeared out of nowhere. Caroline had seen him come in with that woman Wendy and the rest of the Riva's Seafood staff right at seven. He seemed to be intent on having the greatest night of his life.

Bobby held the tray out to him, magnanimously. "I brought enough for everybody!" he yelled. Caroline tried to slink away, but Bobby mustered up all of his courage and grabbed her hand. "Stay," he said. "If you want to."

"I'm working," she said.

"But there's no more shrimp." Something about the way he said it, the way he was pleading with her to stay by his side, the simplicity of his desire for her company . . . it was one of the most romantic things Caroline had ever heard. **But there's no more shrimp.**

Caroline will think of that moment later on tonight, when she and Bobby have sex in the coat closet by the front door. No one will know they are there. And Bobby will cradle her hair in his hands to make sure her head doesn't hit the wall behind them. And it will be tender and sweet. And when they are in the throes of passion, cramped up together in that tiny space, barely air between them, Bobby will say, very quietly, "I never thought I'd have a chance with a girl like you," and Caroline's heart will flutter.

They will not know what the future holds or if their paths will ever cross again. But they will feel that—for one night at least—someone has seen them as they have always wanted to be seen. And that will be enough.

One tray of coke being passed around the party quickly became two trays of coke being passed around the party. And, just as swiftly, it was six trays of coke, waitresses offering blow like it was hors d'oeuvres.

To Kit, it felt like one moment she was at a fancy kegger and then she blinked and suddenly everyone around her was high as fuck and believing their own myths about themselves. **I am the greatest. I am the funniest. I have it going on.**

Kit was offered a line of coke by no fewer than three waitresses before she finally said, "I'm good. Stop offering me cocaine, thanks."

She walked to the patio by the firepit because she wanted some fresh air and because Ricky was there. She figured she should give him an opportunity, if that was what you could call it. If he was even interested. Which now she was thinking maybe he wasn't.

"Uh, hi," Ricky said as she stood next to him. He had a small dab of feta dip on the very corner of his lip and Kit wondered if she should tell him.

"Hi," she said.

"Yeah," Ricky said. He looked down at his sneakers. Then realized what he was doing and looked back up. "I mean, yeah. Totally hi."

Kit smiled. Maybe he was interested.

"You have a tiny bit of feta," she said, pointing. "On your lip."

He took a napkin from the table behind them and wiped it off. "That makes sense," he said. "Because now is the moment that I'm finally talking to my dream girl, so yeah, cheese on my face sounds about right."

Kit blushed. Ricky smiled.

And Kit started to think this was all a lot easier than she'd made it out to be.

Nina was standing next to Brandon in the living room. He was holding tightly on to her hand and whispering into her ear.

"Thank you," he said. "For making me the happiest man in the world."

It didn't sit right with her, the finality in his tone. "I think we still have a lot we have to talk about," she said.

"Of course," Brandon said, pulling her closer to him. "I know I have a lot of making up to do. I'm just thankful to be given the chance. I'm grateful you're allowing me to right my wrongs."

Nina smiled, uncertain what else to say. She wasn't quite sure how he ever possibly could right his wrongs. But she supposed she had told him she would let him try.

"So, Bran, tell us," said a lanky guy in a striped rugby shirt and salmon-colored chinos. He was standing next to a guy in Bermuda shorts and buckskin shoes. Every year more and more preppies were showing up at her parties and if she was honest with herself, she knew it was Brandon's influence. "Think you'll grab another Slam title next month?"

The front door opened and Nina looked up to find that the person coming across the threshold was a great excuse to leave Brandon's side. Her closest friend, fashion model Tarine Montefiore.

Eyes turned to look at the singularly gorgeous woman that had just walked in. Most people recognized her from her multiple covers of **Vogue** and **Elle,** her contract with Revlon. But even those who could not place her knew she had to be one of the most beautiful women in the world. With dark hair, warm brown eyes, and cheekbones that looked like they could cut you, Tarine seemed carved of marble, with too many casual perfections to be human.

Her hair hung long and straight, her eyes were shadowed in silver and black, her lips were covered in a high clear gloss. She was wearing a white microdress and a black leather motorcycle jacket. She had on black pumps that would have broken anyone else's ankles if they took a single step but she glided into the room effortlessly.

And then there was the accent. Tarine had been born in Israel to Spanish Jewish parents and then moved to Paris when she was eleven, Stockholm at sixteen, and to New York City when she turned eighteen. She had an accent entirely her own.

She and Nina had met on a **Sports Illustrated** swimsuit shoot in Panama City a couple years ago. They posed together in yellow bikinis sitting on opposite sides of a dinghy. The photo became so well known, two guys had parodied it on **SNL.**

Nina had liked Tarine instantly. Tarine would tell Nina which photographers were handsy and which agents tried to screw their clients. She would also tell Nina not to smile too wide or she'd show her lower, crooked teeth. Tarine was kind, even when being kind meant not being very nice.

Nina was very happy to see Tarine standing in front of her. And she was surprised when the door opened again and behind Tarine came Greg Robinson.

She had never met Greg personally. But she knew who he was. He'd worked with her father. He was the producer behind the biggest hits of the past two decades. Sam Samantha. Mimi Red. The Grand Band. Greg was the one creating these people, creating their music. He'd even had a few hits of his own back in the late sixties.

Greg put his hand on Tarine's shoulder comfortably—and that is when Nina realized her twenty-seven-year-old friend was dating a man who was at least fifty.

Nina made her way over and Tarine smiled at her. Nina leaned in and gave her friend a tight hug. "I'm so glad you made it," she said.

"Yes, well, I know it is the party of the century," Tarine said.

"Greg, hi," Nina said, shaking his hand. "Welcome."

"It's a pleasure," Greg said. "I'm fond of your father. Some of my first big jobs were on his records. Great guy."

Nina flashed her perfected smile. Brandon spotted them all and came to join the conversation.

"Hi, Tarine," he said, raising his glass to her.

"Brandon," Tarine said, her face blank. "A surprise."

Brandon smiled and introduced himself to Greg. Greg shook Brandon's hand and then looked around the living room, clocked the DJ.

"Any chance I can get behind that deck?" Greg asked.

Nina turned in the direction Greg was looking, at first not sure what he meant.

"Greg cannot stand it when another soul is in charge of what he is listening to," Tarine said, holding Greg's hand.

Brandon looked at their hands, intertwined together, for a moment too long, and something about the way he did it gave Nina the impression that he was less surprised about their age difference, and more surprised that Tarine was dating a black man.

"Are you kidding?" Brandon said, recovering quickly. "We would love to have you in charge of the ones and twos."

Nina wasn't sure what she cringed at more. Brandon trying to sound like Greg Robinson or Brandon saying "we" so casually.

"I'll take you over," Brandon said.

"I don't want to upset your guy. I'm sure he's great," Greg said.

"No," Brandon said, waving Greg off. "He gets paid either way. He'll understand **the** Greg Robinson is here."

Greg laughed and then the two of them walked in the direction of the DJ, with the intention of breaking his heart.

"I need your best red wine, my love," Tarine said, the moment they were out of earshot. "Not the low-shelf stuff you give to everyone. The stuff you reserve for people like me, please. It has been that kind of day."

Nina laughed. Tarine could be completely and utterly obnoxious. But Nina simply didn't mind. She admired the way Tarine never pretended to be anything she wasn't, the way she was so confident in exactly who she had chosen to be, as if there were never any other option.

"I do not mean to be rude," Tarine said. "Obviously. But there are men smoking cigarettes in saggy pants outside. I cannot drink the same wine as them."

Nina laughed. "They're drinking Coors from a keg."

Tarine frowned and it was clear to Nina that she had never heard of Coors, did not have a context for it other than to know it was beneath her. "I suspect you are proving my point," Tarine said.

Nina took her friend by the hand and brought her around the foyer to a small hidden door under the stairs. She hit four digits on the keypad and showed Tarine the wine cellar.

"Choose whatever you want," Nina said and then she slipped her hand out of Tarine's. "Just close it up after you take your bottle."

"Do not think you are leaving me here," Tarine said.

The music changed abruptly, from New Wave to Top 40. Nina watched as a rush of young women came running through the kitchen on their way to the living room. Tarine and Nina overheard one of them say, "No way is Greg Robinson here! No way!" The whole party got louder, everything elevated: the melody, the beat, the screams of excitement.

"I was going to see how things were faring outside," Nina said as she pointed toward the lawn.

Tarine shook her head, raising her voice above the din herself. "No, you are not. You are going to stand here with me while I choose my bottle and then we are going to go somewhere and you are going to tell me why Brandon is here. I thought we were done with that snake."

Nina felt a bit nauseated at the thought of having to explain. She wanted to make a joke. But Tarine was not someone you could brush off. Nina wondered, for a moment, how one became like that. What did it take? To say exactly what you meant? To feel comfortable in the middle of causing discomfort? To not feel—so intrinsically as to be as vital to yourself as your blood—that it was your responsibility to make things smooth and pleasant for everyone?

Tarine looked at Nina more pointedly, waiting for Nina to explain herself. Nina shrugged and said, "I love him."

Tarine turned and looked at her, furrowing her eyebrows, not buying it.

Nina rolled her eyes and tried a different answer, one closer to the truth. "It's just easier this way," she said.

"Easier?" Tarine asked.

"Yeah, just, like, not as complicated and . . . just easier."

Tarine frowned and then pulled a bottle of Opus One. "I am taking this," Tarine said. "All right?"

Nina nodded. Tarine shut the door and pulled Nina through the crowd of people to the kitchen counter. She ruffled through Nina's knife drawer and cooking utensils until Nina found a wine opener.

A cocktail waitress came by offering wine on one tray and lines of coke on the other and Tarine waved her off. "I have what I need, thank you."

Nina stared at the tray of coke as the cocktail waitress snaked her way farther through the kitchen. She wondered when, exactly, that had happened. People couldn't just do coke off the coffee tables anymore?

Tarine turned the corkscrew and then pulled the cork out.

The people around them turned at the sound. Some of them watched for a moment too long, these two beautiful women standing next to each other. Both tall and tan and lean and sparkling. Then they all went on with the rest of their conversations.

Nina saw the girl in the purple dress again, standing alone near the chips. She'd noticed her earlier, coming in the door. Now, the girl met her eye, somewhat timidly. Nina got the distinct impression the girl wanted her attention, would have loved the opportunity to talk to her.

Increasingly, Nina was feeling like the party attracted people who wanted her to provide them a good story to tell. They wanted to be able to say they met "the girl from the poster" or "the girl from the T-shirt ad" or "Mick Riva's daughter" or "Jay Riva's sister" or "Brandon Randall's wife" or whatever other way they wanted to define her.

"Do you ever wish you could be invisible for five minutes?" Nina asked Tarine.

Tarine looked at her, considered her. "No," she said. "That sounds like a nightmare." Tarine poured herself a glass and suddenly, Kyle Manheim pulled up between the two of them.

"Hey, Nina," he yelled over the music. "Great party."

"Thanks," Nina said.

"Can I get in on that?" Kyle called to Tarine as he held out his empty cup.

Tarine looked at Kyle, sizing him up, and then said, decisively, "Not going to happen."

Kyle walked away and Tarine took a sip of her wine. She closed her eyes as she tasted it, as if everything else could wait. When she opened her eyes back up, she said to Nina, "Today has not been easy. I found wrinkles between my breasts."

Nina laughed. "What are you even talking about?"

Tarine put her wineglass on the counter and

surreptitiously pulled the top of her dress down. Nina had to admit she could see the faintest set of lines along her friend's cleavage.

"I am getting old. The offers are going to start to dry up," Tarine said.

"Oh, stop it," Nina said. "You still have plenty of time."

"Three more years, tops," Tarine said, and Nina knew this was probably right. In the world they lived in, they had to make hay while the sun shined because once the sun set, it got very cold and dark indeed.

But part of Nina ached for that time, the time when people stopped looking, stopped caring. Part of her wished she could take her beauty and hand it over to someone else, someone who wanted it.

"Three years is still a long time," Nina said.

"I am not sure I agree," Tarine said.

"So is that why you're with Greg?" Nina asked, quietly. "Some security?"

Tarine shook her head. "I am with Greg because I find his gray hair sexy and I like talking to a man that has been alive long enough to have had interesting experiences. I do not need anyone's money. I have a lot of it and I use what I have to make more of it."

Nina smiled. "I shouldn't have expected anything less."

"No, you should not have," Tarine said.

It surprised Nina that Tarine had been accumulating money in such a purposeful way. It had never really occurred to Nina to try to secure outlandish wealth for her future. She had only ever wanted money because it solved problems. Anything more than that seemed superfluous, like extra air.

"I cannot believe you took him back," Tarine said, grabbing her glass again and folding her arms. She looked right at Nina, square in the eye. "You know what? I am going to do you a favor and tell you what your problem is."

"Oh, I have a lot of problems," Nina said.

Tarine shook her head. "No, you do not actually. That is what is so remarkable. You have just one very big one. Most people, all of these people here," Tarine said, pointing in the general direction of everyone surrounding them, "all of us have thousands of little flaws. I have a lot of them. For instance, I am very judgmental but I am also very absentminded, and that is just the start of it."

Nina did think of Tarine as judgmental but she didn't see it as a problem. And she would never have thought of Tarine as absentminded. "But you," Tarine said. "With you, it is just the one problem. And it affects everything you do and, Nina, I am sorry to say this but I hate it about you."

"All right," Nina said. "Go on and tell me."

Tarine sipped her wine and then said, "I suspect you have not lived a single day for yourself."

Ricky Esposito knew only two ways to woo a woman. One was reciting Shakespearean sonnets. And the other was doing a magic trick.

Ricky chose magic. And so he was rummaging through the kitchen drawers of Nina's home, looking for a deck of cards, while Kit drank her club soda out on the patio alone, granting half smiles to the half strangers that littered her sister's lawn.

Kit spotted Vanessa talking to Seth over by the grill.

Vanessa had seemed so sad earlier. But then Vanessa had told Kit she was "determined to meet someone new," and Kit had decided not to push her on what "new" meant. If she was getting over Hud, great. Now Vanessa was laughing as if Seth Whittles was the funniest guy in the world. She had her hands in her hair, playing with a section of it by her face. Kit watched as Vanessa put her hand on Seth's shoulder and pushed him ever so slightly, teasing him. For a moment, Kit felt a flash of dread. **Was she going to have to act like Ricky was funny? Ugh.**

She thought of Nina gazing up at Brandon like she was proud to stand next to him. She thought of the way her mother used to talk about her father like he was the second coming of Christ.

She couldn't be like that.

She turned away just as Seth kissed Vanessa and suddenly Ricky appeared in front of her, flushed, with a deck of cards in his hand, catching his breath.

"Pick a card, any card," he said, and as he said it, Kit regretted every single choice she'd made that had brought her to this moment. This is what she had always wanted to avoid: being forced to pretend men were interesting.

Kit looked at Ricky and then at the cards fanned out perfectly in front of him. She grabbed one from the middle.

"Do I look at it?" she asked, with a sigh.

"I know it seems lame, but humor me. I've practiced this a lot and I might just blow your mind."

Kit smiled and, despite herself, began to root for him. She looked at the card. The eight of diamonds. "OK," she said. "I've got it."

Ricky offered the deck back to her, this time cut in two. "All right, put it back," he said, gesturing to the lower half. Kit did as she was told and Ricky shuffled. Her card was now lost, one among many.

Ricky palmed the cards in his hands and as he did it, Kit found herself distracted by the commotion around the pool. She couldn't see what was happening but it seemed like things were getting loud.

Ricky held up a card from the top of the deck with flair. "Is this your card?" he asked. A three of clubs.

Kit shook her head. She had wanted him to get it right, she realized. She had wanted him to dazzle her. "No, sorry."

Ricky smiled. "Oh, OK." He flicked the deck like his finger was a magic wand and picked up the card again. It was now an eight of diamonds.

The tiniest charge ran through Kit. "Wow," she said, genuinely impressed. She did not know how he had changed the three of clubs into the eight of diamonds. She knew it must be something simple but she couldn't begin to suspect what it was.

"Do you want to know how I did it?" Ricky asked, pleased to have pleased her.

"Aren't you supposed to never reveal it?" Kit asked.

Ricky shrugged and so Kit stepped in closer, shortening the distance between them.

"All right," she said. "Show me."

Ricky pulled the deck out again and did it in slow motion. When he revealed the true sleight of hand necessary for the illusion—picking up two cards and making it look as if they were only one—Kit was close enough to notice that he smelled like fresh laundry.

"That's all there is to it," Ricky said, showing her the way he held the cards. "It's called a double lift."

"That's rad," Kit said. He smelled really good. How did he do that?

"I can show you how to do it," Ricky said. "If you want."

"Nah," she said. "But do it again. I want to see if I can spot when you do it."

She did not actually care. She just wanted to smell the sleeve of his T-shirt. She just wanted to feel the thrill of his interest.

It was then that Ricky took a step closer, and with haste and trepidation, kissed her. His lips were soft and gentle.

But as his body moved against hers, Kit knew in her gut this was all wrong. This wasn't it. Whatever "it" was supposed to be.

Because she liked Ricky—she did. He was sweet and sort of embarrassing in a lovely way. But the second his lips hit hers, she knew that she had never truly wanted to kiss him.

She was pretty sure she did not want to kiss any guy at all.

Suddenly, Kit felt desperate to quiet the voice that she now realized had been calling to her for years. And so, she kissed Ricky Esposito harder. She put her arms around him and pushed her chest against his, as if, if she really tried, she could deny everything she knew was true.

Tarine had gone in search of a good joint so Nina hung out in the kitchen, talking to a couple of movie producers. She was almost positive that both of them were named Craig.

"Your 1980 calendar is hands down the greatest calendar of all time," First Craig said. He was stockier, meatier, but strong. He looked like he probably worked out two hours a day.

Nina smiled, acting flattered, pretending she cared.

"I mean . . . July?" Second Craig said. He was blond with a square jaw, even his posture was arrogant. "The one in the white bikini . . ." He whistled.

"I **still** think about it," First Craig said.

"That's nice," Nina said dryly. And then she quickly added a "What?" in the opposite direction, as if she heard someone calling to her from the stairs. "I'll be right there!" And then she smiled and left them in the kitchen.

When she got to the stairs, she saw Brandon out by the front door talking to some Olympic runner Nina knew she was supposed to remember. But instead of going to join the conversation, she turned and went up the steps, looking for a moment of peace. That was all right, wasn't it?

She walked past a couple making out against the

wall of her hallway. She smiled at the two former child stars sitting on the floor rolling a joint.

When she got to her bedroom, she shut the door behind her. She went into the master bathroom and stood at her mirror. She reapplied her lipstick and smacked her lips.

Was Tarine right?

How do you live a day for yourself? Nina didn't know. She imagined what a day of her life would look like if she were living only for herself. Maybe going somewhere on her own. Like the coast of Portugal. Just her and the sunshine, a good book, and her Ben Aipa swallowtail surfboard. Small pleasures. She'd spend her time surfing and then eating good bread. And cheese.

But really, Nina just wanted peace and quiet so long-lasting and secure that it might even settle into her bones.

"Excuse me?"

Nina turned toward her bedroom door, the one that had been closed just a moment before. Now it was open and there was a young woman standing in the hallway, one hand on the doorknob.

The girl in the purple jersey dress.

"Nina?" the girl said.

"Yes?"

The girl was short—and young, maybe seventeen or eighteen. Her hair was dark blond, her skin was alabaster and perfectly clear, as if she had never spent a day in the sun.

"I was wondering if I could . . ." The girl's fingers were shaking. And with each word the girl said, her voice became more uneven. "I was wondering if I could talk to you. Just for a moment."

"Um," Nina said. "Sure, come on in. What can I do for you?"

As Nina was looking at the girl standing in front of her, the answer was already beginning to come to her. But she couldn't quite grasp it yet.

"I wanted to . . . well," the girl said, wringing her hands and then catching herself doing it. "My name is Casey Greens," she said.

"Hi, Casey." Nina could hear the slight edge in her own voice. She tried to hide her wariness better. "You seem like you want to say something."

And that's when Nina saw it. Or, maybe more accurately, realized what she had already seen. Casey's lips.

A big lower lip, full like an overstuffed cushion.

Casey Greens did not look anything like Nina or Jay or Hud or Kit or Mick. Except for that lip.

And Nina's heart sank.

Casey spoke up. "I think Mick Riva might be my father."

• • •

Casey Greens didn't belong here. In Malibu, of all places. With the rich people and their perfect bodies. She knew that. She could feel it with every step she took on the thick, expensive carpet. She'd never stood on anything that plush, that soft before. She had grown up in a world of worn-out shag carpeting.

Shag carpeting and wood paneling and screen doors that still let in bugs. She came from a home of warmth even when it was cold, a home of beauty even though it was categorically hideous. Her town was called Rancho Cucamonga. Her parents were Bill and Helen. Her home was a California ranch. It had a birdhouse built on the top of it.

She was an only child, good at getting straight A's—the kind of kid who liked spending Saturday night with her parents. Her mom made the very best tuna casserole in the world. And Casey would ask for it every year on her birthday. She understood that she had lived a pretty sheltered life—right up until she lost both of her parents in one fell swoop.

Casey still heard the term in her head, woke up with it in her mind and fell asleep with it in her ears, even weeks after her parents' car accident: **died on impact.**

Her parents—her deceased parents—hadn't prepared her for a life without them. They hadn't prepared her for loneliness, for true adulthood, for the shocking revelations that would now have to come to light.

Casey had always known she was adopted, that her biological mother had died during childbirth. But she didn't know much more. And that was OK with her. She had parents. Until she didn't.

Days after the funeral, she was packing up her parents' things, trying to determine what to do with the life they all had shared. What was she supposed to do with her father's clothes? Where was she supposed to put her mother's antiperspirant? She was packing and unpacking, repacking. She was caught in a whirl of thoughts. The statements "Leave everything exactly where it is" and "Get all of it out of my sight" fought for dominance in her heart and head.

She sat down on the floor and closed her eyes. And she got the wild idea to do something that had never occurred to her: to look for her birth certificate.

It took an hour and a half to find. It was in a locked box underneath a few other papers.

Casey grabbed it and looked at it. Casey Miranda Ridgemore was her given name. Her birth mother had been named Monica Ridgemore. The space for the father's name was blank.

The next thing Casey found was a photo of a young woman. Blond, gorgeous. Big eyes, high cheekbones, an all-American kind of smile.

When Casey turned the photo over to see what was on the back, in handwriting she didn't recognize, it said, "Monica Ridgemore. Died August 1st, 1965." Below the date was another note. "Claims the baby is result of a one-night stand with Mick Riva."

Mick Riva? Casey thought she must be reading it wrong. She must be misunderstanding. **Mick Riva?**

She pulled out the R volume of her mother's encyclopedia set just to make sure she wasn't insane.

Riva, Mick—singer, songwriter, born 1933. Considered one of the greatest American recording artists of all time, Mick Riva (né Michael Dominic Riva) came to fame in the late 1950s and swept the charts with his romantic ballads and smooth vocals. His chart-topping success, classic good looks, and impeccable style has made him one of the most notable icons of the twentieth century.

Casey closed the book.

It took her a couple of weeks to come to terms with the idea. In moments when she felt she could get out of bed, she stared at her face in the mirror, compared it to the album cover she found in her father's pile of records. Sometimes she thought she saw something, other times she thought she was crazy.

Even if there was legitimacy to the idea, what was she supposed to do? Track down one of the most famous singers in the world and confront him?

But then, three weeks ago, she saw someone named Nina Riva on the cover of **Now This.** It said she was the daughter of Mick Riva and lived in Malibu, California. And Casey thought, **Malibu isn't very far at all.**

Before her parents died, Casey had been accepted at UC Irvine to start in the fall. After her parents died, she knew going away to college was the only thing she had left in the world. College would have to be where she began again.

But after she packed up her truck and headed for freshman orientation, Casey drove past the entrance for the 15 South that would take her to Irvine. She found herself getting on the 10 West, headed for Malibu.

What am I doing? she thought. **Do I think I'm just going to somehow find this Nina Riva person?**

Still. She kept driving.

When she hit the coastline, she drove up and down PCH trying to find the grocery store in the photo. The one Nina had been walking out of.

In the article it had said that Nina and her three siblings had lost their mother almost ten years before. And when she looked at the photo of Nina again, she detected sadness in her eyes, perhaps a world-weariness. Casey figured she was probably imagining it. But still, she reasoned, Nina must know how it felt to lose a parent.

There aren't many grocery stores in Malibu. It wasn't long before Casey found the right one. She walked in and stood in line with nothing in her hands. When she got to the cashier she said, "Sorry to bother you. Do you know Nina Riva?"

The cashier shook her head. "I mean, I've seen her but I don't know her."

Casey tried this with every cashier she saw, as well as the butcher, the entire bakery department, and the shift manager. Until finally someone said, "Why don't you just go to Riva's Seafood?"

Casey drove out to the restaurant she'd just learned

about, parked her car, and walked in. She stared at every single customer, every single server. She went up to the counter. "Is Nina here?"

A blond woman with a name tag that said WENDY looked up at her and shook her head. "No, sorry, hun."

Dejected, Casey walked out to her truck. She was crazy! Driving to Malibu? Trying to track down a famous model with a famous father? That's what stalkers do!

Casey backed out of the parking lot and turned south. She stopped at a gas station to fill her tank, trying to decide if she was filling it up to go home or to go to her first day of school in Irvine or to drive off a cliff.

She got out of the car and asked the cashier to put twenty dollars on pump number two. She went back to her car and put the nozzle in her gas tank and pressed the trigger on the hose. Which is when Casey overheard two men at the pump next to her.

"Are you going to the Riva party tomorrow night?" the tall one asked.

"No doubt, man."

"Let me get that address from you."

The second man laughed as he pulled the nozzle out of his gas tank. "Craig, you know if you don't know the address you aren't invited."

"So give me the address, what's it to you?"

"Everyone in Malibu is going to be there and you're gonna be sitting on your ass alone 'cause you don't know where Nina lives."

"Dude, give me the address. You owe me after I hooked that shit up for you with the girl from Gladstones."

After that, the second man spouted the address like money coming out of an ATM: "28150 Cliffside Drive."

There it was. Casey had come all that way and fate had provided. She had slept in her truck that night, parked on the side of the road on the coastline. And then this morning, she had gone through all of her packed clothes and pulled out the only decently cool dress she owned.

And here she was.

• • • •

"Who did you say your mother was?" Nina asked.

As Nina had listened to Casey's story, her mouth had gone dry. She started doing calculations in her head based on how old this girl was. She'd have been born after Mick left the final time. And Nina had no idea what messes her father had gotten into since then. So she was about as much of an expert about this as Casey herself.

"I actually don't know that much about her," Casey said. "All I know is that her name was Monica Ridgemore. She died giving birth to me, I think." Casey pulled her purse open and took out the photo, handing it to Nina.

"She was really young when she had me," Casey said. "I mean, she was as old as I am now."

Nina wasn't sure what good the photo would do her, why she'd even asked about Casey's mother. But still, she took it in hand and studied it.

Monica, at least in the photo, was young and blond and pretty in a very conventional way. When Nina looked at the photo, she saw where Casey's big eyes came from.

But there was also so much about Casey that Nina couldn't place. She didn't have either Monica's or Mick's cheekbones or either of their coloring, neither of their noses. In fact, Casey didn't look like Mick Riva at all except for her lower lip.

She turned the photo and read the back. **"Claims the baby is result of one-night stand with Mick Riva."** There had to be a lot of women who fantasized about an affair with Mick Riva, right?

Nina hoped, for Casey's sake, that the claim was wrong. She hoped there was a better man out there, waiting for Casey to find him and tell him she was his daughter. She handed the photo back and sighed with her whole body, resigning herself to the futility of this exercise. There was no way to know.

Nina gestured for Casey to have a seat in one of the leather chairs by the window, and Casey sat down with such deference and appreciation that Nina realized she should have offered her a seat quite a while ago.

Nina took a seat next to her and wasn't sure what to say next. What did Casey want?

"Quite a night," Nina said.

"Yeah, I guess so," Casey responded.

The two were quiet for some time—both of them wondering what on earth they could possibly say next. In the silence, they simply watched the party unfolding on the lawn below them.

Chaos was simmering. The music was deafening and people were in various states of undress. There must have been a hundred people in the pool. Someone had rigged the jets in the Jacuzzi to ricochet off of serving plates and spray people on the lawn.

There was a young woman sitting by the grill, reading a book. Casey looked closer. "Is that the girl from **Flashdance**?" she asked.

Nina nodded. "Jennifer Beals, yeah. Love her."

Casey's eyes went wide for a moment. **What a world.**

Nina spotted Jay talking to a very tall blond woman. He seemed to be showing her the ocean from the cliffside.

"See that guy?" Nina said. "The tall one talking to the blond woman? There on the side?"

Casey leaned in. "Yeah."

"That's my brother Jay."

"Oh, OK," Casey said, nodding.

"So he might be . . ."

"Might be my brother, too."

Nina looked at Casey, trying to process how bizarre this conversation was. "Yeah," she said. "Might be your brother, too."

Nina looked for Kit and spotted her talking to someone on the far corner of the patio. Nina put her finger up to the window. "The girl in the crop top and Daisy Dukes talking to that skinny guy . . ."

"Potentially my sister?" Casey asked.

Nina nodded. And then she started looking for Hud. She scanned the area, cataloged every person she could see. She could not find his broad shoulders and barrel chest anywhere. "I'm trying to find my brother Hud, but . . . Doesn't look like he's down there."

As she kept looking, Nina thought of what would have happened if Hud's biological mother had never left him in June's arms. Would he have shown up? At some point? Wanting to meet them? Wanting to know about his father?

Nina imagined feeling like a stranger to him, imagined him feeling like a stranger to her. What a loss that would have been—to have gone her whole life not knowing this person who felt like he owned one third of her heart. To not have been there during Hud's obsession with Frisbee or to see how excited he was when he got his first camera, to not know Hud's gentleness, to not know that Hud can't eat too much vinegar or he starts to sweat. He was hers.

Nina looked at Casey. Did some of the same blood run through their veins? Nina didn't know. She was not sure if she thought Casey might really be her sister or not. But if Casey was, Nina was already sad for what they had lost.

Casey continued to look out the window, stealing glances at Nina. She was trying to gauge just what, exactly, was going on in Nina's mind. She was reminded that she did not know the woman whose bedroom she was currently sitting in. She had no basis for trying to guess at her inner thoughts.

"Sorry for crashing your party," Casey said.

Nina shook her head. "Everyone's invited. Sounds like you might even belong here."

Casey gave a downcast smile. And Nina did, too. And their smiles were completely different, nothing alike.

"My mother died, too," Nina said. "She was the only parent I had. **We** had. So I . . . I'm sorry. No one should have to go through that. What you went through."

Casey looked at Nina and felt like she wanted to melt into her arms. Maybe this had been all she wanted. Just someone who understood, someone to tell her she didn't have to pretend to be OK.

Nina reached out and took Casey's hand for just a moment. She squeezed it and then let it go.

And then the two of them—somewhere between strangers and kin—watched the party in silence from the second-floor window.

Midnight

Mick Riva was standing in front of the mirror in his bedroom straightening his tie.

He looked good for fifty and he knew it. His once jet-black hair was now more salt than pepper. His once smooth face now creased at his forehead, eyes, and mouth. His good looks had not faded but instead had grown roots.

He was wearing a black suit and thin black tie—the look he had been known for for decades, the look he had perfected.

Beside him, on his vanity table, was the demo of three songs he'd recorded for his new album. All of them had been softly rejected by his record company. They'd sent a mostly sycophantic note that included the very **un**sycophantic kicker "We worry these tracks are too 'classic Mick Riva.' But what excites us is looking forward: Who is the Mick Riva of the 1980s?"

Just looking at the thing made him mad. How had it come to pass that someone like him—a luminary—was expected to listen to the musings of a twenty-something A & R guy with pierced ears and a preoccupation with synthesizers?

Angie would have fought back and made them release the tracks—and any others he decided to record. But unfortunately, they were no longer together.

Angie, as both his manager and his sixth wife, had always understood that Mick just needed to be allowed to do his thing and the world would come running. It had been working for the past thirty years. Angie always got that.

He wished he could go back in time and warn himself not to cheat on her, or not to let her find out, or maybe, perhaps, not to fall for her back in 1978, when she was just the young new redhead in his manager's office. Because now he was not quite sure who was supposed to fight his battles for him.

When you fall in love with your manager's assistant, fire your manager, promote his gorgeous assistant, marry her, and then divorce her, you're left with no wife or manager.

Which is how Mick got to be fifty years old and living alone with his butler, Sullivan. Just him and Sully in this white-brick and ivy mansion that Angie had picked out and decorated. She had loved the oversized eat-in kitchen. Now Mick refused to let Sully make him dinner because he didn't want to feel pathetic sitting at the table all by himself. It was a table for six.

The other day he'd had the thought that it would be nice to have a big family, have all of his kids come over for Sunday dinner. They could fill the place up, make it feel alive in there again. He thought about calling them. Nina, Jay, Hud, and Katherine.

They were young adults now. He could understand them, maybe offer them advice, or be useful to them all. Maybe they would like that, too.

He had been considering picking up the phone.

But then he had received a handwritten letter in the mail.

• • •

Despite the fact that there were no invitations for the Riva party, Kit did actually send one invitation every year.

Sometime in mid-August, she would take a piece of notebook paper and write down the date and the time and the address. And then she would write, "You are cordially invited to the Riva party."

And she would address it to her father.

Mick Riva
380 N Carolwood Drive
Los Angeles, California 90077

After decades on the road, he had settled down in a home in Holmby Hills, less than thirty miles from his children. Five years ago, Kit had tracked him down. And since then, every single year, she addressed that envelope the exact same way.

This year was the first year he'd noticed.

•   •   •

Mick slipped his dress shoes on, grabbed his keys, and walked out the door.

He got in his brand-new black Jaguar and put his foot on the gas. He sped down Sunset Boulevard, toward the ocean, with a handwritten invitation sitting on the passenger's seat.

It was just after midnight when Wendy Palmer took off her dress and slipped off her underwear. She stood there, bare, in the backyard, just to the side of the Jacuzzi, and then began to slowly step down into the steaming water.

The far corner of the Jacuzzi was in the far corner of the pool, which was in the far corner of the lawn. So only a few people saw her, at first.

Soon, Wendy was submerged in the bubbling water, floating over to the only other people in the Jacuzzi at that moment.

The two men stopped talking to each other in order to look at her. She smiled and raised her eyebrows ever so slightly. "Hi."

Stephen Cross and Nick Marnell both stared at her, instantly intrigued. They were the bassist and drummer of a British New Wave band with the number three song in the country.

This was not the first time they'd found themselves in a Jacuzzi with a naked woman.

"Hi," Nick said.

"Hello," Stephen said slowly.

Wendy kissed Nick first. And then Stephen. And then moved them all into a spot where people could watch before continuing with her plan.

"Are we really doing this?" Nick mouthed to Stephen.

And Stephen shrugged.

And so it began. Just as Wendy wanted.

Wendy had come to the party with the intention of having sex with two hot guys while people watched. She didn't want people to watch her for **their** sake. She wasn't trying to entertain anyone. She was not there for anyone's amusement but her own. This was something she'd always wanted to do. She'd thought about doing it from time to time when she got a little too drunk or found herself pressed up against a man, wishing they weren't alone. But she'd known when she woke up that morning that if she was ever actually going to do it, it had to be tonight.

Because the Riva party was Wendy's last hurrah.

It was time to leave Los Angeles. She had made the decision to give up on her acting career, quit her job at Riva's Seafood, and end the lark once and for all. Soon, her partying days would be over, too.

She'd grown homesick for Oregon. And she had finally decided that it was time to go home and marry the son of her father's best friend.

His name was Charles and he had loved her since they were children. She, a waiflike blond girl with a headband. He, a brown-haired, round-faced sweetheart who always picked up his toys. Now, Wendy was small-town gorgeous in a big city. And Charles was losing his hair at the age of twenty-six.

Last Christmas, Charles had confessed to Wendy that he still loved her. "If you told me to wait, I would . . ." he'd said in the hallway of her parents' house on Christmas Eve, just as her mother was setting the ham down for dinner. "I'd wait if there was even a small chance."

Wendy had kissed Charles on his cheekbone. And they'd both walked away from it suspecting she would make her way back to him.

When she returned to L.A. right after New Year's, she could smell the smog the second she landed at the airport. Her studio apartment depressed her. She kept being called in to audition for the roles of nagging girlfriends and nagging wives. She kept losing the parts to Valley girls who raised their voices at the ends of their sentences as if everything they said was a question. The only part she scored was to writhe around in a bikini on top of a sports car. They had teased her hair with so much Aqua Net, she had to wash it four times afterward.

When her agent told her that at the age of twenty-six she was too old to play Harrison Ford's girlfriend, Wendy knew she was going home.

She would marry the sweet man with the thinning hair and the money. And she would have kind-hearted children, whom she would love with all of her heart. And she would probably gain some weight. She would lose herself for long stretches of time, when the rush of dance recitals and sleepovers and basketball games took over with such force that her own personality began to drift away. But that was all OK by her. That life now sounded sort of wonderful.

This morning, she had booked a one-way ticket to Portland. She was leaving L.A. for good next Tuesday.

But first, she needed to fuck two rock stars in a Jacuzzi while everyone watched.

Lara had gone to the bathroom at least ten minutes ago, so Jay was killing time. He was by the fireplace in the living room talking to Matt Palakiko, a retired surfer. As a teenager, Jay had idolized Matt. He'd even stuck some of the photos of Matt's greatest waves on his bedroom wall. But now Matt was a father to twins and lived back home on the Big Island of Hawaii. He was in L.A. for the week taking meetings about licensing his name for swimwear.

Jay was listening to Matt talk about how the purity of surfing had returned to him when he stopped competing.

"But that's a ways off for you, man. You have a long career ahead of you," Matt said. "Everybody's saying so."

"Thank you," Jay said, nodding.

"And, look, if you play it right, a decade from now you could be doing some of the shit I'm doing, putting your name on stuff, taking paychecks. Everyone's throwing money around now. It's like there's too much of it all of a sudden. It's all just gonna get bigger and bigger. And I'm telling you, sometimes the financial security and the peace is even sweeter than the victory. I get up every day and surf because I want to. Not because I have to. Do you know how long it's been since I could say that?"

"Right," Jay said. "I bet."

"When it's just you and the wave, and you're not thinking about stats or training or . . ."

Jay was half listening, fixated on his uncertain future, the one he still could not bear to say out loud to anyone but Lara. His retirement wouldn't be like Matt's. He had to retire **and** give up the act itself. There was no real "purity" to exchange for what he was losing. He was just losing everything.

Jay had only begun to be considered one of the best—his career was just taking off. It had been for only a couple years he'd even had all of this attention. But it had not taken him long to acclimate to the adulation. And now, his heart was going to cost him the very thing that made him feel exceptional.

He was the eldest son of Mick Riva—wasn't he supposed to be the best at something? For a moment, Jay considered the idea that he would rather die being great than live being ordinary. He wasn't sure he could bear the stain of obscurity.

"Look, I gotta head out," Matt said, looking at his watch. "I got a flight back home in the morning. If I miss it, my wife will kill me."

"All right, man, take care," Jay said, and then he added, "I'd love to come out there and pick your brain sometime. You know, about the boards you're shaping. What you're up to now that you're, you know . . ."

"Old?"

Jay smiled. "Retired."

"Sure thing, man. Talk soon."

Just as Matt walked away, Jay felt a hand intertwine itself with his.

"Sorry, the line took forever," Lara said. "There are way too many people at this party. Is it always like this?"

Jay looked around, taking note of the bodies in the rest of the house. People were starting to pack themselves tight into small spaces. Couples had taken refuge on the stairs and girls were sitting on the floor. Through the windows it was plain to see that the front lawn was as packed as the back.

"Actually," Jay said. "This **is** a lot. Even for this party."

"Is there somewhere more quiet we can go?" Lara asked.

"Yeah," Jay said. "Of course. What were you thinking? The beach?"

"The beach feels a little . . ." Lara made a face that Jay tried desperately to discern. What did she mean? The beach was too romantic? Too cheesy? Too cold? Too dark? He wasn't sure.

"All right," Jay said and he took her by the hand and out the front door, past the partiers, past the valets, and then into the relative quiet darkness of the makeshift parking lot the attendants had made of his sister's side yard.

He walked right past two people making out with

a fervor that struck him as immensely funny until he realized it was Kit's friend Vanessa and that DJ they'd hired. He instantly looked away and then found himself looking back, stunned at the intensity. He had no idea Vanessa had it in her.

"Uh," Jay said, trying to forget what he'd seen. "Let's go to Hud's truck." Jay's own car had no top and no doors, but he knew Hud's truck would be unlocked. They headed straight for it.

Jay didn't just want to get Lara alone because he wanted to have sex with her. Yes, if Lara made a move on him, if she laid her long bare legs across him, he would strike. But he also wanted to talk to her. He wanted to ask her how she had been and what she was up to and did she think she would still like him if he was a nobody? He wanted to find out where she grew up and what her favorite movie was.

Jay came upon Hud's truck in the second row, toward the very back of the pack. He pulled Lara toward it, and opened the door for her. There wasn't much room and Lara had to squeeze into the ten-inch crack between door and frame. She managed. And when Jay shut the door behind him, they were finally alone.

"Hi," Jay said.

"Hi." Lara smiled.

Then neither of them said anything more. They simply looked at each other, comfortable and silent.

"You're different than I thought you'd be," Lara said, finally.

"What does that mean?" Jay asked. He shifted slightly so he could face her, bending his knee and resting his leg on the bench seat.

Lara shrugged softly. "You're much calmer than I figured."

"Calmer?" Jay asked. He was eager to know how he seemed to her, eager to see himself reflected in her eyes.

Lara laughed. "You seemed arrogant," she said. "Before I really knew you."

"And I don't seem arrogant to you now?" It was a new feeling, this desire to glean what the other person wanted from you and then find a way to be it. If she liked arrogance, he would play it up. If she didn't, he'd be the most humble guy she'd ever met.

Lara shook her head. "And you're quieter than I thought, too."

"You thought I was a loud dickhead," Jay said, smiling.

Lara laughed and lifted her hand to her earring, playing with it. "I did," she said.

"Are you disappointed?" Jay asked.

"No, I'm not disappointed. That's not what I meant at all," Lara said. Her voice was reassuring. "I guess what I'm saying is that people are surprising. I always thought you were cute even when you were a loud dickhead. But I like that you're not. You're more complicated than that."

Jay knew this was a compliment despite the fact that he had never aspired to complexity. "Complicated, huh? I don't know about that." What had happened to all the artificial indifference he normally relied on? Maybe this was the new him. Maybe he was becoming more like Hud.

Hud was always better with women than Jay. Jay slept with more women, hotter women, too. But Hud knew how to love them. Jay hadn't known to be envious of that kind of skill until now. Until all he wanted was to know Lara, earn her trust.

Could they take vacations together? Would she come to Hawaii? His days surfing the North Shore were probably over but could he teach her to surf in the gentle, nonthreatening waves of Waikiki? He wanted to bring her to his favorite café in Honolua Bay. He wanted to order her **haupia.**

"I've been trying to impress you," Jay admitted.

"Impress me?" Lara said. There was delight in the wrinkle of her eyes, in the curved edges of her lips.

"Yeah," Jay said, nodding. His head was down but his eyes were up and focused right on her. "Ever since . . ."

"That night," Lara said.

"Yeah, ever since that night, I haven't been able to stop thinking about you."

"You haven't?"

Jay knew he was a fish on a hook, that she was reeling him in. He wanted to be reeled in. It felt **good** to be drawn in, to become intoxicated. It was the first time he'd ever desired someone so strongly, and he liked the feeling, the sweet ache of this specific wanting.

"I can't stop thinking about you," he said. "I've . . . I've gone into the Sandcastle I don't even know how many times, trying to run into you."

"I know," she said, smiling. He had been exposed and it thrilled them both.

He leaned toward her and put his lips to the spot on her cheekbone that bumped right up to her eye. It was hard like bone and smooth like velvet.

"Is it crazy to think I might love you?" Jay whispered in her ear.

"It sounds a little crazy, yeah," Lara said, laughing. "You don't know me all that well."

Jay was barely listening to her. He was lost in the commotion of his own heart.

"I don't know . . ." he said, kissing her collarbone and running his hands up her legs. "I think I know enough."

He kissed her on the mouth and held her in the front seat of his brother's truck. He thought of what they were about to do as more than just sex. It was a way for him to show her what he felt for her. It was a connection, a sacred act. He put his hands slowly up Lara's shirt, unbuttoned his pants, kicked off his shoes. Lara's skirt was pushed up to her hips. And Jay slipped his hands underneath. He gingerly, and with great appreciation, slipped her underwear off, leaving it hanging at her feet.

"Do you have a condom?" Lara asked.

He didn't. But he figured Hud might have some in the car. He turned to the dashboard and grabbed the keys from where the valet had left them. He took the smallest key and fit it in the glove box. With a turn, the box fell open with a thud. And there were condoms. Three. All in a row, in their shiny foil packets. Jay picked them up, ready to tear one off.

But then.

Jay grabbed the photo in the glove box that had now entered his field of vision, only to see that it was a full **stack** of photos. Photos of his ex-girlfriend blowing his brother.

Photos that broke his already malfunctioning heart.

Hud and Ashley had taken their shoes off and neither one of them knew where they'd left them. They had walked so far down the beach that they did not exactly recognize where they were in the dark.

Hud had already asked her a list of questions. "How long have you known?" **Three days.** "How far along?" **Seven weeks.** "Was it the weekend we went to La Jolla?" **I think so.** "Are we ready to be parents?" **I don't know how to know something like that.**

And now, as they walked hand in hand along the water, they were both quietly considering two futures: one with a baby and one without.

Hud was thinking about renting a house; an Airstream was no place to raise a child. He was thinking about a two-bedroom and he imagined himself painting a nursery yellow. He thought of the sort of master bedroom his mother had. He had always liked that it had two sinks in the bathroom. He had always liked the idea of a mother and a father, together, at those sinks, every night.

Hud suddenly stopped, and Ashley stopped with him.

"What's the first thing you thought?" he asked her. "When you found out? When the test tube turned whatever color it turns."

"It's a ring that appears at the bottom."

"Well, then, when the ring appeared. What was the first thought that popped into your head?"

"Well, what was the first thing in your head? When I told you?" Ashley said.

"Honestly?"

"Yes."

"I thought, **How is it possible to love something that fast?** Because I feel like the minute you said it, I felt it. And that doesn't make any sense at all."

Ashley's eyes started to water and when she smiled, a tear fell.

"You didn't think, **Oh shit,** or **Fuck,** or **How do I get out of this?**" Ashley asked, wiping her tears away.

"No," Hud said, pulling her toward him. "Did you?"

"No," she said, shaking her head. "Not once."

"So we're having a baby," Hud said, holding her.

"We're having a baby."

And they stood there, the cold water swirling up and chilling their ankles, smiling at each other.

There would be rocking chairs and swaddles, mashed bananas and high chairs, the pride of a first step. There would be a wild and beautiful future.

But for now, right now, Hud had no choice but to stop dancing around a lie. His families, old and brand-new, were his to reconcile, his to fight and fight for. And he would do that now. He did not necessarily feel up to the task, but that hardly mattered.

"Should we turn back?" he asked.

Ashley looked up at him and gave him a gentle smile. She leaned into him farther, held his hand tighter. "All right," she said.

It was time to tell Jay the truth.

1:00 a.m.

Brandon was in the guest bathroom of his own home looking in the mirror. He was pretty buzzed already, heading straight to drunk. And he was staring at himself wondering how he had made so many mistakes in such a small span of time.

How could he have done all of this to Nina? She had weathered so many things so young and he had always liked to think of himself as the beginning of good things for her. He liked to think that maybe, in some small way, he was her knight in shining armor.

And then, like a moron, he'd started sleeping with Carrie Soto. There should be a way to undo your fuck-ups. Not just redeem yourself for them but actually undo them, make them so that they never happened. He wanted to take back every second of heartbreak he'd caused his wife. She did not deserve any of it, had done nothing to deserve his complete and disastrous breakdown. He wished the world would let them all just pretend the whole thing never happened.

Brandon stared into the mirror and looked at his face, looked at the lines that had started to form. Every day of your life feels like you're climbing up the mountain. And then you get there and you stay for a bit. And it's nice at the top. But then you start sliding down the other side.

He hadn't seen that part coming. And it had hit him hard.

• • •

This had all started because, nine months ago, Brandon had been the number one seed in the Australian Open. Then he lost in the second round in an upset to a seventeen-year-old Scandinavian named Anders Larsen.

From his first serve, Brandon had begun to worry that he was spinning out. He used his signature sling-shot, something very few players could return. It cut fast and clean across the court.

But Larsen returned it.

It knocked Brandon off his feet, having to volley back and forth for the point. Point went to Larsen. So did the next one.

The serve after that, he double-faulted. He found himself growing angry, looking at this teenager in front of him. The crowd started muttering, some of them cheering for Larsen.

Larsen smiled at Brandon as he waited, crouched over and ready.

It went through Brandon's mind that all the papers were anticipating Brandon and Kriek in the finals but now it was looking like he might not even make it past round two.

He began overthinking. His shoulder started feeling tight. For a moment it was as if his muscles did not remember. His serve got looser, slower. Every time he hit a forehand without spin, without precision, he grew more and more angry. Every backhand that missed his intended mark pushed him further into his own head and out of the game.

Break point.

When he missed the return on Larsen's last volley, he instantly felt the cameras on him. He'd felt this way before, trapped by the camera. The feeling had been manageable enough to shake off when the camera had caught him in victory, or even in a loss to a worthy opponent. But this had been a slaughter. He was Goliath and he had just lost to David.

Larsen turned to the stands and shook his fists in the air, having beaten the current number one player in the world. The crowd cheered.

Brandon, as he usually did in his rare moments like this, held his face tight, showing no sign of distress. He walked, his whole body tense, to the net.

But this time, try as he might, he could not muster a smile as he shook that little fuck's hand.

He knew his father would have been disappointed by his lack of sportsmanship. But that was the least of his problems.

As he slinked into the locker room, his coach, Tommy, trailed behind him. "What the fuck was that! I've never seen you so in your head! You don't have much time left on the court if that's all you have to bring!"

Brandon was silent, his heart pounding. Tommy shook his head and left. And when he was gone, Brandon punched a hole in the wall of the men's locker room.

Obviously, he'd lost before. But in the second round of a tournament he was supposed to win?

• • •

Brandon had gone home to Nina. But the second he opened the front door and saw her, he could not stand the look on her face. Her eyes were wide and welcoming; her mouth was turned down softly in a kind frown. "How are you doing?" she had asked him.

He'd wanted to jump out of his skin. Nina had put her arms around him and hugged him. And then she'd put her hand to his face. "You are a great man," she'd said. "You've already proven that. I mean, you have ten Grand Slams. That's unbelievable."

Brandon had taken her hand and moved it away from his face. "Thank you," he'd said, as he got up and went to take a shower. He could not bear to look at her.

Next up, in January, he was out in the third round at the U.S. Pro Indoor. **Fucking McEnroe.** Then he lost in straight sets at the Davis Cup in March; the U.S. team didn't even make it to the quarterfinals. At the Donnay Open, he lost in the semifinals and chucked his racket on the ground. It made headlines. He pulled out of Monte Carlo on account of his shoulder.

Brandon stopped coming home directly after his matches. He told Nina he had to visit his mother or his brother in New York. He made plans for himself and Tommy to stay longer in Buenos Aires and Nice. When he did finally come home, he would talk to Nina about dinner, and the restaurant, and her siblings, and his travel plans, and her schedule, and what art to buy for the downstairs den. He would not talk to her about tennis. He would not tell her his shoulder was killing him. He would sneak out to doctor's appointments—never told her he'd begun getting cortisone shots.

He was supposed to be indestructible. He was supposed to be humble despite being brilliant, affable despite his sheer domination on the court. He was not supposed to be out in the early rounds and pitied by his wife.

Enter: Carrie Soto.

Carrie Soto was considered the greatest female tennis player of all time. Brandon had met Carrie before but they had never had a conversation until one day back in May in Paris. He was at the French Open without Nina because he'd insisted she stay home.

He was sitting on a bench outside the locker room at Roland-Garros just before his first match, adjusting the sweatband on his head. Carrie Soto walked by him, with her tense body and perfect posture in her tennis whites.

Her dark hair was pulled back, under her visor. Her rosy skin, wide eyes, and button nose made her seem cute. But then when she got in earshot of Brandon, she leaned over and said to him, "Your nice guy routine doesn't fool me. You're as bloodthirsty as the rest of us. Get your serve in line, and murder them all."

Brandon turned and looked at her, his eyes wide.

She smiled at him. And he smiled back.

Brandon won his first match. Then another. And by the skin of his teeth, over the course of two weeks, he earned the Coupes de Mousquetaires. When he won the last match of the finals, he pumped his fist into the air.

Meanwhile, Carrie Soto crushed every single opponent she had with force and determination. She grunted with every serve, yelped as she volleyed, dove with abandon, smearing her tennis whites with the red clay of the court. And she won the Coupe de Suzanne Lenglen.

The night after he won, Brandon ran into Carrie at

their hotel, the two of them raging champions pacing in an elevator. Brandon felt victorious and vulnerable, gleeful and unguarded.

"I told you you could be vicious," Carrie said, grinning.

"I guess you've got my number," Brandon said.

There was a pause as the elevator rose. When it stopped at Brandon's floor, he said, "Let me know if you want to split something from the minibar."

Ten minutes later they were in his room.

Carrie Soto was on top of him, and he could feel her muscles in his hands. He could feel, as she moved, how hard her thighs were, how tight her butt was, how swollen her calves and forearms were. He could feel, as he touched her, her strength and agility. He was holding her power in his hands.

And for one small moment, while he was lying underneath her, he thought he'd found the other half of himself.

When he woke up the next morning, his head throbbed with the realization of what he had done. But just before Carrie left Paris, she told him she thought, just maybe, this could be something serious. And that made him wonder if all of this wasn't just cheating but perhaps something else, like a love affair.

He'd never thought it before, but maybe Nina was wrong for him. Maybe that was why she made him feel so small. And maybe Carrie was right for him. That was why she made him feel so strong.

So he kept seeing her. In L.A., in New York, in London. And soon Brandon had convinced himself that Carrie was his good-luck charm.

After they both won at Wimbledon, Brandon was flying high. He'd won clay and grass courts in the same year. Nearly unheard of. **"This,"** Tommy said, "is the Brandon I know."

The tabloids caught Carrie and him celebrating their wins together that night outside the Wimbledon ball. He was in a tux. Carrie was in a navy blue gown. They were kissing beside a car. His hand was on her ass.

Carrie saw the photos first and bought off the photographer and the magazine. She traded the photos for an exclusive with her. But afterward, she told Brandon that she was in love with him and it was time to "shit or get off the pot."

Brandon felt rushed. He wasn't sure he was ready to commit to leaving Nina. But he was at a crossroads in more ways than one, and he suspected that if he stayed with Nina, happiness and satisfaction might just soften him too much, enough that he might not fight hard enough against the descent of his talent.

If he stayed with Carrie, the best of his times on the court might be yet to come.

So, Brandon flew home. He walked into his massive house and headed right up the stairs to get his things.

He was hoping Nina wasn't home. But he found

her in the bedroom, reading a travel guide to Bora-Bora. She was wearing his boxer shorts. He could barely look at her.

"Hi, honey," she said, sweetly.

He went straight to the closet. He had to move fast; he had to get this over with quickly for the both of them. And he did not think he could bear to look at her. He was not sure he'd keep his nerve. "I'm sorry, Nina," he said. "But I'm leaving."

"What are you talking about?" she said, the bubbliness still in her voice.

He did not remember what she said after that. He had simply run away.

He went right to the Beverly Hills Hotel. And when he got to Carrie's suite, he kissed her at her front door and said, "I love you. I choose you."

The whole thing with Nina had been hideous and unbearable. But it had been necessary. And it was done.

• • •

Brandon stayed with Carrie and found that an entire new life had been mapped out for him within days.

In the mornings, they would both have protein smoothies and a handful of raw almonds and then go to the gym together. They started training at the same courts side by side at the Bel-Air Country Club. Brandon's cortisone shot was wearing off sooner than he'd anticipated, but if at any time Brandon started to slow down his serves or miss a few volleys in a row, Carrie would notice and yell to him from her court, without missing a beat of her own, "Get it together, Randall! You're either a champion or a fuckup. There is no in-between!" And he would run faster, hit more cleanly.

In the afternoon, they dealt with business, calling their agents, discussing endorsement deals, approving travel, sending correspondence.

By seven every evening, they were out the door, ready to go to dinner. The two of them were usually at a party, charity function, or gala by nine. They talked almost exclusively about how much Carrie hated her rival, Paulina Stepanova.

One night, in the middle of the night, Brandon woke up with his shoulder throbbing. They'd had an intense practice in the morning and a gala for Cedars-Sinai Medical Center in the evening, and then they'd come home and made love before turning out the lights.

Suddenly, at three in the morning, the pain was excruciating. He called down for ice but it did not do much to help. He popped a few meds. But the pain was getting sharper, throbbing harder.

He woke Carrie up, in a panic. "What if Wimbledon was my last slam?" he asked her.

"That would be catastrophic," Carrie said. "You only have twelve." And then she turned her body away from his and went to bed.

He ached for the tenderness of Nina.

He fell asleep just in time to wake up to Carrie throwing a towel at him. "Do we cry about the pain? Or do we man up and play through it? Car leaves for the court in fifteen."

He got up, got dressed, and kept her pace all day. And then the next and the next and on it went.

Brandon had lived his life beside Carrie for another four weeks and two days.

But then, again last night, the ache in his shoulder had woken him up. This time it was a searing, burning pain. Every second before the meds kicked in was agonizing. He had made an appointment for another shot and he knew that would help for a little while. But he understood, in some disturbingly clear way, that the clock was ticking. Even if he staved off the decline as long as possible, even if he won more championships than any other human in history, someday, his body was going to break down, because everyone's did.

And who would love him then?

It took him two and a half hours to fall asleep. And then that morning, he had been woken up at 6:00 to hear Carrie talking to room service saying, "Don't send salted nuts. I don't want salt in the morning. You sent salted nuts yesterday after I asked you three times not to! If you can't send the right type of nuts, maybe you should be in another field of work." Then she hung up the phone.

Brandon had laid his head back on his pillow. She

was not a kind person. He wasn't even sure she was a good person. Before he knew what he was doing he opened his mouth. "Oh my God," he said. "You're awful. What the fuck have I done?"

He got out of bed and started gesticulating wildly, going on about what an uptight ice woman she was. "I've made every wrong turn a person could make!" he said, standing in his boxers. "I don't think I love you. I'm not sure I have ever loved you. Why would I think this was where I wanted to be? I don't want to be with a woman who screams at people!"

Carrie stared at him like he had two heads. And then she said, "No one is making you stay here, you gigantic fucking prick."

Brandon considered her words and realized she was right. No one had made him sleep with her. No one had made him leave his wife for her. He'd done it all himself. But he simply could not, for the life of him, remember why any of that had felt like such a good idea.

"I think I should go," he said.

"Be my guest," Carrie said, gesturing to the door. "And feel free to fuck right off."

Brandon grabbed his things, and left.

He trained that morning at a different court. He took a long, punishingly hot shower. Then he sat in the locker room in his towel for an hour, immobile, considering what to do.

All he could think of was how good it felt when

Nina rubbed her hands through his hair, or the look on her face when she told him she'd love him forever.

Right then and there, he had made up his mind to get her back.

And he had! And now everything would be OK. As long as Carrie Soto left them alone.

Nina and Casey were sitting in silence when someone opened the door.

"Nina?"

They both turned to see Tarine. "You need to come downstairs," she said.

"Why?"

"It is Carrie Soto."

Nina was already tired. "What about her?"

"She is on your front lawn throwing clothes and threatening to light them on fire."

• • •

Nina started down the stairs, making her way through the crowd with Tarine.

Greg Robinson had the music up so loud it was shaking the ground, vibrating the very foundation of the house. People were dancing with such fervor in the living room that the picture frames were bouncing against the walls.

It was Nina's house, Nina's carpet they were standing on, her stairs supporting them, her booze they were drinking, her food they were eating. And yet, each person in Nina's way remained in her way until she tapped them on the shoulder, or nudged herself through. She found herself growing more and more annoyed. Her husband's mistress was on the front lawn and she couldn't even get outside to deal with it because there was a group of pro surfers smoking pot in her foyer.

"Excuse me!" Tarine said. "Get out of the way!" The surfers moved immediately.

When Nina finally made her way to the front of the house, she looked out to the driveway to see her husband trying to calm a woman who was waving her arms around and ranting.

Carrie Soto, in white track pants and a white-and-green T-shirt, was standing on the gravel in her driveway with Brandon's clothes dumped in a pile. Nina could see Brandon's favorite black Ralph Lauren polo off to the side, saw his lucky white sweatband lying on the rocks. He loved that sweatband.

He came back to me but left his sweatband with her?

"Brandon, I swear to God, you need to stop being such an asshole. I really might just burn all of your shit to the ground," Carrie said.

The crowd outside was entirely focused on Carrie, giving her a wide berth. People were coming around from the sides of the house to see what the commotion was. Nina could feel the people behind her peering over her head to see more.

"Carrie, please," Brandon was saying. He was standing just at the foot of the steps, his arms up in defense. "Let's talk about this like adults."

Carrie started laughing. Not maniacally, not angrily, but rather with genuine amusement. "I **am** the adult, Brandon. I am the one who told you not to leave your wife unless you were serious about us, do you remember that?" Brandon started to say more but Carrie interrupted. "Do you remember me telling you that I would not allow myself to be a home wrecker unless you and I were truly in love? That this was forever? Do you remember me telling you that?"

Brandon nodded. "Yes, but Carrie—"

"No, don't 'yes, but' me. You're an asshole, Brandon. Do you get that?"

"Carrie—"

"What did I tell you when we first slept together, Brandon? What did I say? Did I say to you that I wasn't going to sleep with another woman's husband unless it was for something real?"

"Yes, but—"

"And did I tell you that you better not fuck with my heart? Did I tell you that, Brandon?"

"Carrie—"

"I believe my exact words, you son of a bitch, were 'If I fall in love with you, don't fuck me over.'"

"I don't know if—"

"No, don't argue with me. That is what I said."

"OK, that is what you said. But—"

"You woke up this morning after making love to me the night before and when I got off the phone with room service to order us raw almonds, you said,

and I quote, 'Oh my God. You're awful. What the fuck have I done?' And then you left."

"Carrie, please. Can we talk about this in private?"

Carrie looked around, taking in the crowd that was forming. Then she looked behind Brandon, to the front door, where she saw Nina. Her face fell.

Brandon turned and saw Nina, too. "Nina—" he said.

"Nina," Carrie interrupted. "I am sorry. I shouldn't have taken up with him and I shouldn't be airing all of this dirty laundry and ruining your party."

Nina continued staring at Carrie but didn't say anything. How was it that this woman could shout out every thought running through her head? Why was it that Carrie Soto felt entitled to scream?

In that moment, Nina was not mad or jealous or embarrassed or anything else she might have expected. Nina was sad. Sad that she'd never lived a fraction of a second like Carrie Soto. **What a world she must live in,** Nina thought, **where you can piss and moan and stomp your feet and cry in public and yell at the people who hurt you. That you can dictate what you will and will not accept.**

Nina, her entire life, had been programmed to **accept.** Accept that your father left. Accept that your mother is gone. Accept that you must take care of your siblings. Accept that the world wants to lust after you. **Accept accept accept.** For so long, Nina had believed it was her greatest strength—that she could withstand, that she could endure, that she would accept it all and keep going. It was so foreign to her, the idea of declaring that something was unacceptable.

Nina thought of herself driving to someone else's house to scream on their front lawn while a whole party's worth of people watched. It was so impossible that she couldn't even summon a mental picture.

But Carrie had this fire within her. Where was Nina's fire? Had it ever been there? And if so, when did it go out?

Her husband had slept with Carrie last night and then Nina had taken him back this evening. What was wrong with her? Was she just going to accept it all? Just accept every piece of bullshit thrown at her for the rest of her life?

When Nina opened her mouth to speak, her voice was flat and calm and controlled. "I think you two need to leave," she said.

Brandon wasn't sure he'd heard her right. Carrie didn't hear her at all.

"I think you two need to leave," Nina said again, this time louder.

"Honey, no," Brandon said, trying to move toward her.

Nina put up her hand. "No. Nope," she said calmly. "Leave me out of this. You two can have each other."

"I don't want him," Carrie said. "I just wanted him to know that you can't treat people like dirt and think they are just going to take it."

Nina hated how small she felt in that moment, for having taken him back.

"How dare you come to this house?" Tarine said to Carrie. Her voice was loud and angry and when Nina looked at her, she could tell that Tarine had been seething for quite some time.

"For what it's worth, I hate myself," Carrie said to Nina and Tarine. "And I know I shouldn't be here. I'm just really sick and tired of people thinking they can treat me like I don't have a heart. Like mine doesn't break, too."

Nina looked at her and nodded. She understood Carrie Soto, understood she was heartbroken, understood that in another world they might even be friends. But they were in this world. And they were not friends.

"You have no right going around acting like you're Mr. Nice Guy. You're an asshole," Carrie said to Brandon. "All I wanted to do was give you back your stuff and tell you that. But then you pissed me off trying to shoo me away like some shameful secret. Like **you** didn't come on to me. Like you didn't start this whole thing."

Carrie turned around and walked back to her Bentley, which she'd left running, the driver's door still open. "I'm sorry, everyone," she said. "I really am."

She backed her car up, bumped against a palm tree, put it in drive, and took off.

Brandon watched her drive out of sight, and then, wearing a look of shock and embarrassment, moved toward his wife.

Nina put up her hands again, in front of everyone. "You need to go, too."

"Nina, honey, it's over with Carrie."

"I don't care. Please, Brandon, just go."

Nina was relieved to hear herself say it, relieved she was capable of **this.**

"You can't kick me out!" Brandon said. "It's my house! This is my house."

"So then take the house," Nina said. "It's yours."

And the moment she relinquished that stupid cliff-side monstrosity and the tennis star that came with it, Nina Riva felt one hundred times lighter.

There was finally enough air within her for a fire to ignite.

Casey Greens looked at herself in the mirror of Nina's master bathroom, splashing her face with cold water and then drying it with a lush taupe towel. Everything in this house was so nice. The towels were so soft, the rooms were so big. She looked at the floor-to-ceiling windows and the mirrored walls and the thousand thread count pillowcases.

But Casey ached for her old world, where the pillows were a little scratchy and the windows were small and always sort of stuck with humidity and old paint, where dinner was always a little overcooked. Where her mom got every question wrong on **Jeopardy!** every night, but they all sat on the couch together and had fun listening to her guess hopelessly anyway.

If Casey could—if the devil ever bartered—she would have sold her soul to leave this place and have her parents back. She felt a wave of despair coming toward her, ready to take her under. This had been happening on and off since she lost them. Casey had learned that the best thing to do was to brace herself for every rush of grief. She would let the sadness and sorrow wash over her, smother her. She held on tight, knowing all she could do was feel the pain until it passed.

She opened her eyes and looked at herself in the mirror once more.

Maybe she didn't belong here. Maybe she didn't belong anywhere, wouldn't belong anywhere. Ever again.

Nina walked back into the house trying to pretend she had not just suffered the indignity of her husband's mistress on her front lawn. And then she went right through the kitchen, opened up the pantry door, and walked in.

There, among the bags of rice and the cans of tomato sauce, Nina closed her eyes and settled herself. While the pantry door hummed with the sounds of the Eurythmics and the noise of people talking and laughing still penetrated the space, it was quiet enough to find stillness. Nina rested her famous ass on a stack of paper towel rolls and pulled her shoulder blades in toward each other, fixing her posture, releasing some of the tension from her back.

For fuck's sake. Her husband had returned, his mistress had shown up, she might have a long-lost sister, and her brother was sleeping with her other brother's ex-girlfriend. She just wanted the night to be over.

The pantry door opened, showering Nina with light and sound. She looked up to see Tarine standing in front of her with a bottle of wine and two glasses.

"Hi, doll," Tarine said as she slipped in and shut the door behind her. She pulled on the cord hanging above their heads. The light went on.

"Brandon is upstairs, packing up your things," Tarine said. "He is drunk, obviously. And he thinks he is kicking you out of the house."

Nina laughed. She had no choice but to find it funny.

Tarine sat down next to Nina and grabbed a cork-screw from her jacket pocket. She started opening up the bottle of sauvignon blanc. Once the cork was popped, she poured some wine into a glass and handed it to Nina, then poured one for herself.

"Someone took the rest of the Opus One," Tarine said. "These people are animals. I got us a white this time."

Nina took it but didn't drink out of it yet.

"Drink up," Tarine said as she took a sip of her own. "We are celebrating your Declaration of Independence."

Nina looked at Tarine and a small smile crept out of the corner of her mouth. She took a sip. And then she drank some more. **Good God,** she could drink the whole bottle right now.

"I didn't expect him to come back," Nina said.

"I know."

"Once he left . . . I don't know, our relationship felt over for me. I was mourning it."

"Rightfully so."

"And I've been really sad," Nina added. "That I . . . that I meant so little to someone who had made me believe I meant so much."

Tarine grabbed Nina's hand and squeezed it.

"But there was no part of me that wanted him back," Nina said, finally looking Tarine in the eye.

Tarine smiled. "Good," she said with a firm nod.

Nina lifted her wineglass to her lips again. She could smell the sweet astringency of the contents of the glass and she felt like she could get lost in it. And then she had this image, suddenly, of her mother on the couch in front of the television. Her blood ran cold.

Nina put the glass down. "When he showed up here tonight, do you know what I thought?" she said.

"What?"

"I went, **Oh fuck, now we have to do this whole song and dance?**"

Tarine smiled. "But you do not."

"No," Nina said. "I don't, do I?"

She didn't have to do any of this. The victimization, the acceptance of bullshit, the leaving your heart in the hands of an asshole yet again. She could just decide not to.

Nina smiled. She had to sit with that one for a moment. It was almost too good to be true.

Jay dropped the photos back into the glove box and tried to pretend that he hadn't seen them. That it hadn't happened. That it wasn't true. That his brother wouldn't **do that.**

He must be misunderstanding the photos. He must be. Because he could not possibly believe that his brother was not only that much of an asshole but also that much of a liar.

He tried to put the thoughts out of his head by moving on top of Lara, by refocusing his attention on her. But as he put his hand up her skirt, as he unzipped his own pants, the thought just kept reverberating in his head, that he couldn't possibly deny what he'd seen with his own two eyes.

Lara moved from under Jay and pushed him down onto the bench seat. He let her do whatever it was she wanted to do, lost in his own thoughts, hoping desperately she could take him somewhere else.

Lara climbed on top of him and began to move, her shirt lifted to expose her breasts, her skirt around her hips. The top of her head kept hitting the ceiling of the truck and Jay, trying so very hard to focus on Lara, couldn't help but wonder if Hud had fucked Ashley in this truck, just like this. If Ashley's head had also hit the ceiling.

When they were both done, Lara leaned off him, pulled down her shirt and her skirt, and said, "You're nearly catatonic. What's the matter?"

Jay looked at her as he sat up. "I think my brother is sleeping with my ex-girlfriend," he said. "And lying about it. Earlier tonight, he sold me some bullshit about wanting to ask her out. And I said no. And now I find out he's probably been fucking her this whole time."

Lara sat up straighter, surprised. "I'm sorry," she said, putting her hand on his back.

Jay's anger raged inside his chest but Lara's soothing hand helped calm him. "If I had to find out about this shit, I'm glad it's with you," he said.

Lara smiled but Jay noticed that it didn't look very sincere. It was like the smile you give to the guy who bags your groceries.

"I meant what I said earlier," he said. "About thinking I might love you."

"Jay . . ." she said.

"I guess I'm saying that I do, love you. I love you."

Jay was expecting Lara to smile or get a little weepy or blush. Women had pressured him to say it before and he never had. But now here he was, saying it. And he was excited for whatever would come next, however happy it would make her. But, instead, he watched as her eyes went blank and her smile stiffened.

"I . . . I don't know that we feel the same way about each other," she said.

Jay shook his head, confused. "Wait, what?"

"I'm sorry."

Jay's face hardened slowly but steadily, from a warm, languid pool to a glacier. "Wow," he said, stunned.

"Jay, I really am sorry. I think I misunderstood what you were looking for."

"I wasn't **looking** for anything," he said, moving away from her, putting his shoes back on. "But clearly you're not the person I thought you were, so whatever."

"Jay, that's not—"

"No, I should have known," he said as he opened the driver's side door and hopped out of the truck. He stood with both feet on the ground, looking at Lara, who had not moved from her seat. "That's why I didn't tell anybody about us. Because I knew you were this kinda girl. I knew you weren't the kind of girl you marry."

Jay could think of no bigger insult and so he felt he'd reclaimed some sense of power after lobbing it at her. But she seemed unfazed.

"All right," Lara said, putting her hand on the door handle.

"Get out of my brother's car," Jay said, his voice rising.

"Please be careful," Lara said as she got up. "I'm worried about your heart."

Jay narrowed his eyes and slammed the door shut.

"I guess I should go," Lara said. They stood on either side of the truck looking at each other.

"I honestly don't care what you do," Jay said before

walking away, swiftly at first, eager for distance. He slowed down when he got closer to the front door of the house. There were clothes all over the yard and people milling around, holding their drinks, smoking their cigarettes, all consumed with talking about something. But Jay wasn't listening.

Just as he got to the front door, he turned around, to see if Lara was still there.

He saw her getting her car from the valet. She took her keys, got in the front seat, and began to drive off.

When she turned onto the road and out of sight, Jay thought he'd feel better, but he didn't. Of course, he didn't.

Mick took a right onto PCH off Chautauqua but he did not bother to use his blinker. Speeding up the highway, ocean to his left, mountains to his right, he turned his attention briefly to the invitation.

He found himself growing a tiny bit nervous, his heart beating an irregular rhythm.

He was preparing his apologies in his head, framing and reframing his past actions to create a story his kids would understand, one they could forgive. Now was the time for them all to run down to the ocean and baptize themselves in the sea and start again.

He was doing this for himself, yes. But he was doing this for them, too. What broken family—no matter how shattered or tattered or bruised beyond recognition—does not ache to be reunited? What child, no matter how lost or abandoned, does not ache to be loved?

Mick pulled up to the red stoplight at Heathercliff Road. And when it turned green, he turned left without his blinker.

Kit was standing in the outdoor bathroom staring at the stars. Ricky was sucking on her neck so hard she was pretty sure she was going to end up with a hickey.

She couldn't look at him. She couldn't bear to. So she kept looking up at the night sky, trying to find the Big Dipper.

• • • •

Ricky could not believe his good fortune. He was here, making out with Kit Riva, in an outdoor shower. **Kit Riva. In an outdoor shower.** He wanted to take her out on romantic dates to Italian restaurants, and buy her flowers, and go surfing with her, and just generally be in her presence all the time.

Ricky was so flabbergasted and ahead of himself, so enchanted and eager, that it was almost as if his excitement could sustain them both.

Almost.

Ricky was no Don Juan but he'd been with women before. He'd had a high school dalliance, a college girlfriend. He knew how it felt when a girl was as excited to be with you as you were to be with her. And Ricky was starting to worry—because of the way Kit wasn't looking him in the eye, the way she kept freezing up when he touched her, the way she moved her pelvis farther from him—that she didn't really want to be here.

Ricky stood back for a moment and tried to get Kit to look at him, but she averted her gaze.

"Kit?" Ricky said.

"What?" she asked.

"Are you sure you want to do this?"

"Why wouldn't I want to do this?" Kit said.

"I don't know." Ricky shrugged. "I was just getting the impression maybe you weren't into it."

"Well, I am," Kit said.

"OK," Ricky said. "If you're sure."

"I'm sure," she said and she pulled him to her and kissed him again.

• • •

Kit was hiding, and she knew it.

She understood, very clearly, that once she admitted to herself she didn't like kissing Ricky, she would have to admit she didn't want to kiss men at all. That she didn't like their roughness, their smell, the coarseness of their faces. That she'd never once looked at a man and desired him.

She knew that as soon as she pulled away from Ricky Esposito, she was going to have to accept that she had always, her entire life, desired softness. Curves and smooth skin and long hair and soft lips. She had always ached to be touched with gentle hands.

Kissing Ricky felt all wrong because he wasn't Julianna Thompson. He wasn't Cheryl Nilsson. Or Violet North. He wasn't even Wendy Palmer, the waitress at the restaurant with whom Kit always felt a thrill when they shared a shift. She wished, for just one moment, he was that cocktail waitress she'd met earlier tonight, the one with the red hair. Caroline. But Kit kept kissing Ricky, hoping some internal desire would kick in, even though she knew that she had all the answers she'd been looking for.

Kit knew now—in her heart, in her body—that she liked girls the way other girls like boys. All she had done this evening by finally kissing a boy was show herself just how much she'd never cared about kissing a boy at all.

She pulled away from Ricky. "You're right. I can't do this."

"OK," Ricky said, backing off. "Sorry if I pushed you or anything."

"No," Kit said. "It's fine. I . . ." She wasn't sure how to finish her sentence and so, instead, she sat down on the bench in the shower.

Ricky sat down next to her.

"I'm sorry," she said. "I don't think I'm . . . this kind of person."

"What kind of person?"

Kit wasn't sure how to say it or even what she wanted to say. "The sort of person that wants to make out with a dude in an outdoor shower right now."

Ricky nodded, forlorn but keeping a smile on his face as best he could. "OK," he said. "I got it."

"It's not you," Kit said.

Ricky looked at her. She was finally looking him in the eye. "But I should take the hint that this is probably it for us, huh?"

Kit smiled at him, kindly. "I think maybe we should think of ourselves as friends."

Ricky nodded and stared at his own feet.

"But, like, real friends," Kit added, trying to get his attention back. "Like I sincerely mean that. If I was going to like a guy . . . I think it would be you."

Ricky cocked his head to the side, not quite sure what she was trying to tell him.

"Ricky . . ." Kit said, unsure if she could even complete the sentence she was starting. But didn't she have to start somewhere? And wasn't this the safest place to start? With someone she could avoid for the rest of her life if need be? "It really isn't you. It's . . ."

Ricky caught her eyeline. "It's what? You can tell me, honestly. I'm a really good listener."

Kit closed her eyes and let it fly. "What if I told you I like . . . girls?" She opened her eyes, unsure what she might see on Ricky's face.

Ricky was quiet for a moment. All Kit could discern was surprise.

"That makes sense. Girls are hot," he said, nodding. And then he laughed.

And Kit laughed, too. She threw her head back and cackled, her shoulders moving up and down as the laugh ran through her.

Ricky looked up at her and felt even more drawn in, the way her eyes looked so warm and bright, the way her smile created little dimples on her cheeks. He had been so close to the girl he'd always wanted. And now he understood it truly was **never** going to happen. **But that's how life goes,** Ricky thought. You don't always get the things you want.

"Thank you," Kit said. "Thank you for that."

"Hey, that's what friends are for, right?" he told her.

"I guess so," Kit said. "Yeah."

"So, look, here's the real question: If we are actually friends, as you say . . . does that mean you might teach me to surf?" he asked her.

Kit laughed. "You don't know how?" She really did like him. He was easy to be around.

"I'm not very good," Ricky said. "Certainly not as good as you."

"Nobody's as good as me," Kit said.

And Ricky laughed. "I know! So you gotta teach me."

Kit smiled at him and hoped that one day she might meet a girl like Ricky. Someone kind. Someone who didn't have anything to prove. She had so much to prove. There wasn't any room for anyone else to prove much.

"All right," Kit said. "I'll teach you."

And then she leaned over, and she kissed Ricky on the cheekbone. It was the first time Kit had kissed someone with all of her heart.

Tarine had been wrong. Brandon wasn't packing Nina's things. He had taken a bottle of Seagram's upstairs and sat down in the first open bedroom, one of the guest rooms. And now he was wallowing on the floor.

This was the room he'd imagined would belong to his first child. Now, he was sitting in it, crying by himself, back against the nightstand, drinking whiskey out of the bottle.

What the fuck is the matter with you, Brandon? Either one of those women would have made you happy, would have given you more than you ever deserved. How did you fuck that up?

God, this was bad. He really didn't want to be left alone at the end of all this.

He drank more of his whiskey and gagged at the sheer amount that was flowing down his throat. He wiped his mouth.

He had to fix this. He had to get one of them back. He had to. And he could! He knew he could. All he had to do was convince one of them that he wasn't a shit. Which was easy enough because he really had not been that much of a shit until recently. Even the tabloids would tell you, he really was a good guy!

He just needed to listen to his gut and choose the

love of his life. And then he would get her back and be a good husband and have children and win more titles and have his life look just like it looked on the pages of the magazines. Just like it was supposed to.

Brandon Randall was about to pass out but once he woke up, world, watch out. He was gonna go get one of those women back if it was the last thing he did.

Jay was searching for Hud everywhere.

He scanned the crowds in every room, pushing through people giving him dirty looks at being moved aside, smelling cigarette smoke and skunkweed, body odor and perfume. Hud was not in the front yard, downstairs, or upstairs. He was not in the backyard as far as Jay could see through the windows.

Jay made it back to the bottom of the landing. He turned to a brunette woman in a polka-dot dress smoking a joint. "Have you seen Hud?" Jay said.

"Who's Hud?" the woman asked, completely uninterested.

Jay looked at her sideways. "Who the fuck are you?" he asked her.

"Heather," she said, smiling.

"Well, Heather, Hud is my brother and he's fucking my girlfriend and I need to find him."

Heather put out her hand, offering Jay the butt of her joint. "You need this more than I do."

"No, thank you."

"Are you sure?"

Jay frowned and took the joint from her. He put it to his lips and pulled in the smoke. He closed his eyes, let it permeate his lungs, sink into his body. He opened his eyes back up.

"Do you feel better now?" Heather asked him.

Jay thought about it. "No. Not at all."

"OK," Heather said, shrugging. "Well, that's all I got." She turned away from him and resumed her conversation with the Laker Girl she'd been talking to. "OK, but, like, Larry Bird is good though."

Jay closed his eyes and pinched his nose, wondering why the fuck anyone would be defending the Celtics, but he didn't have time to fight her on it.

He made his way to the backyard again, still trying to find Hud. He was still seething inside but his rage had nowhere to go. He tried to relax, tried to calm himself down. He didn't see Hud anywhere.

Now Vanessa was sitting in the lap of Kyle Manheim, making out with him. **Jesus, Vanessa.** Jay made a note to himself to tell her she could do better than Kyle. But for now he simply tapped her on the shoulder.

Vanessa turned and looked at him. "Hey," she said. She seemed tipsy but far from blotto.

"Have you seen Hud?" Jay asked her.

Vanessa shook her head. "No. And you know what? I don't care that I haven't seen him. How's that? For once in my life, I can honestly say I just don't care."

Jay had already stopped listening. His eye caught sight of the cliff's edge and the stairs to the beach. "Yeah, cool."

He walked, slowly and deliberately, making eye contact with no one until he got to the edge of the lawn.

He looked down at the water, at the sand. On the beach, he saw two people in an embrace and he could instantly recognize the asshole he was looking for. **Hud.**

Jay's rage turned red hot once again as he realized Ashley was there with him. This was fucking rich.

Jay watched them start to make their way up the stairs to the backyard. He paced around, talking himself up and down, unsure of what he would do when they reached the top.

Mick pulled his car into the driveway of his daughter's house. He handed his keys over without even looking at the valet's face.

He stood in the driveway, gazing up at the full scope of Nina's home, and fixed the knot of his tie.

Mick was surprised by the sheer size of the house. Nina's husband must have bought it. Brandon something. The tennis player. He felt his hackles go up.

"Are you . . ." Eliza Nakamura said to Mick as he walked past her, toward the front door.

Mick looked at her. She was good-looking. If it had been the right time, he might have given her his signature smolder, lifted the edges of his famous lips to give her a grin. But Mick had learned nearly twenty-five years ago that his gravitational pull was such that he had to repel anyone he did not wish to actively attract.

"Not now," he said to the young woman.

Eliza turned away from him, annoyed, and moved on. She would tell people for the rest of her life that she'd met Mick Riva once and he was a dickhead.

Mick did not care if people thought he was an asshole as long as they left him alone when he did not want them and flocked to him when he did. He ignored each and every person in the front yard who stared at him as he walked by them and headed straight over the threshold of his daughter's mansion.

There was an audible gasp from one of the cocktail waitresses when she saw him. That made the two bartenders over by the record players look up toward the door and they both did double takes.

Seeing the bartenders out of the corner of his eye, Greg Robinson, still rippin' it up, moved his eye to the door and saw a legend he once knew years before standing there. His hand slipped and the record scratched.

Then everyone in the living room looked up at the door—a house full of stars all staring at the biggest star in the room.

The gasps and whispers started and within approximately forty-five seconds of Mick placing his foot in the house, the entire party knew he was there.

The entire party except for Casey Greens, who was hiding upstairs in the master bedroom, and Kit, who was with Ricky Esposito in her sister's outdoor shower, and Jay, who was outside looking for Hud, and Hud, who was down at the beach, and Nina, who had locked herself in the pantry.

Hud spotted Jay out of the corner of his eye as he was making his way up the stairs with Ashley. The moment he saw him, his heart dropped. It was clear that Jay already knew what he'd resolved to tell him. Jay had the gait and the fury of a man recently made aware.

Hud turned back to Ashley briefly as they came up the path. He looked at her with warning and apology, and in his glance she knew what he was trying to tell her. **This is going to get worse before it gets better.**

Hud put his feet on the grass at the edge of the lawn and Ashley followed him and then stepped aside, out of the line of fire.

Jay was in Hud's face in no time. "You are a real piece of shit," Jay said. "You know that?"

"I know," Hud said. He did not ask how much Jay knew or how Jay knew. He understood those questions would only serve to make things worse.

Jay shook his head, trying to speak but finding himself dumbfounded. What on earth could he possibly say that would come close to conveying his rage?

"Ashley and I are together," Hud said. Ashley watched his face as he spoke, stunned at the forthrightness of his words, the evenness of his voice. "I fucked up in how I handled it. I lied to you and I went behind your back and I am sorry. But I love her."

Hud caught Ashley's eye for a brief second. "And she loves me."

"Are you kidding me?" Jay screamed, losing control of his voice as he continued to speak, its volume rising higher and higher with every second. "That's your defense?"

Hud stepped closer to his brother and had a moment of sharp clarity. He would see this thing through, he would face every moment of it. And he would come out the other side with a brother and a wife and a child.

"I'm an asshole," Hud said. "I admit it."

"That doesn't even begin to—"

"No, it doesn't. You're right. But I need you to understand something. I'm not going to stop seeing her," Hud said. "And I'm not going to let you stop speaking to me."

A crowd had started to form and Jay was conscious of it—of the fact that every single person who became privy to this conversation was aware of his humiliation.

"So tell me what you need from me in order to put this behind us."

"What I need from you?" Jay said. "What I need from you is to stop sleeping with my ex-girlfriend!"

"No," Hud said, shaking his head. "My answer is no."

When Jay lunged for Hud, it was not graceful. It was sloppy and scrappy and ugly. But it was effective. Before Hud even realized that his brother was aiming for him, his back was slammed down onto the lawn.

Jay swung with reckless abandon but Hud did not fight back. Hud's upper-arm strength alone could have crushed his brother's windpipe, shattered a rib. The lone joy of being the stocky one was that you were the stronger one. Jay on top of Hud—punching and elbowing and grabbing for whatever limbs he could—was like a whippet on a pit bull. But Hud would not further shame his brother.

Jay and Hud had borne witness to the full scope of each other's lives. They had lived in the same rooms, wished on the same stars, breathed the same air, been taught and reared by the same mother and teachers. Been abandoned by the same father.

They had traveled the same beaches, trespassed in the same oceans, surfed the same waves, stood on the same boards. Made love to the same woman.

But they were not the same men. They were not haunted by the same demons, they were fighting for different things.

Ashley screamed as Jay's fist made a crack against Hud's nose.

"Fuuuuuuck!" someone screamed from the crowd that had gathered. Others gasped as the blood started to trickle down.

"Oh my God," one of the women said over and over. "Someone do something!"

"Punch him again!" a man called from the back.

Some people started cheering for Jay. Others yelled at Hud to fight back. Ashley wept. And the two brothers—aching and bruised and bleeding—continued on.

Nina decided it was time to leave the pantry if only because the air was getting stale. But also because if this party wasn't going to end anytime soon, she was at least going to try to enjoy it.

"All right," she said, standing up. "Let's go join the land of the living."

"You do not have to," Tarine said.

"I want to," Nina said, holding her hand out for Tarine to lift herself up.

"I suppose I should check on Greg anyway," Tarine said.

Nina opened the pantry door to see three girls standing by the breakfast nook, looking at her strangely. "It's my pantry," she said. "I can hide in it if I want to."

She could hear a commotion out in the backyard but decided to ignore it. Instead, she walked toward the entryway and then stopped dead in place at what she saw.

Dad?

He was standing with his back to her but Nina recognized him instantly. His back was broad and sturdy and his shoulders were wide enough that, even with a jacket on, you could make out the perfect triangle they formed with his waist. His hair was grayer now, but the back of his head still looked exactly the way it had when she used to watch him watching television or running along the sand.

She felt both intense familiarity and staggering strangeness as she looked at him—this man she knew so well, this man she barely knew at all. The combination made Nina feel dizzy.

She pulled herself back behind the corner. "What the fuck is my dad doing here?" Nina asked. It was a rhetorical question, though she would have welcomed an answer.

"Your father?" Tarine said, truly shocked.

Tarine couldn't help but peek around the corner to see for herself. "Wow," she said, stunned. "Mick Riva. My God."

Nina pulled her back. "Why on earth would he be here?"

"I assure you, I have no clue," Tarine said, peeking again.

Nina searched for any reason that might explain it. "Maybe he needs a kidney or something."

Tarine looked at Nina to see if she was kidding. Nina was dead serious. "I suppose that is possible," Tarine said.

"Does he look sick?"

Tarine leaned over to get another look. Mick had turned around and Tarine could see his face. It was rugged and tan, all smiles. "No," Tarine said. "Actually, he looks quite handsome."

Nina was surprised at the pride she took in this fact. "Old?" she asked.

Tarine looked again. "He looks just like he does in the magazines."

This Nina found to be the most helpful piece of information. If her father looked like he did in the magazines, then, in some way, Nina did know her father. Even if it was barely more than most Americans.

When she could hear her father's voice booming around the corner, Nina decided that she did not want to see him or talk to him or find out what he wanted. At least not at the moment.

"OK," Nina said. "I don't have to deal with this right now if I don't want to."

"Yes, that is exactly right," Tarine said.

Nina spotted a plate of cheese on the kitchen counter. "I'm going to eat this," she said. She threw a hunk of cheddar into her mouth. **Hello, old friend.** Then she set her sights on the Brie.

Nina breathed in deep and then picked up the entire tray of cheese, ready to carry it with her. She set out to alert her siblings that their father was there, like she was a surfer girl Paul Revere. **Mick is coming.**

She did not immediately spot her brothers or her sister. And so, her first stop would be upstairs, to talk to the only person at this party who had actually been looking for Mick Riva.

2:00 a.m.

Vaughn Donovan walked in the front door already quite drunk. He was accompanied by an entourage that included his agent, his business manager, and four of his friends. As had become common for him, the women in the room all took note within a few minutes of his entrance. He threw an upward nod to say hi to a few of them, and then flashed his million-dollar smile. It felt good to be a movie star.

Back in high school in Dayton, Ohio, Robert Vaughn Donovan III did not make the football or the baseball team. But the moment he stepped into the school auditorium, he had found a home. With his quick wit and charmingly exasperated delivery of almost every line, he had the drama kids in stitches.

His dad's college roommate was a Hollywood agent

and by the time he was twenty, Robby had booked his second audition, started going by Vaughn, and swiftly made a career of starring in movies as the cute and nonthreatening boy next door who finally gets the girl.

Vaughn was now twenty-five years old and a bona fide star. But, while he would never admit it to anyone, he still sometimes felt like he needed to sleep with as many beautiful women as possible, go to as many Hollywood parties as possible, make as many movies as possible, as if someone was going to hit a buzzer and send him back to Dayton at any moment.

Vaughn rolled up the sleeves of his blazer and stepped farther into the foyer just as Nina rounded the corner and started up the stairs.

"Whoa," he said as he saw her. "The actual Nina Riva is here in front of me this very second. Everyone's dream girl."

"Vaughn," Nina said, holding the cheese plate with one hand and putting the other out to shake. "Hi."

He was even more handsome up close. His boyish blue eyes were bright and clear. His shaggy brown hair was perfectly contained under his porkpie hat. His jawline was sharp but his skin was soft and pristine. Most people, Nina knew, lost some of their luster when you met them in the flesh. But Vaughn Donovan was gorgeous.

Vaughn took her hand and shook it. "I'm a big fan of yours," he said. "Big fan."

"Why, thank you," Nina said, nodding. "I loved your last movie. **Wild Night.** It was great."

"Thanks," Vaughn said, smiling. "We're thinking about doing a sequel. Maybe you can be in it."

"Oh, that's so nice of you," Nina said. "Um, listen, I have to run real quick but I'll be back down soon and we should talk."

Vaughn nodded. And then as Nina turned away, he grabbed her arm. He took his other hand and brushed the edge of her shirt, just at the top of her rib cage. "This one isn't as **soft to the touch** as I was hoping," he said with a smile, then he winked at her.

Nina stared at him. She cycled through two breaths. "All right, Vaughn. I'll be seeing ya," she said and walked, briskly, up the stairs.

Just then, Vaughn's business manager came out from the kitchen with four beers. He punched a hole in the bottom of one of the cans with a pen and put it to Vaughn's mouth.

Vaughn cheerily popped the tab and shotgunned it. When he was done, he threw the can on the floor and shook his head. "Woooot!" he said. "Let's get fucked up!"

A blond waitress walked by with coke and Vaughn smiled at her and took a line. She batted her eyes at him.

Bridger Miller came around the corner. "Whoa, man!" Bridger said, giving Vaughn a high five. They had not ever met before but fame is a secret club; everyone knows **of** one another.

"Bridger! Big fan, man!" Vaughn said. "I saw you in **Race Against Time.** The scene where you scale that building was unreal."

"Thanks, thanks," Bridger said, nodding. "I didn't see your new one yet but my agent said it's funny as hell."

Vaughn smiled, pleased. "One day, maybe I'll do the action thing."

Bridger laughed. "Better than me trying to do comedy, I'll tell you that."

One of Vaughn's friends, who happened to be standing by the china cabinet, said, "Hey, Vaughn! Weren't you saying earlier that you wanted to play Frisbee?"

Before Vaughn could respond, his buddy took a plate out of the cabinet and flung it across the room to the opposite wall. It smashed into chunks and shards before its pieces even hit the floor.

Everyone turned to look at the cause of the commotion. But when Bridger chuckled, so did everyone else.

"Fuckin' A, man," Vaughn said, laughing. He strode over to the cabinet, picked a plate up himself, and threw it at the wall.

Bridger grabbed two more and flung them in quick succession. The two high-fived.

"All right!" Vaughn said.

Bridger grabbed another plate. "Everybody, let's do this!"

Nina walked into her bedroom and locked the door behind her.

"Cheese?" she said to Casey, offering her the tray.

"I'm good," Casey said. She felt sort of embarrassed to still be up there, in Nina's bedroom. "Sorry, I didn't know where else to go," Casey added, by way of explanation.

"Don't worry about it," Nina said. "But, listen, Mick is downstairs."

Casey looked shocked. If Nina had wondered whether Mick being here had anything to do with Casey, the expression on Casey's face cleared it up.

"What do you mean Mick's here? Like right now?" Casey said.

"Yeah," Nina said as she walked into her closet. She kept the door open so she could continue to talk. There, she took off her gauzy shirt and her tight skirt and her oxygen-depriving tights and her torturous high heels. She stood in a bra and thong and then took both of those off, too. She grabbed a pair of white cotton underwear and pulled them up her legs and then put on a jock bra. She put on a pair of heather gray sweatpants, elastic at both the waist and the ankles. And a faded neon blue T-shirt that said O'NEILL across the chest.

Men were bullshit—**people** were bullshit—and Nina was not going to live through bullshit while wearing high heels a single second longer.

"I don't know why he's here," Nina said. "But he's here."

Casey felt a rush of anxiety. She wasn't even sure she wanted to meet Mick Riva yet, let alone figure out what to say to him.

Nina threw herself onto her bed and lay on her back, staring at the ceiling. "I suppose you could go downstairs right now and ask him if he's your dad," Nina said. But even as she said it, she felt a twinge. It bothered Nina, the idea that Casey might manage to have more of a direct relationship with Mick than she did, that Casey might be unafraid to do the very thing Nina was avoiding. Saying hello.

Nina watched as Casey sat down on the bed next to her. "What is he like?" Casey asked.

Nina continued to stare up at the ceiling and answered as best she could. "I think he's an asshole. But I can't be sure. I don't actually know him well enough to say."

Casey watched as Nina continued to stare at the ceiling and breathe deeply, her chest rising high and falling.

"He sounds like a real winner," Casey said as she lay down on her back next to Nina, staring up at the ceiling, too.

Nina turned to Casey. "Listen, I'm not sure . . . I

mean, if you're looking for family, there might be better ones to pick."

Casey turned to Nina and smiled gently. "That's not exactly how family works, is it?"

"No," Nina said, shaking her head. "No, I guess it's not."

Mick reached the sliding glass door to the lawn and looked out at the crowd. He could tell someone was beating the shit out of someone else. But it wasn't until he made his way to the edge of the circle that had formed around them that he suspected it might be his sons.

As he looked at the two men grappling on the ground, he had to admit an ugly truth to himself: It was not so easy, to recognize your own children after twenty years away.

He knew Jay from the magazines, much the same way he knew Nina. He wasn't one hundred percent sure that the one on the ground was Hud. But, Mick reasoned, you probably don't go to these lengths to beat the shit out of someone unless they are close enough to have really gotten under your skin. So he made an educated guess.

As for his youngest . . . He would not have recognized her if she were standing right next to him.

Which she was.

Kit had left Ricky behind when she heard her brothers yelling and made her way to the front of the crowd. She was stunned to see that not only was Jay pummeling Hud . . . but that her father was standing there watching him do it.

She stood, frozen, next to him. Her eyes were wide, her fingers were stiff as her pinkie grazed the arm of his jacket. She could not believe she was in the presence of this larger-than-life figure who had hovered over her her entire life, and yet had been so long out of reach. There he was. She could extend her pinkie just . . . one half a centimeter . . . farther . . . and . . . touch him.

And then in an instant, he was gone, lunging forward and pulling his older son off his younger one. It wasn't difficult for Mick to get hold of Jay—Jay's body was all limbs, easy to grab and throw down onto his back.

Hud put his hands to his nose as Ashley ran toward him. He looked up to see who had stopped the fight.

Jay got ahold of himself and looked up to see who had pulled him off.

"Dad?" the two of them said at the same time, with the same inflection.

Kit found this sort of preposterous. **Dad?**

Some of the crowd began to disperse now that the fight was over. But a lot of people stuck around, shamelessly gawking at Mick Riva, in the flesh.

"Will you sign this napkin?" Kyle Manheim asked, the second he could get close enough. He handed Mick a pen he'd scrounged up from some girl's purse.

Mick rolled his eyes and scribbled across the cocktail napkin and handed it back. A line had started to form. Mick shook his head. "No, no, that's it, no more autographs." Everyone groaned, acting as if they had been denied a basic human right, but still, they began to wander off.

"All right, get up, you two," Mick said, offering an arm to each of his sons. This, too, mystified Kit as she watched, that he could offer a boost now, having offered so little for so long.

Hud and Jay each took the arm he offered and pulled themselves onto their feet.

Hud took a quick catalog of his injuries: He was pretty sure his nose was broken and could feel he had a black eye, a nicked eyebrow, and a sliced lip. His ribs were bruised, his legs were sore, his abdomen tender. When he tried to breathe deeply, he almost collapsed.

Jay had a gash on his chin, a bruised tailbone, and a shattered ego.

Ashley moved closer to Hud, as if to try to take care of him. But as she took a step in his direction, she saw him flinch. And she understood that her presence, at least right now, could only make things worse.

She turned from him and Hud breathed her name. But she kept walking, pushing through the onlookers.

She wanted a place to cry alone. As she made her way into the kitchen, she considered going out to her car. But it would take forever for the valets to extract it from the maze of vehicles they had parked on the front lawn. Instead, she cut in line to the bathroom, sat down on the toilet lid, and bawled her eyes out.

• • •

"What are you doing here?" Jay asked his father. His chin stung as the air hit the fresh cut and he wondered just how bad Hud was feeling.

"I got an invitation," Mick said.

"There are no invitations," Hud said. "And even if there were . . ." He didn't finish the sentence. He couldn't. He didn't know the man in front of him well enough to insult him to his face.

"Well, I got one," Mick said. "But who cares about that? Why are you two beating the life out of each other?"

"It's not . . ." **It's not any of your business.** "It's a . . ." Jay found himself at a staggering loss for words. He looked over at his brother.

Hud looked back at him—bloodied and purple and hunched over, trying hard not to breathe too deeply—but clearly just as confused. And in Hud's confusion, Jay found solace. He was not crazy. This was, in fact, beyond comprehension.

"You can't just walk in here and start asking questions like that," Kit said. Mick, Jay, and Hud all turned at the sound of her voice. Her stance was wide, her shoulders were squared, her face showed neither awe nor shock.

"Who are you?" Mick said, but then the moment it came out of his mouth he knew the answer. "I mean, I—"

"I'm your daughter," Kit said with a tone of amusement. It did not surprise her, his not knowing. But she found herself desperate to hide how much it still stung.

"I know that, Katherine," he said. "I'm sorry. You grew up even more beautiful than I envisioned." He smiled at her in a way that she assumed was supposed to convey some sort of charming embarrassment. And in that smile, Kit saw the magnetism her father wielded. Even when he failed, he won, didn't he?

"We call her Kit," Jay said.

"Her name is Kit," Hud added.

"Kit," Mick said, directing his attention back to her and putting his hand on her shoulder. "It suits you."

Kit moved away from her father's hand and laughed. "You have no idea what suits me."

"I was the first person to hold you the day you were born," Mick said to her gently. "I know you like I know my own soul."

Kit found his intensity—his presumed connection with her—unsettling. "I'm the one who has invited you to this party for the past four years," she said.

Hud looked at Jay and said, under his breath, "Did you know that?" Jay shook his head.

"Why are you only here now?" Kit asked.

Kit had looked forward to writing that invitation every year. She felt powerful doing it, as if she was both brazen and valiant. She was daring him to show up. Daring him to show his face around here. She felt vindicated every time he didn't.

Every year he ignored that invitation, it renewed

her indignation. It was one more good reason to dislike the motherfucker. It was one more reason not to bother worrying if he was OK or if he missed them. It was one more reason she wouldn't have to show up at his funeral. And it felt good.

But him here, now. **This wasn't how it was all supposed to go.**

"I want to see if we can . . . be a part of one another's lives," he said. "I've missed you all so much." He looked directly at Kit as he spoke, and his eyes misted, and his mouth turned down. For a split second, Kit's chest ached, imagining a world of pain that her father might have lived in without them. **Did it hurt him? To be away? Did he think of them? Did he feel their absence every day? Had he picked up the phone a hundred times but never dialed?**

But then Kit remembered that her father had taken a stab at acting back in the late sixties. He'd been nominated for a Golden Globe—that's how good he was.

"No," Kit said shaking her head. "Listen, I'm sorry," she said, sincerely. "I know that I invited you. It was my mistake. I think that you should go."

Mick frowned but remained undeterred. "How about this?" he said. "Let's all go someplace quiet and talk."

He could see that Kit was about to reject this plan and he put his hands up in surrender. "And then I'll go. But despite everything we've been through, you are my children. So, please, let's just talk for a moment. Maybe down by the beach, away from the party. That's all I'm asking. You all have a few minutes for your old man, don't you?"

Kit looked to Jay, Jay looked to Hud, Hud looked at Kit.

And then the three of them took the stairs down to the beach with their father.

Casey was telling Nina the story of the time she got stuck on a Ferris wheel with her first boyfriend when Nina heard people in the hallway saying Mick Riva had broken up a fight in the backyard.

"Did you hear that?" Nina said to Casey.

"Hear what?" Casey asked.

"It sounded like someone said Dad broke up a fight outside."

Nina got up and walked to the window and Casey followed.

Casey had never experienced that: the use of "Dad" as opposed to "my dad." There had been only herself growing up, no one to compare notes with, share parents with. And then here Nina was, sharing the word with her.

Nina stood at the window and looked down at her yard.

The pool was half-empty—all of the people who'd been splashing in it had transferred much of the water onto her yard. There were plastic cups all over the place. Huge areas of her lawn were covered in broken porcelain. Blue and white chargers and dinner plates and teacups and saucers were all in pieces around her palm trees. Nina thought it was sort of fitting that her wedding china had been destroyed.

"I never liked that china," she told Casey. "Brandon's mother insisted that I had to pick out something floral but I think having fine china is sort of silly. And anyway, I wanted the bird pattern."

"Why didn't you get the birds, then?" Casey asked.

Nina looked at her and frowned. "I . . ." she began to say, but then changed the subject. "Do you smoke?" she said, pulling out a pack of cigarettes from her nightstand drawer. She offered one to Casey.

"Oh, no but, uh . . . OK," Casey said. She took the unlit cigarette from Nina's hand and put it to her mouth.

Nina lit it and then lit her own.

Casey took a drag and coughed. "You were saying . . ." she said once she caught her breath. "About the birds. Why didn't you get them?"

Nina looked at Casey and then out the window, considering the question. The crowd was starting to shift, and as it did, Nina saw something startling. Her brothers, her sister, and her father, all together, walking down the stairs to the beach.

"Because I'm a doormat," Nina said. "I'm a human doormat." She put her cigarette out. "Fuck it. You stay here. I'm gonna go talk to Mick Riva."

3:00 a.m.

Ted Travis was hell-bent on self-destruction.

He was the biggest, highest-paid star on network TV but none of that had mattered to him since his wife died last year. He felt like he was falling apart inside—sobbing alone in his huge house, hiring hookers, shoplifting, upgrading from the occasional coke binge to a full-blown speed addiction—but all of the chaos of his soul wasn't showing on the outside.

When he looked in the mirror, he could see he was just getting handsomer and handsomer. Turns out, he looked even better with gray hair than he had with brown. Sometimes, when he looked at his own reflection, he could hear the ghost of Willa's voice in his head, laughing, telling him he had no right to age so well without her. Drinking quieted it.

At Nina's party, Ted had already downed half a bottle of whiskey, lost four grand on a bet to that girl from **Flashdance,** and then fallen asleep fully clothed in the shallow end of the pool. Someone had cannonballed into the water and woken him up. He climbed out.

But then: her.

A forty-three-year-old script supervisor named Victoria Brooks.

He came across her in the living room when his clothes had just stopped dripping. She was tall and lean and didn't have a single curve on her body. She had bleached blond hair and dark eyebrows and a face that was positively breathtaking in profile.

"Ted," he said, putting out his hand as he walked up to her.

Vickie rolled her eyes. "Yeah, I know who you are."

"And you are?"

"Vickie."

"Beautiful name. Let me get you a drink," Ted said as he gave her his TV smile.

Vickie blew her cigarette away from both of them, her left hand pinning a highball of vodka and soda against her right arm. "I have one, thanks."

"What do I have to do to get a smile out of you?" he asked her.

Vickie rolled her eyes again. "Sober up, maybe. You've embarrassed yourself about ten times already tonight."

Ted laughed. "You're right about that. I keep trying

to find a way to enjoy myself. But it's pointless. I'm too goddamn sad all the time."

Vickie finally looked Ted in the eye.

She was sad, too. God, she was sad. Her husband had died in a boating accident seven years ago and she had resigned herself to loneliness since then. She was not willing to love again, if this was how it felt.

"One drink," Vickie said, surprising herself.

Ted smiled. He got her a fresh vodka soda, straightened his damp clothes, and went back to her.

"I want to take you out," he said. "So what should I do to convince you? Are you a grand gesture sort of lady?"

Vickie sighed. "I guess so? But I'm not going on a date with you."

Ted smiled exactly the way he did on **Cool Nights.** He was just going through the motions but he was good at pretending. That's why they paid him so much money to do it.

"C'mon, I might just charm you. Watch this." He started looking around for the easiest way to make a scene. He settled on swinging from the chandelier.

Ted handed Vickie his drink and started climbing onto the mantel. He pointed at a surfer by the coffee table. "Hey, man, pass me the chandelier, would you?"

The guy, content to play along, stood on top of the coffee table and grabbed the base of the chandelier, slowly moving it toward Ted. Ted grabbed a handful of the crystals on the bottom.

"Vickie, let me take you to dinner!" he said. And

then he swung himself across the room, hanging on for dear life. He hit the opposite wall and then let go, crashing onto the sofa with the howl of an injured animal.

Vickie found herself running to him.

"Are you OK?" she said. "Come on, get up." She put her arms around Ted to help him.

The warmth of her hands made him feel, for one half second, no longer alone. Instead of standing up with her, he pulled her down to him. "Can I kiss you?" he said and when she smiled, he did it. She felt his soft lips on hers and she did not balk. A thrill ran through her like a bolt.

She pulled back, speechless. And then, drunk and confused and momentarily desperate for the very thing she thought she'd never want again, she kissed him once more. It may have looked absurd from the outside, but it felt sort of magical to the two of them. The surprise of sincere desire.

The people around them cheered as another idiot decided to try to swing from the chandelier.

But Ted was already planning his next escapade. "Have you ever stolen something, Vickie?" he asked, as his eyebrows went up and a smile crept over his face.

Ashley wiped her eyes, pulled herself together, and walked out of the bathroom. She stepped over broken glass and crushed pita, hummus smeared across the tiles of the floor. She went out to the front stoop and gave her ticket to the valet.

For some reason, she felt strongly that the baby was a boy. And she liked the name Benjamin. If it did turn out to be a girl, maybe something like Lauren.

The rest of it . . . who knew? Jay would forgive Hud or he wouldn't. Hud would come back to her, or he wouldn't. They would be a family or they wouldn't. This would all work out or it wouldn't. But there would be a Benjamin or a Lauren. She and her Benjamin or her Lauren . . . they'd be OK.

The valet brought Ashley her car and she got in and drove away.

As she pulled out onto PCH, "Hungry Heart" started playing through her speakers and Ashley felt just the tiniest bit of hope. Your whole world can be falling apart, she thought, but then Springsteen will start playing on the radio.

• • •

Ricky Esposito was back hanging out near the food, eating plain crackers since the cheese plate was gone. He was trying to decide if he should just leave. He'd struck out with the girl of his dreams and he wasn't yet in the mood to set his sights on another.

Vanessa de la Cruz walked into the kitchen.

"Oh, I'm starved," she said, grabbing a cracker. "Who took all the cheese?" Her hair was a mess, her eye makeup was smudged. Ricky had seen her around with Kit before. There was something so quirky about her.

"Fun night?" Ricky asked.

Vanessa nodded. "Greatest night of my fucking life," she said.

Ricky laughed.

"I'm serious," Vanessa said, eating a cracker. "I spent so much time thinking I was in love with one guy. One guy! And I just decided to get over it and it was like the whole world opened up. I made out with five dudes tonight. Five. They will tell legends about me one day."

Ricky laughed again.

"None were a love match, unfortunately," she said. "But, you know, I have to be patient. Rome wasn't built in a day."

Ricky laughed once more—she was funny. "No, I guess not."

Vanessa looked at him, actually looked at him, for the first time since they'd started talking. "You're the one! Kit's guy!" Vanessa said suddenly. "Did she kiss you?"

Ricky nodded. "But I don't think she saw fireworks."

Vanessa bent her head to the side, surprised and disappointed. "Really? She seemed into you."

Ricky smiled and shook his head. "She's definitely not into me."

Vanessa considered him. "She should be. You're cute."

"Oh, well, thank you," Ricky said, unconvinced.

"No, I'm serious. I didn't see it before, because you dress like a middle schooler."

"Thank you?"

"I just mean, you know, you could dress cooler."

Ricky looked at his T-shirt and khakis. "I guess so."

"You're sure Kit's not into you?"

"I'm positive. She said all we will ever be is friends."

Vanessa cocked her head to the side again. "I'm sorry. Those Rivas will break your heart."

Ricky took a sip of the beer he'd been nursing. "I'll be all right."

Vanessa nodded. "I can tell you from experience that you definitely will."

"Good God, Nina actually lives on the edge of a cliff," Mick said, as he moved down the stairs.

"Yeah," Jay said. "It's a pretty great location. Sick waves."

"Sick waves?" Mick asked. "Oh, right. Yeah. I bet."

Mick didn't surf. He didn't get the appeal. It seemed like an odd way to spend your life, riding a piece of wood in the ocean. It certainly didn't seem like a thing to bank your fortune on the way it seemed his children had. Had none of them considered that talent like Mick's might be hereditary? Surely one of them must have a voice. He would have been happy to help them break into the industry.

In one phone call, he could set them up with a career most people would kill for, could set them up for life. He could give his children things that most people only dream of.

He had not been perfect as a father, that much was obvious. But if the goal for any generation is to do better than the one before them, then Mick had succeeded. He had given his children more than he had ever been given. He reminded himself of this as his feet hit the sand. He was not so bad.

He moved out of the way, letting Kit and Hud and Jay all join him on the shoreline. He kicked off his shoes, pulled off his socks, cuffed his pants. It had been a long time since he had been on the beach at night. Being on the beach at night was for young romantics and troublemakers.

Mick felt perfectly fine no longer being young. He liked the gravitas of age, liked the respect it afforded him. And if getting on in years was supposed to make you afraid of dying, he wasn't doing it right. The prospect of death didn't bother him at all. He had no plans to bribe the Grim Reaper.

In fact, in some perverse sort of way, Mick was quite looking forward to the aftermath of his passing. He knew the nation would mourn him. He would be called a legend. Decades later people would still know his name. He had achieved that rare level of fame that allows a person to transcend mortality.

What Mick was afraid of was becoming irrelevant. He found himself paralyzed by the thought that the world might pass him by while he was still in it.

"All right, Mick, we're here. What do you want to say?" Kit said. She glanced at her brothers, who would not look at each other. Kit wanted to know why Jay had beaten the shit out of Hud, but at the moment, there were more important things.

"You can call me Dad, you know," Mick said to her.

"I can't, actually, but let's move on," Kit said.

Hud, in grave pain and wishing he had access to Percocet and maybe a couple of stitches, found himself unsure what to say—or whether he was even physically capable of saying it. And so, he kept quiet.

"I know we haven't been close," Mick started. "But I'd like for us all to get to know each other a little bit."

Kit rolled her eyes, but Jay was listening. He sat down on the cold sand of the beach and crossed his legs. Mick put his hands down on the sand and sat, too. Hud didn't think he could sit without his ribs causing agonizing pain. Kit just refused.

"Go ahead," Jay said.

"Shouldn't someone find Nina?" Hud asked.

Mick guessed that Nina would be the hardest to win over. He figured it would be easier to divide and conquer, so he plunged ahead. "Listen to me, kids," he said. "I know I wasn't as available as I should have been but—"

"You weren't **available** at all," Kit reminded him.

Mick nodded. "You are right. I wasn't there for you during things that no child should have to live through." This was the first time Mick had acknowledged the loss of their mother, and both Hud and Kit found it hard to look him directly in the eye as he said it. The two of them still held pockets of grief in their bodies that bubbled up at inopportune moments. Kit, particularly, grieved the way some people drink, which is to say: rarely but always alone and to excess. So she could not keep Mick's gaze at that very moment because she did not want to cry.

But Hud found the easiest way through pain is, in fact, through it. And he let the tears fall when they came. When he thought of his mother and the despair he'd felt in those months after she was gone, those months where they waited for their father to attempt any kind of rescue . . . Hud could do nothing but **feel** it. And so he turned away for the exact opposite reason his sister did. He turned away so no one would see him tear up. And then he wiped his eyes and turned back.

Jay wasn't looking away at all. He was listening, intently, hoping his father had something to say that might make anything better. Anything at all.

"I've made mistakes," Mick said. "And I can . . . I can try to explain them, and I can tell you my own problems, about the screwed-up way I was raised. But none of that matters. What matters is that I'm here now. I'd like to be a proper family. I want to make things right."

Mick had envisioned the possibility that upon his saying this, one of them might run into his arms and hug him tight. He had an image in his head that this would be the beginning of Sunday dinners together when he was in town, or maybe celebrating Christmas at his place in Holmby Hills.

But none of his children appeared to have budged very much yet. And so he pushed forward. "I'd like us to start over. I want to try again."

Hud was struck by Mick's word choice. **Try.**

"Can I ask a serious question?" Kit asked. "I'm

not trying to cause trouble. I just genuinely don't understand something."

"OK," Mick said. He had stood up and was now resting against the rocks of the cliff.

"Are you in AA? Is this part of your twelve steps or something?" she asked. She could not quite imagine what had prompted all of this. But it might make sense to her if it was in service of something else. If he was here to make himself feel better, to tie up loose ends or something. That she could understand. "I mean, why now? You know? Why not yesterday or last year or six months ago or how about when our mother fucking died?"

"Kit," Hud said. "Don't talk like that."

"But our mother did die," Kit said. "And he left us to fend for ourselves."

"Kit!" Jay said. "You asked him a question—let him answer it."

Mick shook his head. "No," he said. "I'm not in any kind of program that requires me to make amends."

"Then what are you after?" Kit asked.

"I'm not after anything," Mick said, defensively. "Why is that so hard to believe? Why don't my own children understand that I just want us to be a part of each other's lives?"

Jay spoke up. "That's not what we're saying, Da—"

Hud cut him off. "Kit's just asking what's changed. Actually I want to know, too. So I guess **we're** asking," he said, his voice becoming softer and yet more focused, **"what's changed?"**

Before Mick could answer, Nina's feet hit the sand.

She hadn't heard Mick's apology or his appeals. But she could guess what they entailed. She'd overheard the same things as a child. His talk of having lost his way and owning up to his mistakes and asking for another chance. She didn't need to see the live show—she'd seen in it previews.

"I'll tell you what's changed for him. Nothing," Nina said.

They all turned toward her. None of them were surprised to see her. They all had more or less hoped she'd find them here. But they were a little taken aback by her sweatpants and her general demeanor. What Nina was this?

"Nothing has changed, right, Dad?" Nina said, looking right at him.

"Hi, Nina-baby," Mick said, walking to her.

This was his first time seeing her up close as an adult. And he was overcome by the affection he felt for her face.

He saw himself in it—in the lips and the cheekbones and the tanned skin. But he saw June in it, too. He could see her in Nina's eyes and her brows and nose.

He missed June. He missed her so much. He missed her roast chicken and the way she had always smiled when he walked in the door. He missed the smell of her. The way she loved to love the people around her. Her death had shocked him. He'd always imagined that he could one day come home to her.

If she was still alive, he'd be with her right now. He'd have come to her tonight, maybe even sooner.

To look at Nina, as Mick did now, was to have proof that June had lived.

He moved closer to Nina, ready to hug her. But she put her hands up, stopping him. "You're fine where you are," she said.

"Nina," Mick said, aggrieved.

Nina ignored him. "Guys, if you want to know why he's here, it's really simple," she said to her siblings. Then she redirected her attention to her father. "You're here because you want to be, right?" she asked him. "Because you woke up this morning and you got a wild hair up your ass to try to be a decent guy."

Mick flinched. "That is absolutely not—"

"Hold up," she said. "I'm not done." She continued, her voice strong and rising. "It's awfully convenient that you're suddenly interested in us once we're all adults, once we no longer need anything from you."

"I told you that's not—"

"I said I wasn't done."

"Nina, I am your—"

"You are fucking nothing."

Kit's mouth dropped and Jay's and Hud's eyes went wide. The three of them watched their father's face as he moved through stages of shock. The air carried only the sounds of the crashing waves in front of them and the light cacophony of the party above.

Nina spoke again. "You are a big somebody to the

world, Dad. We all know that. We live with it every goddamn day. But let's be clear about one thing, you are not anybody's father."

Kit looked at Nina, trying to catch her eye. But Nina would not break her gaze. She stared only at Mick.

It would not be her that bent and broke anymore.

Casey left the bedroom and started walking down the stairs. She was restless and didn't know what to do with herself.

She walked past a couple making out so aggressively that she couldn't be sure they weren't having sex. But she was almost positive both of them were anchors on the nightly news and she resolved to never watch Channel 4 again.

When she got to the living room, she saw a group of people swinging from the chandelier like they were swashbucklers. Just as two people grabbed on and let it fly, the entire thing came off the ceiling, plaster and crystal covering the floor and the table and the heads of everyone underneath it.

There was a hole where the chandelier had been, exposing the inner frame of the house.

Casey reversed course. As she started to move through the dining room on her way to the kitchen, she noticed a vase had been shattered and two paintings had fallen off the wall.

When she finally made her way into the kitchen, she saw the floor was covered in tiny shards of chips and crackers that had been crushed under dancing feet. Empty wine bottles were rolling around on the

ground. Two grown men sat on the island counter-
top, washing their feet in the sink.

"My editor says he thinks my manuscript could be
the defining novel of the MTV Generation," one of
them said.

As the two of them hopped off the counter and
left the room, Casey got to work. She stood next to
the stove, stacking empty trays, using a sponge to
wipe up crumbs. Her mother had always tidied the
house when she felt out of sorts. She remembered
that her father had known to ask her mother what
was wrong when he found her cleaning the drum of
the washing machine.

The world may have taken her parents but—as
cruel as it was—at least it had left her the memory of
them. It did not rob her of the ability to remember
Memorial Day 1980 at Dodger Stadium, when her
father spilled mustard on his shirt and then laughed
and squirted some on hers so he wouldn't be the only
one. It had not stolen the scent of Wind Song that
her mother used to wear or how their home always
smelled like Pine-Sol. It could not take away her father's many pairs of reading glasses, left all over the
house, collecting, disappearing, and reproducing.

Casey knew that, in a few years, the memories
would begin to fade. She might forget whether her
father had spilled mustard or ketchup. She might lose
the ability to recall the exact smell of Wind Song. She
might even forget about the reading glasses altogether
after a while, as much as it pained her to admit it.

She knew that she could not sustain her life fueled only by the memories of those she once loved. Loss would not propel her forward. She had to go out and live. She had to find new people.

She tried to imagine her parents doing what she was doing right now, crashing a famous party in Malibu. She could not even picture it. But she understood that while the circumstances were almost unrecognizable, she did still have the instincts they'd given her. After all, when they could not have a child, they went out in search of one. They had taught her that family is found, that whether it be blood or circumstance or choice, what binds us does not matter. All that matters is that we are bound.

And that was why Casey was there. In search of family, just as her parents once had been.

Casey slowly put down the sponge, turned from the counter, and walked outside.

She was going to walk down those terrifying steps. The ones that appeared to lead to the very edge of the earth.

Brandon Randall woke up and realized he had passed out on the guest bedroom floor. He looked at his watch. It was half past three in the morning. He stood up, a little dizzy, and remembered he had to win back the love of his life.

He put his shoes back on. He fixed his hair. And then he walked downstairs and out the front door to where all of the vehicles were parked.

"I need my car," he said to the valet.

"Sir," the valet said. "You don't seem like you should be driving."

"Just get me my car," Brandon said. "The silver Mercedes, up there at the front."

Brandon had been the first one to arrive and so his car was packed in, quite firmly, behind at least a hundred others.

"It's going to take a while," the valet warned.

The key stand was left unmanned as the valet began the job of getting Brandon's car out. The other valets were busy with other people. Brandon stood alone, lost in his own impaired thoughts, and started to forget why he was waiting there.

What had he been hanging around for? **Oh, right. A car.**

Fuck it. Brandon helped himself to a set of keys

he saw with a Jaguar key chain and then used them to unlock the black Jag right in front of him.

And without delay, Brandon Randall drove off in Mick Riva's car to go profess his love to Carrie Soto.

• • •

Tarine was sitting on Greg's lap and nuzzling his neck while he continued to kick out the jams. But as she turned her head away, she saw the unmistakable sight of Vaughn Donovan taking the Lichtenstein off the wall and then . . . peeing on it.

She started to wonder if maybe this party was getting out of control.

Mick was taken aback by his daughter's anger but he was not deterred.

"You're right," he said, looking at his firstborn. "I have not been a father to you all. I have not been here when I should have been."

Nina looked away, toward the water. Mick turned to the rest of his kids and switched tactics. "How about this? I won't ask for your forgiveness or ask you to make any promises. I'm just asking to get to know you all, a little bit."

They all turned to one another and then to Nina. **Did they owe him that much?** Nina wasn't sure. Maybe you owe your parents nothing, maybe you owe them everything. But she was overwhelmed by her certainty that if her mother were in her place, she would give him a chance.

"OK, fine," Nina said. And then she turned to her shed, opened the lock, pulled out an array of towels, and threw down a couple of surfboards. They hit the ground with a muffled thud.

Nina sat down on a surfboard, her feet on the sand, her elbows perched over her knees. Everyone else followed suit.

The five of them sat like that, on Nina's longboards,

and let the fresh air surrounding them grow stale with their silence.

"Quite a beating you took there, son," Mick said finally, unsure where to start. He figured he'd address the elephant in the room.

Hud nodded, felt his lip. The blood was dry; flecks crumpled off. "Yeah," he said, not looking directly at his attacker. "I guess."

"What happened here?" Mick said.

"It's not really anyone's business, is it?" Jay said.

"I don't know," Kit said. "I'm pretty interested."

Mick looked to Kit and saw, for the first time, what his daughter looked like when she smiled. She looked just like him—that crinkle in her eye was so familiar. And yet, what an enigma she was. The youngest, the newest, the one he did not know. She was so boyish, in a way that Mick wasn't sure was a good thing. But she looked like trouble, and that drew Mick in.

What has she inherited from me? he wondered. He suspected it was boldness, a sense of entitlement to say whatever she wanted. How had he given it to her so passively? And yet, there it was.

He hadn't even needed to be there in order to help form his children.

"This does seem like something we should talk about," Nina said, gesturing to Hud's eyes and the way he was cradling his ribs. "Are you OK? Do you need a doctor?"

"I'm not sure," Hud said. "I mean, no. Not yet at

least." He was trying not to cause any alarm. He knew that right now what he needed to do was play it cool. He was worried about Ashley, about where she was, about how she was feeling. He needed to take care of her, and he would, but for now, he knew she would be OK. She was the kind of woman who was always going to be OK. It was half of why he loved her.

"Seriously though," Kit pushed. "What happened?"

Hud looked to Jay.

"He's sleeping with Ashley," Jay said, his voice flat.

Kit gasped.

"Who is Ashley?" Mick said.

"Jay's ex-girlfriend," Kit offered up. "Who dumped him."

"She didn't dump me, all right?"

"Look, I handled it all wrong," Hud admitted.

"There was no right way to handle it," Jay said as he turned to him. "You just shouldn't have done it."

"Seems like a fair point," Mick said. "Women shouldn't come between brothers."

Hud rolled his eyes at his father passing judgment on anything. But it was Jay who spoke up, seething with rage. "Shut up, Dad. You have absolutely no idea what you're talking about."

"I was agreeing with y—"

"I don't care! Hud can fuck all my ex-girlfriends ten times in front of me and I'd still like him more than I like you."

Mick felt a pinch in his chest.

"Hud and Ashley, huh?" Kit said. Sometimes, she

just couldn't stop herself from poking at things to see if they twitched. "I don't quite see it. She seems a little . . . I don't know . . . boring."

"Would you quit it, Kit?" Hud snapped. "You have no idea what you're talking about. She's not boring, she's shy. She's sweet and thoughtful and funny. So shut up." Hud wasn't going to bring up the fact that she was also the mother of his child. He needed to wait until that would be received as a good thing. He needed that news to make people happy, not furious. "I love her. I am in love with her."

Jay turned to his brother, finally listening to what Hud had been trying to tell him all night. **He loved her?** Jay had never loved Ashley. Not even close. "How long have you two been"—Jay wasn't quite sure of the word he wanted to use—"going around behind my back?"

Hud looked at the sand, stared at how his toes got lost beneath it. "A long time," he said.

Mick watched his sons. He himself had punched little shits that so much as looked at one of his dates. He'd also screwed almost all of his friends' wives.

"The two of them seem pretty serious," Nina chimed in. "Doesn't seem like something Hud just did on a whim."

"You knew?" Jay said, his blood starting to boil again.

Nina shook her head. "No, but I saw them in the yard a few hours ago."

"You should have told me," Jay said.

"Jay, it's not her fault," Hud said.

"Shut up, Hud," Jay added.

"Seriously? You're arguing over Ashley?" Kit asked.

"Shut up, Kit," both Hud and Jay said.

"Sorry," Kit said. "I'm just saying that of all things for the two of you to get in a fight over, I'm surprised it's some girl."

"She's not just some girl," Hud said, exasperated. "That's what I'm trying to say. I want to marry her."

To Mick, this seemed like the mad ravings of a pussy-whipped twenty-something. "Hud, you're twenty . . ." Mick paused, realizing he didn't know exactly how old his son was.

"I'm twenty-three," Hud said.

"Right," Mick said. "That's what I was going to say."

"You don't know how old he is. You don't know how old any of us are," Kit said. "Just admit it. You don't need to pretend so much."

"I'm not pretending. They are twenty-three," Mick said. "I knew that."

Jay corrected him. "I turned twenty-four two weeks ago."

"Right," Mick said. His shoulders slumped. "Sorry. I forgot you two aren't actually twins."

Kit shook her head. "You are ridiculous. But at least now you're telling the truth," she said. "How do you ration it out? You get four honest moments a day?"

Mick laughed, despite himself. "Yeah, but I try to keep a couple in the reserve," he said, grinning out of the side of his mouth.

The sound that came out of Kit's mouth was somewhere between a scoff and a laugh. Mick locked eyes with her and could tell she was almost about to smile. "What do you want me to say, all right? We all know I'm a shit. It's not news. I've been a shit my whole life."

Kit looked him in the eye now. He knew she was finally, actually listening. "I wish I was a better man," he said. "But I was just never capable of it. I really did try, sometimes. But it was like putting lipstick on a pig. Some people are just shits, and I'm a shit."

Hud found it hard to be mad at someone who was suddenly being so transparent. Jay found it refreshing, the idea that it was OK to admit you suspected yourself of being a dickhead, deep inside. Nina had to stop herself from rolling her eyes.

"Honestly, it never quite made sense why a woman as good as your mother picked me, but, you know, I did lay it on pretty thick when I met her," he said. "The second I saw her, with her big brown eyes, I thought, **Let me just try to be whoever she wants. Let me just pretend I can be good enough for her.** And I really did become that person for a little while there. I know I failed at the end but . . . I did try."

Nina turned and looked at her father. Mick caught her eye and relaxed into the softness of her gaze. "She deserved better," he said softly. "I hope she knew that."

Nina watched her father's face. She watched his long eyelashes as he blinked, remembering looking at them as a child.

"She didn't," Nina said, her voice almost as quiet as breath. "She didn't know that."

Mick nodded, his eyes to the ground. "I know," he said. "I know."

Nina watched as his eyes turned glassy, as the corners of his mouth turned down. She began to understand something she had never suspected. He was sorry. For what he'd done to all of them.

Nina started to open her mouth, to say something, when she heard a rustling from behind her.

Everyone turned their heads to see a girl in a purple dress coming down the stairs.

4:00 a.m.

Tarine Montefiore was—for a brief moment in the chaos of the night—looking at her paramour, and wondering if she wanted to spend her life with him. He had, just earlier that day, asked her to marry him.

She had always liked older men and always liked spending her time with people who knew more than she did. She figured it came down to the fact that her father had been such a brilliant man. Tarine's father was a linguistics professor who brought his whole family on his journeys, teaching in universities on three continents. And, through David Montefiore, Tarine had come to learn about the world. She felt she understood so much about life and culture that no man her own age could keep up with her. Also, her father was twenty years older than her mother.

Taylor Jenkins Reid

So she liked that Greg's skin was a bit rougher, that it hung differently on his body. She liked the taste of decades of cigarettes on his tongue, the creeping gray in his hair. She liked that when he put his hands on her ass, she knew that he could feel its relative youth.

So maybe, Tarine reasoned, there was a future here.

Tarine would retire from modeling soon. She would plan their wedding, plan their honeymoon. Maybe they could travel the world for a while, then settle down in a Santa Barbara Spanish–style home in Beverly Hills. They would have no children—about this Tarine was adamant. And then, soon enough after their wedding, she would get back to work. She needed a second act.

She had already had an offer for her own day-time talk show. She thought that could be a great next step. She was also considering designing a line of aerobics wear. There were a lot of things that might be interesting.

Tarine knew that Greg would be a good partner in all of this, in anything she decided to do. He would be behind her, he would believe in her and support her. They would have so much fun together, every day of their lives.

As she thought of it, a smile spread across Tarine's face. She leaned over to Greg while the two of them stood behind the record player.

"If we do this—marriage—you should know . . . I will not always be faithful. I do not expect you to be either."

Greg smiled and nodded. "All right. I understand."

"But I will promise to be by your side for the rest of our lives. That will be my promise."

"That's all I'm asking. It's all I want."

She kissed his earlobe. "OK, then I will marry you," she whispered.

Greg smiled wide and grabbed her shoulders. He kissed her. "I love you," he said.

"I love you, too," Tarine told him. "With all of my heart."

Just then, someone flung a Waterford crystal vase into the sliding doors of the kitchen, where it shattered everywhere.

"OK," Tarine said. "That is enough!"

There must have been a million tiny pieces of crystal all over the floor. Clearly, it was time for Nina to shut down this party. Tarine looked around for Nina, but she couldn't find her. Then, she checked for any of Nina's siblings and found none of them, either. And Brandon was gone, too.

There was no one in charge.

Vanessa came up to Tarine. "Are you looking for the Rivas?" she asked.

"I can't find a single one of them."

"Neither can I. I've been looking for Kit for a half hour. Can't find anybody. But I don't think Nina will be happy."

Tarine frowned. It would have to be her that put a stop to this.

"Greg," Tarine said. "Turn off the music, please."

Greg nodded and cut the sound. People groaned but no one headed for the door. They didn't really need the music anymore.

There were models crying in the corners and rock stars smoking weed on the stairs. There were writers fighting in the dining room and pop stars having sex in the bathrooms and studio execs passed out on the sofas. There were surfers puking on the lawn. Actors throwing wineglasses like footballs. TV stars putting on Nina's clothes and pocketing her jewelry. One of the kids from **Family Ties** was lying in the middle of the fallen chandelier singing "Heart of Glass" and staring up at the hole left in the ceiling.

"Let's get rid of the caterers," Vanessa said. "Maybe stop the flow of booze at least."

Tarine nodded and the two of them proceeded to tap every single bartender and cocktail waitress on the shoulder and send them home.

But as the last one was out the door, Vanessa and Tarine turned back to the party and saw no discernible difference. It was still loud, things were still getting ruined.

"THE PARTY IS OVER," Tarine yelled, cupping her hands to her mouth to project her voice.

No one moved but Kyle Manheim. He ran out the front door, sheepishly waving goodbye to Vanessa as he did so. She winked at him as he scurried by. The rest of them barely even looked up.

"Do you all care about anything other than yourselves?" Vanessa asked.

Tarine shook her head. "Of course they do not," she said. "You people are revolting."

Greg came up behind her and grabbed her hand. "Maybe we should go, honey," he said. "This isn't your problem."

Just then, a bullet came through the living room door and hit the mirror above the fireplace.

Vanessa and Tarine ducked. Greg followed suit, putting his arms over the both of them. Then the three of them stood back up to see Bridger Miller with a rifle in one hand and his other hand up in the air, as if showing he meant no harm. "I found it in a trunk upstairs. I thought it would shoot BBs," he said, laughing. "I didn't realize it was a real gun, I swear."

"Everyone out, now!" Tarine yelled. "Or I'm calling the cops."

Two girls got scared and ran out the door. Seth Whittles came running in after hearing the gunshot and grabbed the gun out of Bridger's hand.

"What the fuck are you doing, man?" Seth yelled at him. "You could have killed someone."

"I wasn't going to kill anyone!" Bridger said. But then he walked away, no longer interested.

"Yeah," Seth said, turning to Tarine and Vanessa. "Call the cops."

Vanessa walked right into the kitchen, picked up the receiver, and dialed the police.

"Yes, Officer?" she said, suddenly at a loss. "We need you to . . . come here. . . . Well, we need someone to . . . There's a party, you know? And it's . . ." She could not seem to figure out what to say that wouldn't get Nina in trouble. "Can you just come?"

Tarine grabbed the phone out of Vanessa's hand. "Please send multiple police units to 28150 Cliffside Drive. There is a party here of over two hundred people and it has gotten out of control."

Casey had been making her way down the rickety stairs when she noticed everyone looking at her. She lost her focus and took a wrong step, tumbling the last few feet. Mick instinctively caught her.

And, because he caught her, Casey thought for a moment that Mick **must** be her father. But by the time Casey straightened herself out, she remembered that life doesn't work that way.

"You OK?" he asked her.

"Yeah," she said, nodding. She stood up, but couldn't put weight on her ankle. "Thanks."

"Casey, are you all right?" Nina asked, running to her.

"Who the fuck is Casey?" Kit mouthed to Jay. Jay shook his head, **No idea.** But both of them felt a twist in their chests, watching their sister take such special care of someone they had never met before in their lives.

Hud wasn't paying attention. He was calculating how long he could bear it before he had to get to the hospital. His nose needed to be reset. He could just tell. He tried to pinch the very top of the bridge of it, wondering if that would stop the throbbing. It didn't. So he let go and looked up to see Casey hobbling toward him.

He was unclear on exactly who she was. But by the time Nina got Casey safely seated next to her on the surfboard, Hud had figured it out.

Maybe he was intuitive or maybe he saw Casey's lips. Or maybe the reason Hud made the leap was because he, of all people, knew there had to be more children like him, Mick's kids who weren't from June.

"Sorry, everyone," Casey said. She was overwhelmed, somewhat from the shock of the fall but mostly from trying to take in the faces of the people she had been anticipating meeting all night. Jay was skinnier, Hud was . . . much more beat up. And yet, Kit seemed to match perfectly with the picture Casey had had in her mind. She always assumed there would be at least one Riva who looked at her with suspicion. And here she was.

"What, exactly, is going on?" Kit asked.

Mick, too, was confused.

"This is Casey Greens," Nina said.

Casey waved and half smiled, not looking directly at any of them.

Nina lacked the energy to ease them all into it. She had spent so much of her young life being tactful and gentle and making things OK. But Nina couldn't fix everything, could she? **For fuck's sake.** "She's probably our sister."

Everyone was surprised, but it was Jay who spoke up. "What the hell are you talking about?"

Mick ignored Jay's incredulity. "Casey?" Mick said to the girl.

Casey nodded.

"Care to fill me in here, hun?"

Casey began searching for the words. But Nina jumped in and Casey felt taken care of, like she was being wrapped up in a soft blanket.

"She was adopted in 1965," Nina said. "She was raised by the Greens family in Rancho Cucamonga."

Nina nudged Casey and put her hand out. Casey handed her the photograph of her mother.

"This is her mom," Nina said. "I mean, her birth mother. You can see on the back, someone wrote a note that you are her father."

Hearing the phrase **birth mother** gave Hud the very strong instinct to stand up and sit next to Casey. He had so many things he wanted to ask her.

Nina offered Mick the photo and Mick took it from her hands gently, as if he was reluctant to touch it. He looked at it, front and back.

"Her name was . . ." Nina realized she had forgotten. "What was her name?"

Casey found her voice. "Monica Ridgemore," she said, and it really sank in that she was talking to Mick Riva. One of the most famous men in the world. A man she'd seen on billboards and on TV her entire life. "She would have been eighteen. Apparently, she told people that she was carrying Mick Riva's baby. Your baby."

Hud wondered just how many other children his father had fathered. Jay wondered whether the girl was lying. And Kit wondered how they all could possibly be descended from the man in front of them. They were nothing like him.

"I don't want anything from you," Casey said. "Any of you. Well, not money or anything like that. I have enough money."

She had so much less than any one of the Riva kids had at that very moment. She had such a small fraction of what Mick had that you couldn't calculate it in whole percentages.

"I'm here because . . ." Casey found it difficult to keep going. She knew the words she wanted to say, she just didn't know if she could withstand the ache of saying them. **I don't have anyone else.** Mick looked up from studying the photo and saw that Casey had her mother's eyes.

"She's looking for family," Nina said. "Sound familiar?"

Mick gave a shy and bittersweet smile, his eyes downcast. He looked at Nina and then Casey. And then back down at the photo.

He tried to place the face in the picture. Had he slept with this woman—Monica Ridgemore—in 1964 or '65? Those were big years for him. He'd toured all over the world. He'd slept with a lot of women. Some of them were groupies. And, yes, some of them had been young.

Mick looked up from the photo and at Casey, at her eyes and her cheekbones and her lips. There was something familiar about her—but that was a feeling Mick had all the time. He had met so many people in his lifetime that, years ago, it had begun to feel like there were no strangers anymore. Just different versions of the same person over and over.

It was just as likely that Mick had slept with Monica and forgotten about it as it was that Monica had made it up.

"I don't know," he said, finally. He watched Casey's eyes close and her chest fall as she understood she would find no answer tonight. "I'm sorry, Casey. I know that's probably not what you wanted to hear. But the truth is that I just don't know."

It broke them all a tiny little bit—Nina, Jay, Hud, Kit, and Casey. There was no end to the ways he could disappoint.

Six police officers arrived in three squad cars.

They drove through the quiet streets of Point Dume, their sirens off, their lights silently cascading over the high fences and hedges.

When they got to Nina's door, they knocked. If they'd been at an out-of-control party in Compton, they would not have knocked. Leimert Park, Inglewood, Downtown, Koreatown, East L.A., Van Nuys, they would have walked right in. But this was Malibu, where the rich white people live. And rich white people get the benefit of the doubt and all of its many benefits.

The door opened just as Sergeant Eddie Purdy's knuckles grazed it. Sergeant Purdy was stocky and stout with a face covered in stubble unless he shaved twice a day. He gazed up to see the gorgeous woman in front of him.

"Oh, thank God you are here," Tarine said. "You need to do something. Now they are on the roof, trying to ride surfboards like sleds into the pool."

There was broken glass and vomit and passed-out half-naked bodies and two people doing lines off a silver platter. The female Channel 4 news anchor was crying into a bowl of dip.

"Ma'am, is this your home?" Sergeant Purdy asked.

"No, it is not."

"Is the owner of the home here?"

"We are still looking for her," Tarine said. Vanessa was outside, on the hunt.

"Well, can you help us to find out where she might be?" he said. "I need to speak with whoever is the owner first."

Tarine stood up, trying to explain herself more clearly. "I just told you, I do not know where Nina is, but I think the more urgent issue is to get things under control."

"Could she be upstairs?" Sergeant Purdy asked. He directed some of the men to look around the party.

"Sir, there's an asshole around here shooting up mirrors," Tarine said. "Can we focus on that?"

"Ma'am, please watch your language."

"Are you even listening?" Tarine asked. "I do not know who has the gun now. Bridger Miller shot out the sliding glass doors. So please do something."

"Ma'am," Sergeant Purdy said. "I'm going to need you to calm down. Now, where did you last see the owner of the house?"

"Sir, I have told you already. I do not know where Nina is. She is probably with her father. Mick Riva showed up here a little while ago."

"Mick Riva owns this home?" Sergeant Purdy looked back to his men and raised his eyebrows, as if to say this was an important detail he'd uncovered. "Ma'am, that would have been good to mention earlier."

"He does not own the home. His daughter owns the home."

Sergeant Purdy's voice was growing more impatient. "Tell us where Mr. Riva is."

"Why?" Tarine asked. "Do you want an autograph?"

Vanessa came around the corner. "I was thinking maybe they are—" She spotted the cops. "Oh, good. You can help us. Someone peed on a Lichtenstein. **A Lichtenstein.**"

"I understand, ma'am," Sergeant Purdy said, though by the way he said it, it was clear to everyone, including his men, that he did not know what a Lichtenstein was.

There was a crash from upstairs and then a loud splash. It sounded like someone had thrown or ridden a surfboard off the roof.

"Are you going to do something now or what, Officer?" Tarine asked.

"Ma'am, adjust your tone. I could have you arrested for speaking to me like that."

"Oh, I do not think so," Tarine said.

Purdy's men now started chattering around him, laughing without looking him in eye. Vanessa understood things were about to take a turn.

"Ma'am, I admit you're awfully pretty. And I'm sure you're in charge wherever you go. I bet it's a sight to watch. But you're not in charge here, all right?" He smiled at Tarine, and what grated at her most was that it was such a genuine smile. "So you will speak to me with respect, hun, or we are going to have a very big problem."

"Officer . . . if you could just—" Vanessa started but Tarine interrupted her.

"Maybe if you actually did your job, instead of standing around like this," she said, "I would not need to speak to you at all."

"I'm not messing around anymore. You're making me angry," Purdy said as he moved toward her. "So you better watch that mouth."

Tarine could feel the space between them narrowing; she could feel Purdy's eyes on her. "Excuse me?" she said. "I was the one who called you here. I have done nothing wrong."

She leaned away from him as she spoke, trying to maintain her personal space.

Purdy moved in closer. "You sure are a ball-buster, aren't you?" And then he took his left hand and brought it up to her face and looked her in the eye as he smoothed her hair behind her ear. "There. That's better."

Tarine pulled her hand back and slapped Sergeant Eddie Purdy across the face.

Jay looked at his father and felt the anger begin to pour out of him. "Do you even know how many children you have?" he snapped.

There were so many thoughts rushing through his head, so many appalling scenarios he was only now considering. Specifically, it was the first time in Jay's life that it had occurred to him that there might be more than just the four of them. He felt smaller and smaller by the second.

"Let's not get into all of this," Mick said, shaking his head.

His children just continued to stare at him.

"I have had three paternity suits brought against me," Mick said, finally. "And all of them turned out not to be me."

"That's your answer?" Kit asked.

Mick lowered his eyes and then looked at Kit.

Kit shook her head. "You're a real prize, **Pops.**"

There was something about the mocking way Kit referred to him that took Mick's breath away.

Why weren't these kids even a little happy to see him? He had never treated his parents this way. No matter what his mother did, no matter where his father went, he was always glad when they came back.

"Two women I was with terminated their pregnancies, that I know of," Mick said.

"Charming," Kit said sharply.

Mick tried to ignore her. "Another woman had a miscarriage. But I was generally very careful. Especially after I left your mother the last time. I was very, very careful."

"Do you want a prize or something?" Kit asked.

"Will you listen to me? I'm trying to answer your question. I'm trying to explain something to you. I tried my best to be responsible about it. I always told women I slept with that I didn't want any children. I said, 'If I had any interest in being a dad, I'd go home to my kids.'"

The beach went deadly silent.

"Wow," Kit finally said, her fury raging inside her with such a fervor that her cheeks were turning red. "You know what?" she continued. "That's fine. Thanks for clearing it up. Because I always did kind of wonder if you loved us, and now we know."

Mick shook his head, but she kept talking. "It's fine. We had each other. We barely noticed you were gone."

Mick could see the pain in his stoic daughter's face—the way her chin quivered, the way her eyes narrowed. He had worn the same face himself as a child, wondering the same thing, coming to the same conclusion.

Mick shook his head again. "You're misunderstanding me."

"I'm not really sure how that's possible, Dad," Hud said. "You seem clear that you never wanted to be our father until now."

"It had nothing to do with want!" Mick said, his voice beginning to rise. "That's what I'm trying to tell you! I'm trying to tell you that if I could have been a dad, I would have been your dad. I wanted to be a father to you all. But I **couldn't. I couldn't** be a father.

"This is something you have to understand about being a parent—some people just aren't cut out for it. Some people don't have what it takes. And I didn't. But I'm here now. And I'm hoping that we can make something of all this. I just . . . I simply couldn't before. But now I think I have what it takes. And I want to be a part of your lives now. I want to . . . get dinners and, I don't know, spend holidays together or whatever it is that families do. I want that."

Suddenly, Nina started cackling. Laughing like a madwoman, like the women they used to burn at the stake.

"Oh my God," Nina said, putting her hands in her hair, shaking her head. "I almost fell for it. I forgot your words mean nothing. That you just say whatever you want, but you're never prepared to do anything meaningful, at all."

"Nina . . ." Mick said. "Please don't say that. I'm trying to explain to you why I wasn't capable of being a father until now."

Nina shook her head. "If you were any kind of real

parent, you would know that **capable** has nothing to do with it."

Mick frowned at her and sighed.

"Do you think Mom felt **capable** of raising four children on her own? Holding her head up high when the whole world knew you'd left her, **twice**? Making all of the money, and doing all of the housework, and helping each of us with our homework? Making every single one of our birthdays special despite having no money and no time? Remembering that Jay likes chocolate cake with buttercream and Kit likes coconut cake and Hud likes yellow cake with chocolate frosting? Always having the perfect number of candles?

"Do you think **I** felt capable of taking it all over after she fucking **drowned**? Do you think I felt capable of trying to pay all the bills and still scraping up enough money for coconut at the fucking Malibu Mart? Do you think I felt capable of holding each one of these guys as they woke up in the middle of the night remembering that they had essentially been orphaned? Do you think I wanted to drop out of high school so I could do it all? That I wanted to be twenty-five years old without a high school diploma?"

Mick flinched as he heard this, and when Nina saw the pinched look on his face, it pissed her off.

"I didn't feel capable of any of that! But did that matter? Of course not. So I've gotten up every single day since Mom died—and even a lot of the days before that—and I have done what needed to be done.

Capable is a question I never had the luxury of asking. Because my family needed me. And unlike you, I understand how important that is."

"Nina—" Mick tried to interject.

"You think I want to be here selling photos of my ass and living on this fucking cliff? No, I don't. I want to be in Portugal somewhere living in a shack on the beach, riding waves and eating the catch of the day. But I don't. I stay here. That's what it means to be a family. **Staying.** Not just strolling into a party after midnight expecting a hug."

"Nina, you're right. I'm a weak—"

"Must be nice. To be able to be weak. I wouldn't know."

At this, Kit smiled to herself and quickly rested her chin on her hand in order to hide it.

Nina continued. "You have no idea what it takes to stand by anyone. You certainly don't know what it takes to stand by a child. Mom did that. And when Mom couldn't, I tried to finish the job. No, scratch that. I didn't **try** to finish the job. I **did** finish the job. Because look at them. They are all talented and smart and good—and, sure, we're not perfect. But we have integrity. We know something about loyalty. We are there for each other.

"And all of that is because Mom and I did a great job. You . . . you have done nothing despite how capable you probably could have been if you gave half a shit. But because you weren't here, we learned how to go on without you."

Nina took a moment and closed her eyes. And then she looked back up at her father. "It's not my place to speak for the rest of us, Dad, so I'll just say this for me: There's no room for you in my life anymore. And I don't owe it to you to make any space."

When Nina stopped speaking, she dried the tears off her cheeks with her hands and then wiped her hands on her sweatpants. She caught her breath and settled her chest. As she stood there, she felt a peace take over, as if by speaking her anger, she had freed it from where it had been living in her body. It was as if her tendons were loosening, leaving behind a new softness within her in places that had long ago hardened.

Mick watched his daughter's face begin to calm. And he wanted so badly to move to her and hold her, to hug her, like he had when she was six years old, when they were just a few miles down this very beach running with that kite. But he knew better than to make a single step toward her.

"Do you all feel this way?" Mick asked the rest of his children.

Nina looked away from her father, toward the ocean, and wiped her eyes again.

Kit looked at the sand as she nodded. Hud, bruised inside and out, looked at his father. "I think it's just . . ."

"It's too late, Dad," Jay said.

It hurt Jay to say it. He felt bad for his father. He felt bad for his siblings. But more than anything, it made Jay so sad to be offered a father **now** when he had needed one so badly before. The man in front of him had never been the man he'd yearned for. The man he'd yearned for had never existed. And that was a pain unto itself.

Mick pursed his lips and nodded, absorbing it all. He looked at his children. His firstborn, who had raised her siblings and gone on to make a career for herself. His older son, who was now renowned in a field beyond Mick's own grasp. His third born, who had found a way to succeed in this world despite his rocky beginning. His fourth born, who appeared to have inherited the things he liked about himself the most without any contact with him at all. And even this young girl, the one who may or may not be his, who appeared to have faced so much of what he, himself, had faced at her age, but with so much more grace than he ever had.

"OK," Mick said. "I get it."

He needed his children now that he was alone. Now that he was afraid he wasn't going to matter very soon. Now that he had a house that echoed.

But they didn't need him.

"I never meant for you to grow up feeling alone, feeling . . . like you had no one to rely on," he said, momentarily covering his eyes with the pads of his fingers. "I can't imagine you'd believe me but I swear that was the very last thing I wanted."

At this, Mick's voice started to crack. "My dad stepped out on my mom a lot," he said. "He left for long stretches of time. And my mom . . . she would forget about me for days. They both would."

Nina looked away from her father and watched a family of dolphins swim past them all, diving in and out of the water in tandem. She loved how they always moved in a pack, in one direction. They never cared what was happening on the shore, they just kept going. Dolphins had been swimming along the shore in Malibu well before she was born and they would be swimming along the shore here in Malibu well after she left, and she took comfort in that.

"Then they both died when I was your age, Casey," Mick said. "At the same time. Just like . . . Just like you. Just like you all, really. My mother . . . She got mad at my father one afternoon shortly after he took up with a waitress at the deli. She set the linens on fire. I wasn't there. So I don't know exactly what happened. But I've always thought it was probably just to upset my old man. But then . . . then it grew out of control too quickly.

"I was eighteen. I came home from school and our apartment was gone, burned to the stilts. They were both dead."

Mick looked up at the sky, then back at his children. "In an instant, I was on my own. I didn't graduate high school either," he said, looking at Nina.

Nina looked her father in the eye and her face tightened. She felt for him. But it made her even more angry, that he had allowed her to lose what he himself had lost. He had—all along—known the cost of it and had done nothing to stop it from happening to her, too.

"I don't think I ever really knew how it felt to be loved until I met your mother. I was born to people who never cared, people who couldn't even be bothered to not set the house on fire.

"Anyway, I'm whining about it like I've got some sob story. That's not my point. My point is that . . . I know how it feels to wonder. If anyone loves you, if you matter at all. And I should never have done that to you. I set out to make sure you never felt that way," he said, a lump forming in his throat. "But . . . I don't know . . . somehow it still happened.

"When I found out your mother died, I just wanted it to go away. I didn't want to believe it. I wanted to still imagine her with you. I did not want to face that I had failed you and that the world had taken the only good parent you had. So I just . . . ignored it. I pretended it wasn't true. And then I got the notice that you'd filed for guardianship, and I . . . I felt like the decision had been made for me."

"You never even acknowledged it," Nina said.

"Every day I didn't call just made it that much more shameful I hadn't called. But . . . that was about me. Not about you. And what I'm getting at here is that I used to think the way my parents treated me was because I wasn't worth loving or I wasn't . . . good enough. But . . ." Mick closed his eyes and shook his head. "What I did—the way I failed you, I guess—it wasn't because you didn't deserve to be taken care of. It was because of me. My parents weren't ever able to tell me that, and so I've never been sure. But I'm here right now and I can make sure you know: You deserved better. You deserved the world."

Mick's eyes welled up and he looked each of them in the eye, even Casey. "Every minute of your lives you were loved," he said as his chin started to quake. He put his hands together in a prayer motion and put them to his chest and said, "If I exist on this earth, someone loves you. I'm just . . . I'm a very selfish man but I promise you all—I love you. I love you so much."

The sky was just beginning to lighten. Nina was so tired.

"I think the problem, Dad," she said, with an unexpected warmth in her voice, "is that your love doesn't mean very much."

Mick closed his eyes. And he nodded. And he said, "I know, honey. I know. And I'm sorry."

Sergeant Purdy put handcuffs on Tarine as she screamed at him.

"Are you kidding me?" she shouted.

"You accosted a police officer," he said, and then he pulled her hands behind her back. The movement turned her elbows out and threw her off balance. Tarine tripped on the step in front of her and fell down. He unceremoniously pulled her up, and as he did, he dragged her body toward him, tight against his torso. He smiled.

Vanessa snapped. Without thinking, she pushed him. "Don't touch her again!" she said.

The cop behind Purdy grabbed Vanessa by both of her arms and cuffed her, pulling her arms tight behind her.

Greg came back around the corner at the same time Ricky came into the living room, wondering what all of the commotion was about.

"What the hell is going on?" Greg yelled. "Let her go!"

Instinctually, Ricky lunged forward and pushed both cops off the women. Purdy fell back, the other cop barely moved. "You get off of them!" Ricky said. "I don't care what badge you're wearing!"

Purdy looked at Ricky, and Ricky instantly understood this was going to cost him. But he stood tall as both cops moved toward him, and remained stoic as they pulled his arms behind his back and cuffed him.

He winced at the tightness of the restraints themselves, but as he did, Tarine caught his eye and mouthed **Thank you.** Vanessa smiled at him. Greg gave Ricky a nod, and the remaining crowd cheered.

Tarine, Vanessa, and Ricky were all going to jail. But at least they'd put up a fight.

Then the police raided the house.

They got the two actors hallucinating from LSD on the tennis courts (Tuesday Hendricks and Rafael Lopez, possession), the one supplying coke (Bobby Housman, possession with intent to distribute), the two throwing serving trays like oversized ninja stars (Vaughn Donovan and Bridger Miller, vandalism), the naked woman blowing a drummer in the middle of the lawn (Wendy Palmer, indecent exposure, lewd conduct), the ones with pockets full of what were clearly Nina's and Brandon's belongings (Ted Travis and Vickie Brooks, grand larceny), and the one holding a gun (Seth Whittles, possession of a loaded firearm without a license).

There were so many of them that the cops had to call in a police van. They loaded each of them in as they cleared out the rest of the house. Bridger stared daggers at Tuesday the second he saw her. Tuesday refused to look at him, focused entirely on Rafael. Ted and Vickie tried to hold hands in handcuffs. Bobby nodded at Wendy. Wendy smiled kindly at Seth. Vaughn was trying not to vomit.

Ricky was seated next to Vanessa, pushed together tight, almost no room between them.

"Weird night," he said to her.

"Yeah," she said. "Weird night. But thank you, for, you know, standing up to that cop for me."

"Oh, yeah," Ricky said. "Sure. I mean, anytime."

Vanessa smiled and leaned over and kissed Ricky on the lips. "Maybe we could hang out sometime," she said.

Ricky nodded. "How about tomorrow night, assuming we're not both in jail?"

"Excellent," Vanessa said.

The two of them sat there, handcuffed next to each other, smiles creeping across their faces. And in this way, the very end of the night contained its own kind of beginnings.

Tarine was the last one escorted to the van.

"I'm going to come get you," Greg called to her. "I'll be right behind the van."

"Please!" she yelled, as the doors were shut. "These people are crazy."

On the way to the precinct, the cops came across a crashed black Jaguar on the side of the road. The hood was crunched around a tree, the engine smoking.

They arrested the very drunk but completely unscathed Brandon Randall (driving while intoxicated).

Thirteen arrests, hundreds of people kicked out of
the house, and the Rivas nowhere to be found.

By the time the clock struck 5:00 A.M., the party
of the decade was over.

5:00 a.m.

The six of them sat on the beach in silence for a while, no one quite ready to move.

They had the answers to the questions Nina, Jay, Hud, Kit, and even Mick had held in the backs of their minds for the past two decades. **Would he ever come back? Could he belong to them once more?**

Yes. But no.

And so they all sat quietly as the world shifted and settled within each of them.

After what felt like hours, Nina stood up and wiped the sand off her legs. The Santa Ana winds were gearing up, she could feel it against her shoulders. "It's getting cold," she said.

The six of them put the surfboards back in the shed and started climbing back up the cliff.

• • •

Jay was reeling from almost everything that had happened over the past twelve hours. He was having trouble processing what had taken place, and he knew it would be some time until he truly understood it all. But there was one thing that felt clear to him now: He did not want to be anything like his father.

There had been so many times over the past years that Jay had hoped his father's glory or prestige might have rubbed off on him. But now he could see plainly, he did not want to indulge that about himself the way his father had.

In fact, despite everything, he had to admit if there was a man in his life to look up to, it had always been Hud. As difficult as that felt to swallow at that given moment, it was still undeniably true.

As Hud struggled up the stairs, Jay came up behind. He put his arm out to help and said, in a voice that was not a whisper, but was not heard by anyone else, "I need you to be sorry."

"I am," Hud told him.

"No, you have to be so sorry that I know you'll never lie to me again, so that I know I can still trust you forever. Like nothing has changed."

Hud looked at his brother and allowed his sorrow to surface. Jay could see the pain in his brother's face and body, and he knew Hud well enough to know that it wasn't the broken ribs. "I am that sorry," Hud said.

"OK," Jay said. "We're OK." And with that, Jay took the full weight of his brother's body onto his shoulder and helped Hud up the cliff.

• • •

All this talk of their father made Hud think of their mother. And he thought of the story she used to tell him, how he had been handed to her, and she had held him as he cried, and loved him right then and there.

She had chosen to love him and it had changed his life.

Hud would love his child the way his mother had loved him: actively, every day, and without ambiguity.

And maybe twenty-five years from now, all of them plus a whole new generation of Rivas would be right here on this very beach. And maybe there would be another reckoning. Perhaps his children would tell him he'd been too permissive or he'd been too strict, he'd put too much emphasis on **x** when it should have been **y.**

He smiled to think of it, the ways in which he would mess this whole thing up. It was inevitable, wasn't it? The small mistakes and heartbreaks of guiding a life? His mother had screwed up almost as much as she'd succeeded.

But the one thing he knew in his bones was that he would not leave.

His child—his children, if he was lucky—would know, from the day they were born, that he was not going anywhere.

• • • •

Kit, despite herself, did feel something for her father. She did not like him, per se. But she was happy to have learned that he had a soul, however imperfect. Somehow, knowing her father wasn't all bad made her like herself more, made her less afraid of who she might be down in the unmined depths of her heart.

As they made their way up the stairs, Kit pushed ahead of everyone as only little sisters can and then stopped when she got to Casey.

She slowed down, and as she passed her she said, "Excuse me."

Later on, Kit would look back on that moment—that time they were all walking, mostly in silence, back up the stairs with their father—as the moment their family rearranged, made room for Casey to stay, made room for Nina to go.

Kit tapped Nina on the shoulder. "Hey," she whispered.

"Hi," Nina said.

"What's the place in Portugal?" Kit asked.

"Huh?" Nina said.

"The place in Portugal. Where you said you wanted to go and eat the catch of the day."

"Oh," Nina said. "I don't know. I was just talking."

"No, you weren't," Kit said. "I know you."

"It doesn't matter."

"It was the most honest you've ever been," Kit said. "It matters more than anything."

Nina turned, and looked at her sister. "It's Madeira. I've always wanted to live in Madeira in a tiny house on the water, the kind of place where you only go into town once a week to buy food. I'd love to be somewhere where no one knows who I am or who my dad is and no one has my posters on their wall and I can eat anything I want to. And I can cut all my hair off if I feel like it and maybe be a gardener or a landscaper. Something outside. Where no one knows I was married to Brandon. And when the waves are good, I'm always in the water."

Kit saw it in perfect Technicolor. The thing they could all do for Nina.

• • •

Mick knew that if he really loved his kids, he would leave them alone. That seemed easy, that seemed doable. He thought of it as his own redemption.

And so, as he made his way up the steps, he decided he'd hug each of them, give them his direct phone number, tell them he would be there if they wanted to go get lunch, and then get in his Jag and drive away.

He turned to Casey, just as his feet hit the grass, and he said, "I'll take a paternity test. If you want. Just let me know."

Casey, still finding this night beyond belief and sad and a tiny bit thrilling, smiled at him. Then, just in case he was her father, she grabbed his hand and squeezed it.

• • •

As the family came up to the lawn, the remaining cops shined their lights on the faces of Mick and his five children. And it was then that, for one of the first times in their lives, they saw why it's good to have Mick Riva as your father.

They all went inside and, after ten minutes of smiles and handshakes and autographs and polite laughing at inane stories, the cops resolved to be on their way.

"We had some arrests," Sergeant Purdy said. "Nobody you'd miss, I can't imagine. Vandals, really."

Nina wasn't sure what to say to that and she wondered who the cops had arrested. "Thank you, Officers," she said. She showed them to the front door.

Then she turned and looked at her family. Her brothers had blood crusted on their faces, her sister had a hickey—**what?**—and there were two more bodies than there'd been at the beginning of this whole thing.

"All right," Mick said. "I believe this is my cue to leave."

He entertained the fantasy that someone might try to stop him. He wasn't too surprised when no one did.

He hugged his sons first, and then his possible daughter, and then the one with the big mouth, and then as he got to the front door, the one who had saved the family he had started.

"Thank you," Mick whispered in her ear as he pulled Nina to him. "For the person you've been your entire life. And all that you've done."

And then, before Nina could even realize she was crying, he was gone.

Nina sat down on the steps facing the door and her brothers and sister sat down next to her.

"You OK?" Hud asked.

Nina looked up at him, so many feelings dancing around inside her, out of the grasp of words. "I mean . . ." she said and then gave up.

"Right," he said.

"Me, too," Kit added.

"Yeah," Jay said.

Casey stood by the door.

Hud looked at her there, alone and unsure, on the threshold. "Come on, sit down. I don't care who your dad is. You're one of us."

Kit scooted over to make room. And when Casey sat down next to Nina, Jay squeezed her shoulder. Nina patted her knee.

She needed someone to love her. And they could do that. That would be very easy for them to do.

June was gone. Yet here she was, living on through her children.

6:00 a.m.

It took exactly fifty-two minutes for them to convince Nina to leave. The five of them were all standing around the island in the kitchen, eating from the cracker tray.

Kit pitched the initial idea. "What if you just left and went to Portugal right now?"

Hud was silent. Casey wasn't sure what to say. And Nina dismissed it over and over again.

Until Jay started echoing Kit.

"It's not actually that crazy, Nina," he said. "You don't want to live here. Especially now. You don't want to be with Brandon. You don't want all the attention. You don't want any of this and you also don't want to have to explain yourself to everyone. So leave. Don't tell anybody. Just go."

"You're saying I leave my things, my bank account, my house. And no one will have any idea where I am?" Nina said.

"I mean, that's not exactly what we are saying," Hud said.

"Brandon will know where I am, won't he? So he'll still be a problem. People still know who Dad is. Everyone is going to know I got cheated on. Everyone's gonna know my husband left me for Carrie fucking Soto."

"Can I just say . . ." Casey stepped in. "That she seems like, as my mother used to say when she was really mad, **a real asshole**?"

"Yes, you can," Nina said. "Yes, you can say that."

Kit saw then that there was a version of Nina—the nice girl who always said the nice thing—who was gone. And there was a slightly new Nina—who agreed when someone said the woman that fucked her husband was an asshole. And Kit thought, for both the old Nina and this new Nina, she wanted Portugal.

"Will you just listen to me?" Kit said. "It's actually pretty simple."

"OK," Nina said, exasperated. "Go ahead."

"We don't want people tracking you down. We want them to leave you alone. So we make it really ambiguous. You leave now. The party got out of control. I'm sure it will be in the papers. And people will think you ran off with someone or something."

"Or that I died."

"I mean, maybe," Hud said, conceding the unlikely possibility.

"So, fine," Kit said. "People say you died. Who cares? That just means they will leave you alone. We know you're not dead. We'll tell Mick you're not dead. I can tell Tarine or whoever you want. We'll tell anyone that will keep the secret. But then you take some cash, you drive to the airport, and you get a one-way ticket to Portugal. Get yourself a small house. Or whatever. See if you like it. If you don't, then you'll come home. And if you do, then stay as long as you want. And we will come visit you. All the time. And no one would even question it because the surfing is great there. Hud and Jay would probably go all the time anyway for surf shoots and shit. I'll tag along. We will see you all the time. We will come stay with you for weeks sometimes. We'll always be in your hair."

"I can't leave," Nina said. "I can't leave you all. You . . ." **Need me.**

"No," Kit said. "Not anymore. We love you and we want you around. But, Nina, you don't need to take care of us anymore."

"She's right," Hud said. "Kit's right."

And that is when Nina started to wonder if this wasn't such a crazy idea. She started to wonder if she could just go. It felt daring to even imagine.

"Kit's right. You should go, Nina," Jay said. "It's totally not like you to do it. And that's exactly why you have to."

Nina was listening to him. He could tell.

"You've spent your whole life making up for Mom and Dad. We don't talk about it very much but . . . Mom didn't make it easy either. But I have always known that it didn't matter how drunk Mom got or whether Dad came home because you would always be there."

"I've known that, too," Hud said.

"I've known it my entire life," Kit said. "I know it now. And I'll know it even if you live on a beach in Madeira."

Casey stepped in. "I barely know you and you've made me feel that way. It seems like it's just the way you are."

Kit looked at Casey and could see that Casey cared about her family, cared about Nina already. Kit wondered what it would be like to be someone's older sister, to pass along the stuff you've figured out. She could do that. She **wanted** to do that.

"What if they find my car at the airport at some point and track me down?" Nina asked.

Kit started smiling. They'd moved on to logistics.

"My truck," Casey said. "It's parked down the road, way past the bluffs. I was . . . I was intimidated by the valets. And . . . all the fancy cars." Casey walked over to her purse and pulled out her keys. "It's a red pickup with three quarters of a tank of gas. Registered in my dad's name. Should get you to whatever airport you want to leave from."

"And then, you know, go. Fly to Portugal and do

something for you. For once. Just for a little while," Kit said.

It was the "little while" that got her. She could go for a **little while.** There would be no harm in a **little while.**

"What about the restaurant?" Nina asked. "Who is going to make sure everything runs—"

"We'll sell the restaurant," Kit said. "I'm sorry but we need to sell it and take the money. Mom hated that place. She never wanted it for us. Let Ramon take it over—he actually cares about it. We should let it go. We don't have to live life the exact same way Mom did or Grandma did. It's ours to do with what we want and I say you go to Portugal and let us sell the damn thing, please."

Nina looked at Hud. Hud looked at Jay. "Yeah," Jay said. "Kit's right. Mom wouldn't want you to stay here so you could run the restaurant. Mom would have hated that."

That was true, wasn't it? And yet here Nina was, holding on to it simply because her mother had carried it before her.

Nina suddenly had a picture in her head. It was as if June had given her a box—as if every parent gives their children a box—full of the things they carried.

June had given her children this box packed to the brim with her own experiences, her own treasures and heartbreaks. Her own guilts and pleasures, triumphs and losses, values and biases, duties and sorrows.

And Nina had been carrying around this box her whole life, feeling the full weight of it.

But it was not, Nina saw just then, her job to carry the full box. Her job was to sort through the box. To decide what to keep, and to put the rest down. She had to choose what, of the things she inherited from the people who came before her, she wanted to bring forward. And what, of the past, she wanted to leave behind.

And so, she put down the restaurant. Just as her mother would have wanted her to. And when she let it go, she let it go for June, too.

"Yeah," Nina said. "You're right. We don't need to keep the restaurant."

And as quickly as she understood all of this, she also understood that eventually, she would have to open the box her father had given her, too, the one she had all but thrown away.

One day, when the world made a bit more sense to her, she would have to go through that box and try to see if there was anything inside worth saving. Maybe there wasn't much. But maybe there was more than she thought.

Hud smiled at Nina. "Go, Nina, seriously. Go."

Was there even a good excuse to say no? Nina was having a hard time thinking of a single reason to stay except the people standing in front of her.

"I can be the Nina now," Jay said. "Let me. Know that no matter where you are, no matter what happens, you and these guys will always be safe because of me."

"And me," Hud said.

"And me," Kit said. "And Casey," she added as she put her arm around Casey's shoulders.

And so, Nina, breathless and stunned at the joy daring to bloom within her, pulled her siblings to her, and decided to go. Just for a little while.

7:00 a.m.

Mick Riva couldn't find his Jaguar. There were still a few cars left in the side yard but none of them were his, and none of them had keys. And he didn't want to bother his kids.

So, as he stood at the entrance to his daughter's driveway, where the gravel met the road, he smoked his last cigarette, and then decided to walk to PCH, where he would hitch a ride.

Mick Riva, hitching a ride. **What a riot.** He'd make someone's day.

He took the final drag of the cigarette, blew out the smoke, and threw the butt in the air. It cascaded over the gravel drive and landed, softly, in the bushes.

The dry, arid desert bushes of Malibu. On a morning plagued by Santa Ana winds. In a land of scrub brush. In a town under constant threat of combustion. In an area of the country where a tiny spark could destroy acres. In a region that yearns to burn.

And so, with the very best of intentions, Mick Riva walked away, having no idea he had just set fire to 28150 Cliffside Drive.

Before the smoke had become visible, Hud and Jay hugged Nina and told her they loved her and would see her soon. And then Jay drove Hud to the hospital.

As they sat in the waiting room, Jay told Hud the very thing he had been afraid to tell anyone.

"I have cardiomyopathy," he said and then explained what it meant: that he would have to stop surfing.

"But you're going to be OK?" Hud asked. His eyes were starting to water and Jay couldn't quite stand to see his brother cry at that moment.

"Yeah," Jay said, nodding. "I'll be OK. I'm just gonna find something else to do with my life, I guess."

Hud shook his head. "I mean, no worries there. You're good at almost everything you do."

Jay smiled and breathed in deeply. "But, I . . ." he said, having a hard time finding the words. "I've just been . . . worried. About letting you down."

"Me?"

"We're a team."

Hud smiled and then came clean himself. "I actually think pretty soon I won't be able to travel as much."

"What do you mean?"

"I . . . I don't know the best way to tell you this. And I swear, I just learned it tonight but . . ."

Jay knew. He knew it a half second before Hud said it.

"Ashley's pregnant."

Jay closed his eyes and laughed. "You've got to be kidding me," he said.

Hud shook his head. "I'm dead serious."

Jay nodded. "Wow. Well, you know what they say. If you're gonna sleep with your brother's ex-girlfriend, make sure you knock her up while you're at it."

Hud laughed and then grabbed his rib cage and caught his breath. "I don't think they say that."

"No, they don't." Jay stared at his shoes for a moment and then back to his brother.

"Are we still cool?" Hud asked.

Jay nodded. "Look, I still think you're a dick. And I'm probably going to think that for a while. But yeah, we're OK. We'll be fine."

They were quiet for a moment, the world still recalibrating between them.

"So I guess we're both sticking around Malibu for a while then."

Hud nodded. "Yeah, although . . ." he said. "I was actually thinking of photographing Kit. Seeing if I can sell the photos to **Surf.**"

"Kit? Really?"

"She's good, Jay," he said. "She's . . . outrageously good."

Jay nodded slowly, realizing he already knew that.

"Yeah, OK," he said, thinking of how brash Kit could be in the water, how daring. He was imagining just how great the photos could be—she'd be something new and exciting, like Nina had been but she'd be bold, going for big waves and sharper moves, like him. Maybe she was the best of all of them. **Maybe,** Jay thought for a second, **she's the whole point.**

"She's good and we'll help her be the best," Jay said. "Maybe one day Kit takes the Triple Crown. Maybe that's our new goal."

Hud put out his hand and Jay shook it, and they ushered in the next chapter of the Riva dynasty.

Two hours later, after Hud's nose had been reset, Jay drove him to Ashley's house.

There, at her front door, Hud Riva got down on one knee and proposed. Jay watched from the car as Ashley said yes.

• • •

Before the smoke had become visible, Casey gave Nina the keys to her truck and hugged her and thanked her for being exactly the kind of person Casey had needed at that very moment.

"I'm glad I met you," she said, "if only for a few hours."

Nina smiled. "It's certainly been an intense time, hasn't it? This is a real baptism by fire."

Kit hugged Nina and told her she loved her and would see her soon. "You have to do this," she said.

And Nina understood, maybe for the first time, that letting people love you and care for you is part of how you love and care for them.

"Case and I are going out to breakfast," Kit said. "Please don't be here when we get back."

Nina smiled, tears forming in her eyes. Kit started to cry but wiped the tears away. As Kit and Casey headed for the door, Kit's hand hit the knob and she couldn't go just yet. She turned and ran back to her older sister.

"I'll always love you," she said. "No matter who you are or what sort of life you want." One day, she knew, she would tell her sister all that she was just learning about who **she** was. They both had plenty of time for understanding all the ways they'd both changed tonight. "I love you just for being, whoever that is."

"Oh, kiddo," Nina said, the tears now falling from her face. "Back at ya."

Kit pulled her sister into her arms, squeezed her so tight that it felt like they might fuse together, and then pulled away and left her there, to leave on her own.

• • •

Before the smoke had become visible, Nina Riva took one last look around the house—at the shattered glass and the ruined paintings, the chandelier on the floor and the broken lamps. She felt unbridled glee at it not being her problem. She relished the thought of not being the one who had to clean it up, not having to live on a cliff, not having to look at Brandon ever again.

She grabbed a few things and threw them in a bag. She held Casey's keys in her hand, and walked down the road to the red pickup truck.

It hurt to leave, but Nina knew that most good things come with a pinch or an ache.

All she had ever needed was her family. Her siblings. And maybe, now that they didn't need her, she could find some peace and quiet. Some sunshine. Some privacy.

After all, her family had grown up. And wasn't this the day you always looked toward? When the kids were grown and your life was yours to take.

The flames traveled over the gravel and dirt to find the grass and leaves and wood they needed.

They started to inhale the house, climbing up its sides, passing over windows in favor of the roof. They took hold of the paintings, the clothes, the broken glass inside. They seized the white walls and the ivory couches, the ecru carpets. The wine cellar, the barbecue, the lawn, the tennis court.

28150 Cliffside Drive burned in vivid orange and gray, the smell of carbon wafting out over the sea.

By the time the fire had fully claimed the estate and started rolling down the coastline, Greg had gotten Tarine out of jail, Kit and Casey had tracked down Ricky and Vanessa and bailed them out, Seth's mom had picked him up, Caroline had sprung Bobby, Vaughn's and Bridger's agents had freed them and started responding to reporters asking for comment, Ted's business manager had shown up to help him and Vickie, Tuesday's publicist had come to get her and Rafael, and Wendy's brother had taken her home and already hired her a lawyer.

By the time the firefighters arrived, Brandon was out on bond and already in the hotel room of Carrie Soto. They turned on the TV to see his home in flames on the morning news.

As Point Dume was evacuated—neighbors leaving their homes holding their children and photo albums, their dogs packed in the way backs of their luxury station wagons—the blaze roared into the sky. It began reaching its fingers out for treetops and the second stories of other properties, clutching whole homes in its grasp.

The people of Malibu knew how to evacuate. They'd done this before. They would do it again.

By the time the fire was contained—the mansion turned to a charred, wet frame, the neighbors' homes singed and covered in ash, the sky stained gray, firefighters wiping their brows—the lady of the house was nowhere to be found.

Nina Riva was midflight.

She would read about the fire later in an American paper and clutch her chest, relieved no one had been hurt. She would think of the damage and the distress it must have caused.

But she would understand that it was one fire, in a long line of fires in Malibu since the dawn of time.

It had brought destruction.

It would also bring renewal, rising from the ashes.

The story of fire.

ACKNOWLEDGMENTS

I am a different writer today than I was two years ago when I started this book. And that is because of the insight and direction of my compassionate and brilliant editor, Jennifer Hershey. Jennifer, your guidance feels like a gift I have been given and I'm incredibly grateful for it.

To Kara Welsh and Kim Hovey, thank you for making me feel so **at home** at what is such a stunningly excellent publishing house. To Susan Corcoran, Leigh Marchant, Jennifer Garza, Allyson Lord, Quinne Rogers, Taylor Noel, Maya Franson, Erin Kane, and the rest of the incredible people at Ballantine, you blow me away with your thoughtful ideas, your attention to detail, and the fact that you care. Thank you from the bottom of my heart for that. To Carisa

Hays, it has been a crazy beginning, hasn't it? I'm incredibly fortunate to have you in charge of where I go. To Paolo Pepe, you are killing it with these covers. I could not be any more in love. Thank you.

Theresa Park, my queen and also my agent, I am so appreciative of your belief in me. You so beautifully translate that belief into an excitement that is infectious, high expectations that fuel me to push harder, and the world's best handwritten Christmas cards. You keep my feet on the ground and yet you help me to keep aiming higher. I could not ask for more.

Emily Sweet, Andrea Mai, Abby Koons, Alex Greene, Ema Barnes, Celeste Fine, and the rest of the Park + Fine team, I still marvel at how well you all knock it out of the park on a daily basis. But I also feel like you all are a really great reality show that I get to watch from three thousand miles away and then do reunion shows when I'm in NYC. I guess what I'm saying is that I just **like** you all very much.

To Sylvie Rabineau and Stuart Rosenthal, are you happy that the Mick Riva saga has come to its full conclusion? (Or has it? I make no promises.) Thank you for fighting so hard for my stories and my characters. I can feel it every time we talk and it means the world.

Brad Mendelsohn! Your fingerprints are all over this one. Thank you for letting me grill you that day at Nate 'n Al's, my key Malibu surfing consultant. My goal for the future is to keep you busy but not so busy that you don't still have time to get in the waves.

I, however, will not be going with you. The Pacific Ocean is freezing, you don't talk about that enough. Anyway, thank you, friend. For all that you've done and will continue to do for this story.

To the Peanuts, thank you for believing in me and for helping me process my life. I'm not sure I'd be adjusting very well without you all. You are some of the rare people who have known all the versions of me. And this current version of me really needs that. I hope I can do the same for you.

To Rose, Warren, and Sally, these books don't exist without you all stepping in and taking such good care of Lilah so I can write. Thank you for listening to me talk about this story, for always being there for me, and for being such incredible grandparents (and a great-grandparent!) to Lilah. Extra special thanks go to Rina and Maria for taking such good care of Lilah that she misses you when you're not around. I have the privilege of being able to work because of the support system I have in all of you. There are not enough thank-yous for that.

To my brother Jake, there's so much to thank you for that it seems silly to try. But I will say this: Thank you for being the person by my side through everything, and from the beginning. Thank you for sorting through the boxes with me.

To Alex, every day when I sit down at the computer, I strive to be the writer you think I am. Thank you for sharing each and every moment of my career with your whole heart. You show up for me when things are tough and you revel in the success with me, too, never taking a single moment for granted. I need that. And thank you for having so much respect for what I do and what I need in order to do it. Case in point, you are watching Lilah right now, the two of you having a picnic in the front yard, so that I can finish this book—a moment two years in the making. I know when I come outside and tell you I'm finished, you will cheer. And it's only then that I will know it's truly done.

And lastly, to Lilah. I think you sort of understand that I'm a writer now. You know how to read my name on book covers. And recently somebody said the word "Daisy" and you said, "Jones and the Six?" So it's easier for me to see how, one day, you might read this book and understand what I'm trying to tell you. But just for fun, let me make it perfectly clear: I may mess up sometimes. And I will not be perfect. But I will stand by your side, with my hand out for you to hold, for as long as you'll have me. I'm yours.

ABOUT THE AUTHOR

TAYLOR JENKINS REID is the author of **Daisy Jones & The Six, The Seven Husbands of Evelyn Hugo, One True Loves, Maybe in Another Life, After I Do,** and **Forever, Interrupted.** She lives in Los Angeles with her husband, their daughter, and their dog.

taylorjenkinsreid.com
Facebook.com/taylorjenkinsreidbooks
Twitter: @tjenkinsreid
Instagram: @tjenkinsreid

To inquire about booking Taylor Jenkins Reid for a speaking engagement, please contact the Penguin Random House Speakers Bureau at speakers@penguinrandomhouse.com.